Nora Roberts is the number one *New York Times* best-selling author of nearly two hundred novels. Under the pen name J.D. Robb, she is the author of the *New York Times* bestselling futuristic suspense *In Death* series starring Lieutenant Eve Dallas. There are more than 300 million copies of her books in print, and she has had over 150 *New York Times* bestsellers to date.

Visit her website at www.noraroberts.com

D1639299

Vengeance in Death

Nora Roberts

writing as

J.D. Robb

PIATKUS

PIATKUS

First published in the United States 1997 by Berkley Publishing Group
a division of Penguin Putnam Inc., New York
First published in Great Britain in 1997 by Piatkus Books
This paperback edition published in 2007 by Piatkus Books
Reprinted 2004 (twice), 2005, 2006, 2007, 2008

A CIP catalogue record for this book is available from the British Library

ISBN 978-0-7499-3413-2

Typeset in Times by Palimpsest Book Production Limited,
Polmont, Stirlingshire
Printed and bound in Great Britain by CPI Mackays, Chatham ME5 8TD

Papers used by Piatkus Books are natural, renewable and recyclable
products made from wood grown in sustainable forests and certified
in accordance with the rules of the Forest Stewardship Council.

Mixed Sources
Product group from well-managed
forests and other controlled sources
www.fsc.org Cert no. SGS-COC-004081
© 1996 Forest Stewardship Council
FSC

Piatkus Books
An imprint of
Little, Brown Book Group
100 Victoria Embankment
London EC4Y 0DY

An Hachette Livre UK Company
www.hachettelivre.co.uk

www.piatkus.co.uk

Vengeance is mine; I will repay, says the Lord.

ROMANS 12:19

Vengeance is in my heart, death in my hand.

SHAKESPEARE

Chapter One

The business of murder took time, patience, skill, and a tolerance for the monotonous. Lieutenant Eve Dallas had them all.

She knew the act of murder required none of these. All too often a life was taken on impulse, in rage, for amusement, or simply out of stupidity. It was the last of these, in Eve's mind, that had led one John Henry Bonning to throw one Charles Michael Renekee out a twelfth-story window on Avenue D.

She had Bonning in Interview and calculated that it would take another twenty minutes tops to shake a confession out of him, another fifteen to book him and file her report. She might just make it home on time.

'Come on, Boner.' It was her veteran cop talking to veteran bad guy. Level ground, her turf. 'Do yourself a favor. A confession, and you can go for self-defense and diminished capacity. We can tie this up by dinnertime. I hear they're serving pasta surprise in lockup tonight.'

'Never touched him.' Bonning folded his oversized lips, tapped his long, fat fingers. 'Fucker jumped.'

With a sigh, Eve sat down at the little metal table in Interview A. She didn't want Bonning to lawyer himself and gum up the works. All she had to do was keep him from saying those words, steer him in the direction she was already heading, and she had a wrap.

Second-rate chemi-dealers like Bonning were invariably

slow-witted, but sooner or later he'd whine for a representative. It was an old shuffle-and-dodge, as timeless as murder itself. As the year 2058 stumbled to an end, the business of murder remained basically unchanged.

'He jumped – a quick gainer out the window. Now why'd he do that, Boner?'

Bonning furrowed his ape-sized forehead into deep thought. 'Because he was a crazy bastard?'

'That's a good guess, Boner, but it's not going to qualify you for round two of our stump-the-cops sweepstakes.'

It took him about thirty pondering seconds, then his lips stretched out into a grin. 'Funny. Pretty funny, Dallas.'

'Yeah, I'm thinking of moonlighting as a stand-up. But, going back to my day job, the two of you were cooking up some Erotica in your porta-lab on Avenue D, and Renekee – being a crazy bastard – just got some hair up his ass and jumped out a window – right through the glass – and dived twelve stories, bounced off the roof of a Rapid Cab, scared the living shit out of a couple of tourists from Topeka in the backseat, then rolled off to leak his brains onto the street.'

'Sure did bounce,' Bonning said with what passed for a wondering smile. 'Who'da thought?'

She didn't intend to go for murder one, and figured if she went for murder two the court-appointed rep would bargain Bonning down to manslaughter. Chemi-dealers greasing chemi-dealers didn't make Justice flip up her blindfold and grin in anticipation. He'd do more time for the illegals paraphernalia than he would for the homicide. And even combining the two, it was doubtful he'd do more than a three-year stretch in lockup.

She folded her arms on the table, leaned forward. 'Boner, do I look stupid?'

Taking the question at face value, Bonning narrowed his eyes to take a careful study. She had big brown eyes, but they

2

weren't soft. She had a pretty, wide mouth, but it didn't smile. 'Look like a cop,' he decided.

'Good answer. Don't try to hose me here, Boner. You and your business partner had a falling out, you got pissed off, and you terminated your professional and personal relationship by heaving his dumb ass out the window.' She held up a hand before Bonning could deny again. 'This is the way I see it. You got into, maybe dissing each other over the profits, the methods, a woman. You both got hot. So maybe he comes at you. You've got to defend yourself, right?'

'Man's got a right,' Bonning agreed, nodding rapidly as the story sang to him. 'But we didn't get into nothing. He just tried to fly.'

'Where'd you get the bloody lip, the black eye? How come your knuckles are ripped up?'

Bonning stretched his lips into a toothy grin. 'Bar fight.'

'When? Where?'

'Who remembers?'

'You'd better. And you know you'd better, Boner, after we run the tests on the blood we scraped from your knuckles, and we find his blood mixed with yours. We get his DNA off your fat fingers, I'm going for premeditated – maximum lockup, life, no parole.'

His eyes blinked rapidly, as if his brain was processing new and baffling data. 'Come on, Dallas, that's just bullshit. You ain't gonna convince nobody I walked in there thinking to kill old Chuckaroo. We were buds.'

Her eyes steady on his, Eve pulled out her communicator. 'Last chance to help yourself. I call my aide, have her get the test results, I'm booking you on murder one.'

'Wasn't no murder.' He wanted to believe she was bluffing. You couldn't read those eyes, he thought, wetting his lips. Couldn't read those cop's eyes. 'It was an accident,' he claimed, inspired. Eve only shook her head. 'Yeah, we were busting a little and he . . . tripped and went headlong out the window.'

'Now you're insulting me. A grown man doesn't trip out a window that's three feet off the floor.' Eve flicked on her communicator. 'Officer Peabody.'

Within seconds Peabody's round and sober faced filled the communicator screen. 'Yes, sir.'

'I need the blood test results on Bonning. Have them sent directly to Interview A – and alert the PA that I have a murder in the first.'

'Now hold on, back up, don't be going there.' Bonning ran the back of his hand over his mouth. He struggled a moment, telling himself she'd never get him on the big one. But Dallas had a rep for pinning fatter moths than he to the wall.

'You had your chance, Boner. Peabody—'

'He came at me, like you said. He came at me. He went crazy. I'll tell you how it went down, straight shit. I want to make a statement.'

'Peabody, delay those orders. Inform the PA that Mr Bonning is making a statement of straight shit.'

Peabody's lips never twitched. 'Yes, sir.'

Eve slipped the communicator back in her pocket, then folded her hands on the edge of the table and smiled pleasantly. 'Okay, Boner, tell me how it went down.'

Fifty minutes later, Eve strolled into her tiny office in New York's Cop Central. She did look like a cop – not just the weapon harness slung over her shoulder, the worn boots and faded jeans. Cop was in her eyes – eyes that missed little. They were a dark whiskey color, and rarely flinched. Her face was angular, sharp at the cheekbones, and set off by a surprisingly generous mouth and a shallow dent in the chin.

She walked in a long-limbed, loose-gaited style – she was in no hurry. Pleased with herself, she raked her fingers through her short, casually cropped brown hair as she sat behind her desk.

She would file her report, zing off copies to all necessary parties, then log out for the day. Outside the streaked and narrow window behind her, the commuter air traffic was already in a snarl. The blat of airbus horns and the endless snicking of traffic copter blades didn't bother her. It was, after all, one of the theme songs of New York.

'Engage,' she ordered, then hissed when her computer remained stubbornly blank. 'Damn it, don't start this. Engage. Turn on, you bastard.'

'You've got to feed it your personal pass number,' Peabody said as she stepped inside.

'I thought these were back on voice ID.'

'Were. Snaffued. Supposed to be back up to speed by the end of the week.'

'Pain in the butt,' Eve complained. 'How many numbers are we supposed to remember? Two, five, zero, nine.' She blew out a breath as her unit coughed to life. 'They'd better come up with the new system they promised the department.' She slipped a disc into the unit. 'Save to Bonning, John Henry, case number 4572077-H. Copy report to Whitney, Commander.'

'Nice, quick work on Bonning, Dallas.'

'The man's got a brain the size of a pistachio. Tossed his partner out the window because they got into a fight over who owed who a stinking twenty credits. And he's trying to tell me he was defending himself, in fear for his life. The guy he tossed was a hundred pounds lighter and six inches shorter. Asshole,' she said with a resigned sigh. 'You'd have thought Boner would have cooked up the guy had a knife or swung a bat at him.'

She sat back, circled her neck, surprised and pleased that there was barely any tension to be willed away. 'They should all be this easy.'

She listened with half an ear to the hum and rumble of the

early air traffic outside her window. One of the commuter trams was blasting out its spiel on economical rates and convenience.

'Weekly, monthly, yearly terms available! Sign on to EZ TRAM, your friendly and reliable air transport service. Begin and end your work day in style.'

If you like the packed-in-like-sweaty-sardines style, Eve thought. With the chilly November rain that had been falling all day, she imagined both air and street snarls would be hideous. The perfect end to the day.

'That wraps it,' she said and grabbed her battered leather jacket. 'I'm clocking out – on time for a change. Any hot plans for the weekend, Peabody?'

'My usual, flicking off men like flies, breaking hearts, crushing souls.'

Eve shot a quick grin at her aide's sober face. The sturdy Peabody, she thought – a cop from the crown of her dark bowl-cut hair to her shiny regulation shoes. 'You're such a wild woman, Peabody. I don't know how you keep up the pace.'

'Yeah, that's me, queen of the party girls.' With a dry smile, Peabody reached for the door just as Eve's tele-link beeped. Both of them scowled at the unit. 'Thirty seconds and we'd have been on the skywalk down.'

'Probably just Roarke calling to remind me we've got this dinner party deal tonight.' Eve flicked the unit on. 'Homicide, Dallas.'

The screen swam with colors, dark, ugly, clashing colors. Music, low octave, slow paced, crept out of the speaker. Automatically, Eve tapped the command for trace, watched the Unable to Comply message scroll across the bottom of the screen.

Peabody whipped out her porta-link, stepping aside to contact Central Control as the caller spoke.

'You're supposed to be the best the city has to offer, Lieutenant Dallas. Just how good are you?'

'Unidentified contact and/or jammed transmissions to police

officers are illegal. I'm obliged to caution you that th... transmission is being traced through CompuGuard, and it's being recorded.'

'I'm aware of that. Since I've just committed what worldly society would consider first-degree murder, I'm not overly concerned about minor nuisances like electronic violations. I've been blessed by the Lord.'

'Oh yeah?' Terrific, she thought, just what she needed.

'I have been called on to do His work, and have washed myself in the blood of His enemy.'

'Does He have a lot of them? I mean, you'd think He'd just, what, smite them down Himself instead of enlisting you to do the dirty work.'

There was a pause, a long one, in which only the dirge played through. 'I have to expect you to be flippant.' The voice was harder now, and edgier. Temper barely suppressed. 'As one of the godless, how could you understand divine retribution? I'll put this on your level. A riddle. Do you enjoy riddles, Lieutenant Dallas?'

'No.' She slid her gaze toward Peabody, got a quick, frustrated head shake. 'But I bet you do.'

'They relax the mind and soothe the spirit. The name of this little riddle is Revenge. You'll find the first son of the old sod in the lap of luxury, atop his silver tower where the river runs dark below and water falls from a great height. He begged for his life, and then for his death. Never repenting his great sin, he is already damned.'

'Why did you kill him?'

'Because this is the task I was born for,'

'God told you that you were born to kill?' Eve pushed for trace again, fought with frustration. 'How'd He let you know? Did He call you up on your 'link, send a fax? Maybe He met you in a bar?'

'You won't doubt me.' The sound of breathing grew louder, strained, shaky. 'You think because you're a woman in a position of authority that I'm less? You won't doubt me for much longer. I contacted you, Lieutenant. Remember this is in my charge. Woman may guide and comfort man, but man was created to protect, defend, to avenge.'

'God tell you that too? I guess that proves He's a man after all. Mostly ego.'

'You'll tremble before Him, before me.'

'Yeah, right.' Hoping his video was clear, Eve examined her nails. 'I'm already shaking.'

'My work is holy. It is terrible and divine. From Proverbs, Lieutenant, twenty-eight seventeen: "If a man is burdened with the blood of another, let him be a fugitive until death; let no one help him.' This one's days as a fugitive are done – and no one helped him.'

'If you killed him, what does that make you?'

'The wrath of God. You have twenty-four hours to prove you're worthy. Don't disappoint me.'

'I won't disappoint you, asshole,' Eve muttered as the transmission ended. 'Anything, Peabody?'

'Nothing. He jammed the tracers good and proper. They can't give us so much as on or off planet.'

'He's on planet,' she muttered and sat. 'He wants to be close enough to watch.'

'Could be a crank.'

'I don't think so. A fanatic, but not a crank. Computer, run buildings, residential and commercial with the word *luxury*, in New York City, with view of the East River or the Hudson.' She tapped her fingers. 'I hate puzzle games.'

'I kind of like them.' Brows knit, Peabody leaned over Eve's shoulder as the computer went to work.

Luxury Arms
Sterling Luxury
Luxury Place
Luxury Towers

8

Eve pounced. 'Access visual of Luxury Towers, on screen.'

Working . . .

The image popped, a towering spear of silver with a glint of sunlight off the steel and shimmering on the Hudson at its base. On the far west wide, a stylish waterfall tumbled down a complex arrangement of tubes and channels.

'Gotcha.'

'Can't be that easy,' Peabody objected.

'He wanted it easy.' Because, Eve thought, someone was already dead. 'He wants to play and he wants to preen. Can't do either until we're in it. Computer, access name of residents on the top floor of the Luxury Towers.'

Working . . . Penthouse is owned by The Brennen Group and is New York base for Thomas X. Brennen of Dublin, Ireland, age forty-two, married, three children, president and CEO of The Brennen Group, an entertainment and communications agency.

'Let's check it out, Peabody. We'll notify Dispatch on the way.'

'Request backup?'

'We'll get the lay of the land first.' Eve adjusted the strap on her weapon harness and shrugged into her jacket.

The traffic was just as bad as she'd suspected, bumping and grinding over wet streets, buzzing overhead like disoriented bees. Glide-carts huddled under wide umbrellas and did no business she could see. Steam rolled up out of their grills, obscuring vision and stinking up the air.

'Get the operator to access Brennen's home number, Peabody. If it's a hoax and he's alive, it'd be nice to keep it that way.'

'On it,' Peabody said and pulled out her 'link.

Annoyed with the traffic delays, Eve sounded her siren. She'd have had the same response if she'd leaned out the window and shouted. Cars remained packed together like lovers, giving not an inch.

'No answer,' Peabody told her. 'Voice-mail announcement says he's away for two weeks beginning today.'

'Let's hope he's bellied up to a pub in Dublin.' She scanned the traffic again, gauged her options. 'I have to do it.'

'Ah, Lieutenant, not in this vehicle.'

Then Peabody, the stalwart cop, gritted her teeth and squeezed her eyes shut in terror as Eve stabbed the vertical lift. The car shuddered, creaked, and lifted six inches off the ground. Hit it again with a bone-shuddering thud.

'Goddamn piece of dog shit.' Eve used her fist this time, punching the control hard enough to bruise her knuckles. They did a shaky lift, wobbled, then streamed forward as Eve jabbed the accelerator. She nipped the edge of an umbrella, causing the glide-cart hawker to squeal in fury and hotfoot in pursuit for a half a block.

'The damn hawker nearly caught the bumper.' More amazed than angry now, Eve shook her head. 'A guy in air boots nearly outran a cop ride. What's the world coming to, Peabody?'

Eyes stubbornly shut, Peabody didn't move a muscle. 'I'm sorry, sir, you're interrupting my praying.'

Eve kept the sirens on, delivering them to the front entrance of the Luxury Towers. The descent was rough enough to click her teeth together, but she missed the glossy fender of an XRII airstream convertible by at least an inch.

The doorman was across the sidewalk like a silver bullet, his face a combination of insult and horror as he wrenched open the door of her industrial beige city clunker.

'Madam, you cannot park this . . . thing here.'

Eve flicked off the siren, flipped out her badge. 'Oh yeah, I can.'

His mouth only stiffened further as he scanned her ID. 'If you would please pull into the garage.'

Maybe it was because he reminded her of Summerset, the butler who had Roarke's affection and loyalty and her disdain, but she pushed her face into his, eyes glittering. 'It stays where I put it, pal. And unless you want me to tell my aide to write you up for obstructing an officer, you'll buzz me inside and up to Thomas Brennen's penthouse.'

He sucked air through his nose. 'That is quite impossible. Mr Brennen is away.'

'Peabody, get this . . . citizen's name and ID number and arrange to have him transported to Cop Central for booking.'

'Yes, sir.'

'You can't arrest me.' His shiny black boots did a quick dance on the sidewalk. 'I'm doing my job.'

'You're interfering with mine, and guess whose job the judge is going to think is more important?'

Eve watched the way his mouth worked before it settled in a thin, disapproving line. Oh yeah, she thought, he was Summerset to a tee, even though he was twenty pounds heavier and three inches shorter than the bane of her existence.

'Very well, but you can be sure I will contact the chief of police and security about your conduct.' He studied her badge again. 'Lieutenant.'

'Feel free.' With a signal to Peabody, she followed the doorman's stiff back to the entrance, where he activated his droid backup to man the post.

Inside the shining silver doors, the lobby of the Luxury Towers was a tropical garden with towering palms, flowing hibiscus and twittering birds. A large pool surrounded a splashing fountain in the shape of a generously curved woman, naked to the waist and holding a golden fish.

The doorman keyed in a code at a glass tube, silently

gestured Eve and Peabody inside. Unhappy with the transport, Eve stayed rooted to the center while Peabody all but pressed her nose against the glass on the ascent.

Sixty-two floors later, the tube opened into a smaller garden lobby, no less abundant. The doorman paused by a security screen outside double arched doors of highly polished steel.

'Doorman Strobie, escorting Lieutenant Dallas of the NYPSD and aide.'

'Mr Brennen is not in residence at this time,' came the response in a soothing voice musical in its Irish lilt.

Eve merely elbowed Strobie aside. 'This is a police emergency.' She lifted her badge to the electronic eye for verification. 'Entrance is imperative.'

'One moment, Lieutenant.' There was a quiet hum as her face and ID were scanned, then a discreet click of locks. 'Entrance permitted, please be aware that this residence is protected by SCAN-EYE.'

'Recorder on, Peabody. Back off, Strobie.' Eve put one hand on the door, the other on her weapon, and shouldered it open.

The smell struck her first, and made her swear. She'd smelled violent death too many times to mistake it.

Blood painted the blue silk walls of the living area, a grisly, incomprehensible graffiti. She saw the first piece of Thomas X. Brennen on the cloud-soft carpet. His hand lay palm up, fingers curled toward her as if to beckon or to plead. It had been severed at the wrist.

She heard Strobie gag behind her, heard him stumble back into the lobby and the fresh floral air. She stepped into the stench. She drew her weapon now, sweeping with it as she covered the room. Her instincts told her what had been done there was over, and whoever had done it was safely away, but she stuck close to procedure, making her way slowly over the carpet, avoiding the gore when she could.

'If Strobie's finished vomiting, ask him the way to the master bedroom.'

'Down the hall to the left,' Peabody said a moment later. 'But he's still heaving out there.'

'Find him a bucket, then secure the elevator and this door.'

Eve started down the hall. The smell grew riper, thicker. She began to breathe through her teeth. The door to the bedroom wasn't secure. Through the crack came a slash of bright artificial light and the majestic sounds of Mozart.

What was left of Brennen was stretched out on a lake-sized bed with a stylish mirrored canopy. One arm had been chained with silver links to the bedpost. Eve imagined they would find his feet somewhere in the spacious apartment.

Undoubtedly the walls were well soundproofed, but surely the man had screamed long and loud before he died. How long had it taken, she wondered as she studied the body. How much pain could a man stand before the brain turned off and the body gave out?

Thomas Brennen would know the answer, to the second.

He'd been stripped naked, his hand and both his feet amputated. The one eye he had left stared in blind horror at the mirrored reflection of his own mutilated form. He'd been disemboweled.

'Sweet Jesus Christ,' Peabody whispered from the doorway. 'Holy Mother of God.'

'I need the field kit. We'll seal up, call this in. Find out where his family is. Call this in through EDD, Feeney if he's on, and have him put a media jammer on before you give any details. Let's keep the details quiet as long as possible.'

Peabody had to swallow hard twice before she was sure her lunch would stay down. 'Yes, sir.'

'Get Strobie and secure him before he can babble about this.'

When Eve turned, Peabody saw a shadow of pity in her

eyes, then it was gone and they were flat and cool again. 'Let's get moving. I want to fry this son of a bitch.'

It was nearly midnight before Eve dragged herself up the stairs to her own front door. Her stomach was raw, her eyes burning, her head roaring. The stench of vicious death clung to her though she'd scrubbed off a layer of skin in the locker room showers before heading home.

What she wanted most was oblivion, and she said one desperate and sincere prayer that she wouldn't see the wreckage of Thomas Brennen when she closed her eyes to sleep.

The door opened before she could reach it. Summerset stood with the glittery light of the foyer chandelier behind him, his tall bony body all but quivering with dislike.

'You are unpardonably late, Lieutenant. Your guests are preparing to leave.'

Guests? Her overtaxed mind struggled with the word before she remembered. A dinner party? She was supposed to care about a dinner party after the night she'd put in?

'Kiss my ass,' she invited and started passed him.

His thin fingers caught at her arm. 'As Roarke's wife you're expected to perform certain social duties, such as assisting him in hosting an important affair such as this evening's dinner.'

Fury outdistanced fatigue in a heartbeat. Her hand curled into a fist at her side. 'Step back before I—'

'Eve darling.'

Roarke's voice, managing to convey welcome, amusement, and caution in two words, stopped her curled fist from lifting and following through. Scowling, she turned, saw him just outside the parlor doorway. It wasn't the formal black that made him breathtaking. Eve knew he had a leanly muscled body that could stop a woman's heart no matter what he wore – or didn't wear. His hair flowed, dark as night and nearly to his shoulders, to frame a face she often thought belonged on a Renaissance painting. Sharp bones, eyes bluer than prized cobalt, a mouth fashioned to spout poetry, issue orders, and drive a woman to madness,

In less than a year, he had broken through her defenses, unlocked her heart, and most surprising of all, had gained not only her love but her trust.

And he could still annoy her.

She considered him the first and only miracle in her life.

'I'm late. Sorry.' It was more of a challenge than an apology, delivered like a bullet. He acknowledged it with an easy smile and a lifted eyebrow.

'I'm sure it was unavoidable.' He held out a hand. When she crossed the foyer and took it, he found hers stiff and cold. In her aged-whiskey eyes he saw both fury and fatigue. He'd grown used to seeing both there. She was pale, which worried him. He recognized the smears on her jeans as dried blood, and hoped it wasn't her own.

He gave her hand a quick, intimate squeeze before bringing it to his lips, his eyes steady on hers. 'You're tired, Lieutenant,' he murmured, the wisp of Ireland magical in his voice. 'I'm just moving them along. Only a few minutes more, all right?'

'Sure, yeah. Fine.' Her temper began to cool. 'I'm sorry I screwed this up. I know it was important.' Beyond him in the beautifully furnished parlor she saw more than a dozen elegant men and women, formally dressed, gems winking, silks rustling. Something of her reluctance must have shown on her face before she smoothed it away, because he laughed.

'Five minutes, Eve. I doubt this can be as bad as whatever you faced tonight.'

He ushered her in, a man as comfortable with wealth and privilege as with the stench of alleys and violence. Seamlessly he introduced his wife to those she'd yet to meet, cued her on the names of those she'd socialized with at another time, all the while nudging the dinner party guests toward the door.

Eve smelled rich perfumes and wine, the fragrant smoke

15

from the applewood logs simmering discreetly in the fireplace. But under it all the sensory memory stink of blood and gore remained.

He wondered if she knew how staggering she was, standing there amid the glitter in her scarred jacket and smeared denim, her short, untidy hair haloing a pale face, accenting dark, tired eyes, her long, rangy body held straight through what he knew was an act of sheer will.

She was, he thought, courage in human form.

But when they closed the door on the last guest, she shook her head. 'Summerset's right. I'm just not equipped for this Roarke's wife stuff.'

'You are my wife.'

'Doesn't mean I'm any good at it. I let you down. I should've—' She stopped talking because his mouth was on hers, and it was warm, possessive, and untied the knots in the back of her neck. Without realizing she'd moved, Eve wrapped her arms around his waist and just held on.

'There,' he murmured. 'That's better. This is my business.' He lifted her chin, skimming a finger in the slight dent centered in it. 'My job. You have yours.'

'It was a big deal though. Some whatzit merger.'

'Scottoline merger – more of a buyout, really, and it should be finalized by the middle of next week. Even without your delightful presence at the dinner table. Still, you might have called. I worried.'

'I forgot. I can't always remember. I'm not used to this.' She jammed her hands in her pockets and paced down the wide hall and back. 'I'm not used to this. Every time I think I am, I'm not. Then I come walking in here with all the megarich, looking like a street junkie.'

'On the contrary, you look like a cop. I believe several of our guests were quite impressed with the glimpse of your weapon under your jacket, and the trace of blood on your jeans. It's not yours, I take it.'

16

'No.' Suddenly she just couldn't stand up any longer. She turned to the steps, climbed two and sat. Because it was Roarke, she allowed herself to cover her face with her hands.

He sat beside her, draped an arm over her shoulders. 'It was bad.'

'Almost always you can say you've seen as bad, even worse. It's most always true. I can't say that this time.' Her stomach still clenched and rolled. 'I've never seen worse.'

He knew what she lived with, had seen a great deal of it himself. 'Do you want to tell me?'

'No, Christ no, I don't want to think about it for a few hours. I don't want to think about anything.'

'I can help you there.'

For the first time in hours she smiled. 'I bet you can.'

'Let's start this way.' He rose and plucked her off the step up into his arms.

'You don't have to carry me. I'm okay.'

He flashed a grin at her as he started up. 'Maybe it makes me feel manly.'

'In that case . . .' She wound her arms around his neck, rested her head on his shoulder. It felt good. Very good.

'The least I can do after standing you up tonight is make you feel manly.'

'The very least,' he agreed.

Chapter Two

The sky window above the bed was still dark when she woke. And she woke in a sweat. The images in the dream were muddled and blurred. All too glad to have escaped them, Eve didn't try to clarify the dream.

Because she was alone in the big bed, she allowed herself one quick, hard shudder. 'Lights,' she ordered. 'On low.' Then sighed when the dark edged away. She gave herself a moment to settle before checking the time.

Five-fifteen A.M. Terrific, she thought, knowing there would be no return to sleep now. Not without Roarke there to help beat the nightmares back. She wondered if she'd ever stop being embarrassed that she had come to depend on him for such things. A year before she hadn't even known he existed. Now he was as much a part of her life as her own hands. Her own heart.

She climbed out of bed, grabbing one of the silk robes Roarke was constantly buying her. Wrapping herself in it, she turned to the wall panel, engaged the search.

'Where is Roarke?'

Roarke is in the lower level pool area.

A swim, Eve thought, wasn't a bad idea. A workout first, she decided, to smooth away the kinks and the dregs of a bad dream.

With the objective of avoiding Summerset, she took the elevator rather than the stairs. The man was everywhere, sliding out of shadows, always ready with a scowl or a sniff. A continuation of their confrontation the night before wasn't the way she wanted to start her day.

Roarke's gym was fully equipped, giving her all the options. She could spar with a droid, pump up with free weights, or just lay back and let machines do the work. She stripped out of the robe and tugged herself into a snug black unitard. She wanted a run, a long one, and after tying on thin air soles she programmed the video track.

The beach, she decided. It was the one place other than the city she was completely at home. All the rural landscapes and desert vistas, the off-planet sites the unit offered made her vaguely uncomfortable.

She started out at a light trot, the blue waves crashing beside her, the glint of the sun just peeking over the horizon. Gulls wheeled and screamed. She drew in the moist salt air of the tropics, and as her muscles began to warm and limber increased her pace.

She hit her stride at the first mile, and her mind emptied.

She'd been to this beach several times since she'd met Roarke – in reality and holographically. Before that the biggest body of water she'd seen had been the Hudson River.

Lives changed, she mused. And so did reality.

At mile four when her muscles were just beginning to sing, she caught a movement out of the corner of her eye. Roarke, his hair still damp from his swim, moved into place beside her, matching his pace to hers.

'Running to or away?' he asked.

'Just running.'

'You're up early, Lieutenant.'

'I've got a full day.'

He lifted a brow when she increased her pace. His wife had a healthy competitive streak, he mused, and easily matched her stride. 'I thought you were off.'

'I was.' She slowed, stopped, then bent at the waist to stretch out. 'Now I'm not.' She lifted her head until her eyes met his. It wasn't only her life now, she remembered, or her reality. It was theirs. 'I guess you had plans.'

'Nothing that can't be adjusted.' The weekend in Martinique he'd hoped to surprise her with could wait. 'My calendar's clear for the next forty-eight hours, if you want to bounce anything off me.'

She heaved out a breath. This was another change in her life, this sharing of her work. 'Maybe. I want to take a swim.'

'I'll join you.'

'I thought you just had one.'

'I can have two.' He skimmed a thumb over the dent in her chin. The exercise had brought color to her cheeks and a light sheen to her skin. 'It's not illegal.' He took her hand to lead her out of the gym and into the flower-scented air of the pool room.

Palms and flowing vines grew lushly, surrounding a lagoon-styled pool sided with smooth stones and tumbling waterfalls.

'I've got to get a suit.'

He only smiled and tugged the straps from her arms. 'Why?' His graceful hands skimmed her breasts as he freed them and made her brows raise.

'What kind of water sport did you have in mind?'

'Whatever works.' He cupped her face in his hands, bent to kiss her. 'I love you, Eve.'

'I know.' She closed her eyes and rested her brow against his. 'It's so weird.'

Naked, she turned and dove into the dark water. She stayed under, skimming along the bottom. Her lips curved when the water turned a pale blue. The man knew her moods before she did, she thought. She did twenty laps before rolling lazily to her back. When she reached out, his fingers linked with hers.

'I'm pretty relaxed.'

'Are you?'

'Yeah, so relaxed I probably couldn't fight off some pervert who wanted to take advantage of me.'

'Well then.' He snagged her waist, turning her until they were face to face.

'Well then.' She wrapped her legs around him and let him keep her afloat.

When their mouths met, even the whisper of tension fled. She felt loose and fluid and quietly needy. Sliding her fingers up, she combed them through his hair – thick, wet silk. His body was firm and cool against hers and fit in a way she'd nearly stopped questioning. She all but purred as his hands skimmed over her, just hinting of possession.

Then she was underwater, tangled with him in that pale blue world. When his mouth closed over her breast, she shivered with the thrill of sensation, from the shock of being unable to gasp in air. And his fingers were on her, in her, shooting her to a staggering climax that had her clawing toward the surface.

She gulped in air, disoriented, delirious, then felt it whoosh out of her lungs again when his clever mouth replaced his fingers.

The assault on her system was precisely what she'd wanted. Her helplessness. His greed. That he would know it, understand it, and give was a mystery she would never solve.

Her head dipped back to lay limply on the smooth side of the pool as she simply wallowed in the pleasure he offered her.

Slowly, slyly, his mouth roamed up, over her belly, her torso, her breasts, to linger at her throat where her pulse beat thick and fast.

'You've got amazing breath control,' she managed, then trembled as gradually, inch by inch, he slipped inside her. 'Oh God.'

He watched her face, saw the heat flush her cheeks, the flickers of pleasure move over it. Her hair was slicked back, leaving it unframed. And that stubborn, often too serious mouth, trembled for him. Cupping her hips, he lifted her, moved in deep, deeper to make her moan.

21

He rubbed his lips over hers, nibbled at them while he began to move with an exquisite control that tortured them both. 'Go over, Eve.'

He watched those shrewd cop's eyes go blind and blurry, heard her breath catch then release on something like a sob. Even as his blood burned, he kept his movements achingly slow. Drawing it out, every instant, every inch until that sob became his name.

His own release was long and deep and perfect.

She managed to drag her hands out of the water and grip his shoulders. 'Don't let go of me yet. I'll sink like a stone.'

He chuckled weakly, pressed his lips to the side of her throat where her pulse still danced. 'Same goes. You should get up early more often.'

'We'd kill each other. Miracle we didn't drown.'

He drew in the scent of her skin and water. 'We may yet.'

'Do you think we can make it over to the steps?'

'If you're not in a hurry.'

They inched their way along, staggered up the stone steps to the apron. 'Coffee,' Eve said weakly, then stumbled off to fetch two thick terry robes.

When she came back, carrying one and bundled into the other, Roarke had already programmed the AutoChef for two cups, black. The sun was staining the curved glass at the end of the enclosure a pale gold.

'Hungry?'

She sipped the coffee, hummed as the rich caffeine kicked. 'Starving. But I want a shower.'

'Upstairs then.'

Back in the master suite, Eve carried her coffee into the shower. When Roarke stepped into the criss-crossing sprays with her, she narrowed her eyes. 'Lower the water temp and die,' she warned.

'Cold water opens the pores, gets the juices flowing.'

'You've already taken care of that.' She set the coffee on a ledge and soaped up in the steam.

She got out first, and as she stepped into the drying tube, shook her head as Roarke ordered the water to drop by ten degrees. Even the thought of it made her shiver.

She knew he was waiting for her to tell him about the case that had kept her out the night before and was taking her back on her day off. She appreciated that he waited for her to settle in the sitting area of the suite, a second cup of coffee in her hand and a plate loaded with a ham and cheese omelette waiting to be devoured.

'I really am sorry about not showing up for the deal last night.'

Roarke sampled his own buttermilk pancakes. 'Am I going to have to apologize every time I'm called away on business that affects our personal plans?'

She opened her mouth, closed it again, and shook her head. 'No. The thing is I was headed out the door – I hadn't forgotten – and this call came in. Jammed transmission. We couldn't track.'

'The NYPSD has pitiful equipment.'

'Not that pitiful,' she muttered. 'This guy's a real pro. You might have had a tough time with it.'

'Now, that's insulting.'

She had to smirk. 'Well, you might get a chance at him. Since he tagged me personally, I wouldn't put it past him to contact me here.'

Roarke set his fork aside, picked up his coffee, both gestures casual though his entire body had gone to alert. 'Personally?'

'Yeah, he wanted me. Hit me with some religious mission crap first, Basically, he's doing the Lord's work and the Big Guy wants to play with riddles.' She ran the transmission through for him, watching his eyes narrow, sharpen. Roarke was quick, she reflected as she saw his mouth go grim.

'You checked the Luxury Towers.'

'That's right, penthouse floor. He'd left part of the victim in the living area. The rest of him was in the bedroom.'

She pushed her plate aside and rose, raking a hand through her hair as she paced. 'It was as bad as I've ever seen, Roarke, vicious. Because it was calculated to be ugly, not because it was uncontrolled. Most of the work was precise, like surgery. Prelim from the ME indicates the victim was kept alive and aware during most of the mutilation. He'd been pumped up with illegals – enough to keep him conscious without taking the edge off the pain. And believe me, the pain must have been unspeakable. He'd been disemboweled.'

'Christ Jesus.' Roarke blew out a breath. 'An ancient punishment for political or religious crimes. A slow and hideous death.'

'And a goddamn messy one,' she put in. 'His feet had been severed – one hand gone at the wrist. He was still alive when his right eye was cut out. That was the only piece of him we didn't recover at the scene.'

'Lovely.' Though he considered his stomach a strong one, Roarke lost his taste for breakfast. Rising, he went to the closet. 'An eye for an eye.'

'That's a revenge thing, right? From some play.'

'The Bible, darling. The lord of all plays.' He chose casual pleated trousers from the revolving rack.

'Back to God again. Okay, the game's revenge. Maybe it's religious, maybe it's just personal. We may zero in on motive when we finish running the victim. I've got a media blackout at least until I contact his family.'

Roarke hitched up the trousers, reached for a simple white linen shirt. 'Children?'

'Yeah, three.'

'You have a miserable job, Lieutenant.'

'That's why I love it.' But she rubbed her hands over her face. 'His wife and kids are in Ireland, we think. I need to track them down today.'

'In Ireland?'

'Hmm. Yeah, seems the victim was one of your former

24

countrymen. I don't suppose you knew a Thomas X. Brennen, did you?' Her half smile faded when she saw Roarke's eyes go dark and flat. 'You did know him. I never figured it.'

'Early forties?' Roarke asked without inflection. 'About five-ten, sandy hair?'

'Sounds like. He was into communications and entertainment.'

'Tommy Brennen.' With the shirt still in his hand, Roarke sat on the arm of a chair. 'Son of a bitch.'

'I'm sorry. It didn't occur to me that he was a friend.'

'He wasn't.' Roarke shook his head to clear away the memories. 'At least not in more than a decade. I knew him in Dublin. He was running computer scams while I was grifting. We crossed paths a few times, did a little business, drank a few pints. About twelve years ago, Tommy hooked up with a young woman of good family. Lace curtain Irish. He fell hard and decided to go straight. All the way straight,' Roarke added with a crooked grin. 'And he severed ties with the less . . . desirable elements of his youth. I knew he had a base here in New York, but we stayed out of each other's way. I believe his wife knows nothing of his past endeavors.'

Eve sat on the arm opposite him. 'It might have been one of the past endeavors, and one of those less desirable elements, that's responsible for what happened to him. Roarke, I'm going to be digging, and when I dig how much of you am I going to uncover?'

It was a worry, he supposed. A mild one to him. But, he knew, it would never be mild to her. 'I cover my tracks, Lieutenant. And, as I said, we weren't mates. I haven't had any contact with him at all in years. But I remember him. He had a fine tenor voice,' Roarke murmured. 'A good laugh, a good mind, and a longing for family. He was fast with his fists, but never went looking for trouble that I recall.'

'Looking or not, he found it. Do you know where his family is?'

He shook his head as he rose. 'But I can get that information for you quickly enough.'

'I'd appreciate it.' She rose as he shrugged into the casual elegant shirt. 'Roarke, I'm sorry, for whatever he was to you.'

'A touchstone perhaps. A song in a smoky pub on a rainy night. I'm sorry, too. I'll be in my office. Give me ten minutes.'

'Sure.'

Eve took her time dressing. She had a feeling Roarke would need more than ten minutes. Not to access the data she'd asked for. With his equipment and his skill he'd have it in half that time. But she thought he needed a few moments alone to deal with the loss of that song in a smoky pub.

She'd never lost anyone even remotely close to her. Maybe, Eve realized, because she'd been careful to let only a select few become close enough to matter. Then there had been Roarke, and she'd had no choice. He'd invaded, she'd supposed, subtly, elegantly, inarguably. And now . . . she ran a thumb over the carved gold wedding ring she wore. Now he was vital.

She took the stairs this time, winding her way through the wide halls in the big, beautiful house. She didn't have to knock on his office door, but did so, waiting until the door slid open in invitation.

The window shields were up to let in the sun. The sky behind the treated glass was murky, hinting that the rain wasn't quite finished. Roarke manned the antique desk of gleaming wood rather than the slick console. The floors were covered with gorgeous old rugs he'd acquired on his journeys.

Eve slipped her hands into her pockets. She was almost accustomed to the grandeur she now lived in, but she didn't know what to do with Roarke's grief, with the self contained quiet sorrow.

'Listen, Roarke—'

'I got you a hard copy.' He nudged a sheet of paper across the desk. 'I thought it would be easier. His wife and children

26

are in Dublin at the moment. The children are minors, two boys and a girl. Ages nine, eight, and six.'

Too restless to sit, he rose and turned to stare out at his view of New York – quiet now, the light still dull, the skies almost still. He'd brought up visuals of Brennen's family – the pretty, bright-eyed woman, the rosy-cheeked children. It had disturbed him more than he'd anticipated.

'Financially they'll be quite comfortable,' he said almost to himself. 'Tommy saw to that. Apparently he'd become a very good husband and father.'

She crossed the room, lifted a hand to touch, then dropped it. Damn it, she was no good at this, she thought. No good at knowing if comfort would be welcomed or rejected. 'I don't know what to do for you,' she said at length.

When he turned, his eyes were brilliantly blue, and fury rode in them along with the grief. 'Find who did this to him. I can trust you for that.'

'Yeah, you can.'

A smile touched his lips, curved them. 'Lieutenant Dallas, standing for the dead, as always.' He skimmed a hand through her hair, lifting a brow when she caught it.

'You'll leave this to me, Roarke.'

'Have I said otherwise?'

'It's what you haven't said that's just beginning to get through.' She knew him, knew him well enough to understand he would have his own ways, his own means, and very likely his own agenda. 'If you've got any ideas about going out on your own, put them to bed now. It's my case, and I'll handle it.'

He ran his hands up her arms in a way that made her eyes narrow. 'Naturally. But you will keep me apprised? And you know that I'm available for any assistance you might require.'

'I think I can stumble through on my own. And I think it would be best if you took a step back from this one. A long step back.'

He kissed the tip of her nose. 'No,' he said pleasantly.

'Roarke—'

'Would you prefer I lied to you, Eve?' He picked up the hard copy while she fumed, handed it to her. 'Go to work. I'll make a few calls. I'd think by the end of the day I should have a complete list of Tommy's associates, professional and personal, his enemies, his friends, his lovers, his financial status, and so forth.' He was leading her across the room as he spoke. 'It'll be easier for me to accumulate the data, and it'll give you a clear picture.'

She managed to hold her ground before he pushed her out the door. 'I can't stop you from accumulating data. But don't step out of line, pal. Not one inch.'

'You know how it excites me when you're strict.'

She struggled back a laugh and nearly managed a glare. 'Shut up,' she muttered, and shoved her hands in her pockets and she strode away.

He watched her, waited until she'd disappeared at the stairs. Cautious, he turned to the security monitor and ordered view. The laughter was gone from his eyes as he watched her jog down the steps, snag the jacket Summerset had laid back over the newel post for her.

'You're forgetting an umbrella,' he murmured, and sighed when she walked into the thin drizzle unprotected.

He hadn't told her everything. How could he? How could he be certain it was relevant, in any case? He needed more before he risked tangling the woman he loved in the ugliness of his own past, his own sins.

He left his office, heading for the communications room that was both expansive and illegal. Laying his palm on the security screen, he identified himself then entered. Here, the equipment was unregistered and any activity would be undetected by the all-seeing eye of CompuGuard. He needed specifics in order to plan his next step, and sitting in the deep U of a sleek black control center, he began.

Invading the system of NYPSD was child's play for him. He sent a silent apology to his wife as he accessed her files, dipped into the medical examiner's office.

'Crime scene video on screen one,' Roarke ordered, easing back. 'Autopsy report, screen two, primary investigating officer's report, screen three.'

The horror of what had been done to Brennen swam on screen, made Roarke's eyes go cold and flat. There was little left of the young man he'd known a lifetime before in Dublin. He read Eve's clipped and formal report without emotion, studied the complex terms of the preliminary report from the ME.

'Copy to file Brennen, code Roarke, password my voiceprint only. Off screen.'

Turning, he reached for his in-house tele-link. 'Summerset, come up please.'

'On my way.'

Roarke rose, moved to the window. The past could come back to haunt, he knew. Most often it remained in some ghostly corner waiting to strike. Had it slipped out to strike Tommy Brennen? he wondered. Or was it just bad luck, bad timing?

The door slid open and Summerset, bony in black, stepped through. 'Is there a problem?'

'Thomas Brennen.'

Summerset's thin lips frowned, then his eyes cleared into what was nearly a smile. 'Ah yes, an eager young hacker with a love of rebel songs and Guinness.'

'He's been murdered.'

'I'm sorry to hear that.'

'Here in New York,' Roarke continued. 'Eve is primary.' Roarke watched Summerset's mouth set and flatten. 'He was tortured, kept alive for the pain. Disemboweled.'

It took a moment, but Summerset's already pale face whitened a shade more. 'Coincidence.'

'Maybe, hopefully.' Roarke indulged himself by taking a

slim cigarette from a japanned case, lighting it. 'Whoever did it called my wife personally, wanted her involved.'

'She's a cop,' Summerset said with a lifetime of disdain in his voice.

'She's my wife,' Roarke returned, the edge in his voice scalpel sharp. 'If it turns out it isn't coincidence, I'll tell her everything.'

'You can't risk that. There's no statute of limitations on murder – even justifiable murder.'

'That'll be up to her, won't it?' Roarke took a long drag, sat on the edge of the console. 'I won't have her working blind, Summerset. I won't put her in that position. Not for myself, not for you.' The grief slipped back into his eyes as he looked down at the flame at the tip of the cigarette. 'Not for memories. You need to be prepared.'

'It's not me who'll pay if the law means more to her than you. You did what needed to be done, what had to be done, what should have been done.'

'And so will Eve,' Roarke said mildly. 'Before we project, we need to reconstruct. How much do you remember about that time, and who was involved?'

'I've forgotten nothing.'

Roarke studied Summerset's stiff jaw, hard eyes and nodded. 'That's what I was counting on. Let's get to work then.'

The lights on the console twinkled like stars. He loved to look at them. It didn't matter that the room was small, and windowless, not when he had the hum of the machine, the light of those stars to guide him.

He was ready to move on to the next one, ready to begin the next round. The young boy who still lived inside him reveled in the competition. The man who had formed out of that boy prepared for the holy work.

His tools were carefully set out. He opened the vial of water blessed by a bishop and sprinkled it reverently over the laser, the knives, the hammer, the nails. The instruments of divine vengeance, the tools of retribution. Behind them was a statue of the Virgin, carved in white marble to symbolize her purity. Her arms were spread in benediction, her face beautiful and serene in acceptance.

He bent, kissed the white marble feet.

For a moment he thought he saw the gleam of blood on his hand, and that hand shook.

But no, his hand was clean and white. He had washed the blood of his enemy away. The mark of Cain stained the others, but not him. He was the lamb of God after all.

He would meet with another enemy soon, very soon, and he had to be strong to bait to trap, to wear the mask of friendship.

He had fasted, made the sacrifice, cleansed his heart and mind of all worldly evils. Now he dipped his fingers into a small bowl of holy water, touched his fingers to his brow, his heart, left shoulder, then right. He knelt, closing a hand over the cloth scapular he wore. It had been blessed by the Pope himself, and its promise of protection from evil comforted him.

He tucked it tidily under the silk of his shirt where it could rest against warm flesh.

Secure, confident, he lifted his gaze to the crucifix that hung above the sturdy table that held the weapons of his mission. The image of the suffering Christ gleamed silver against a cross of gold. A rich man's visual aide. The irony of owning an image carved from precious metals of a man who had preached humility never touched him.

He lighted the candles, folded his hands, and bending his head prayed with the passion of the faithful, and the mad.

He prayed for grace, and prepared for murder.

Chapter Three

The Homicide bullpen at Cop Central smelled like day-old coffee and fresh urine. Eve wound her way through the jammed-in desks, barely registering the buzz of chatter from detectives working their 'links. A maintenance droid was busily mopping up the ancient linoleum.

Peabody's cube was a dimly lighted two-foot square in the far corner. Despite its size and location, it was as ruthlessly organized and tidy as Peabody herself.

'Somebody forget where the toilets are?' Eve asked casually, and Peabody turned from her dented, police issue metal desk.

'Bailey had a sidewalk sleeper in for questioning on a knifing. The sleeper didn't like being held as a witness and expressed his displeasure by emptying his bladder on Bailey's shoes. From all reports, said bladder was unusually full.'

'Just another day in paradise. Is the sweeper report in on Brennen yet?'

'I just gave them a nudge. It should be coming through shortly.'

'Then let's start with the security discs from the Luxury Towers and Brennen's apartment.'

'There's a problem there, Lieutenant.'

Eve cocked her head. 'You didn't get them?'

'I got what there was to get.' Peabody picked up a sealed bag containing a single disc. 'The Towers's security, penthouse level, for the twelve-hour period before the discovery of Brennen's body and the SCAN-EYE in Brennen's place were disengaged, and empty.'

Eve nodded and took the bag. 'I should have figured he wouldn't be that stupid. Did you download the incoming and outgoing calls from Brennen's tele-link?'

'Right here.' Peabody handed over another disc, neatly labeled.

'My office. We'll run them and see what we've got. I'm going to give Feeney a call,' Eve continued as they headed out of the bullpen. 'We're going to need the Electronic Detective Division on this.'

'Captain Feeney's in Mexico, Lieutenant. Vacation?'

Eve stopped, scowled. 'Shit, I forgot. He's got another week, doesn't he?'

'Just over that. In your lovely cliffside villa. To which your devoted aide has yet to be invited.'

Eve lifted a brow. 'You got a yen to see Mexico?'

'I've seen Mexico, Dallas, I've got a yen to let a hot-blooded caballero have his way with me.'

Snorting, Eve unlocked her office door. 'We wrap this case up in good time, Peabody, I'll see if I can arrange it.' She tossed the discs on her already disordered desk, then shrugged out of her jacket. 'We still need someone from EDD. See who they can spare who knows his stuff. I don't want some second-grade tinkerer.'

Peabody got out her communicator to make the request while Eve settled behind her desk, slipped the disc of Brennen's communications into her unit.

'Engage,' she ordered after remembering her password. 'Playback.'

There was only one call, an outgoing on the day before Brennen was murdered. He'd called his wife, talked to his children. And the simple, intimate domestic chatter of a man and the family he was planning to join made Eve unbearably sad.

'I have to contact the wife,' Eve murmured. 'Hell of a way to start the day. Best get it done now before we have a media leak. Give me ten minutes here, Peabody.'

'Yes, sir. EDD is sending over a Detective McNab.'

'Fine.' When her door shut and she was alone, Eve took a long breath. And made the call.

When Peabody came back ten minutes later, Eve was drinking coffee while she stood staring out her skinny window. 'Eileen Brennen's coming back to New York, bringing her kids. She insists on seeing him. She didn't fall apart. Sometimes it's worse when they don't crumble, when they hang on. When you can see in their eyes they're sure somehow you've made a mistake.'

She rolled her shoulders, as if shrugging off a weight, then turned. 'Let's see the security disc. We could catch a break.'

Peabody unsealed the disc herself and engaged it. Seconds later both she and Eve were staring at the computer screen.

'What the hell is that?' Eve demanded.

'It's – I don't know.' Peabody frowned at the figures moving over the screen. The voices were raised but solemn and in a foreign tongue. At the center was a man in black, robe over robe, with two young boys in white beside him. He held a silver goblet in his hand as he stood before an altar draped with black cloth and white flowers and candles. 'A ritual? Is it a play?'

'It's a funeral,' Eve murmured, studying the closed and gleaming casket beneath the raised platform. 'A funeral Mass. I've been to one. It's a Catholic thing, I think. Computer, identify ceremony and language on disc.'

Working . . . Ceremony is Catholic Requiem Mass
or Mass for the Dead. Language is Latin. This section
depicts offertory chant and ritual in which—

'That's enough. Where the hell did you get this disc, Peabody?'

'Straight out of the security room at the Luxury Towers, Dallas. It was coded, marked, and labeled.'

'He switched them,' Eve muttered. 'The son of a bitch switched discs on us. He's still playing games. And he's damn good at it. Computer, stop run, copy disc.' Shoving her hands in her pockets, Eve rocked back on her heels. 'He's having fun with us, Peabody. I'm going to have to hurt him for that. Order a sweep of the security room, and arrange to confiscate all discs for the appropriate time period.'

'All discs?'

'All discs, all floors, all levels. And I want the report from the uniforms who handled the door-to-doors on the Towers.' She pocketed the copy her computer spat out. 'And I'm going to see what the hell's keeping the initial sweeper report.'

She reached for her 'link just as it beeped. 'Dallas.'

'You were quick, Lieutenant. I'm impressed.'

Eve only had to blink to have Peabody ordering a transmission trace. Eve smiled thinly at the colors swimming across her screen. This time the music was a chorus of voices in a language she now recognized as Latin. 'You did quite a job on Brennen. Looked like you enjoyed yourself.'

'Oh, I did, believe me, I did. Tommy was quite a singer, you know. He certainly sang for me. Listen.'

All at once the room was full of screams, inhuman, weeping screams that had ice skating up Eve's spine.

'Beautiful. He begged for his life, then he begged me to end it. I kept him alive for four hours giving him time to relive his past sins.'

'Your style lacks subtlety, pal. And when I nail you, I'll have enough to keep you from pulling a mentally defective. I'll get you straight, and I'll push for a cage on Attica Two. The facilities there make on-planet cages look like country clubs.'

'They caged the Baptist, but he knew the glory of Heaven.'

Eve searched her threadbare memory of Bible stories. 'He's the one who lost his head to a dancing girl, right? You willing to risk yours to a cop?'

'She was a harlot.' He mumbled the words so that Eve had to lean close to hear. 'Evil in a beautiful form. So many are. He withstood her, her temptation, and was martyred pure.'

'Do you want to be martyred? To die for what you call your faith? I can help you with that. Just tell me where you are.'

'You challenge me, Lieutenant, in ways I hadn't expected. A strong-minded woman is one of God's greatest pleasures. And you're named for Eve, the mother of mankind. If only your heart was pure, I could admire you.'

'You can save the admiration.'

'Eve was also weak in spirit and caused the loss of Paradise for her children.'

'Yeah, and Adam was a wimp who couldn't take responsibility. Bible hour's over. Let's get on with it.'

'I look forward to meeting you – though it can't be for a little while yet.'

'Sooner than you think.'

'Perhaps, perhaps, Meanwhile, another riddle. A race this time. The next sinner is still alive, still blissfully unaware of his punishment. By his words, and God's law, he will be condemned. Heed this. A faithful man will abound with blessings, but he who hastens to be rich will not go unpunished.' He's gone unpunished long enough.'

'For what?'

'For a lying tongue. You have twenty-four hours to save a life, if God wills it. Your riddle: He's fair of face and once lived by his wits. Now those wits are dulled as like poor old Dicey Riley, he's taken to the sup. He lives where he works and works where he lives, and all the night serves others what he craves most. He traveled across the foam but closes himself in a place that reminds him of home.

36

Unless you find him first, his luck runs out tomorrow morn. Better hurry.'

Eve stared at the screen long after it went blank.

'Sorry, Dallas, no good on the trace. Maybe the e-detective can do something with it when he gets here.'

'Who the hell is Dicey Riley?' Eve muttered. 'What does he mean "sup"? Like supper? Food maybe. Restaurants. Irish restaurants.'

'I think that's an oxymoron.'

'Huh?'

'Bad joke,' Peabody offered with a sick smile. 'To lighten the mood.'

'Right.' Eve dropped in her chair. 'Computer, list name and locations for all Irish restaurants in the city. Hard copy.' She swiveled in her chair. 'Contact Tweeser – she was head sweeper on Brennen. Tell her I need something, anything. And have a uniform go over to the Towers and get those security discs. Let's move.'

'Moving,' Peabody agreed and headed out.

An hour later, Eve was pouring over the sweeper's report. There was little to nothing to study. 'Bastard didn't leave so much as a nose hair to scoop up.' She rubbed her eyes. She needed to go back to the scene, she decided, walk through it, try to visualize it all. All she could see was the blood, the gore, the waste.

She needed to clear her vision.

The Biblical quote had come from Proverbs again. She could only assume that the intended victim wanted to be rich. And that, she decided, narrowed it down to every single sinning soul in New York City.

Revenge was the motive. Money for betrayal? she wondered. Someone connected to Brennen? She called up the lists Roarke had accessed and transmitted, scanned the names of Thomas Brennen's associates, friends.

No lovers, she mused. And Roarke would have found any if they'd existed. Thomas Brennen had been a faithful husband, and now his wife was a widow.

At the sharp rap on her doorjamb, she glanced up, frowned distractedly at the man grinning at her. Midtwenties, she judged, with a pretty-boy face and a love of fashion.

He barely topped five-eight even in the neon yellow air boots. He wore denim above them, pants that bagged and a jacket that showed frayed cuffs. His hair was a bright new minted gold that flowed into a waist-length ponytail. He had half a dozen small, glinting gold hoops in his left earlobe.

'You took a wrong turn, pal. This is Homicide.'

'And you'd be Dallas.' His bright, eager grin pinched twin dimples into his cheeks. His eyes were a misty green. 'I'd be McNab, with EDD.'

She didn't groan. She wanted to, but suppressed it into a quiet sigh as she held out a hand. *Good Christ* was all she could think, as he took it with fingers twinkling with rings. 'You're one of Feeney's.'

'Joined his unit six months ago.' He glanced around her dim, cramped office. 'You guys in Homicide really got squeezed in the budget cuts. We got closets bigger than this in EDD.'

He glanced over, then beamed a fresh smile as Peabody stepped up beside him. 'Nothing like a woman in uniform.'

'Peabody, McNab.'

Peabody took a long, critical study, scanning glints and glitters. 'This is the EDD dress code?'

'It's Saturday,' McNab said easily. 'I got the call at home, thought I'd swing in and see what's up. And we're a little loose over at EDD.'

'Obviously.' Peabody started to squeeze by him, narrowing her eyes when he grinned again.

'With three of us in there, we'll be standing in sin. But I'm game.' He shifted enough to let her by, then followed, letting his gaze skim down to judge curves.

Not bad, thought McNab. Not bad at all.

When he lifted his gaze and encountered Eve's stony stare, he cleared his throat. He knew Eve Dallas's reputation. She didn't tolerate bullshit. 'What can I do for you, Lieutenant?'

'I've got a homicide, Detective, and I may have another by this time tomorrow. I need a trace on communication. I need a location. I need to find out how the hell this prick is jamming our lines.'

'Then I'm your man. Calls coming in on this unit?' At Eve's nod, he moved closer. 'Mind if I take your chair, see what I can do?'

'Go ahead.' She rose, moved aside for him. 'Peabody, I've got to get over to the morgue this afternoon. Try to head off Mrs Brennen, get a statement. We're going to split the restaurant list between us. We're looking for someone who works and lives on the premises, someone who emigrated into New York, and someone with a possible connection to Thomas Brennen. I've got a list of Brennen's nearest friends and associates. Narrow it down, and narrow it fast.' She handed Peabody a hard copy.

'Yes, sir.'

'And check close on anyone named Riley – or Dicey.'

McNab stopped the under-the-breath humming that seemed to be the theme song of every electronics man Eve knew. 'Dicey Riley?' he said and laughed.

'I miss the joke, McNab?'

'I don't know. 'Dicey Riley' is an Irish pub song.'

'Pub?' Eve's eyes narrowed. 'You Irish, McNab?'

She caught the slight flare of insult flicker over his pretty face. 'I'm a Scotsman, Lieutenant. My grandfather was a Highlander.'

'Good for him. What's the song mean – what's it about?'

'It's about a woman who drinks too much.'

'Drinks? Not eats?'

'Drinks,' he confirmed. 'The Irish Virus.'

'Shit. Well, half these are pubs anyway,' Eve said as she looked down at her own list. 'We'll run another check on Irish bars in the city.'

'You'll need a twenty man task force to hit all the Irish pubs in New York,' McNab said easily, then turned back to his work.

'You just worry about the trace,' Eve ordered. 'Peabody, run the names and locations for the bars. The uniform back yet with the discs from the Towers?'

'He's en route.'

'Fine, have the bars broken down geographically. I'll take the south and west, you take north and east.' Even as Peabody left, Eve turned to McNab. 'I need something fast.'

'It's not going to be fast.' His boyish face was grim with purpose now. 'I've already gone down a couple of layers. There's nothing. I'm running a scattershot trace on the last transmission that came through. It takes time, but it's the best way to trace through a jam.'

'Make it take less time,' she snapped. 'And contact me as soon as you break through.'

He rolled his eyes behind her back as she strode out. 'Women,' he muttered. 'Always wanting a miracle.'

Eve hit a dozen bars as she worked her way down to the medical examiner's building. She found two bar owners and three crew who lived above or behind the business. As she pulled her unit into a third-level parking space at the ME's, she called up Peabody.

'Status?'

'I've got two possibles so far, and my uniform's going to smell like smoke and whiskey for the next six months.' Peabody grimaced. 'Neither of my possibles claims to have known Thomas Brennen or to have an enemy in the world.'

'Yeah, I'm getting the same line. Keep at it. We're running out of time.'

40

Eve took the stairs down, then coded herself into security. She avoided the discreet, flower-laden waiting area and moved straight into the morgue.

The air there was cold, and carried the sly underlayer of death. The doors might have been steel and sealed, but death always found a way to make its presence known.

She'd left Brennen in Autopsy Room B, and since it was unlikely he'd taken himself off anywhere, she approached the security panel, holding up her badge for the scan.

Autopsy in progress, Brennen, Thomas X. Please observe the health and safety rules upon entering. You are cleared, Dallas, Lieutenant Eve.

The door clicked, then unsealed with a whoosh of chilly air. Eve stepped in to see the trim and dapper form of Dr Morris, the ME, gracefully removing Brennen's brain from his open skull.

'Sorry we're not finished up here, Dallas. We've had a flood of check-ins without reservations this morning. People – ha, ha – dying to get in.'

'What can you tell me?'

Morris checked the weight of the brain, set it aside in fluid. His waist-length braid made a curling line down the back of his snowy white lab coat. Under it he wore a skin suit of virulent purple. 'He was a healthy fifty-two-year-old man, and had once suffered a broken tibia. It mended well. He enjoyed his last meal about four and a half hours before death. Lunch, I'd say. Beef soup, bread, and coffee. The coffee was drugged.'

'With?'

'A midline soother. Over-the-counter tranq. He'd have felt pretty relaxed, maybe with a slight buzz.' Morris manually logged data into his portable log and spoke to Eve across the white and mutilated remains. 'The first injury would have been the severed hand. Even with the soother in his system, that would have caused shock and quick, traumatic blood loss.'

Eve remembered the walls of the apartment, the ghastly sprays of blood. She imagined the severed arteries had spurted and pumped like a fire hose on full.

'Whoever hacked him stopped the blood jet by cauterizing the stump.'

'How?'

'My guess would be a hand torch.' He grimaced. 'It was a messy job. See where it's all blackened and crispy from the stump to the elbow. Say ouch.'

'Ouch,' Eve murmured and hooked her thumbs in her pockets. 'What you're telling me is Brennen basically collapsed after the first attack – which accounts for the little to no sign of struggle in the apartment.'

'He couldn't have fought off a drunk cockroach. Victim was restrained by his remaining wrist. Drugs administered were a combination of adrenaline and digitalis – that would keep the heart beating, the brain conscious while he was worked over.' Morris blew out a breath. 'And he was worked over good. Death didn't come quick or easy for this Irish rover.'

Morris's eyes remained mild behind his safety goggles. He gestured with a sealed hand to a small metal tray. 'I found that in his stomach along with his lunch.'

Eve frowned down at the tray. The object was about the size of a five-dollar credit. It was glossy white with a bright green image painted on it. On the other side was an oblong shape that met at one end with crossed lines.

'A four-leaf clover,' Morris supplied. 'It's a symbol for good luck. Your murderer has a strong and nasty sense of irony. On the back – that funny shape? Your guess is as good as mine.'

'I'll take it with me.' Eve slipped the token into an evidence bag. 'I intend to ask Dr Mira to consult on this case. We need a profile. She'll contact you shortly.'

'Always a pleasure to work with Mira, and you, Lieutenant.' The communication band on his wrist buzzed. 'Death Palace. Morris.'

'Mrs Eileen Brennen has arrived and requests to view her husband's remains.'

'Take her on into my office. I'll be there shortly.' He turned to Eve. 'No use her seeing the poor bastard like this. You want to interview her?'

'Yes.'

'Use my office as long as you need it. Mrs Brennen can see the body in twenty minutes. He'll be . . . presentable by then.'

'Thanks.' She headed for the door.

'Dallas.'

'Yeah?'

'Evil is – well, it's not a term I like to toss around like candy. Kind of embarrassing.' He moved his shoulders. 'But the guy who did this . . . it's the only word I can think of that fits.'

Those words played back in Eve's head as she faced Eileen Brennen. The woman was trim and tidy. Though her eyes were dry, her face was waxy pale. Her hands didn't shake, but neither could they be still. She tugged at the gold cross that hung on a thin chain to her waist, tugged at the hem of her skirt, combed fingers through her wavy blond hair.

'I want to see the body you found. I insist on seeing it. It's my right.'

'You will, Mrs Brennen. We're arranging that. If I could have a few minutes of your time first, it would be very helpful.'

'How do I know it's him? How do I know it's my Tommy until I see him?'

There was no point in offering hope. 'Mrs Brennen, we've identified your husband. Fingerprints, DNA, and the visual ID of the doorman at the Luxury Towers. I'm sorry, there's no mistake. Please sit down. Can I get you anything? Some water.'

'I don't want anything. Nothing.' Eileen sat with a little jerk, her hands closing and unclosing. 'He was to join us today, in Dublin. Today. He only stayed back in New York this past week to finish up some business. He was coming today, stopping off in London first last night.'

'So you weren't expecting him until today.'

'No. He didn't call last night, he was supposed to call from London, but sometimes he gets busy.' She unclasped her purse, shut it again, repeating the movement over and over. 'I didn't think anything of it. I didn't think anything of it,' she repeated and fisted her hand over the cross until the rounded points dug into her palm.

'So you didn't try to contact him?'

'The children and I, we went out to dinner and to an entertainment center. We got home late, and Maize was cross. I put her to bed and went to sleep. I just went to sleep because I was tired and I didn't even think of Tommy not calling from London.'

Eve let her wind down, then sat across from her in one of Dr Morris's soft brown cloth chairs. 'Mrs. Brennen, can you tell me about the business your husband stayed in New York to see to?'

'I don't – I don't know that much about it. I don't understand all of that. I'm a professional mother. I have children to raise, three houses to run. We have another home in the country. In the west of Ireland. I don't understand business. Why should I?' she demanded in a voice that cracked.

'All right. Can you tell me if your husband mentioned anyone who concerned him? Someone who threatened him or disturbed him.'

'Tommy doesn't have enemies. Everyone likes him. He's a fair man, a kind-hearted one. You've only to ask anyone who knows him.' Her eyes, a pale blue, focused on Eve's face

44

again, and she leaned forward. 'You see, that's why you must be wrong. You must have made a mistake. No one would hurt Tommy. And the Luxury Towers is very secure. That's why we chose it for our home in New York. So much crime in the city, and Tommy wanted me and the children safe.'

'You met your husband in Ireland.'

Eileen blinked, distracted. 'Yes, more than twelve years ago. In Dublin.'

'Did he still have friends from that time, associates?'

'I . . . he has so many friends. I . . .' She passed a hand over her eyes. 'There would always seem to be someone who'd call hello to him if we were out. And sometimes he'd go to a little pub when we were in Dublin. I don't care much for pubs, so I didn't often go. But he'd get a yearning now and then and go in for an evening.'

'What was the pub?'

'The name? The Penny Pig, I think it's called.' Suddenly Eileen gripped Eve's arm. 'I have to see him. I have to.'

'All right. Just give me a moment. I'll be right back.' Eve stepped outside the office, pulled out her communicator. 'Peabody.'

'Lieutenant.'

'The Penny Pig. Any of the pubs on your list by that name?'

'Just a second . . . no, sir. Nothing with Pig at all.'

'Just a thought. Keep at it. I'll be in touch.' She shifted, contacted Dr Morris. 'She needs to see him.'

'He's as good as he's going to get here. I'll pass you both through.'

Eve opened the office door. 'Mrs Brennen. If you'll come with me now.'

'You're taking me to him.'

'Yes.'

As much for support as guidance, Eve took Eileen's elbow. Their footsteps echoed down the white-tiled corridor. At the

45

door, Eve felt the woman stiffen and brace. Heard her draw in a breath and hold it.

Then they were inside. Morris had done what he could, but there was no disguising the trauma. There was no way to soften death.

Eileen let out the breath in one choked sob. Just one, then she drew it in again and gently pushed Eve's supporting hand aside.

'It's my Tommy. This is my husband.' She stepped closer, approaching the white-sheeted figure as if he were sleeping. Eve said nothing when Eileen traced fingertips over her husband's cheek. 'How can I tell our babies, Tommy? What will I tell them?'

She looked over at Eve, and though her eyes swam, she seemed determined to hold onto her tears. 'Who could have done such a thing to such a good man?'

'It's my job to find out. I will do my job, Mrs Brennen. You can rely on that.'

'Finding out won't bring Tommy back to me or our children. Finding out's too late, isn't it?'

Death, Eve thought, made everything too late. 'It's all I have for you, Mrs Brennen.'

'I don't know if it can be enough, Lieutenant Dallas. I don't know if I can make it be enough.' She bent over, softly kissed her husband's lips. 'I always loved you, Tommy. From the first.'

'Come with me now, Mrs Brennen.' Eileen didn't resist as Eve took her arm. 'Come outside. Who can I call for you?'

'I – my friend Katherine Hastings. She lives . . . she has a place on Fifth Avenue, a shop. Noticeable Woman.'

'I'll call. I'll have her come and meet you here.'

'Thank you. I need . . . someone.'

'Do you want some water now? Coffee?'

'No, just to sit down.' And she all but collapsed into a stiff-backed chair in the waiting area. 'Just to get off my feet.

46

I'll be fine.' She looked up, blue eyes swimming in a white face. 'I'll be all right. I have the children, you see. I have to be all right.'

Eve hesitated, then pulled the evidence bag out of her pocket. 'Mrs Brennen, have you ever seen this before?'

Eileen concentrated on the token as if it were a rare piece of art. 'No. That is, of course I've seen a shamrock before, but not this little button.'

'Shamrock?'

'Of course, that's what it is. A shamrock.'

'How about this?' Eve turned the token over.

'A fish.' She closed her eyes now. 'A symbol of the Church. Will you call Katherine now, please? I don't want to be here anymore.'

'Right away. Just sit and try to rest a minute.'

Eve rushed through the call to Katherine Hastings, offering little explanation. She was skimming her hard copy of the pub list as she did so. She had no Penny Pig, no Four-Leaf Clover, nothing with fish or church. But she had three locations with Shamrock in the name.

She snagged her communicator. 'Peabody, concentrate on locations with Shamrock in the name.'

'Shamrock, Lieutenant?'

'It's a hunch. Just do it.'

Eve walked into the Green Shamrock at three P.M. She'd missed the lunch crowd – if there'd been one – and found the small, dark pub nearly deserted. A couple of sad-looking customers sat huddled over thickly foamed beers at a back table while they played a desultory game of gin. Though she saw no on-site gambling license displayed, she ignored the piles of credits beside the mugs of beer.

A young woman with a white apron and rosy cheeks was whistling as she wiped tables. She smiled at Eve, and when she spoke Eve heard that lovely lilt of Roarke's native land.

'Good afternoon to you, miss. Can I get you a menu? It's just sandwiches this time of day, I'm afraid.'

'No, thanks.' There was no one manning the bar, but Eve slid onto a stool before pulling out her badge. She saw the young waitress's eyes widen.

'I haven't done anything. I'm legal. I have papers.'

'I'm not with Immigration.' From the hasty relief on the girl's face, Eve imagined the papers were still wet, and likely fake. 'Are there rooms for rent on the premises? Do any of the employees, or the owner, live on-site?'

'Yes, ma'am. There are three rooms. One in the back and two upstairs. I have one upstairs myself. It's up to code.'

'Who else lives here – what's your name?'

'I'm Maureen Mulligan.'

'Who else lives on-site, Maureen?'

'Well, Bob McBride did until last month when the boss fired him for laziness. Bob had a hard time lifting a pint, you see, unless it was up to his own lips.' She smiled again and began to scrub at the bar industriously. 'And now there's Shawn Conroy who takes the back room.'

'Would he be back there now?'

'I just looked a bit ago, and he wasn't about. He should be in here now, half hour ago his shift started.'

'You want to show me his room, Maureen?'

'He's not in any trouble, is he? Shawn drinks a bit, but he's a good worker and does his best.'

'I want to make sure he's not in trouble. You can call your boss, Maureen, and clear showing me in the back.'

Maureen bit her lip, shifted from foot to foot. 'Well, then I'd have to say as how Shawn's not in for his shift, and there'd be hell to pay then, wouldn't there? I'll show you the room if you want to see it. Shawn doesn't do illegals, Lieutenant,' she continued as she led the way through a door beside the laminated bar. 'The boss, he's strong against illegals and sloth. There's not much more will get you the ax around here, but either of those'll do it in a wink.'

She unlocked the door with an old-fashioned key from a chain at her waist.

It wasn't much, just a bunk-style bed, a cheap dresser, and a streaked mirror. But it was surprisingly neat. A quick look in the closet assured Eve that the absent Shawn hadn't packed up and left.

She walked to the dresser, idly opened a drawer. Shawn had one pair of clean underwear and two mismatched socks. 'How long has he been in the U.S.?'

'Shawn, why, two or three years at least, I'm thinking. He talks about going back to Dublin, but—'

'That's where he's from?' Eve asked sharply. 'He's from Dublin?'

'Yes, he says he was born and raised there and came to America to make his fortune. Not much of a fortune yet for Shawn,' she continued with a sunny smile. Her gaze shifted to the empty bottle of brew on the nightstand. 'That's probably why. He likes the drink a bit more than it likes him.'

'Yeah.' Eve glanced at the bottle as well, then her gaze sharpened on what sat beside it. Her muscled tensed as she picked up the enameled token. 'What's this, Maureen?'

'I don't know.' Maureen angled her head and studied the green shamrock on the white background. And on the back, the fish. 'A lucky piece, I suppose.'

'Have you seen it before?'

'No. Looks new, doesn't it? It's so shiny. Shawn must have just picked it up. Always looking for luck, Shawn is.'

'Yeah.' Eve closed her fist around the token. She was very much afraid luck had run out.

Chapter Four

'I need you to think, Maureen. I need you to be calm and clear.'

Huddled in a neatly patched chair in her own little room above the Green Shamrock, Maureen wet her lips. 'I'm not going to go to jail or be deported?'

'You're not in any kind of trouble. I promise you.' Eve edged forward in her chair. 'Help me out here, Maureen, help Shawn out, and I'll pull some strings and get you real papers. You won't have to worry about Immigration ever again.'

'I don't want anything to happen to Shawn, truly I don't. He was never anything but nice to me.' Her eyes darted over to where Peabody stood by the door. 'I'm a little nervous, you see. Cops make me a little nervous.'

'Peabody's a pussycat. Aren't you, Peabody?'

'Tame as a tabby, Lieutenant.'

'Help us out here now, and think back. When did you last see Shawn?'

'I'm thinking it must have been last evening when I went off my shift. You see, as a rule, Shawn comes on midday like. I'm on from eleven – that's when we open – until eight. I have two thirty-minute breaks. Shawn he works through till half ten most nights. Then he comes back on at one and works the after-hours—'

She shut up like a clam in seawater.

'Maureen,' Eve began with straining patience. 'I'm not

worried about the after-hours business. It's no concern of mine if the bar stays open past its licensing limit.'

'Well, we do a bit of after-hours business now and again.' She began to wring her hands. 'I'll be fired for sure if the boss finds I've told a cop such a thing.'

'Not if he doesn't get any heat from it. Now you saw Shawn last night, before you went off shift at eight.'

'I did, yes. When I finished up, he was behind the bar and he said something like, "Maureen, me darling, don't you be letting that young buck steal any of my kisses."'

At Eve's lifted brow, Maureen flushed. 'Oh, he didn't mean anything by it, Lieutenant. He was just joking like. Shawn, he's forty years old or more, and there isn't anything like that between us. I have a sort of young man. I mean . . .' She fumbled again, looked nervously at the silent Peabody. 'He is a man, a young man, and I'm seeing him lately. We're getting to know each other, and Shawn, he knew I had a date last night, so he was just teasing me.'

'All right, so you saw Shawn when you left at eight. Then—'

'Oh wait!' Maureen threw up her hands. 'I saw him again. I'd forgotten. Well, not "saw" so much. I heard him when I got in from seeing Mike – my young man – that is, the young man I'm seeing lately. I heard Shawn talking when I came in, you see.'

She beamed, pleased as a pup who'd done its master's bidding.

'Who was he talking to?'

'I don't know. You see, I have to pass his room to get to the steps to come up to mine. It would have been right about midnight, and Shawn would have been on his break before the after-hours shift. The building's old, you see, so the walls and doors aren't really thick or soundproofed well. So I heard him and another man talking in Shawn's room.'

'Did you hear what they said?'

51

'Not really. I was just passing, but I remember being glad that Shawn sounded happy. He was laughing and he said something about something being a fine idea and he'd be there for certain.'

'Are you sure he was talking to a man?'

Maureen furrowed her brow. 'It was more an impression. I didn't hear the words from the other, just a rumble of voice. But deep, like a man's. I didn't hear more than that because I came up here to get ready for bed. But I know it was Shawn talking. It was his laugh. He has a big laugh, does Shawn.'

'Okay, who covers the tables after your shift?'

'Oh, that's Sinead. She comes on at six and we work the two hours together, then she handles the tables alone until closing. Sinead Duggin, and she lives only a couple blocks over on Eighty-third, I think. And the barkeep who works the busy time with Shawn is a droid. The boss, he only uses the droid for the busy times. They're costly to maintain.'

'All right, Maureen, have you noticed anyone new coming into the bar over the last week or two, striking up a conversation with Shawn?'

'We get new people in from time to time, and some come back. Some of them talk and some don't. Most will talk a bit to Shawn because he makes a friendly drink, you see. But I don't recall anybody in particular.'

'Okay, you can go on back to work. I may have to talk to you again. If you remember anything, anything at all, or anyone, you'll get in touch with me.'

'I will, yes. But Shawn can't have done anything really wrong, Lieutenant,' she added as she rose. 'He's not a bad sort, just a bit foolish.'

'Foolish,' Eve mused, turning the token in her fingers as Maureen hurried out. 'And unlucky. Let's get a uniform to stake out the bar just in case we're wrong and Shawn's been out all day wheeling a deal or making love to a woman. We'll go see if Sinead Duggin is any more observant than Maureen.'

'The riddle guy, he said you had until tomorrow morning.'

Eve rose, tucking the token away. 'I think we can safely assume he cheats.'

Sinead Duggin lighted a skinny silver cigarette, narrowed hard green eyes, and blew jasmine-scented smoke in Eve's face. 'I don't like talking to cops.'

'I don't like talking to assholes.' Eve said mildly, 'but I spend half my life doing it. Here or at Cop Central, Sinead. Up to you.'

Sinead shrugged thin shoulders, the movement nudging apart the poppy-strewn robe she wore. Absently she tugged it tight and, turning, padded barefoot into her cramped one-room apartment.

It wasn't cramped with furniture. There was the Murphy bed, open and unmade, that she'd crawled out of when Eve had battered at the door. Two small chairs, two narrow tables. But every surface, window sills included, was jammed with things.

Obviously. Sinead liked things. Colorful things. Bowls and plates and statues of fuzzy little dogs and cats. The tassels of the two floor lamps were heavy with dust. Scatter rugs were piled like jigsaw puzzles over the floor. Sinead sat cross-legged on the bed, hefted up an enormous glass ashtray that would have made a fine blunt instrument, and yawned hugely.

'So?'

'I'm looking for Shawn Conroy. When did you see him last?'

'Last night. I work nights.' She scratched the instep of her left foot. 'I sleep days.'

'Who did he talk to? Did you see him with anyone in particular?'

'Just the usual. People come in looking for a bottle or a glass. Shawn and I oblige them. It's honest work.'

Eve dumped a week's worth of clothes off a chair and

sat. 'Peabody, open those blinds. Let's get some light in here.'

'Oh, Jesus.' Sinead covered her eyes, hissing when the blinds zipped up and sun shot in. 'That stuff'll kill ya.' Then she let out a long sigh. 'Look, cop, Shawn's a drunk right enough. But if that's the worst you can say about a body, it's a fine life after all.'

'He went back to his room on his break. Who went with him?'

'I didn't see anyone go with him. I was working. I tend my business. Why do you care?' Her eyes cleared slowly as she lowered her hand. 'Why do you care?' she repeated. 'Something happen to Shawn?'

'That's what I'm trying to find out.'

'Well, he was right as rain last night, I can tell you that. Cheerful enough. Said something about an outside gig in the offing. Money heading his way.'

'What kind of gig?'

'Private parties, classy stuff. Shawn had a yen for classy stuff.' Sinead tapped out her cigarette then immediately lighted another. 'He came back from his break grinning like a cat with a bowl full of canaries. Said he'd put in a word for me if I was interested.'

'A word where, with who?'

'I wasn't paying attention. Shawn's always talking big. He was going to be tending bar, serving the finest wines and such at a party for some high flyer.'

'Give me a name, Sinead. He was bragging, full of himself. What name did he drop?'

'Well, hell.' Irritated, but caught up, Sinead rubbed her forehead with her fingers. 'An old mate, he said. Someone from Dublin who'd made it big. Roarke,' she said, jabbing with the smoldering cigarette. 'Of course. That's why I thought it was just Shawn bullshitting as usual. What would a man like Roarke be wanting with the likes of Shawn?'

54

It took all Eve's control not to leap up from the chair. 'He said he'd talked to Roarke?'

'Christ, my mind's not awake.' She yawned again when an airbus with a faulty exhaust farted outside the window. 'No, I think he said . . . yeah, he was saying how Roarke sent his man to do the deal. And the pay was fine. He'd be out of the Shamrock and into the high life before long. Take me along for the ride if I wanted. Shawn and me, we bumped together a few times when the mood struck. Nothing serious.'

'What time did you close up the Shamrock?' As Sinead's gaze slid away, Eve ground her teeth. 'I don't give a shit about the after-hours license. I need the time you last saw Shawn, and where he went.'

'It was about four this morning, and he said he was going to bed. He was to meet the man himself today and needed to look presentable.'

'He's playing with me.' Eve slammed into her vehicle, rapped a fist against the wheel. 'That's what the bastard's doing, playing with me. Throwing Roarke's name into the mix. Goddamn it.'

She held up a hand before Peabody could speak, then simply stood staring out the window. She knew what she had to do. There was no choice for any of them. She snatched up the car 'link and called home.

'Roarke residence,' Summerset said in smooth tones, then his face went stony. 'Lieutenant.'

'Put him on,' she demanded.

'Roarke is engaged on another call at the moment.'

'Put him on, you skinny, frog-faced son of a bitch. Now.'

The screen switched to the pale blue holding mode. Twenty seconds later, Roarke was on. 'Eve.' Though his mouth curved, the smile didn't touch his eyes. 'Problem?'

'Do you know a Shawn Conroy?' She saw it in his face before he answered, just a flicker in those dark blue eyes.

'I did, years ago in Dublin. Why?'

'Have you had any contact with him here in New York?'

'No. I haven't seen or spoken to him in about eight years.'

Eve took a calming breath. 'Tell me you don't own a bar called the Green Shamrock.'

'All right. I don't own a bar called the Green Shamrock.' Now he did smile. 'Really, Eve, would I own something quite so clichéd?'

Relief had the weight dropping out of her stomach. 'Guess not. Ever been there?'

'Not that I recall.'

'Planning any parties?'

He angled his head. 'Not at the moment. Eve, is Shawn dead?'

'I don't know. I need a list of your New York properties.' He blinked. 'All?'

'Shit.' She pinched her nose, struggling to think clearly. 'Start with the private residences, currently, unoccupied.'

'That should be simple enough. Five minutes,' Roarke promised and ended transmission.

'Why private residences?' Peabody wanted to know.

'Because he wants me to find it. He wants me there. He's moved quickly on this one. Why hassle with a lot of security, cameras, people. You get a private home, empty. You get in, do your work, get out.'

She flipped her 'link to transmit when it beeped.

'Only three unoccupied at the moment,' Roarke told her. 'The first is on Greenpeace Park Drive. Number eighty-two. I'll meet you there.'

'Just stay where you are.'

'I'll meet you there,' he repeated, and broke transmission.

Eve didn't bother swearing at him, but swung the car away from the curb. She beat him there by thirty seconds, not quite enough time for her to bypass the locks with her master code.

The long black coat he wore against the bite of wind flowed like water, snapped like a whip. He laid a hand on her shoulder, and despite her scowl kissed her lightly. 'I have the code,' he said and plugged it in.

The house was tall and narrow to fit the skinny lot. The ceiling soared. The windows were treated to ensure privacy and block UV rays. At the moment, security bars covered them so that the sunlight shot individual cells onto the polished tile floors.

Eve drew her weapon, gestured Peabody to the left. 'You're with me,' she told Roarke, and started up the curving flow of the staircase. 'We're going to talk about this later.'

'Of course we are.' And he wouldn't mention, now or then, the illegal nine-millimeter automatic he had in his pocket. Why distress the woman you loved with minor details?

But he kept a hand in that pocket, firm over the grip as he watched her search each room, watched those cool eyes scan corner to corner.

'Why is a place like this empty?' she wanted to know after she'd assured herself it was indeed empty.

'It won't be next week. We're renting it, furnished, primarily on the short term to off-planet businesses who don't care to have their high execs in hotels. We'll furnish staff, droid or human.'

'Classy.'

'We try.' He smiled at Peabody as they descended the stairs. 'All clear, Officer?'

'Nothing here except a couple really lucky spiders.'

'Spiders?' Lifting a brow, Roarke took out his memo and plugged in a note to contact the exterminators.

'Where's the next place?' Eve asked him.

'It's only a couple of blocks. I'll lead you over.'

'You could give me the code and go home.'

He brushed a hand over her hair as they stepped outside. 'No, I couldn't.'

The second home was back off the street, tucked behind now leafless trees. Though houses crowded in on either side, residents had sacrificed their yards for privacy. Trees and shrubs formed a high fence between buildings.

Eve felt her blood begin to stir. Here, she thought, in this quiet, wealthy arena, where the houses were sound-proofed and protected from prying eyes, murder would be a private business.

'He'd like this one,' she said under her breath. 'This would suit him. Decode it,' she told Roarke, then gestured for Peabody to move to the right.

Eve shifted in front of Roarke, opened the door herself. That was all it took.

She smelled fresh death.

Shawn Conroy's luck had run out in a gorgeously appointed parlor, just off a small, elegant foyer. His blood stained the wild roses climbing over the antique rug. His arms were stretched wide as if in supplication. His palms had been nailed to the floor.

'Don't touch anything.' She gripped Roarke's arm before he could step inside. 'You're not to go in. You'll contaminate the scene. You give me your word you won't go in or I'll lock you outside. Peabody and I have to check the rest of the house.'

'I won't go in.' He turned his head, and his eyes were hot with emotions she couldn't name. 'He'll be gone.'

'I know. We check the house anyway. Peabody, take the back. I'll do upstairs.'

There was nothing and no one, which was what she'd expected. To give herself a moment alone with Roarke, she sent Peabody out to the unit for her field kit.

'He wants it to be personal,' she began.

'It is personal. I grew up with Shawn. I knew his family. His younger brother and I were of an age. We chased some of the same girls on the streets of Dublin, and made them sigh in dark alleys. He was a friend. A lifetime ago, but a friend.'

'I'm sorry. I was too late.'

Roarke only shook his head, and stared hard at the man who'd once been a boy with him. Another lost boy, he thought. Eve turned away, pulled out her communicator. 'I have a homicide,' she said.

When her hands and boots were clear sealed, she knelt in blood. She could see that death had come slowly, obscenely to Shawn Conroy. His wrists and throat had been slashed, but not deeply, not so that the blood would gush and jet and take him away quickly. He would have bled out slowly, over hours.

He was sliced, neatly, almost surgically from breastbone to crotch, again so that the pain would be hideous, and release would be slow. His right eye was gone. So was his tongue.

Her gauge told her he'd been dead less than two hours.

She had no doubt he'd died struggling to scream.

Eve stood back as the stills and videos of the body and scene were taken. Turning, she picked up the trousers that had been tossed aside. They'd been sliced off him, she noted, but the wallet remained in the back pocket.

'Victim is identified as Shawn Conroy, Irish citizen, age forty-one, residence 783 West Seventy-ninth. Contents of wallet are victim's green card and work permit, twelve dollars in credits, three photographs.'

She checked the other pocket, found key cards, loose credits in the amount of three dollars and a quarter, a slip of torn paper with the address of the house where he'd died. And an enameled token with a bright green shamrock on one side and a line sketch of a fish on the other.

'Lieutenant?' The field team medic approached. 'Are you finished with the body?'

'Yeah, bag him. Tell Dr Morris I need his personal attention on this one.' She slipped the wallet and the pocket contents into an evidence bag as she glanced over at Roarke. He'd said nothing, his face revealed nothing, not even to her.

Automatically, she reached for the solvent to remove the blood and sealant from her hands, then walked to him.

'Have you ever seen one of these before?'

He looked down into the bag that held what Shawn had carried with him, saw the token. 'No.'

She took one last scan of the scene – the obscenity in the midst of grandeur. Eyes narrowed, she cocked her head and stared thoughtfully at the small, elegant statue on a pedestal with a vase of pastel silk flowers.

A woman, she mused, carved out of white stone and wearing a long gown and veil. Not a bridal suit, but something else. Because it seemed both out of place and vaguely familiar she pointed. 'What is that – the little statue there?'

'What?' Distracted, Roarke glanced over. Puzzled, he stepped around a field tech and might have picked it up if Eve hadn't snagged his hand. 'The BVM. Odd.'

'The what?'

His laugh was short and far from humorous. 'Sorry. Catholic shorthand. The Blessed Virgin Mary.'

Surprised, she frowned at him. 'Are you Catholic?' And shouldn't she have known something like that?

'In another life,' he said absently. 'Never made it to altar boy. It doesn't belong here,' he added. 'My decorating firm isn't in the habit of adding religious statues to the rental units.'

He studied the lovely and serene face, beautifully carved in white marble. 'He put it there, turned it just so.'

He could see by the cool look in Eve's eyes that she'd already come to the same conclusion. 'His audience,' she agreed. 'So, what was he, like showing off for her?'

Roarke might not have thought of himself as Catholic or anything else for too many years to count, but it sickened him. 'He wanted her to bless his work, I'd say. It comes to the same thing more or less.'

Eve was already pulling out an evidence bag. 'I think I've seen another just like this – at Brennen's. On the wife's dresser, facing the bed. It didn't seem out of place there, so I didn't really notice. There were those bead things you pray with, holos of the kids, a statue like this, silver-backed hairbrush, comb, a blue glass perfume bottle.'

'But you didn't really notice,' Roarke murmured. Some cops, he mused, missed nothing.

'Just that it was there. Not that it shouldn't have been. Heavy,' she commented as she slipped the statue into the bag. 'Looks expensive.' She frowned at the markings on the base. 'What's this, Italian?'

'Mmm. Made in Rome.'

'Maybe we can run it.'

Roarke shook his head. 'You're going to find that thousands of these were sold in the last year alone. The shops near the Vatican do a bustling business on such things. I have interests in a few myself.'

'We'll run it anyway.' Taking his arm, she led him outside. It wouldn't help for him to watch the body bagged and readied for transport. 'There's nothing for you to do here. I have to go in, file the report, do some work. I'll be home in a few hours.'

'I want to talk to his family.'

'I can't let you do that. Not yet. Not yet,' she repeated when his eyes went narrow and cold. 'Give me a few hours. Roarke . . .' Helplessly she fell back on the standard line. 'I'm sorry for your loss.'

He surprised her by grabbing her close, pressing his face into her hair and just holding on. Awkwardly she smoothed her hands over his back, patted his rigid shoulders.

'For the first time since I met you,' he murmured so she could barely hear, 'I wish you weren't a cop.'

Then he let her go and walked away.

She stood out in the freshening wind, smelled hints of the winter to come, and bore the miserable weight of guilt and inadequacy.

*

Roarke was closed in his office when she arrived home. Only the cat greeted her. Galahad twined affectionately between her legs as she shrugged out of her jacket, hitched her bag more securely on her shoulder.

It was just as well she was alone, Eve decided. She still had work. Since she was obviously pathetic at comforting her husband, she'd be a cop. There, at least, she knew her moves.

Galahad came with her, bounding up the steps despite his girth as she headed for the suite of rooms where she often worked and sometimes slept when Roarke was away from home.

She got coffee from the AutoChef, and as much because Galahad looked so hopeful as for her own appetite, ordered up a tuna sandwich. She split it with the cat, who fell on it as if he hadn't eaten in a month, then carried her own to her desk.

She studied the door that connected her office with Roarke's. She had only to knock, she knew. Instead she sat behind her own desk.

She hadn't saved his friend. Hadn't been fast enough or smart enough to prevent death. Nor would she be able to keep Roarke out of the investigation. There would be questions she would have to ask, statements she would have to take.

And the media would know by morning. There was no way to block them out now. She'd already decided to call Nadine Furst, her contact at Channel 75. With Nadine she would get fair coverage. Though Nadine was annoyingly persistent, she was without doubt accurate.

Eve looked at her 'link. She'd arranged for McNab to program her office 'link to transfer transmissions to her home unit for the night. She wanted the bastard to call.

How long would he wait? And when would he be ready to play the next round?

She drank coffee, ordered her mind to clear. Go back to the beginning, she told herself. Replay first round.

She shoved a copy of the initial contact call into her machine, listened to it twice. She had his rhythm, she thought, his tone, his mood. He was arrogant, vain, smart, yes, he was smart and skilled. He was on a holy mission. But conceit was his weak point. Conceit, she mused, and his skewed faith.

She'd need to exploit it.

Revenge, he'd said. An eye for an eye. Revenge was always personal. Both men who were dead had a connection to Roarke. So, logically, did their killer. An old vendetta, perhaps.

Yes, she and Roarke had quite a bit to discuss. He could be a target. The thought of that turned her blood cold, scattered her heartbeat, froze her brain.

She shoved it aside. She couldn't afford to think like a wife, like a lover. More than ever, she needed to be pure cop.

She gave Galahad most of the second half of the sandwich when he came begging, then took out the copies of the security disc for the Luxury Towers.

Step by step, she ordered herself. Every disc, every area covered, no matter how long it took. In the morning she would have Roarke view them as well. He might recognize someone.

She knocked her coffee cup over when she did.

'Stop,' she ordered. 'Replay from zero-zero-five-six. Jesus Christ. Freeze, enhance section fifteen to twenty-two by thirty percent, shift to slow motion.'

She stared as the figure in the trim black suit and flowing overcoat enlarged, as he walked across the sumptuous lobby of the apartment complex. Checked the expensive timepiece on his wrist. Smoothed his hair.

And she watched Summerset step into the elevator and head up.

'Freeze screen,' she snapped.

The time at the bottom read twelve P.M., the afternoon on Thomas X. Brennen's murder.

She ran the lobby disc through, fast-forwarding through hour after hour. But she never saw him come back out.

Chapter Five

She didn't bother to knock, but simply shoved open his door. Her blood was hot, her mind cold.

Roarke could clearly see both temperatures in her eyes. Deliberately and without haste, he flipped his computer manually to hold, closing off his work.

'You're overdoing again,' he said easily, remaining seated as she stalked – a single posse closing in on her man – to his desk. 'Fatigue always steals the color from your face. I don't like seeing you pale.'

'I don't feel pale.' She wasn't sure what she felt. All she could be certain of was that the man she loved, a man she'd taught herself to trust, knew something. And he wasn't telling her. 'You said you hadn't had any contact with Brennen or Conroy. Any contact, Roarke? Not even through a liaison?'

He angled his head. This wasn't the track he'd expected. 'No, I haven't. Tommy because he preferred to sever ties, and Shawn because . . .' He looked down at his hands, spread his fingers, closed them. 'I didn't bother to keep in touch. I'm sorry for that.'

'Look at me,' she demanded, her voice sharp and keen. 'Look me in the face, damn it.' He did, rising now so their gazes were nearly level. 'I believe you.' She whirled away from him as she said it. 'And I don't know if it's because it's the truth, or because I need it to be.'

He felt the nick of her distrust at the edge of his heart.

'I can't help you with that. Would you prefer to do this in Interview?'

'I'd prefer not to do it at all. And don't climb on your golden horse with me, Roarke. Don't you even start.'

He opened the japanned box on his desk, carefully selected a cigarette. 'That would be "high horse," Lieutenant.'

She clenched her fists, prayed for control, and turned back. 'What was Summerset doing at the Luxury Towers on the day of Thomas Brennen's murder?'

For perhaps the first time since she'd met him, she saw Roarke completely staggered. The hand that had just flicked on a silver lighter froze in midair. His just beginning to be annoyed blue eyes went blank. He shook his head once, as if to clear it, then carefully set down both the lighter and the unlit cigarette.

'What?' was all he managed.

'You didn't know.' Her limbs went limp with it. It wasn't always possible to read him, she knew. He was too controlled, too clever, too skilled. But there was no mistaking the simple shock on his face. 'You weren't prepared for that. You had no idea at all.' She took a step closer. 'What were you prepared for? What did you expect me to ask you?'

'Let's just stick with the initial question.' Outwardly his recovery was smooth and quick. His stomach muscles, though, were tightening into oily knots. 'You believe Summerset visited Tommy on the day of the murder. That's just not possible.'

'Why not?'

'Because he would have told me.'

'He tells you everything, does he?' She jammed her hands in her pockets, took a fast, impatient turn around the room. 'How well did he know Brennen?'

'Not well at all. Why do you think he was there that day?'

'Because I have the security discs.' She stood still now, facing him with the desk between. 'I have Summerset in

66

the lobby of the Luxury Towers at noon. I have him getting into an elevator. I don't have him coming back out. The ME puts Brennen's time of death at four-fifty P.M. But the initial injury, the amputation of the hand, is clocked at between twelve-fifteen and twelve-thirty P.M.'

Because he needed something to do with his hands, Roarke walked over, poured a brandy. He stood for a moment, swirling it. 'He may irritate you, Eve. You may find him . . . unpleasant.' He only arched his brows when Eve snorted. 'But you can't seriously believe Summerset is capable of murder, of spending a number of hours torturing another human being.' Roarke lifted the snifter, sipped. 'I can tell you, without a single doubt, that he isn't capable of it, and never has been.'

She wouldn't be swayed by sentiment. 'Then where was your man, Roarke, from noon to five P.M. on the date in question?'

'You'd do better to ask him.' He reached up, pressed a button on a monitor without glancing at it. 'Summerset, would you come up to my office, please? My wife has a question for you.'

'Very well.'

'I've known the man since I was a boy,' Roarke said to Eve. 'I've told you most of it, trusted you with that. Now I'm trusting you with him.'

She felt a fist squeeze around her heart. 'I can't let this be personal. You can't ask that of me.'

'You can't let it be anything else. Because that's exactly what it is. Personal,' he continued, walking to her. 'Intimate.' With fingertips only, he skimmed her cheek. 'Mine.'

He dropped his hand as the door opened.

Summerset stepped inside. His silver hair was perfectly groomed, his black suit ruthlessly pressed, his shoes shone with a mirror gleam.

'Lieutenant,' he said, as if the word was ever so slightly distasteful to his palette. 'Can I help you?'

'Why were you at the Luxury Towers yesterday at noon?'

He stared at her, through her, and his mouth thinned to a line sharp as a blade. 'That is certainly none of your business.'

'Wrong, it's exactly my business. Why did you go see Thomas Brennen?'

'Thomas Brennen? I haven't seen Thomas Brennen since we left Ireland.'

'Then what were you doing at the Luxury Towers?'

'I fail to see what one has to do with the other. My free time is . . .' He trailed off, and his eyes darted to Roarke, went wide. 'Is that where – Tommy lived at the Luxury Towers?'

'You're talking to me.' Eve stepped between them so that Summerset focused on her face. 'I'll ask you again, what were you doing at the Luxury Towers yesterday at noon?'

'I have an acquaintance who lives there. We had an engagement, for lunch and a matinee.'

'All right.' Relieved, Eve pulled out her recorder. 'Give me her name.'

'Audrey, Audrey Morrell.'

'Apartment number?'

'Twelve eighteen.'

'And Ms Morrell will verify that you met at noon and spent the day together?'

His already pale face was slowly going whiter. 'No.'

'No?' Eve looked up, and said nothing when Roarke brought Summerset a glass of brandy.

'Audrey – Ms Morrell wasn't in when I arrived. I waited for a time, then realized she'd . . . Something must have come up.'

'How long did you wait?'

'Thirty or forty minutes.' Some color seeped back into his cheeks now, of the embarrassed sort. 'Then I left.'

'By the lobby exit.'

'Of course.'

'I don't have you on the security discs coming out. Maybe you left by another exit.'

'I certainly did not.'

Eve bit her tongue. She'd tossed him a rope, she thought, and he hadn't grabbed for it. 'Fine, you stick to that. What did you do then?'

'I decided against the matinee. I went to the park.'

'The park. Great.' She leaned back on Roarke's desk. 'What park?'

'Central Park. There was an outdoor art exhibit. I browsed for a time.'

'It was raining.'

'There were inclement weather domes.'

'How did you get from the apartment complex to the park? What kind of transpo?'

'I walked.'

Her head began to throb. 'In the rain?'

'Yes.' He said it stiffly and sipped his brandy.

'Did you speak to anyone, meet someone you know?'

'No.'

'Shit.' She sighed it, then rubbed absently at her temple. 'Where were you at midnight last night?'

'Eve—'

She cut Roarke off with a look. 'This is what I do. What I have to do. Were you at the Green Shamrock last night at midnight?'

'I was in bed with a book.'

'What was your relationship with Shawn Conroy?'

Summerset set the brandy down, stared at Roarke over Eve's shoulder. 'Shawn Conroy was a boy in Dublin years ago. He's dead, then?'

'Someone claiming to represent Roarke lured him to one of Roarke's rental units, nailed him to the floor, and opened up pieces of him. Let him bleed to death.' There was shock on his face, she noted. Good, she wanted him to be shocked.

'And you're going to have to give me a solid alibi, something I can confirm, or I'm going to have to take you in for a formal interview.'

'I don't have one.'

'Find one,' she suggested, 'before eight A.M. tomorrow. That's when I want you at Cop Central.'

His eyes were cold and bitter when they met Eve's. 'You'll enjoy interrogating me, won't you, Lieutenant?'

'Hauling you in on suspicion of a couple of torture murders is just the chance I've been waiting for. The fact that the media will be screaming the news of your connection to Roarke by midday is only a minor inconvenience.' Disgusted, she stalked toward the door that connected her office with Roarke's.

'Eve.' Roarke's voice was quiet. 'I need to speak with you.'

'Not now' was all she said as she closed the door between them. Roarke heard the bad-tempered snick of locks engaging.

'She's already decided I'm guilty.' Summerset drank brandy now, deeply.

'No.' While regret warred with irritation, Roarke studied the panel that closed him off from his wife. 'She's decided she has no choice but to gather the facts.' His gaze shifted to Summerset's, held it. 'She needs to know all of them.'

'That would only worsen the situation.'

'She's entitled to know.'

Summerset set the snifter down, and his voice was as stiff as his spine. 'I see where your loyalties lie, Roarke.'

'Do you?' Roarke murmured as Summerset left him alone. 'Do you really?'

Eve slept in her office suite, and slept poorly. She didn't care that her deliberate avoidance of Roarke was petty. She needed the distance. Well before eight she was at Cop Central. After toying with a bagel the consistency of cardboard and coffee

70

that bore too close a relationship with raw sewage, she shot off a transmission to Peabody with orders to report to Interview Room C.

Prompt as a palace guard, Peabody was already in the small tiled and mirror-walled room checking the recording equipment when Eve came in. 'We've got a suspect?'

'Yeah, we've got one.' Eve filled a pitcher from the water distiller herself. 'Let's try to keep a cork in it until the interview's wrapped.'

'Sure, but who . . .' Peabody trailed off when a uniform brought Summerset and Roarke to the door. Her eyes darted to Eve's, rounded. 'Oh.'

'Officer.' Eve nodded to the uniform. 'You're dismissed. Roarke, you can wait outside, or in my office.'

'Summerset is entitled to representation.'

'You're not a lawyer.'

'His representative isn't required to be.'

She had to consciously unclench her jaw. 'You're making this worse.'

'Perhaps.' He sat, folding his hands on the scarred table, an elegant presence in an unfriendly room.

Eve turned to Summerset. 'You want a lawyer,' she said, spacing her words carefully. 'Not a friend.'

'I dislike lawyers. Nearly as much as I dislike cops.' He sat as well, his bony fingers hitching the knees of his trousers to preserve the knife-edge pleats.

Eve thrust her hands into her pockets before she could pull at her hair. 'Secure the door, Peabody. Recorder, engage.' Taking a deep breath, she began. 'Interview with Summerset – Please state your full name for the record.'

'Lawrence Charles Summerset.'

'Interview with Summerset, Lawrence Charles re case number 44591-H, Thomas X. Brennen and case number 44599-H, Shawn Conroy. Homicides. The date is November seventeen, twenty fifty-eight, time is oh eight hundred point three hours. Present are subject; his chosen representative, Roarke; Peabody, Officer Delia; and Dallas, Lieutenant Eve, conducting interview. Subject has come into Interview voluntarily.'

Still standing, she recited the revised Miranda. 'Do you understand your rights and obligations, Summerset?'

'Perfectly.'

'And you waive legal representation at this time?'

'That's correct.'

'What was your connection with Thomas Brennen and Shawn Conroy?'

Summerset blinked once, surprised she'd shot straight to the heart. 'I knew them, casually, when I lived in Dublin.'

'When was that?'

'Over a dozen years ago.'

'And when was the last time you saw or spoke with Brennen?'

'I couldn't say precisely, but at least a dozen years ago.'

'Yet you were in the Luxury Towers only days ago, the day of Brennen's murder.'

'Coincidence,' Summerset stated with a quick and belligerent lift of his shoulder. 'I had no knowledge that he resided there.'

'What were you doing there?'

'I've alreay told you that.'

'Tell me again. For the record.'

He hissed out a breath, poured water from pitcher to glass with a steady hand. In flat tones he repeated everything he'd told Eve the night before.

'Will Ms Morrell verify your appointment with her?'

'I have no reason to believe otherwise.'

'Maybe you can explain to me why the security cameras caught you in the lobby, walking to the elevators, getting in, and yet there is no visual record of you exiting the building by that route at the time you claim to have left. Or, for that matter, any other time that day.'

72

'I can't explain it.' He folded his perfectly manicured hands again and stared her down. 'Perhaps you didn't look carefully enough.'

Eve had reviewed the tape six times through the night. Now, she pulled up a chair and sat. 'How often have you visited the Luxury Towers?'

'It was my first visit there.'

'Your first,' she said with a nod. 'You've had no occasion to visit Brennen there before?'

'I had no occasion to visit Brennen there at any time, as I was unaware he lived there.'

He answered well, she thought, carefully, like a man who'd skimmed his way through Interview before. She spared a glance at Roarke, who sat silently. Summerset's official record would be clear as a baby's, she imagined. Roarke would have seen to it.

'Why would you leave by an unsecured exit on the day of his death?'

'I did not leave by an unsecured exit. I left the way I came in.'

'The record shows otherwise. It clearly shows you coming in. There is no record of you exiting the elevator on the level where you claim Ms Morrell lives.'

Summerset waved one of his thin hands. 'That's ridiculous.'

'Peabody, please engage and display evidence disc one-BH, section twelve for subject's examination.'

'Yes, sir.' Peabody slipped the disc into a Play slot. The monitor in the wall flickered on.

'Note the time display at the bottom right of the recording,' Eve continued as she watched Summerset walk in and through the attractive lobby of the Luxury Tower. 'Stop disc,' she ordered when the elevator doors shut behind him. 'Continue play, section twenty-two. Note time display,' she repeated, 'and the security label that identifies this area as

73

the twelfth floor of the Luxury Towers. That is the floor in question?'

'Yes.' Summerset's brows drew together as he watched the recording. The elevator doors did not open, he did not walk out. A cool line of sweat dribbled down his spine as time passed. 'You've doctored the disc. You tampered with it to implicate me.'

Insulting son of a bitch. 'Oh, sure. Peabody'll tell you I spend half my time on a case screwing with the evidence to suit myself.' Temper just beginning to brew, Eve rose again, leaned on the table. 'Trouble with that theory, pal, is this is the original, straight out of the security room. I worked with a copy. I've never had my hands on the original. Peabody collected the security discs.'

'She's a cop.' Summerset sneered it. 'She'd do what you ordered her to do.'

'So now it's a conspiracy. Peabody, hear that? You and I tampered with the evidence just to make Summerset's life tough for him.'

'You'd like nothing better than to put me in a cage.'

'At this particular moment, you couldn't be more right.' She turned away then, until she was certain her rapidly rising temper wouldn't rule her head. 'Peabody, disengage disc. You knew Thomas Brennen in Dublin. What was your relationship?'

'He was simply one of many young men and women I knew.'

'And Shawn Conroy?'

'Again, he was one of many young people I knew in Dublin.'

'When was the last time you were in the Green Shamrock?'

'I have never, to my knowledge, patronized that establishment.'

'And I suppose you weren't aware that Shawn Conroy worked there.'

'I was not. I wasn't aware that Shawn had left Ireland.'

She hooked her thumbs in her pockets, waited a beat. 'And naturally, you haven't seen or spoken to Shawn Conroy in a dozen years.'

'That's correct, Lieutenant.'

'You knew both victims, you were on the site of the first murder on the day of Brennen's death, you have, thus far, offered no alibi that can be substantiated for the time of either murder, yet you want me to believe there is no connection?'

His eyes locked coldly on hers. 'I don't expect you to believe anything but what you choose to believe.'

'You're not helping yourself.' Furious, she snagged the token she'd found on Shawn Conroy's nightstand from her pocket, tossed it on the table. 'What's the significance of this?'

'I have no idea.'

'Are you Catholic?'

'What? No.' Pure bafflement replaced the chill in his eyes. 'Unitarian. Mildly.'

'How much do you know about electronics?'

'I beg your pardon?'

No choice was all she could think, and refused to look at Roarke. 'What are your duties for your employer?'

'They're varied.'

'And in these various duties, do you have occasion to send and receive transmissions?'

'Naturally.'

'And you're aware that your employer has very sophisticated communication equipment.'

'The finest communication equipment on- or off-planet.' There was a lilt of pride in his voice.

'And you're very familiar with it.'

'I am.'

'Familiar enough, knowledgeable enough, to cloak or jam in- or outgoing transmissions?'

'Of course I—' He caught himself, set his teeth. 'However, I would have no reason to do so.'

'Do you like riddles, Summerset?'

'On occasion.'

'And would you consider yourself a patient man?'

He lifted his eyebrows. 'I would.'

She nodded and, as her stomach fisted, turned away. Here was the thought, the worry, the grief that had kept her wakeful most of the night. 'Your daughter was murdered when she was a teenager.'

She heard no sound behind her now, not even breath. But if pain had weight, the air grew heavy with it. 'Your current employer was indirectly responsible for her death.'

'He was—' Summerset cleared his throat. Beneath the table his hands had fisted on his knees. 'He was not responsible.'

'She was tortured, she was raped, she was murdered to teach Roarke a lesson, to hurt him. She was no more than a tool, is that correct?'

He couldn't speak for a moment, simply couldn't squeeze the words past the grief that had so suddenly dug claws into his throat. 'She was murdered by monsters who preyed on innocence.' He took one breath, long and deep. 'You, Lieutenant, should understand such things.'

When she turned back her eyes were blank. But she was cold, horribly cold, because she did understand such things all too well. 'Are you patient enough, Summerset, are you clever enough and patient enough to have waited all these years? To have established the relationship, the trust, with your employer, to have gained unconditional access to his personal and professional dealings, and then, using that relationship, that trust, that access, attempt to connect him to murder?'

Summerset's chair dug into the aged linoleum as he shoved back from the table and sprang to his feet. 'You dare speak to me of using. You dare? When you'd use an innocent young girl in this filthy business? And you would stand there and point your finger at the man whose ring you wear and say that he was responsible for the horrors she endured? They were children. *Children.* I'd gladly spend the rest of my life in a cage if it makes him see you for what you are.'

'Summerset.' Roarke stayed seated, but laid a hand on Summerset's arm. His eyes were flat and cool as they met Eve's. 'He needs a moment.'

'Fine. This interview is broken at this time at the request of the subject's representative. Record off.'

'Sit down,' Roarke murmured, keeping his hand on Summerset's arm. 'Please.'

'They're the same, you see.' Summerset's voice trembled with emotion as he lowered himself into a chair. 'With their badges and their bullying and their empty hearts. Cops are all the same.'

'We'll have to see,' Roarke said, watching his wife. 'Lieutenant, I'd like to speak with you, off the record, and without your aide.'

'I won't have it,' Summerset fired up.

'It's my choice. If you'd excuse us, Peabody.' Roarke smiled politely, gestured toward the door.

Eve stood where she was, kept her eyes on Roarke's. 'Wait outside, Peabody. Secure the door.'

'Yes, sir.'

'Engage soundproofing.' When she was alone with Roarke and Summerset, Eve kept her balled hands in her pockets. 'You've decided to tell me,' she said coldly. 'Did you think I didn't realize you knew more than you were saying? Do you think I'm a fucking idiot?'

Roarke read the hurt behind the temper and bit back a sigh. 'I'm sorry.'

'You would apologize to her?' Summerset snapped. 'After what she—'

'Just shut the hell up,' Eve ordered, turning on him with teeth bared. 'How do I know I didn't have it just right? The

77

equipment to jam transmissions, to bypass CompuGuard, is right there in the house. Who knows about it but the three of us? The first victim was an old personal friend of Roarke's, the second another old friend who was killed in one of Roarke's properties. You know everything he owns, everything he does and how he does it. It's been almost twenty years, but that isn't so long for you to wait for payback, to avenge your daughter. How do I know you're not willing to sacrifice everything to destroy him?'

'Because he's what I have left. Because he loved her. Because he's mine.' This time when Summerset picked up his glass, water sloshed to the rim and over onto the table.

'Eve.' Roarke spoke softly even as he felt his heart, and his loyalties, dragged in opposite directions by angry hands. 'Please sit down, and listen.'

'I can listen fine standing.'

'Suit yourself.' Wearily Roarke pressed his fingers to his eyes. The woman fate had handed his heart to was rarely easy. 'I told you about Marlena. She was like a sister to me after Summerset took me in. But I wasn't a child,' he continued, eyeing Summerset with amused affection. 'Or innocent.'

'Beaten half to death,' Summerset muttered.

'I'd been careless.' Roarke shrugged. 'In any case, I stayed with them, worked with them.'

'Running grifts,' she said tightly. 'Picking pockets.'

'Surviving.' Roarke nearly smiled again. 'I won't apologize for that. I told you that Marlena . . . she was still a child, really, but she had feelings for me I'd been unaware of. And she came to my room one night, full of love and generosity. I was cruel to her. I didn't know how to handle the situation so I was clumsy and cruel. I thought I was doing the right thing, the decent thing. I couldn't touch her in the way she thought she wanted. She was so innocent and so . . . sweet. I hurt her, and instead of going back to her own room and hating me for a while as I'd hoped – as I'd thought she would – she went out. Men who

78

were looking for me, men I was arrogant enough to believe I could deal with on my own ground, found her, took her.'

Because a part of him still mourned, and always would, he paused a moment. When he continued his voice was quieter, his eyes darker. 'I would have traded my life for hers. I would have done anything they asked to spare her one moment's fear or pain. But there was nothing to be done. Nothing I was allowed to do. They tossed her on the doorstep after they'd done with her.'

'She was so small.' Summerset's voice was barely a whisper. 'She looked like a doll, all broken and torn. They killed my baby. Butchered her.' Now his eyes, bright and bitter, met Eve's, 'The cops did nothing. They turned their backs. Marlena was the daughter of an undesirable. There were no witnesses, they said, no evidence. They knew who had done it, because the word was everywhere on the street. But they did nothing.'

'The men who had killed her were powerful,' Roarke continued. 'In that area of Dublin, cops turned a blind eye and deaf ear to certain activities. It took me a great deal of time to gain enough power and enough skill to go up against them. It took me more time to track down the six men who had had a part in Marlena's death.'

'But you did track them down, and you killed them. I know that.' And she'd found it possible to live with that. 'What does this have to do with Brennen and Conroy?' Her heart stuttered a moment. 'They were involved? They were involved with Marlena's death?'

'No. But each of them fed me information at different times. Information that helped me find a certain man in a certain place. And when I found the men, two of the men who had raped and tortured and murdered Marlena, I killed them. Slowly. Painfully. The first,' he said with his eyes locked on Eve's, 'I gutted.'

The color drained out of her face. 'You disemboweled him.'

'It seemed fitting. It took a gutless bastard to do what was done to a young helpless girl. I found the second man through some data I bought from Shawn. When I had him I opened him up, one vein at a time, and let him bleed to death.'

She sat now, pressed her fingers to her eyes. 'Who else helped you?'

'It's difficult to say. I talked to dozens of people, gathered data and rumor, and went on. There was Robbie Browning, but I've checked on him already. He's still in Ireland, a guest of the government for another three to five. Jennie O'Leary, she's in Wexford running a bed and breakfast of all things. I contacted her yesterday so she would be on the alert. Jack—'

'Goddamn it.' Eve thumped both fists on the table. 'You should have given me a list the minute I told you about Brennen. You should have trusted me.'

'It wasn't a matter of trust.'

'Wasn't it?'

'No.' He grabbed her hand before she could shove away. 'No, it wasn't. It was a matter of hoping I was wrong. And a matter of trying not to put you in the very position I've just put you in.'

'You thought you could handle it without me.'

'I'd hoped I could. But as Summerset's being set up, that's no longer an option. We need your help.'

'You need my help.' She said it slowly as she tugged her hand free of his. 'You need my help. That's great, that's fine.' She rose. 'Do you think anything you've just told me takes the heat off of him? If I use it, you'll both go into a cage. Murder, first degree, multiple charges.'

'Summerset didn't murder anyone,' Roarke said with characteristic cool. 'I did.'

'That hardly takes the pressure off.'

'You believe him then?'

He's what I have left. She let Summerset's words, the

passion behind them, play back in her head. 'I believe him. He'd never involve you. He loves you.'

Roarke started to speak, closed his mouth, and stared thoughtfully at his own hands. The simple statement, the simple truth behind it rocked him.

'I don't know what I'm going to do.' She said it more to herself, just to hear the words out loud. 'I have to pursue the evidence, and I have to go carefully by the book. Officially. If that comes down to me charging you,' she aimed a level look at Summerset, 'then that's what I'm going to do. The only way you're going to help yourself is to give me everything. You hold back, it works against you. I'm going into this with both hands tied behind my back. I'm going to need yours,' she said to Roarke.

'You have them. Always.'

'Do I?' She smiled humorlessly. 'The evidence points to the contrary. And I'm hell on evidence, Roarke.' She walked to the door but didn't yet disengage the locks. 'I'll clear your bony ass, Summerset. Because that's my job. Because not all cops turn their backs. And because this cop keeps her eyes and ears open.' She shot one last fulminating look at Roarke. 'Always.'

She opened the locks and stalked out.

Chapter Six

Peabody knew when to keep her mouth shut and her thoughts to herself. Whatever had been said in the interview room off record hadn't put her lieutenant in a cheerful state of mind. The lieutenant's eyes were hot and broody, her mouth grim, and her shoulders stiff as a board of black market oak.

Since Eve was currently driving uptown behind the wheel of a not entirely reliable vehicle – and Peabody was in the passenger seat – the lieutenant's aide chose the better part of valor.

'Idiots,' Eve muttered, and Peabody was dead certain she wasn't referring to the stream of jaywalking tourists who barely missed being mowed down by a maxi-bus.

'Trust, my ass.'

At this, Peabody merely cleared her throat and frowned sternly at the smoke-obscured corner of Tenth and Forty-first where a pair of glide-carts were dueling over territorial rights. Peabody winced as the operators rammed their carts together. Metal sang against metal once, twice. At the third butt, a funnel of flame shot skyward. Pedestrians scattered like ants.

'Oops' was Peabody's comment, and she resigned herself when Eve swung her vehicle to the curb.

Eve stepped out into the smoke, caught the scent of scorched meat. The operators were too busy screaming at each other to notice her until she elbowed one of them aside to reach the regulation extinguisher hanging on the corner of the nearest cart.

There was a fifty-fifty shot that it would contain anything but air, but luck fell on her side. She coated both carts with foam, snuffing out the fire and eliciting a stream of furious Italian from one operator and what might have been Mandarin Chinese from the other.

They might have joined forces and jumped her, but Peabody stepped through the stink and smoke. The sight of a uniformed cop had both operators satisfying themselves with threatening curses and vicious glares.

Peabody scanned the crowd that had gathered to watch the show, and furrowed her brow. 'Move along,' she ordered. 'There's nothing more to see here. I always wanted to say that,' she murmured to Eve, but got no quick, answering grin in response.

'Make their day perfect and write them up for creating a public hazard.'

'Yes, sir.' Peabody sighed when Eve walked back to the car.

Ten minutes later, and in silence, they pulled up in front of the Luxury Towers. The droid was on duty at the door and only nodded respectfully when Eve flashed her badge and walked by him. She headed straight to the elevator and stood dead center of the glass tube as it shot them up to the twelfth floor.

Peabody remained silent as Eve pressed the bell at Audrey Morrell's snowy white door. A moment later it was opened by a tidy brunette with mild green eyes and a cautious smile.

'Yes, can I help you?'

'Audrey Morrell?'

'That's correct.' The woman focused on Peabody, the uniform, and lifted a hand to the single strand of white stones around her neck. 'Is there a problem?'

'We'd like to ask you a few questions.' Eve took out her badge, held it up. 'It shouldn't take long.'

'Of course. Please come in.'

She stepped back into a lofty living area made cozy with soft pastel hues and the clever grouping of conversation areas. The walls were crowded with paintings in dreamy, bleeding colors.

She led them to a trio of U-shaped chairs covered in Easter-egg blue.

'May I offer you anything? Coffee perhaps?'

'No, nothing.'

'Well then.' With an uncertain smile, Audrey sat.

This would be Summerset's type was Eve's first thought. This slim, pretty woman wearing a classically simple pale green sheath. Her hair was neatly arranged in smooth waves.

Age was difficult to gauge. Her complexion was creamy and smooth, her hands long and narrow, her voice quiet and cultured. Midforties was Eve's best guess, with plenty of bucks spent on body maintenance.

'Ms Morrell, are you acquainted with a man named Summerset?'

'Lawrence.' Instantly the green eyes took on a sparkle, and the smile grew wider and more relaxed. 'Yes, of course.'

'How do you know him?'

'He attends my watercolor class. I teach painting on Tuesday nights at the Culture Exchange. Lawrence is one of my students.'

'He paints?'

'Quite well, too. He's working on a lovely still life series right now, and I . . .' She trailed off, and her hand went back to twist her strand of rocks. 'Is he in trouble? Is he all right? I was annoyed when he missed our engagement on Saturday, but it never occurred to me that—'

'Saturday? You had an appointment with him on Saturday?'

'A date, really.' Audrey shifted and brushed at her hair. 'We . . . well, we have common interests.'

'Your date wasn't for Friday?'

'Saturday afternoon. Lunch and a matinee.' She let out a breath, worked up a smile again. 'I suppose I can confess, as we're all women. I'd gone to quite a bit of time and trouble with my appearance. And I was terribly nervous. Lawrence and I have seen each other outside of class a few times, but always with art as a buffer. This would have been our first actual date. I haven't dated in some time, you see. I'm a widow. I lost my husband five years ago, and . . . well. I was crushed when he stood me up. But I see he must have had a good reason. Can't you tell me what this is about?'

'Where were you on Friday afternoon, Ms Morrell?'

'Shopping for my outfit for Saturday. It took me most of the day to find just the right dress, shoes, the bag. Then I went to the salon for a manicure, a body polish.' She lifted her hand to her hair again. 'A little highlighting.'

'Summerset claims your engagement was for Friday noon.'

'Friday.' Audrey frowned, shook her head. 'That can't be. Can it? Oh, did I mix the dates?' Obviously distracted, she got up quickly and hurried into another room. She came back moments later with a slim silver-toned datebook. As she coded in, she continued to shake her head. 'I'm certain we said Saturday. Yes, that's what I have here. Saturday, twelve noon, lunch and theater with Lawrence. Oh dear.' She looked at Eve again, her face comically distressed. 'Did he come on Friday, when I was out? He must have thought I stood him up, just as I—'

She started to laugh then, sitting down, crossing her legs. 'How absurd, and the two of us with our pride and feelings crushed just because we didn't have the good sense to call and verify. Why in the world didn't he at least leave a message at the door?'

'I couldn't say.'

'Pride again, I suppose. And shyness. It's so difficult for two shy people to manage.' Her smile faded slowly as she studied Eve's face. 'But surely this isn't a police matter.'

'Summerset is involved in an investigation. It would be helpful if we could verify his movements on Friday.'

'I see. No, I don't,' Audrey corrected. 'I don't see at all.'

'I can't give you a great deal of information at this time, Ms Morrell. Did you know a Thomas Brennen?'

'No, I don't believe so.'

You will, Eve thought. By the evening newscasts everyone would know of Thomas Brennen and Shawn Conroy. 'Who else knew about your date with Summerset?'

Audrey's fingers tangled with her necklace again. 'I can't think of anyone. We're both rather . . . private people. I suppose I did mention to my beauty consultant when I made the appointment that it was for a special occasion.'

'What's your salon?'

'Oh, I always use Classique on Madison.'

'I appreciate your time,' Eve said and rose.

'You're welcome, of course. But – Lieutenant, was it?'

'Yes. Dallas.'

'Lieutenant Dallas, if Lawrence is in any sort of trouble . . . I'd like to help however I can. He's a lovely man. A gentleman.'

'A lovely man,' Eve muttered as they headed back to the elevator. 'A gentleman. Right. Penthouse floor,' she ordered as the tube closed them in. 'I want to go over the scene again. Set your recorder.'

'Yes, sir.' Efficiently, Peabody clipped the minirecorder onto her starched lapel.

Eve used her master code to bypass the police block on Brennen's door. The apartment was dim, the outside light blocked by security screens. She left them in place and ordered the lights to bright.

'It started right here.' She frowned down at the bloodstains on the carpet, the walls, and brought the gruesome image of a severed hand into her mind. 'Why did Brennen let him in? Did he know him? And why did the attacker hack off his hand? Unless . . .'

She circled around, moved back to the door, eyed the direction of the bedroom. 'Maybe it went this way: The killer's an electronics whiz. He's already messed up the cameras. Can't take a chance that some bored security guard scans discs before he can do the job here then get back to them. So he's taken care of that. He's smart, he's careful. He can get into this place easily enough. Bypass the codes, pop the locks. That'd give him a kick, wouldn't it?'

'He likes to be in charge,' Peabody offered, 'Could be he wouldn't want to ask to come in.'

'Exactly. So he lets himself in. What a thrill. The game's about to begin. Brennen comes out, from the kitchen most likely. He's just had lunch. He's caught off guard, and he's a little sluggish from the tranq. But he grew up on the streets, he grew up rough. You don't forget how to take care of yourself. He charges the intruder, but the intruder's armed. The first injury, it could have been no more than a defensive move. Unplanned. But it stops Brennen, stops him cold. There's blood everywhere. Most likely some of it splattered on the intruder. He'll have to clean up, but he'll worry about that later. Now he wants to do what he came for. He tranqs Brennen a little deeper, drags him into the bedroom.'

Eve followed the trail and puddles of dried blood, then stood in the bedroom, eyes keen. She lifted the statue of the Virgin from Eileen's dresser, scissoring the head between her fingers to upend it and check the markings on the base. 'The same. The same as at the Conroy scene. Bag this.'

'Seems kind of – I don't know – disrespectful,' Peabody decided as she sealed the marble image.

'I'd think the Mother of God would find cold-blooded murder a bit more than disrespectful,' Eve said dryly.

'Yeah, I suppose.' Still, Peabody pushed the sealed statue into her bag where she didn't have to think about it.

'Now, he's got Brennen in here, on the bed. He doesn't want his man to bleed to death. He wants to take his time. Gotta stop that bleeding. So he cauterizes the stump, crudely, but it does the job.'

She circled the bed, studying the grisly rust colored stains. 'He gets to work. Secures his man to the bedpost, gets out his tools. He's precise. Maybe he was nervous before, but now he's just fine. Everything is going just as he wants. Now he puts his symbolic audience on the dresser so she has a good view. Maybe he says a prayer to her.'

She frowned, looked back at the dresser, put the statue back in place in her mind. 'Then he gets down to it,' she continued. 'He tells Brennen what he's going to do to him, and he tells him why. He wants him to know, he wants him to piss himself with fear, he wants to be able to smell the pain. This is payback, and payback's the big one. Passion, greed, power, they're all part of it, but revenge drives it all. He's waited a long time for this moment, and he's going to enjoy it. Every time Brennen screams, every time he begs, this guy gets off. When it's done, he's flying. But he's a mess, covered with blood and gore.'

She moved toward the adjoining bath. It sparkled like gems, the sapphire walls, the ruby insets in the tiles, the silver dials and faucets. 'He's come prepared. He had to be carrying a case of some kind, for the knives and rope. He's got a change of clothes in there. He'd have thought of that. So he showers, scrubs himself like a fucking surgeon. He scrubs the bathroom too, every inch. He's a goddamn domestic droid in here. He sterilizes it. He's got plenty of time.'

'We didn't find a single hair or skin cell in here,' Peabody agreed. 'He was thorough.'

Eve turned away, walked back into the bedroom. 'The ruined clothes go back in his case, along with all his nasty tools. He gets himself dressed, watching where he steps. Don't want to get blood on our shiny shoes, do we? Maybe he stops back here for a last look at his work. Sure he does, he wants to take that image away with him. Does he say another prayer? Oh yeah, one for glory. Then he walks out, and he calls a cop.'

'We can review the lobby tapes, check out anyone with briefcases or satchels.'

'There are five floors of offices in this building. Every second person carts in a briefcase. There are fifty-two shops. Every third person has satchels.' Eve moved her shoulders. 'We'll look anyway. Summerset didn't do this, Peabody.' When her aide remained silent, Eve turned impatiently. 'Brennen was five-ten, but he was a hundred and ninety pounds – and a lot of that was muscle. Maybe, just maybe, a skinny, bone-ass fart like Summerset could take Brennen by surprise, but he doesn't have the arm to have severed flesh and bone with one swipe. And one swipe was what it took. Say he got lucky and managed that – how do you figure he hauled dead weight from here to the bedroom, then managed to drag that nearly two hundred pounds of dead weight up two and a half feet onto the bed? He isn't physical enough. He's got strong hands,' she murmured, remembering well how those fingers had gripped her arm from time to time and bruised. 'But he's got no muscle, no arm, and he's not used to lifting much more than a tea tray or his nose in the air.'

Now she sighed. 'And you have to figure that if he's smart enough to play electronic games with us, to fiddle with security discs, he'd have done better than to let himself get tagged walking into the lobby of the murder scene. Why didn't he wipe those discs while he was at it?'

'I hadn't thought of that,' Peabody admitted.

'Somebody's setting him up, and they're setting him up to get to Roarke.'

'Why?'

Eve stared into Peabody's eyes for a long ten seconds. 'Let's seal up here.'

'Dallas, I'm no good to you if you stick blinders on me.'

'I know. Let's seal it up.'

'I need air,' Eve said when they were outside again and Peabody's recorder was tucked away. 'And food. Any objections to getting both in Central Park?'

'No.'

'Don't pout, Peabody,' Eve warned as they climbed back into the car. 'It's not attractive.'

They drove in silence, squeezed into a street level parking spot, and headed off into the denuded trees. The wind had enough kick to make Eve fasten her jacket as they crunched dead leaves under their feet. At the first glide-cart Eve debated between a veggie hash pocket and a scoop of soy fries. She opted for grease while Peabody ordered a single healthy fruit kabob.

'Your Free-Ager's showing,' Eve commented.

'I don't consider food a religious issue.' Peabody sniffed and bit into a pineapple spear. 'Though my body is a temple.'

It made Eve smile. She was going to be forgiven. 'I'm in possession of certain information that, as an officer of the law, I am duty bound to report to my superior. I have no intention of doing so.'

Peabody studied a slice of hothouse peach, slid it off the stick. 'Would this information have relevance in a case currently under investigation?'

'It would. If I share this information with you, you would also be duty bound to report it. Not doing so would make you an accessory after the fact. You'd risk your badge, your career, and very likely some portion of your freedom.'

'It's my badge, my career, my freedom.'

'Yes, it is.' Eve stopped, turned. The wind ruffled her hair as she studied the earnest face, the sober eyes. 'You're a good cop, Peabody. You're on your way to earning a detective's shield. I know that's important to you. I know what mine meant to me.'

She looked away to where two uniformed nannies watched their young charges play on the grass. Nearby a jogger stopped along the path to stretch, to shift the bottle of antimugging spray on his hip when a licensed beggar meandered in his direction. Overhead, a park security copter cruised lazily with monotonous thudding blades.

'This information I have affects me personally, so I've made the choice. It doesn't affect you.'

'With respect, Lieutenant, it does. If you're questioning my loyalty—'

'It isn't a matter of loyalty, Peabody. This is the law, this is duty, this . . .' Heaving a breath, she dropped down on a bench. 'This is a mess.'

'If you share this information with me, will it help me assist you in apprehending the killer of Thomas Brennen and Shawn Conroy?'

'Yes.'

'Do you want my word that said information remains between us?'

'I have to ask for it, Peabody.' She looked over as Peabody sat beside her. 'With regret, I have to ask you to promise me you'll violate your duty.'

'You have my word, Lieutenant. With no regret.'

Eve squeezed her eyes shut for a moment. Some bonds, she realized, were formed quickly and held fast. 'It started in Dublin,' she began, 'almost twenty years ago. Her name was Marlena.'

She related it all, carefully and concisely, using the cop speak that both of them understood best. When it was done, they continued to sit. Eve's lunch lay untouched on her lap. Somewhere deeper in the park birds sang, their voices competing with the drone of traffic.

'I never thought of Summerset having a daughter,' Peabody

said at length. 'Losing her like that. There's nothing worse, is there?'

'I suppose not. But somehow something worse always comes along. Revenge, Marlena to Summerset to Roarke. It fits like a skin suit. A shamrock on one side, the Church on the other. A game of luck, a mission from God.'

'If he set Summerset up, knew he'd be in the Towers, doctored the discs, he had to know about his date with Audrey Morrell.'

'Yeah. People are never as discreet as they think they are, Peabody. My guess is at least half that painting class knew they were eyeballing each other. So, we check out the art students.' She rubbed her eyes. 'I need a list from Roarke – the names of the men he killed. The names of everyone he can think of who helped him track them.'

'Which list do you want me to run?'

It surprised Eve to feel her eyes sting. *Overtired*, she told herself and willed back the tears. 'Thanks. I owe you big for this.'

'Okay. You going to eat those fries?'

With a half laugh, Eve shook her head and passed them over. 'Help yourself.'

'Dallas, how are you going to get around the commander?'

'I'm working on that.' Because it made Eve's stomach uneasy, she rubbed it absently. 'Right now, we have to get back to Central and goose McNab on the jams. I have to deal with the media before this explodes. I need the sweeper's and ME's reports on the Conroy homicide, and I have to have a fight with Roarke.'

'Busy day.'

'Yeah, all I have to do is fit the commander in, and it'll be perfect.'

'Why don't I go harass McNab and you can go bribe Nadine Furst?'

'Good thinking.'

*

Eve didn't have to find Nadine. The reporter was in Eve's office, grinning at Eve's communication center. The guts of it were spread over the desk.

'A little electronic blip, Dallas?'

'Peabody, go find McNab and kill him.'

'Right away, Lieutenant.'

'Nadine, how many times have I told you to stay out of my office?'

'Oh, dozens, I imagine.' Still grinning, Nadine sat down and crossed her shapely legs. 'I don't know why you bother. So, who was Shawn Conroy and why was he killed in Roarke's house?'

'It wasn't Roarke's house, it was one of Roarke's properties, of which he has legion.' She angled her head, lifted her eyebrows meaningfully. 'That's a qualification I'm sure you'll include in your report.'

'My exclusive report.' Nadine smiled her sunny smile. 'Which will include a statement from the primary.'

'You'll get your statement, and your exclusive.' Eve shut the door, locked it.

'Hmm.' Nadine lifted one perfectly arched brow. 'That was entirely too easy. What's it going to cost me?'

'Nothing yet. You're running a tab. The NYPSD is investigating the murder of Shawn Conroy, Irish citizen, unmarried, forty-one years of age, bartender by trade. Following an anonymous tip, the primary in the case – with the assistance of Roarke – discovered the victim in an empty rental unit.'

'How was he killed? I heard it was nasty.'

'The details of the crime are not available to the media at this time.'

'Come on, Dallas.' Nadine leaned forward. 'Gimme.'

'Nope. But the police are investigating a possible connection between this crime and the murder, on Friday last, of communication tycoon – and Irish citizen – Thomas X. Brennen.'

'Brennen? Jesus. Friday?' Nadine leaped to her feet. 'Brennen's been killed? Christ Almighty, he owned majority stock in Channel 75. Holy God, how did we miss this? How did it happen? Where?'

'Brennen was killed in his New York residence. Police are pursuing leads.'

'Leads? What leads? God, I knew him.'

Eve's eyes narrowed. 'Did you really?'

'Sure, I met him dozens of times. Station functions, charity events. He even sent me flowers after – after that business last spring.'

'The business where you nearly got your throat slit.'

'Yes,' Nadine snapped and sat again. 'And I haven't forgotten who made sure I didn't. I liked him, Dallas. Damn it, he's got a wife, kids.' She brooded a moment, pretty fingers tapping her knee. 'The station's going to be in an uproar when this hits. And half the media around the world. How did it happen?'

'At this point, we believe he surprised an intruder.'

'So much for security,' she muttered. 'Walked in on a damn burglary.'

Eve said nothing, pleased that Nadine had jumped to that particular conclusion.

'A connection?' Her eyes sharpened. 'Shawn Conroy was Irish, too. Do you believe he was involved in the burglary? Did they know each other?'

'We'll investigate that angle.'

'Roarke's Irish.'

'So I've heard,' Eve said dryly. 'Off the record,' she began, and waited for Nadine's reluctant nod. 'Roarke knew Shawn Conroy back in Ireland. It's possible – just possible – that the house where Conroy was taken out was being cased. It was furnished – well, as I'm sure you can imagine how well. And the new tenants weren't due to move in for a couple of days. Until we nail things down a bit, I'd like to keep

Roarke's name out of it, or as far in the background as possible.'

'Shouldn't be hard at this point. Every station, and certainly ours, is going to hit with the Brennen story – then we'll do a lot of retrospectives, biographies, that sort of thing. I've got to get this in.'

She leaped up again. 'Appreciate it.'

'Don't.' Eve unlocked the door, opened it. 'You'll pay for it eventually.'

And now, Eve mused, rubbing her temple, she could only hope she could bluff and bullshit her commander with half as much success.

'Your report seems sparse, Lieutenant,' Whitney commented after Eve had finished backing up her written report with an oral one.

'We don't have a lot to work with at this stage, Commander.' She sat, face composed, voice bland, meeting Whitney's sharp dark eyes without a blink. 'McNab from EDD is working on the jams and trace, but he doesn't appear to be having much success. Feeney will be back in about a week.'

'McNab has a very good record with the department.'

'That may be, but so far, he's stumped. His words, Commander. The killer is highly skilled in electronics and communications. It's possible that's his link with Brennen.'

'That wouldn't explain Conroy.'

'No, sir, but the Irish connection does. They knew each other, casually at least, in Dublin some years ago. It's possible they continued, or renewed, the acquaintance in New York. As you've reviewed the tape of the transmissions I received from the killer, you know the motive is revenge. The killer knew them, most likely in Dublin. Conroy continued to live in Dublin until three years ago. Brennen has his main residence there. It would be to our benefit to enlist the aid of the Dublin police to investigate that angle. Something these men did, or some deal they were part of in Ireland in the last few years.'

'Roarke has interests there as well.'

'Yes, sir, but he's had no recent dealings with either Conroy or Brennen. I checked. He's had no business or personal contact with them in a more than a decade.'

'Revenge often takes time to chill.' He steepled his fingers and studied Eve over the tips. 'Do you intend to bring Summerset back into Interview?'

'I'm weighing that option, Commander. His alibi for the time of Brennen's murder is weak, but it's plausible. Audrey Morrell confirmed their date. It's more than possible they confused the times. The manner of Brennen's death, and Conroy's as well, doesn't fit Summerset. He isn't physical enough to have managed it.'

'Not alone.'

Eve felt her stomach stutter but nodded. 'No, not alone. Commander, I'll pursue the leads. I'll investigate Summerset and any and all suspects, but it's my personal belief, and a strong personal belief, that Summerset would do nothing to harm or implicate Roarke in any way. He is devoted – even overly devoted. And I believe, Commander, that Roarke is a future target. He's the goal. That's why I was contacted.'

Whitney said nothing for a moment as he measured Eve. Her eyes were clear and direct, her voice had been steady. He imagined she was unaware that she'd linked her fingers together and that her knuckles were white.

'I agree with you. I could ask you if you'd prefer to be taken off the case, but I'd be wasting my breath.'

'Yes, sir.'

'You'll interview Roarke.' He paused while she remained silent. 'And I imagine there will be no official report of said interview. Be careful how far you bend the rules, Dallas. I don't want to lose one of my best officers.'

'Commander.' She rose. 'His mission isn't complete. He'll

contact me again. I've already got a feel for him, an impression of type, but I'd like to consult with Dr. Mira on a profile as soon as possible.'

'Arrange it.'

'And I intend to work as much as possible out of my home. My equipment there is . . . superior to what's available to me at Cop Central.'

Whitney allowed a smirk to twist his wide face. 'I bet it is. I'm going to allow you as much free rein as I can on this, for as long as I can. I can tell you that time will be short. If there's another body, that time's going to be even shorter.'

'Then I'll work fast.'

Chapter Seven

Halfway up the long, curving drive Eve sat in her car and studied the house that Roarke built. That wasn't entirely accurate, she supposed. The structure would have been there for more than a century, ready for someone with money and vision to buy it. He'd had both and had polished a stone and glass palace that suited him beautifully.

She was at home there now, or more at home than she'd ever imagined she could be. There with the towers and turrets, the graceful lawns and glamorous shrubberies. She lived among the staggering antiques, the thick carpets from other lands, the wealth and the privilege.

Roarke had earned it – in his way. She had done nothing more than tumble into it.

They had both come from the streets and misery, and had chosen different paths to make their own. She had needed the law, the order, the discipline, the rules. Her childhood had been without any of them, and the early years that she had so successfully blanked out for so long had begun to hurtle back at her, viciously, violently, over the past months.

Now she remembered too much, and still not all.

Roarke, she imagined, remembered all, in fluid and perfect detail. He wouldn't allow himself to forget what he'd been or where he'd come from. He used it.

His father had been a drunk. And so had hers. His father had abused him. And so had hers. Their childhoods had been smashed beyond repair, and so they had built themselves into adults at an early age, one standing for the law, and one dancing around it.

Now they were a unit, or trying to be.

But how much of what she had made herself, and he had made himself, could blend?

That was about to be tested, and their marriage, still so new and bright, so terrifying and vital to her, would either hold or fail.

She drove the rest of the way, parking at the base of the old stone steps. She left her car there, where it consistently annoyed Summerset, and carried a small box of file discs into the house.

Summerset was in the foyer. He would have known the moment she'd driven through the iron gates, she imagined. And he would have wondered why she'd stopped for so long.

'Is there a problem with your vehicle, Lieutenant?'

'No more than usual.' She stripped off her jacket, and out of habit, tossed it over the newel post.

'You left it in front of the house.'

'I know where it is.'

'There is a garage for the purpose of storing vehicles.'

'Move it yourself. Where's Roarke?'

'Roarke is in his Fifth Avenue office. He's expected home withing the hour.'

'Fine, tell him to come up to my office when he gets here.'

'I'll inform him of your request.'

'It wasn't a request.' She smirked as she watched Summerset pick up her jacket by the collar with two reluctant fingers. 'Any more than it's a request when I tell you to make no plans to leave the city until further notice.'

A muscle in his jaw twitched visibly. 'You're enjoying this, aren't you, Lieutenant?'

'Oh, yeah, it's a bucketful of laughs for me. A couple of dead guys, one of them slaughtered on my husband's property, both of them old pals of his. I've been breaking up over it all day.' When he stepped forward, her eyes went to dangerous slits. 'Don't get in my face, old man. Don't even think about it.'

The core of his anger simmered out in one terse sentence. 'You interrogated Ms. Morrell.'

'I tried to verify your piss-poor alibi.'

'You led her to believe I was involved in a police investigation.'

'News flash: You *are* involved in a police investigation.'

He drew air audibly through his nose. 'My personal life—'

'You've got no personal life until these cases are closed.' She could read his embarrassment clearly enough, and told herself she didn't have time for it. 'You want to do yourself a favor, you do exactly what I tell you. You don't go anywhere alone. You make certain you can account for every minute of your time, day and night. Because somebody else is going to die before much more time passes if I can't stop it. He wants the finger to point at you, so you make sure it doesn't.'

'It's your job to protect the innocent.'

She'd started up the stairs and now she stopped, turned back until their eyes met. 'I know what my job is, and I'm damned good at it.'

When he snorted she came down two steps. She came down slowly, her movements deliberate, because her own temper was much too close to the boil. 'Good enough to have figured out why you've hated the sight of me since I first walked in that door. Since you understood Roarke had feelings for me. Part A was easy – a first-year rookie could have snagged onto it. I'm a cop, and that's enough for you to hold me in contempt.'

He offered a thin smile. 'I've had little reason to admire those in your profession.'

'Part B was tougher.' She came down another step so that their eyes were level. 'I thought I had that figured, too, but I didn't realize that Part B had a couple of stages. Stage one: I'm not one of the glamorous, well-bred stunners that Roarke socialized with. I haven't got the looks or the pedigree or the style to suit you.'

He felt a quick tug of shame, but inclined his head. 'No, you don't. He could have had anyone, his pick of the cream of society.'

'But you didn't want just anyone for him, Summerset. That's stage two, and I just figured that out this morning. You resent me because I'm not Marlena. That's who you wanted for him,' she said quietly as the color slipped out of his cheeks. 'You hoped he'd find someone who reminded you of her, instead you got stuck with an inferior model. Tough luck all around.'

She turned and walked away, and didn't see his legs buckle, or the way his hand shot out to grip the newel post as the truth of what she'd tossed in his face struck him like a fist in the heart.

When he was sure he was alone, he sat on the steps and buried his face in his hands as the grief he thought he'd conquered long ago flowed through him, fresh and hot and bitter.

When Roarke arrived home twenty minutes later, Summerset was composed. His hands no longer trembled, his heart no longer shuddered. His duties, as he saw them – as he needed to see them – were always to be performed smoothly and unobtrusively.

He took Roarke's coat, approving of the fine and fluid weight of the silk, and draped it over his arm. 'The lieutenant is upstairs in her office. She would like to speak with you.'

Roarke glanced up the stairs. He was sure Eve hadn't put it quite so politely. 'How long has she been home?'

'Less than thirty minutes.'

'And she's alone?'

'Yes. Quite alone.'

Absently he flicked open the top two buttons of his shirt. His afternoon meetings had been long and tedious. A rare tension headache was brewing at the base of his skull.

'Log any calls that come through for me. I don't want to be disturbed.'

'Dinner?'

Roarke merely shook his head as he started up the stairs. He'd managed to put his temper on hold throughout the day, but he felt it bubbling back now, black and hot. He knew it would be best, certainly more productive, if they could speak calmly.

But he kept thinking about the door she'd closed between them the night before. The ease with which she'd done so, and the finality of the act. He didn't know if he would be able to remain calm for long.

She'd left her office door open. After all, Roarke thought sourly, she'd summoned him, hadn't she? She sat scowling at her computer screen as if the information it offered annoyed her. There was a mug of coffee at her elbow, likely gone cold by now. Her hair was disordered and spiky, no doubt disturbed by her restless hands. She still wore her weapon harness.

Galahad had made himself at home on a pile of paperwork on the desk. He twitched his tail in greeting, and his bicolored eyes gleamed with unmistakable glee. Roarke could almost hear the feline thoughts.

Come on in, get started. I've been waiting for the show.

'You wanted to see me, Lieutenant?'

Her head came up, turned. He looked cool, she noted, casually elegant in his dark business suit with the collar of his shirt loosened. But the body language – the cock of his head, the thumbs hooked in his pockets, the way his weight was balanced on the balls of his feet – warned her here was an Irish brawler spoiling for a fight.

Fine, she decided. She was ready for one.

'Yeah, I wanted to see you. You want to shut the door?'

'By all means.' He closed it behind him before crossing the room. And waited. He preferred for his opponent to draw first blood.

It made the striking back more satisfying.

'I need names.' Her voice was clipped and brisk. She wanted them both to know she was speaking as a cop. 'Names of the men you killed. Names of any- and everyone you can remember you contacted to find those men.'

'You'll have them.'

'And I'll need a statement from you, detailing where you were and who you were with during the times of the Brennen and Conroy homicides.'

His eyes went hot, for an instant only, then frosted to brilliant blue ice. 'Am I a suspect? Lieutenant?'

'No, and I want to keep it that way. Eliminating you from the top simplifies things.'

'By all means let's keep things simple.'

'Don't take that line with me.' She knew what he was doing, she thought with rising fury. Oh, she had his number, all right, with his cold and utterly reasonable tone. Damned if he'd shake her. 'The more I can go by the book on this, the better it is for everyone involved. I'd like to fit Summerset with a security bracelet. He'd never agree if I asked, so I'd like you to.'

'I won't ask him to submit to the indignity of that.'

'Look.' She got to her feet, slowly. 'A little indignity might keep him out of a cage.'

'For some, dignity is a priority.'

'Fuck dignity. I've got enough problems without worrying about that. What I need is facts, evidence, an edge. If you keep lying to me—'

'I never lied to you.'

'You withheld vital information. It's the same thing.'

'No, it's not.' Oh, he had her number, he thought, with her stubborn, unbending rules. Damned if she'd shake him.

'I withheld information in the hope I could keep you out of a difficult position.'

'Don't do me any favors,' she snapped as control teetered.

'I won't.' He moved to a dome-topped cabinet, selected a bottle of whiskey, and poured three fingers into a heavy crystal glass. He considered throwing it.

She heard the ice pick fury in his tone, recognized the frigid rage. She would have preferred heat, something hot and bubbling to match her own mood.

'Great, terrific. You go ahead and be pissed off. I've got two dead guys, and I'm waiting for the third. I've got essential information, information vital to the case, that I can't use officially unless I want to come visit you in a federal facility for the next hundred years.'

He sipped, and showed his teeth in a smile. 'Don't do me any favors.'

'You can just yank that stick out of your ass, pal, because you're in trouble here.' She found she wanted to hit something – smash anything – and settled for shoving her chair aside. 'You and that bony droid you're so goddamn fond of. If I'm going to keep both your butts out of the sling, you better get yourself a quick attitude adjustment.'

'I've managed to keep my butt out of the sling by my own devices up until now.' Roarke drained the rest of the whiskey, set the glass down with a snap of glass on wood. 'You know very well Summerset killed no one.'

'It doesn't matter what I know, it matters what I can prove.' Temper straining, she dragged her hands through her hair, fisted them there a moment until her head began to throb. 'By not giving me all the data, you put me a step behind.'

'What would you have done with the data that I wasn't doing myself? And, with my contacts and equipment, doing more quickly and more efficiently?'

That, she thought, tore it. 'You better remember who's the cop here, ace.'

His eyes glinted once, like blue steel in moonlight. 'I'm unlikely to forget.'

'And whose job it is to gather evidence and information, to process that evidence and information. To investigate. You do whatever it is you do with your business, but you stay off my turf unless I tell you different.'

'Unless you tell me?' She saw the quick and vicious flare of violence in his eyes, but stood her ground when he whirled on her, when he closed a fist over her shirt to haul her up to her toes. 'And what if I don't do what I'm told, Lieutenant, what I'm ordered? How do you handle that? Do you walk away and lock the door again?'

'You better move your hand.'

He only yanked her up another inch. 'I won't tolerate locked doors. I've got my limit, and you reached it. If you don't want to share our bed, if you don't want me near you, then you say so. But I'm damned if you'll turn away and lock the door.'

'You're the one who screwed up,' she shot back. 'You pissed me off and I didn't want to talk to you. I'm the one who has to deal with what's going on here, what's gone on before. I have to overlook the laws you've broken instead of carting you off to a cell.' She lifted both hands, shoved hard, and was both surprised and furious when she didn't budge him an inch. 'And I've got to make dinner conversation with a bunch of snooty strangers every time I turn around, and worry about what the hell I'm wearing when I do it.'

'Do you think you're the only one who's made adjustments?' Enraged, he gave her a quick shake, then let her go so he could prowl the room. 'For Christ's sake, I married a cop. Fuck me, a cop. It has to be fate's biggest joke.'

'Nobody held a knife to your throat.' Insulted, she fisted her hands on her hips. 'You're the one who pushed for it.'

'And you're the one who pulled back, and still does. I'm sick of it, sick to death of it. It's always you, isn't it, Eve, who has to make the changes and give way?' Fury shimmered around him in all but visible waves, and when those waves crashed over her, she'd have sworn they had weight. 'Well, I've made changes of my own, and given way more times than I can count. You can have your privacy when you need it, and your neurotic little snits, but I won't put up with my wife closing doors between us.'

The *neurotic little snits* left her speechless, but the *my wife* freed her tongue again. 'Your wife, your wife. Don't you dare say *my wife* in that tone. Don't you dare make me sound like one of your fancy suits.'

'Don't be ridiculous.'

'Now I'm ridiculous.' She threw up her hands. 'I'm neurotic and ridiculous.'

'Yes, often.'

Her breath began to hitch. She could actually see red around the edges of her vision. 'You're arrogant, domineering, egotistical, and disdainful of the law.'

He lifted one amused brow. 'And your point would be?'

She couldn't form a word. What came out was something between a growl and a scream. The sound of it had Galahad leaping from the top of the desk and curling under it.

'Well said,' Roarke commented and decided to have another whiskey. 'I've given up a number of businesses in the past months that you would have found questionable.' He studied the color of the whiskey in the glass. 'True, they were more like hobbies, habits, I suppose, but I found them entertaining. And profitable.'

'I never asked you to give up anything.'

'Darling Eve.' He sighed, found most of his temper had slipped away. 'You ask just by being. I married a cop,' he said half to himself and drank. 'Because I loved her, wanted her, needed her. And to my surprise, I admired her. She fascinates me.'

'Don't turn this around.'

'It's just come full circle. I can't change what I am, and what

I've done. And wouldn't even for you.' He lifted his gaze to hers, held it there. 'I'm telling you not to lock the door.'

She gave a bad-tempered shrug. 'I knew it would piss you off.'

'Mission accomplished.'

She found herself sighing, a weak sound she didn't have the energy to detest. 'It's hard – seeing what had been done to those men, and knowing . . .'

'That I was capable of doing the same.' He set his glass down again. 'It was justice.'

She felt the weight of her badge, tangibly. Not in her pocket but on her heart. 'That wasn't for you to decide.'

'There we part ways. The law doesn't always stand for the innocent and the used. The law doesn't always care enough. I won't apologize for what I did, Eve, but I will for putting you in the position of choosing between me and your duty.'

She picked up her cold coffee and drank it to clear her throat. 'I had to tell Peabody. I had to bring her in.' She rubbed a hand over her face. 'She'll stand with me. She didn't even hesitate.'

'She's a good cop. You've taught me the phrase isn't a contradiction in terms.'

'I need her. I need all the help I can get on this one because I'm afraid.' She closed her eyes, fought to steady herself. 'I'm afraid if I'm not careful enough, not quick or smart enough, I'll walk onto a scene and I'll find you. I'll be too late, and you'll be dead, because it's you he wants. The others are just practice.'

She felt his arms come around her, and moved in. There was the warmth of his body, the lines of it all so familiar now, so necessary now. The scent of him as she gripped him close, the steady beat of his heart, the soft brush of his lips over her hair.

'I couldn't stand it.' She tightened her hold. 'I couldn't. I know I can't even think about it because it'll mess me up, but I can't get it out of my head. I can't stop—'

Then his mouth was on hers and the kiss was rough and hot. He would know that was the tone she needed, that she needed his hands on her, hard, impatient. And the promises he murmured as he tugged her shirt aside were for both of them.

Her weapon thudded to the floor. His beautifully cut jacket followed. She tipped her head back so that his lips could race thrills over her throat as she dragged at his belt.

No words now as they hurried to touch. With greedy little nips and bites they tormented each other. She was panting when he pushed her onto the desk. Paper crinkled under her back.

She reached for him.

'I'm not neurotic,' she managed to say.

He laughed first, delighted with her, delirious for her. 'Of course not.' He closed his hands over hers and drove into her.

He watched her come at the first thrust, those golden brown irises blurring, that slim torso arching up. The shocked pleasure strangled in her throat then shuddered out on his name.

'Take more.' His hands were less gentle than he intended as he lifted her hips, went deeper. 'Take all of me.'

Through the stunning waves of sensation she understood he wanted acceptance, finally and fully, for both of them.

She took all of him.

Later they shared soup in her office. By the second bowl, her head was clear enough to deal with the business at hand.

'I'm going to be working here for the most part for a while.'

'I'll lighten my schedule so I'll be available for you.'

She broke open a roll, buttered it thoughtfully. 'We're going to have to contact the Dublin police. Your name's bound to come up.' She ignored the quick grin he flashed her and bit into the roll. 'Should I expect any surprises?'

'They don't have any more hard data on me than your records show.'

'Which is next to nothing.'

'Exactly. There's bound to be a few members of the guarda with long memories, but there shouldn't be anything too embarrassing. I've always been careful.'

'Who investigated Marlena's murder?'

The amusement died out of Roarke's eyes. 'It was an Inspector Maguire, but I wouldn't say he investigated. He went through the motions, took the bribes offered, and called it death by misadventure.'

'Still, his records might be of some use.'

'I doubt you'll find much, if any. Maguire was one of the many cops in the pocket of the cartel whose territory I trespassed on.' He took the other half of Eve's roll. 'The Urban Wars started later and lasted longer in that part of the world. Even when I was a boy there were pockets of it still being waged, and certainly the results of the worst of it were still in evidence.'

He remembered the bodies, the sound of gunfire screaming through the night, the wails of the wounded, and the sunken eyes of the survivors.

'Those who had,' he continued, 'had in abundance. Those who didn't, suffered and starved and scavenged. Most cops who'd been through the hell of it went one of two ways. Some dedicated themselves to maintaining order. Most took advantage of the chaos and profited.'

'Maguire decided to profit.'

'He was hardly alone. I took plenty of kicks from a beat cop if I didn't have the payoff in my pocket. When you're down to your last punt, you'd as soon have the kick and keep the pound.'

'Did you take any from Maquire?'

'Not personally. By the time I was working the grift and the games, he was riding a desk. He used uniforms as his runners and muscle and collected in comfort.' Roarke sat back with his coffee. 'For the most part I outmaneuvered him. I paid my shot when I couldn't get around it, but I usually stole it back. Cops are easy marks. They don't expect to have their pockets picked.'

'Hmm' was all Eve could say to that. 'Why was Maguire brought in on Marlena?'

'When she was killed, Summerset insisted on calling in the police. He wanted to see the men who had . . . he wanted to see them punished. He wanted a public trial. He wanted justice. Instead he got Maguire. The bastard came sniffing around, shaking his head, clucking his tongue. "Well, well," he said, "seems to me a father should keep a closer eye on a pretty young girl. Letting her run wild like that."'

As the old fury crawled back, Roarke shoved away from the table to rise and pace. 'I could have killed him on the spot. He knew it. He wanted me to try it, then and there while he had six cops around him who'd have broken me to pieces at the first move. His conclusions were that she was an incorrigible, that there were illegals in her system and she'd fallen in with a bad lot who'd panicked and killed her when they'd done with her. Two weeks later he was driving a new car around Dublin Town and his wife had a new haircut to show off her diamond earrings.'

He turned back. 'And six months later, they hooked him out of the River Liffey with enough holes in him for the fish to swim through.'

Her throat had gone dust dry, but she kept her gaze steady. 'Did you kill him?'

'No, but only because someone beat me to it. He was low on my list of priorities.' Roarke came back, sat again. 'Eve, Summerset had no part in what I did. He wasn't even aware of what I planned to do. It wasn't his way – isn't his way. He ran cons, bilked marks, lifted wallets.'

'You don't need to defend him to me. I'll do my best

110

for him.' She let out a breath. 'Starting now by ignoring regulations, again, and using your unregistered equipment to run names. Let's start on those lists.'

He got to his feet, taking her hand and bringing it to his lips. 'It's always a pleasure working with you, Lieutenant.'

'Just remember who's in charge.'

'I've no doubt you'll remind me. Regularly.' He slipped an arm around her waist when she stood. 'Next time we make love, you can wear your badge. In case I forget who's in charge.'

She eyed him narrowly. 'Nobody likes a smart-ass.'

'I do.' He planted a kiss between her scowling eyes. 'I love one.'

Chapter Eight

Eve stared at the list of names on the wall screen in Roarke's private room. The equipment installed there was every hacker's wet dream. He'd indulged himself in aesthetics in the rest of the house, but this room was all business.

Illegal business, she thought, since all its information, research, and communications devices were unregistered with CompuGuard. Nothing that went in or came out of that room could be tracked.

Roarke sat at the U-shaped console, like a pirate, she thought, at the helm of a very snazzy ship. He hadn't engaged the auxiliary station with its jazzy laser fax and hologram unit. She imagined he didn't think he required the extra zip, just yet.

She stuck her hands in her pockets, tapped her boot on the glazed tile floor and read off the names of the dead.

'Charles O'Malley. Murder by disembowelment, August 5, 2042. Unsolved. Matthew Riley. Murder by evisceration, November, 12, 2042. Donald Cagney. Murder by hanging, April 22, 2043. Michael Rowan, Murder by suffocation, December 2, 2043. Rory McNee, murder by drowning, March 18, 2044. John Calhoun, murder by poisoning, July 31, 2044.'

She let out a long breath. 'You averaged two a year.'

'I wasn't in a hurry. Would you like to read their bios?' He didn't call them up, simply continued to sit, staring at the viewing screen across the room. 'Charles O'Malley, age thirty-three, small-time thug and sexual deviant. Suspected of raping his sister and his mother. Charges dismissed through lack of evidence. Suspected of torture-murder of an eighteen-year-old licensed companion whose name no one bothered to remember. Charges dismissed through lack of interest. A known free-lance spine cracker and debt collector who enjoyed his work. His trademark was shattering kneecaps. Marlena's knees were broken.'

'All right, Roarke.' She held up a hand. 'It's enough. I need you to run their families, friends, lovers. With luck we can find a computer jock or communications freak among them.'

Because he didn't want to say their names again, he typed in the request manually. 'It'll take a few minutes. We'll bring up the list of contacts I had on viewing screen three.'

'Who else knew what you were doing?' she asked as she watched names begin to scroll on screen.

'I didn't pop into the pub after and brag about it over a pint.' He moved his shoulders dismissively. 'But word and rumor travel. I wanted it known in any case. I wanted to give them time to sweat.'

'You're a scary guy, Roarke,' she murmured, then turned to him. 'At a guess, then, most anyone in Dublin – hell, in the known universe – could have gotten wind of it.'

'I found Cagney in Paris, Rowan on Tarus Three, and Calhoun here in New York. The wind blows, Eve.'

'Jesus.' She pressed her fingers to her eyes. 'Okay, this won't help. We need to cull it down to interested parties, people with a connection with one or more of . . . your list. People with a grudge against you.'

'A number of people harbor grudges. If it was about me personally, why is Summerset being set up instead of me?'

'He's the bridge. They're walking over him to get to you.' She began to pace while she thought it through. 'I'm going to consult with Mira, hopefully tomorrow, but my take is if this goes back to Marlena, whoever is behind it sees Summerset as the cause. Without him, no Marlena, without Marlena you wouldn't have played vigilante. So you both have to pay. He wants you to sweat. Coming at you direct isn't going to make that happen. He has to know you well enough to understand that. But going after someone who matters to you, that's different.'

'And if Summerset was taken out of the equation?'

'Well, then, it would—' She broke off, heart jumping as she whirled. 'Wait a minute, wait a minute. Don't even think about it.' She slapped her hands on the console. 'You promise me, you have to give me your word you won't help him disappear. That's not the way to play this out.'

He was silent for a long moment. 'I'll give you my word to play this out your way as long as I possibly can. But he's not going in a cage, Eve, not for something I'm responsible for.'

'You have to trust me not to let that happen. If you go that far outside the law, Roarke, I'll have to go after him. I won't have a choice.'

'Then we'll have to combine our skill and our efforts to make sure neither of us has to make a choice. And we're wasting what time we have debating it.'

Seething with frustration, she spun away. 'Damn it, you make the line I have to walk thin and shaky.'

'I'm aware of that.' His voice was tight and warned her she'd see that cold, controlled temper on his face when she turned back.

'I can't change what I am either.'

'And you're a cop first. Well, Lieutenant, give me your professional take on this.' He swung around in his chair, engaging the auxiliary station. 'Display hologram file image, Marlena.'

It formed between them, a lovely laughing image of a young girl just blossoming into womanhood. Her hair was long and wavy and the color of sun-washed wheat, her eyes a clear summer blue. There was the flush of life and joy in her cheeks.

She was tiny was all Eve could think, a perfect picture in her pretty white dress with its scallop of lace at the hem. She carried a single tulip in her china-doll hand, candy-pink and damp with dew.

'There's innocence,' Roarke said quietly. 'Display hologram image, police file. Marlena.'

The horror spilled onto the floor, almost at Eve's feet. The doll was broken now, bloodied and battered and torn. The skin was gray paste with death, and cold from the police camera's passionless eye. They'd left her naked and exposed, and every cruelty that had been done to her was pitifully clear.

'And there,' Roarke said, 'is the ruin of innocence.'

Eve's heart shuddered and ripped, but she looked as she had looked on death before. In the eyes – where even now dregs of terror and shock remained.

A child, she thought, swamped with pity. Why was it so often a child?

'You've made your point, Roarke. End hologram program,' she ordered, and her voice was steady. The images winked away and left her staring into his eyes.

'I would do it again,' he told her. 'Without hesitation or regret. And I would do more if it would spare her what she suffered.'

'If you think I don't understand, you're wrong. I've seen more of this than you. I live with it, day and night. The aftermath of what one person does to another. And after I wade through the blood and the waste, all I can do is my best.'

He closed his eyes and, in a rare show of fatigue, rubbed his hands over his face. 'I'm sorry for that. This has brought too much of it back. The guilt, the helplessness.'

'It's stupid to blame yourself, and you're not a stupid man.'

He let his hands drop. 'Who else?'

She stepped around the console until she stood directly in front of him. 'O'Malley, Riley, Cagney, Rowan, McNee, and Calhoun.' She would comfort now, because now she understood how. Eve put her hands on his shoulders. 'I'll only say this once. I may only mean it once, now, while I've still got her image in my head. You were right. What you did was necessary. It was justice.'

Unspeakably moved, he put his hands on hers, sliding them down so their fingers could link. 'I needed to hear you say it, and mean it. Even if only once.'

She squeezed his hands then turned to the screen. 'Let's get back to work and beat this son of a bitch at his own game.'

It was after midnight when they shut it down. Eve tumbled into sleep the instant her head hit the pillow. But somewhere just before dawn, the dreams began.

When her restless movements woke him, Roarke reached for her. She struggled away, her breath coming in quick little gasps. He knew she was trapped in a nightmare where he couldn't go, couldn't stop the past from cycling back.

'It's all right, Eve.' He gathered her close even as she fought to twist free with her body shuddering, jerking, shuddering.

'Don't, don't, don't.' There was a plea in her voice and the voice was thin and helpless, a child's voice that broke his heart.

'You're safe. I promise.' He stroked her back, in slow and soothing motions, when at last she turned to him. Turned into him. 'He can't hurt you here,' Roarke murmured as he stared into the dark. 'He can't touch you here.'

There was a long, catchy sigh, then he felt the tension drain out of her body. He lay awake, holding her, guarding against dreams until the light began to slip through the windows.

He was gone when Eve awoke, which was usual. But he wasn't in the sitting area as he was most mornings, drinking coffee and scanning the stock reports on the bedroom monitor. Still groggy, she rolled out of bed and hit the shower. Her mind cleared slowly. It wasn't until she stepped out of the drying tube that the dream came back to her.

She stood, one hand reaching for a robe, as it flashed into her mind.

The cold, horrible little room with the red light blinking into the dirty window. Hunger clawing at her belly. The door opening and her father stumbling in. Drunk, but not drunk enough. The knife she'd held to cut the mold off a pitiful hunk of cheese clattering to the floor.

The pain of that big hand smashing over her face. Then worse, so much worse, his body pressing hers into the floor. His fingers tearing, probing. But it wasn't her struggling. It was Marlena. Marlena with her white dress ripped, her delicate features locked in fear and pain. Marlena's broken body sprawled in fresh blood.

Eve looking down at that wasted young girl. Lieutenant Eve Dallas, with her badge displayed on her pocket, studying death one more time. Reaching for a blanket, a thin, stained blanket from the bed to cover the girl. Against procedure, disturbing the crime scene, but she couldn't help herself.

But when she turned, looked down again with the blanket in her hand, it was no longer Marlena. Eve stared down at herself, in death, and let the blanket fall over her own face.

Now she shuddered and bundled quickly into the robe to help chase away the chill. She had to put it away, ordered herself to shut it away. She had a maniac to catch, lives that depended on her doing so quickly. The past, her past, couldn't be allowed to surface and interfere.

She dressed quickly, snagged a single cup of coffee and took it with her to her office.

The door between it and Roarke's was open. She heard his voice, only his, and stepped to the doorway.

He was at his desk, using a headset 'link while he manually

117

keyed data into his computer. His laser fax shot off a transmission, immediately signaled an incoming. Eve sipped her
coffee, imagined him buying and selling small galaxies while
he carried on a conversation.

'It's good to hear you, Jack. Yes, it's been awhile.' Roarke
turned to his fax, skimmed it, then quickly logged and sent a
reply. 'Married Sheila, did you? How many kids did you say?
Six. Christ.' He let out a rolling laugh and, turning back to
his computer, made arrangements to buy the lion's share of a
small, floundering publishing company. 'Heard that, did you?
Yes, it's true, last summer. Aye, she's a cop.' A lightning
grin flashed across his face. 'What black past, Jack? I don't
know what you're talking about. I'm as law-abiding as the
parish priest. Yes, she is lovely. Quite lovely and quite
remarkable.'

Roarke swiveled away from his monitor, ignored the low
beep of an incoming call. 'I need to talk to you, Jack. You've
heard about Tommy Brennen and Shawn? Aye, it's a hard
thing. My cop's connected them, and the connection goes
back to me – to O'Malley and the rest and what happened
to Marlena.'

He listened for a time, then rose and walked to the window,
leaving his communication center humming and beeping.
'That's exactly so. Any ideas on it? If any occur to you, if
you can dig up anything, you can contact me here. Meanwhile,
I can make arrangements for you and your family to get away
for a time. Take your kids to the beach for a couple weeks. I've
a place they'd enjoy. No, Jack, this is my doing, and I don't
want another widow or fatherless child on my conscience.'

He laughed again, but his eyes stayed sober. 'I'm sure you
could, right enough, but why don't we leave that part to my
cop and you and your family get out of Dublin awhile. I'll
send you what you need today. We'll talk again. My best to
Sheila.'

Eve waited until he'd pulled the headset off before she

118

spoke. 'Is that what you're going to do, ship off everyone you think might be a target?'

He set the headset aside, vaguely uncomfortable that she'd heard his conversation. 'Yes. Do you have a problem with that?'

'No.' She crossed to him, set her coffee down so that she could take his face in both hands. 'I love you, Roarke.'

It was still a rare thing for her to use the words. His heart tripped once, then steadied. 'I love you, Eve.'

Her lips curved, brushed his lightly. 'Is that what I am now, "your cop"?'

'You've always been my cop – ever since you wanted to arrest me.'

She tilted her head. 'Did you know that when you were talking to your Dublin friend your accent got thicker, the rhythm of your speech changed. And you said aye instead of yes at least twice.'

'Did I?' He'd been totally unaware of it, and wasn't sure how that sat with him. 'Odd.'

'I liked it.' The hands she held to his face slid around to link behind his neck. Her body bumped his. 'It was . . . sexy.'

'Was it, now?' His hands roamed down, cupped her bottom. 'Well, Eve, me darling, if you're after—' His gaze flicked over her shoulder, and the amusement in them deepened. 'Good morning, Peabody.' Eve jerked, then swore when Roarke held her firmly in place. 'Lovely day.'

'Yes, it . . . I beg your pardon. Sir,' she added lamely when Eve scorched her with a look. 'You said eight sharp, and there was nobody downstairs so I just came up and . . . here I am. And, ah, McNab is—'

'Right behind her.' Leading with a grin, McNab stepped into view. 'Reporting for duty, Lieutenant, and may I say that your house is . . . Holy Mother of God.'

His eyes went so huge, so bright, that Eve reached instinctively for her weapon as he rushed in.

'Would you look at this setup? Talk about sexy. You must be Roarke.' He grabbed Roarke's hand and pumped it enthusiastically. 'It's a pleasure to meet you. I work on one of your 2000MTSs in EDD. What a honey. We're crying for the 5000, but the budget, well, it sucks. I'm rebuilding an old multimedia unit at home – the Platinum 50? That baby rocks. Is that a Galactic MTS?'

'I believe it is,' Roarke murmured, cocking a brow at Eve as McNab rushed over to drool on the communication system.

'McNab, get a grip on yourself,' Eve ordered.

'Yes, sir, but this is ice.' His voice quivered. 'This is a god-damn glacier. How many simultaneous tasks will it perform?'

'It's capable of three hundred simultaneous functions.' Roarke wandered over, more to prevent McNab from playing with his equipment than to give a tour. 'I've had it up to nearly that without any glitches.'

'What a time to be alive. Your R and D division must be paradise.'

'You can put in an application,' Eve said dryly. 'Since if you don't get your ass in there and deal with my unit, you won't have one in EDD.'

'I'm going. You really ought to talk her into upgrading her home unit,' he told Roarke. 'And that thing she works on at Central. It's a supreme junker.'

'I'll see what I can do.' He smiled as McNab sauntered out. 'Interesting associates you have, Lieutenant.'

'If Feeney doesn't get back soon, I'm going to shoot myself. I'm going to keep an eye on him.'

'Peabody,' Roarke said quietly before she could follow Eve out. 'A moment.' He stepped closer, satisfied when he heard Eve arguing with McNab in the adjoining room. 'I'm in your debt.'

She looked him straight in the eye. 'I don't know what you're talking about. The lieutenant, and the department, is grateful for your assistance in our investigation.'

Touched, Roarke took her hand, brought it to his lips. 'Peabody, you are a jewel.'

She flushed, and her stomach fluttered pleasantly. 'Yeah, well, ah . . . you were an only child, right?'

'Yes.'

'Figures. I'd better go keep Dallas from pounding on McNab. Doesn't look good on interdepartmental memos.'

She'd barely turned when Eve's 'link beeped – one long, two short.

'Okay.' McNab began to toy with controls on a small, portable trace unit. 'That's coming into your downtown office – bypassing main control. It's him, yeah, it's him. She's jammed solid.'

'Unjam it,' Eve snapped. 'Fast.' She reached for the 'link. 'Block video,' she ordered. 'Homicide. Dallas.'

'You were quick.' The voice flowed out, a hint of charm, a wealth of amusement. 'Dear old Shawn wasn't even cold when you found him. I'm so impressed.'

'I'll be quicker next time.'

'If God wills it. I'm enjoying the competition, Lieutenant. And I'm coming to admire your strength of purpose. So much so that I've already begun the next stage. Are you up for the challenge?'

'Why don't you play with me directly. Take me on, asshole, and let's see who wins.'

'I follow the plan given me by a higher power.'

'It's just a sick game to you. God has nothing to do with it.'

'I am the chosen.' He took a long breath. 'I hoped you would see, I've wanted you to see, but your eyes are blinded to that because you've accepted worldly acclaim and responsibilities over the spiritual.'

She stared holes into McNab as he muttered under his breath and finessed dials. 'Funny, I didn't see anything spiritual in the way you slaughtered those two men. I've got one for you.

121

From Romans, chapter two verse three. "Do you suppose, O man, that when you judge those who do such things and yet do them yourself, you will escape the judgment of God?"'

'You would dare use His word against me? I am the angel of His justice, and the sword of His fury. Born and bred to deliver His verdict. Why do you refuse to see, to acknowledge?'

'I see exactly what you are.'

'One day you'll kneel before me and weep tears of blood. You'll know the grief and despair only a woman can know.'

Eve glanced at McNab, who was hunched over his equipment and swearing under his breath. 'You think you can get to Roarke? You overstimate yourself. He'll flick you off like a gnat. We've already had some good laughs over it.'

'I can rip out his heart any time I please.' The voice had changed. There was fury in it but the fury was nearly a whine.

'Prove it — he'll meet you. Name the spot.'

There was silence for a long moment. 'You think you can draw me out that way? Another Eve offering forbidden fruit? I'm not the sheep but the shepherd. I have accepted the task, I hold the staff.'

The voice wasn't quite controlled. No, Eve thought, it was fighting for control. Temper and ego. Those were her keys inside him.

'I think you're too much of a coward to risk it. You're a sick, pathetic coward who probably can't get it up unless he uses both hands.'

'Bitch, cop whore. I know what women of your kind do to a man. "For a harlot may be hired for a loaf of bread, but an adulteress stalks a man's very life."'

'I'm getting something,' McNab whispered. 'I'm getting it. Keep him talking.'

'I wasn't offering you sex. I don't think you'd be very good at it.'

'The harlot did. She offered her honor for her life. But God ordered her execution. His will be done.'

He has another one was all Eve could think. She may already be too late. 'You're boring me, pal. Your riddles are boring me. Why don't we just go to the main match, you and me, and see what shakes down?'

'There will be nine before it is accomplished.' His voice grew stronger, like an evangelist's saving souls. 'A novena of vengeance. It's not your time, but hers. Another riddle, Lieutenant, for your petty and secular mind: Pretty girls grow into pretty women, but once a whore, always a whore. They come running when the price is right. You'll find this one in the west, in the year of her crime. How long she breathes depends on her – and you, Lieutenant. But do you really want to save a whore who once spread her legs for the man you spread them for? Your move,' he said and ended transmission.

'He's bouncing the transmission all over hell and back. Goddamn it.' McNab shoved at his hair and flexed his fingers. 'Got him on Orion, into Stockholm, up into Vegas Two, and through Sydney for Christ's sake. I can't pin him. He's got me outequipped.'

'He's in New York,' Roarke said, 'The rest is smoke.'

'Yeah, well, it's damn good smoke.'

Eve ignored McNab and concentrated on Roarke. His face was pale and set, his eyes icily blue. 'You know who he has.'

'Yes. Jennie. Jennie O'Leary. I just spoke with her two days ago. She was once a barmaid in Dublin and now runs a B and B in Wexford.'

'Is that in the west of Ireland?' Even as Roarke shook his head, she was rising, skimming her fingers through her hair. 'He can't want us to go to Ireland. That can't be right. He's got her here, he wants us here. I don't have any authority in Ireland, and he wants me in charge.'

'The West Side,' Peabody suggested.

'Yeah, that would fit. The West Side – in the year of her crime,' she added, looking at Roarke.

'Forty-three. Twenty forty-three.'

'West Forty-third then. That's where we start. Let's move, Peabody.'

'I'm going with you.' Roarke laid a hand on Eve's arm before she could protest. 'I have to. McNab, call this number.' He turned long enough to scrawl a 'link series onto a card. 'Ask for Nibb. Tell him to have a 60K Track and Monitor unit and a 7500MTS sent over, along with his best tech to install it here in my wife's office.'

'There's no 60K T and M,' McNab objected.

'There will be in about six months. We have some test units.'

'Holy shit, 60K.' McNab nearly shuddered with delight. 'I don't need a tech. I can handle it.'

'Have him send one anyway. Tell him I want it up and running by noon.'

When he was alone, McNab looked at the card and sighed. 'Money doesn't just talk. It sings.'

Eve got behind the wheel and took off down the drive the minute the doors were shut. 'Peabody, run all the flops and lc nests on West Forty-third.'

'Licensed companions? Oh, I get it.' She pulled out her personal palm computer and got to work.

'He wants her to die in a whore's surroundings – my guess is the sleazier the better. Roarke, what do you own on West Forty-third that fits the bill?'

Another time he would have made a joke of that. He took out his own ppc and requested the data. 'I own two buildings on West Forty-three. One is a restaurant with apartments above – single-family units, a hundred percent occupancy. The other is a small hotel with a public bar, projected to be refurbished.'

'Name?'

'The West Side.'

'Peabody?' Eve cut over to Seventh and headed downtown.

She nipped through a red light and ignored the blast of horns and pedestrian curses. 'Peabody?' she repeated.

'Working on it: Here. The West Side – that's 522 West Forty-third. Approved for on-site alcohol consumption, private smoking booths. Attached hotel licensed companion approved. Former owner, J.P. Felix, arrested January 2058. Violation of Codes 752, 821. Operating live sex acts without a license. Operating gambling establishment without a license. Property confiscated by City of New York and auctioned September 2058. Purchased by Roarke Industries, and currently up to code.'

'Five twenty-two,' Eve muttered as she winged onto Forty-third. 'Do you know the setup here, Roarke?'

'No.' In his mind he could see Jennie as he'd once known her. Pretty and bright and laughing. 'One of my acquisitions staff viewed and bid on the property. I've only seen the paperwork.'

He looked out the window as a young boy set up a three-card monte game while his adolescent partner scanned for cops and nuisance droids. He hoped they made a killing.

'I have one of my architects working up a plan for remodeling,' he continued. 'I haven't seen them either.'

'Doesn't matter.' Eve jerked the car to a stop, double parking in front of 522. She flipped on the NYPSD blinker, which helped her chances of finding her vehicle in one piece when she came back. 'We'll check at the front desk, see what the clerk can tell us.'

She bypassed the bar, noted grimly that the security plate on the hotel door was broken. The lobby was dim, with a single pathetic plant going from green to sickly yellow in the corner. The thick safety glass that caged in the desk was scratched and pitted. The access door was wide open. The droid on duty was out of operation.

It was easy to see why, as its body was slumped in a chair and its head sat on the counter.

'Goddamn it. He's been here. Maybe he's still here.' She pulled out her weapon. 'We take a floor at a time, knock on doors. Anybody doesn't answer, we go in.'

Roarke opened a drawer under the droid's head. 'Master code.' He held up the thin card. 'It'll make it easier.'

'Good. Use the stairs.'

Nearly every room on the first floor was empty. They found one groggy-eyed lc sleeping off a long night. She'd heard and seen nothing, and made her displeasure at being roused by cops obvious. On the second floor they found the remnants of a wild party, including a fistful of illegals scattered over the floor like abandoned toys.

On the graffiti-strewn stairway heading toward three, they found the child.

He was perhaps eight, thin and pale, with his toes poking out of his ragged sneakers. There was a fresh bruise under his right eye, and a scruffy gray kitten in his lap.

'Are you Dallas?' he wanted to know.

'Yeah. Why?'

'The man said I should wait for you. He gave me a two-dollar credit to wait.'

Her heart picked up rhythm as she crouched down. The aroma there told her the kid hadn't seen bathwater in a number of days. 'What man?'

'The guy who told me to wait. He said how you'd give me another two if I did, and I told you the thing.'

'What thing?'

His eyes scanned her face slyly. 'He said how you'd give me another two.'

'Sure, okay.' Eve dug in her pocket, made certain to keep her tone light, her smile easy. 'So, what's the thing?' she asked as the boy took the credit and fisted it in his grubby hand.

'He said . . .' the boy closed his eyes and recited, '"It's the third but not the last. You're quick but not too fast. No matter how much flash, no matter how much cash, no bastard

126

son of Eire can ever escape his past. Amen."' He opened his eyes and grinned. 'I got it right, told him I would.'

'Good for you. You stay right here and I'll give you another two. Peabody.' She waited until they'd reached the landing. 'Take care of the kid. Call Child Protection Services, then see if you can get any kind of description out of him. Roarke, you're with me. Third victim, third floor,' she said to herself. 'Third door.'

She turned to the left, weapon raised, and knocked hard. 'There's music.' She cocked her head to try to catch the tune.

'It's a jig. A dance tune. Jennie liked to dance. She's in there.'

Before he could move forward, Eve threw up an arm to block him. 'Stand clear. Do it.' She opened the locks and went in low.

The barmaid who had liked to dance was hanging from a cord from the stained ceiling. Her toes just brushed the surface of a wobbling stool. The cord had cut deep into her throat so that blood trickled down her breasts. It was still fresh enough to carry that copper penny smell, still fresh enough to gleam wet against white skin.

Her right eye was gone, and her fingers, bruised and bloodied from dragging at the cord, hung limp at her sides.

The music played, bright and cheerful, from a small recorder disc under the stool. The statue of the Virgin stood on the floor, her marble face turned toward violent death.

'Fucking, filthy bastard. Bloody motherfucking son of a whore.' Roarke's vision went black with rage. He bulled forward, shoving Eve aside, nearly knocking her to her knees when she fought to muscle him back. 'Get out of my way.' His eyes were sharp and cold as a drawn sword. 'Get the hell out of my way.'

'No.' She did the only thing she could think of, and, countering his weight, knocked him back against the wall and rammed his elbow to his throat. 'You can't touch her. Do you understand me? You can't touch her. She's gone. There's nothing you can do. This is for me. Look at me, Roarke. Look at me.'

Her voice barely punched through the thick buzzing in his head, but he dragged his eyes away from the woman hanging in the center of the room and stared into the eyes of his wife.

'You have to let me try to help her now.' She gentled her tone but kept it firm, as she would with any victim. She wanted to hold him, to lay her cheek against his, and instead kept her elbow pressed lightly to his windpipe. 'I can't let you contaminate the scene. I want you to go outside now.'

He got his breath back, though it burned his lungs. Cleared his vision, though the edges of it remained dark and dull. 'He left the stool there. He stood her on the stool so that she could strain just enough to reach it with her toes. She could stay alive as long as she had the strength to reach the stool. She'd have been choking, her heart overworked, the pain burning, but she could stay alive as long as she fought for balance. She'd have fought hard.'

Eve lowered her elbow, laid her hands on his shoulders. 'This isn't your fault. This isn't your doing.'

He looked away from her, forced himself to look at an old friend. 'We loved each other once,' he said quietly. 'In our way. We had a careless way, but one gave the other what was needed, for a time. I won't touch her. I'll stay out of your way.'

When Eve stepped back, he moved to the door. He spoke now without looking at her. 'I won't let him live. Whether you find him or I do, I won't let him live.'

'Roarke.'

He only shook his head. His eyes met hers, once, and what she read in them chilled her blood. 'He's already dead.'

She let him go, promising herself she would talk him

down as soon as she could. With her eyes tightly shut, she trembled once, hard. Then she pulled out her communicator, called it in, and signaled for Peabody to bring up her field kit.

Chapter Nine

When Roarke stepped outside the building, he saw Peabody had the field kit gripped in one hand and the kid's arm gripped in the other. Roarke thought she was wise to keep him in tow. From the look on his face he'd be unlikely to hang around now that he had four in credits in his pocket. At least he'd be unlikely to hang with a uniformed cop.

He forced himself to block the scene he'd just left from his mind and concentrate on this one: 'Got your hands full there, Peabody.'

'Yeah.' She blew out a harassed breath that fluttered her razor-straight bangs. 'The CPS isn't known for being quick on its feet.' She glanced up at the building, longingly. If Eve had called for the field kit, that meant there was a scene to preserve and investigate. And she was stuck baby-sitting. 'I assume it's inadvisable to take the minor back in, so if you wouldn't mind taking the lieutenant her kit . . .'

'I'll mind the boy, Peabody.'

Her eyes simply lit with gratitude. 'That works for me.' With more haste than tact, she handed him over. 'Don't lose him,' she warned and hustled inside.

Roarke and the boy eyed each other with cool calculation. 'I'm faster,' Roarke said, easily reading the intent. 'And I've got more experience.' Crouching, Roarke gave the kitten a scratch behind the ears. 'What's his name?'

'Dopey.'

Roarke felt a smile tug at his lips. 'Not the brightest of the Seven Dwarfs, but the most pure of heart. And what's yours?'

The boy studied Roarke cautiously. Most of the adults in his life only knew Snow White as an illegal happy powder. 'Kevin,' he said and relaxed a little as Dopey was purring hard and loud under the man's long scratching fingers.

'Nice to meet you, Kevin. I'm Roarke.'

The offer of the man's hand to shake had Kevin giggling at once. 'Meetcha.'

The foolish and lovely sound of a child's quick giggle lightened his heart. 'Think Dopey's hungry?'

'Maybe.'

'There's a cart down the block. Let's check it out.'

'He likes soy dogs.' Kevin began to skip along beside Roarke, thrilled beyond belief with his new good fortune. The new bruise was a dark and ugly contrast under the pale gray eyes.

'The only sensible choice for the discriminating palate.'

'You talk fancy.'

'It's a fine way to make people believe you're saying something much more important than you are.'

He held the boy's hand lightly, then let it go when the smoke from the glide-cart puffed into the air. Kevin raced happily ahead, bouncing on his toes when he reached the cart where soy dogs and turkey hash rolls were popping with heat.

'Didn't I tell you not to come around here?' The operator started to shove Kevin aside, snarling when the boy danced expertly out of reach. 'I ain't got no freebies for dirty little boys.' She grabbed up a long-handled, dual-pronged fork, jabbing with it. 'Keep pestering me and I'll chop up that ugly cat and fry its liver.'

'I got money.' Kevin clutched his kitten tighter, but stood his ground. His stomach was rolling with distress and hunger.

'Yeah, yeah, and I shit gold turds. Go beg somewhere else, or I'll blacken your other eye.'

Roarke stepped up, laid a hand on Kevin's shoulder and had the operator shrinking back with one stony stare. 'Can't you decide what you'd like, Kevin?'

'She said she's going to fry Dopey's liver.'

'Just joking with the boy.' The operator grinned hugely, showing off teeth that screamed an abhorrence for basic dental hygiene. 'I've always got a joke and a few tater snacks for the neighborhood kids.'

'You're a regular fairy godmother, I imagine. Box up a half dozen soy dogs, three scoops of fries, a couple of fruit kabobs, a bag of pretzel twists, two jumbo tubes of— What's your drink, Kevin?'

'Orange Fizzy Supreme,' Kevin managed, dumb-founded by the upcoming feast.

'Two, then, and a handful of the chocolate sticks.'

'Yes, sir, right away.' The operator went to work with a vengeance as Kevin stared up at Roarke, eyes wide, mouth agape.

'Want anything else?' Roarke asked as he reached in his pocket for loose credits.

Kevin only shook his head. He'd never seen that much food in one box before. Dopey, inspired by the scents, let out a wild meow.

'Here.' Roarke pulled one of the soy dogs out, handed it to Kevin. 'Why don't you take this. Go back to the lieutenant's car – and wait for me.'

'Okay.'

Kevin turned, took three steps, then, turning back, did something just childish enough to warm Roarke's heart. He stuck out his tongue at the vendor then dashed off.

Roarke hefted the box of food, ignoring the operator's oily chatter. He tossed credits onto the pay board, then stared through the smoke. 'I'm in the mood to hurt someone – too much in the mood, which is why you're still standing. But if you ever lay hands on that boy, I'll hear about it. And it won't be a cat's liver that ends up on the grill. Understood?'

'Yes, sir. Absolutely. Yes.' Her fingers were already snagging up credits, but her eyes stayed warily on Roarke's. 'Didn't know the kid had a dad. Thought he was just another street brat. They're worse than rats around here. Scavenging, making life messy for decent folk.'

'Let's put it this way.' Roarke clamped a hand over the woman's wrist. It took all his control not to give in to the urge to snap it like a dry twig. 'It should take me about thirty seconds to walk back to where the boy's waiting. When I get there, I'm going to turn around. I don't want to see you here.'

'This is my corner.'

'I'd advise you to find another.' Roarke released her and hefted the box. He'd taken no more than two strides when he heard the metallic clang of the cart being moved. It was a small satisfaction. A bigger one was seeing Kevin sitting on the hood of Eve's unit, the cat beside him, and each of them devouring half a soy dog.

Roarke joined them, set the box between him and the boy. 'Dig in.'

Kevin's hand darted toward the box, then jerked back as though he was wary of a trick. 'I can have anything?'

'Whatever you can stomach.' Roarke nipped out a fry for himself and noted that the cart was gone. 'Is she always so unpleasant?'

'Uh-huh. The big kids call her Snitch Bitch 'cause she's always calling the beat droid on them. She keeps a zapper in her cart, too. She was scared of you, though, and you didn't even try to steal anything.'

Roarke took another fry, only lifting a brow as he watched Kevin mow through the chocolate. Life, he thought, was much too uncertain for some to risk saving the best for last.

'Tell me about the man who asked you to wait for Lieutenant Dallas.'

'He was just a guy.' Kevin dug out another soy dog, splitting it in two. Boy and cat ate with the same ferocious concentration and lack of finesse. Then Kevin froze as two black-and-whites turned the corner, sirens screaming. Behind them was an NYPSD crime scene van.

'They won't hassle you,' Roarke said quietly.

'Are you a cop, too?'

Roarke's huge, gut-level laugh had Kevin grinning uncertainly. He would have liked to have slipped his hand into Roarke's again as the cops streamed by, but he was afraid to be thought of as a pussy. He contented himself by scooting just a little closer, and thought fleetingly that the man smelled good, almost as good as the food.

'I needed that.' Sighing hugely, Roarke ruffled the boy's hair. 'A good laugh after a miserable morning. What I am, Kevin, is a grown-up street brat. Here, drink some of this to wash that down before you choke.'

''Kay.' Taking the tube, Kevin sucked up sparkling orange. 'The guy, he talked like you.'

'How?'

'You know, like singing. The way the words go up and down.' He mashed a handful of fries into his mouth.

'You can take the boy out of Ireland,' Roarke murmured. 'What did he look like?'

'Dunno. Kinda tall maybe.'

'Young, old?'

Kevin's answer was a grunt and a shrug followed by a happy belch. 'He musta been hot.'

'Why is that?'

'He had a big long coat on, and a hat, and a scarf thing and gloves. He smelled really sweaty.' Kevin held his nose, rolled his eyes, then, giggling, dug for more food.

'Close your eyes,' Roarke ordered and nearly smiled at the

speed with which Kevin complied. 'What kind of shoes am I wearing? No peeking.'

'Black ones. They're shiny and they don't hardly make any noise when you walk.'

'Good. What kind was he wearing?'

'Black ones, too, with the red swipe. Hightops, like the big kids want all the time. They were beat up some. They're better when they're beat up some.'

'Okay. What color are my eyes?'

'They're really, really blue. Like in a picture.'

'What color were his?'

'I . . . green, I think. Sorta green, but not like Dopey's. Maybe they were green, but they were mean. Not mean like yours were when you talked to Snitch Bitch. His were more scared mean. That's worse, 'cause they hit you more when they're scared mean.'

'So they do,' Roarke murmured and draped an arm around Kevin's shoulders. 'That was well done. Lieutenant Dallas would say you'd make a good cop.'

Kevin belched again, shook his head. 'Shit work.'

'Often,' Roarke agreed. 'Who blackened your eye, Kevin?'

He felt the boy pull back, just an inch. 'Walked into something.'

'I often had that problem when I was your age. Will your mother be looking for you?'

'Nah. She works late, so she sleeps mostly. She gets pissed if I'm around when she's sleeping.'

Gently, Roarke took the boy's chin in his hand until their eyes met. He hadn't saved Jennie, he thought, and would have to live with that. But there were lost children everywhere.

'Do you want to stay here, stay with her?'

To Kevin, the man's face looked like an angel's. He'd seen one on screen once when he'd snuck into a vid-den. 'I got no place else.'

'That's not what I'm asking you,' Roarke said quietly. 'Do

you want to stay here with her, or do you want to go with the CPS?'

Kevin swallowed hard. 'The CPS, they put you in a box, then they sell you.'

'No, they don't.' But it would seem like that, Roarke knew. As a child he had chosen his father's fists over the system. 'Would you like to go somewhere else entirely?'

'Can I go with you? I can work for you.'

'One day maybe.' Roarke ran a hand over the boy's hair. 'I know some people you might like. If it's what you want I can see about having you stay with them. You can take some time to make up your minds about each other.'

'Dopey has to go, too.' Kevin would give up his mother with her unhappy eyes and quick slaps, but he wouldn't give up the cat.

'Of course.'

Kevin bit his lip, turned his head to look up at the building. 'I don't have to go back in there?'

'No.' Not as long as money bought freedom and choices. 'You don't.'

When Eve came out onto the street she was surprised, and a little annoyed, to see Roarke and the boy were still there. They were a few yards up the street, talking with a woman. From the navy blue suit, side arm zapper, and sour expression, Eve pegged her as the social worker for this section of the city.

Why the hell isn't she moving the boy along? Eve wondered. She'd wanted the kid and Roarke gone before the body was brought out and transferred to the morgue.

'All the bagged evidence is stowed, Dallas.' Peabody stepped up beside her. 'They're bringing the victim out now.'

'Go in and tell them to hold for five minutes.'

She started toward them, relieved when she watched the social worker walk off with the boy. To her surprise the kid turned, flashed a killer smile at Roarke, and waved.

136

'CPS took their time, as usual.'

'Neglected children are plentiful – and no more than a chore to some.' He turned and disconcerted her by kissing her long and deep. 'And some find their way alone.'

'I'm on duty here,' she muttered, casting a quick look over her shoulder to see if they'd been observed. 'You should catch a cab, go on home. I'll be heading there shortly, but I've got some stuff—'

'I'll wait.'

'Go home, Roarke.'

'She's already dead, Eve. It won't be Jennie they bring down in a bag, just what once contained her.'

'All right, be hardheaded.' She pulled out her communicator. 'Continue transport.' Still, she did her best to distract him. 'So, what were you huddled with the social worker about?'

'I had some . . . suggestions as to Kevin's foster care facility.'

'Oh?'

'I thought Richard DeBlass and Elizabeth Barrister would do well by him.' He watched Eve's brows draw together. 'It's been nearly a year since their daughter was murdered, since they had to deal with the cancer that had eaten away at their family. Elizabeth mentioned to me that she and Richard were thinking about adoption.'

It had been the DeBlass case that had first brought Eve and Roarke together. She thought of that now – the loss and the gain. 'Life cycles, I suppose.'

Roarke saw the morgue team roll out the body bag. 'What choice does it have? The boy needs a place. His mother knocks him around – when she's around. He's seven – at least he thinks he is. He doesn't know his birthday.'

'How much are you . . . donating to CPS?' Eve asked dryly and made him smile.

'Enough to ensure the boy gets his chance.' He touched

Eve's hair. 'There are too many children who end up broken in alleys, Eve. We have personal experience there.'

'You get involved, it's your heart that gets broken.' But she sighed. 'A lot of good it does to tell you when you've already made up your mind. He had a great smile,' she added.

'He did.'

'I'll have to interview him. Since you're going to see that he gets shipped off to Virginia, I'd better put it higher on my list.'

'I don't think you'll need him. He told me everything he knew.'

'He told you?' Her mouth went grim, her eyes hot and hard. Her cop look, Roarke thought with admiration – and a surprising tug of pure lust. 'You questioned him? Goddamn it, you questioned him about an open case? A minor, without parental permission or a CPS rep present? What the hell were you thinking of?'

'A young boy – and a girl I once loved.'

Eve hissed out a breath and tried to pace off the worst of the heat. After two swings up and down the sidewalk, she felt more controlled. 'You know damn well I can't use anything you got. And if the kid opens his mouth about talking to you, we're in hip-deep shit. The primary investigator is married to you, the prime suspect is in your employ and has your friendship and loyalty. Anything you got the kid to say is tainted.'

'And well aware you would take precisely that view, I took the precaution of recording the entire conversation.' From his pocket he drew a microrecorder. 'You're welcome to take it into evidence, and you yourself have witnessed that I haven't had the time or opportunity to doctor it.'

'You recorded your conversation, with a minor, on an open homicide case.' She threw up her hands. 'That caps it.'

'You're welcome,' he retorted. 'And though you may be reluctant to take it into evidence – though I have no doubt you could get around the letter of the law there – I don't believe you're stubborn enough to ignore it.'

Seething, she snatched the recorder out of his hand and jammed it into her pocket. 'First chance I get, very first chance, I'm heading to midtown and horning in on one of your board meetings.'

'For you, darling Eve, my door is always open.'

'We'll see if you say that with a smile when I fuck up one of your billion-dollar mergers.'

'If I can watch, it would be worth it.' Still smiling, he took something else out of his pocket and offered it. 'Here, I saved you a chocolate stick – which was, under the circumstances, no easy task.'

She frowned at it. 'You think you can bribe me with candy?'

'I know your weaknesses.'

She took it, yanked down the wrapper, and bit in. 'I'm still pissed at you.'

'I'm devastated.'

'Oh, shut up. I'm taking you home,' she said over the next bite. 'And you're staying out of my way while I talk to Summerset.'

'If you'll listen to the recording, you'll see that the man Kevin described wasn't Summerset.'

'Thank you for your input, but I'll just muddle along here. The chances of me getting the commander to take the word of a seven-year-old kid – who no doubt had chocolate breath – over hard evidence is just slightly less likely than me dancing naked in Times Square.'

She started off at a loping stride. 'If Times Square intimidates you,' Roarke began, 'perhaps you could practice the naked dancing at home.'

'Oh, bite me.'

'Darling, I'd love to, but you're on duty.'

'Get in the goddamn car.' She jerked a thumb at Peabody,

139

who was currently doing her best to pretend she was deaf and blind.

'Please, Eve, these public displays of affection must stop. I have a reputation.'

'Keep it up, ace, and I'll give you a public display of affection that'll have you limping for a week.'

'Now I'm excited.' Smiling, Roarke opened the front passenger door, gestured to Peabody.

'Ah, why don't I sit in the back?' Where it's safer, she thought.

'Oh, no, I insist. She probably won't hurt you,' he murmured in Peabody's ear as she ducked in front of him.

'Thanks. Thanks a lot.'

'Just be grateful I don't put up the cage,' Eve snapped when Roarke settled in to the backseat.

'I am. Constantly.'

'Was that a snicker, Peabody?' Eve demanded as she pulled away from the curb.

'No, sir. It's, ah, allergies. I'm allergic to marital disputes.'

'This isn't a marital dispute. I'll let you know when I'm having a marital dispute. Here.' She shoved the last of the chocolate stick at Peabody. 'Eat that and keep it buttoned.'

'You bet.'

Still fired, Eve's eyes met Roarke's in the rearview mirror. 'And you better hope Summerset has an alibi for this morning.'

He didn't, and all Eve could do was pull at her hair. 'What do you mean you went out?'

'As usual I rose at five A.M. and went out for my morning constitutional. As it was market day, I then returned, took one of the vehicles, and drove out to the Free-Agers' market for fresh produce.'

Eve sat down on the arm of a chair in the main parlor.

'Didn't I tell you not to leave the house, not to go anywhere alone?'

'I'm not in the habit of taking orders on my personal routine, Lieutenant.'

'Your personal routine is going to include group showers where even your bony ass will get plenty of attention if you don't start listening to me.'

His jaw muscles fluttered. 'I don't appreciate your crudeness.'

'And I don't appreciate your bitchiness, but we're both stuck. This morning at approximately nine A.M., the body of Jennie O'Leary was discovered, hanged at a location on West Forty-third.'

The high color fury had brought to his cheeks drained. He reached out blindly for support when his knees buckled. Through the buzzing in his head, he thought he heard someone swearing bitterly. Then he was being pushed into a chair and a glass was pressed to his lips.

'Just drink,' Eve ordered, thoroughly shaken. 'Drink it down, get a grip, because if you faint on me, I'm leaving you where you fall.'

It had the effect, as she'd hoped, of snapping him back. 'I'm perfectly fine. I was simply shocked for a moment.'

'You knew her.'

'Of course I knew her. She and Roarke were close for a time.'

'And now she's dead.' Eve's voice was flat, but her heart settled back into place as she scanned Summerset's face and judged him composed again. 'You'd better be able to take me through every step – where you were, what you did, who you saw, who you spoke with, how many goddamn apples you bought. Right now I'm the best friend you have in the world.'

'If that's the case, Lieutenant, I believe I'd like to call my lawyer.'

'Fine, great, you do that. Why not fuck it up all the way?'

She whirled away to stride around the room. 'You listen to me. I'm going out on a limb here because you matter to him. The evidence against you is only circumstantial, but it's piling up. There'll be pressure from the media, which translates into pressure on the department. The PA's going to want to tag someone, and the pile's just big enough on you for orders to come down to hold you for questioning. It's not enough to book you, not yet.'

She paused, frowning into middle distance. 'But once the PA comes aboard, there's a very strong chance they'll pull me off. Either way, I figure we got another week, tops, to nail this down. After that, you're likely to be dealing with another cop.'

Summerset considered, nodded. 'Better the devil you know.'

With a nod, Eve took out her recorder, set it on a table between them, then sat. 'Let's do it, then.'

'I bought a half bushel of apples, by the way.' He very nearly smiled, making Eve blink in surprise. 'We'll be having pie.'

'Yum,' she said.

Ninety minutes later, Eve carried her discs and a screaming headache up to her office. She nearly groaned when she spotted McNab lounging at her desk, his feet up, ankles crossed to show off flower-patterned socks.

'Make yourself at home, Detective.' To accent the invitation, she gave his feet a hard shove.

'Sorry, Lieutenant. Just taking a little break.'

'I'm up against the wall, McNab, which means your butt's right up there with mine. We don't have time for little breaks. Where's Peabody?'

'She's using one of the other rooms in this castle to run your latest victim, and performing other official acts. Tell me, is she really all regulation, or does some of it come off with her uniform?'

Eve walked over to the AutoChef, ordered coffee, hot and

black. 'Are you considering an attempt to divest Officer Peabody of her uniform, McNab?'

'No. No.' He stood up so quickly the quartet of silver wands in his ear clanged together musically. 'No,' he said for a third time. 'It was a matter of some curiosity. She's not my type.'

'Then why don't we dispense with the inappropriate chatter, and get down to work?'

He rolled his eyes behind Eve's back. As far as he could tell, both female officers were ear high in regulations. 'The equipment Roarke had sent over is beyond mag,' he began. 'It took some time to get it installed and programmed, but I've got it doing an auto search and trace on the incoming from this morning. Oh, nearly forgot, you had a couple of 'link transmissions come through while you were out.'

Helpfully, he punched in Recall. 'Nadine Furst, she wants a meet asap. And Mavis, no last name given. She says she'll be coming by tonight.'

'Why, thank you for taking such an interest in my personal communications.'

He let the sarcasm pass. 'No problem. So this Mavis, she's a pal of yours, huh?'

'And she cohabitates with a guy who could break you into very small pieces one-handed.'

'Well, scratch that. So, maybe I could get some lunch while I wait for—' He broke off when the trace unit began to send out high beeps. 'Solid.' He all but leaped behind the desk, tossed his flowing tail of hair over his shoulder, and began to whistle as paper spilled out of the machine. 'Clever bastard, damn clever. Bounced the waves all over hell and back again twice. Zurich, Moscow, Des Moines for Christ's sake, Regis Six, Station Utopia, Birmingham. Gotta love it.'

She'd seen that exact adoring gleam in Feeney's eyes and understood it to be a side effect of working in EDD. 'I don't care where it was bounced to, McNab, where did it bounce from?'

'It's coming, it's coming. Even technology needs a patient hand. New York. Originates in New York. You called it, Lieutenant.'

'Fine it down. Get me an address.'

'Working on it.' He flapped his hands behind him where Eve hovered. 'Give me some room here, though I'd like to mention you smell terrific. Origin of traced transmission New York City, find zone.'

Tracking . . . estimated time to complete, eight minutes, fifteen seconds.

'Begin. I could use a burger. Got any stocked?'

Eve struggled to find patience. 'How do you want it?'

'Rare. A slice of provolone and plenty of mustard – poppy seed roll, pasta salad on the side, and a cup of that wicked coffee.'

Eve drew a breath in, let a breath out. 'What?' she said sweetly. 'No dessert?'

'Now that you mention it, how about—'

'Lieutenant.' Peabody hurried into the room. 'I've got the data on the last victim.'

'In the kitchen, Peabody, I'm fixing the detective his lunch.'

The killing look Peabody aimed at McNab was answered with a cheeky grin.

'How much longer before Feeney gets back?' Peabody wanted to know.

'One hundred and two hours and twenty-three minutes. But who's counting the time?' Eve programmed the AutoChef for McNab's choices. 'What have you got?'

'Victim departed Shannon airport yesterday on a four P.M. transport. Arrived Kennedy-Europa annex at one P.M. EST. She checked into the Palace at approximately two o'clock, into a prepaid suite. It was booked and paid through Roarke Industries.'

144

'Fuck it.'

'At four, the victim left the hotel. I haven't been able to track a cab company who picked her up. Got the name of the doorman who was on duty. He'll be back on in about an hour. The victim left the key to her room at the concierge station. She never picked it back up.'

'Have them block off her room – no one goes in. Get a uniform to stand until we get over there.'

'Already done.'

Eve pulled McNab's lunch out. 'Get yourself something to eat. It's going to be a long day.'

Peabody sniffed at the burger. 'Maybe McNab has taste in something. I'll have one of them. Want anything?'

'Later.' Eve walked back into the office, dropped the plate on the desk. 'Progress.'

'Got the zone nailed, it's searching for sector. We're closing in.' He hefted the burger one-handed, bit in heartily. 'God love us,' he managed over a full mouth. 'From a real cow or I'm a Frenchman. Better than mother's milk. Want a bite?'

'I'll pass. McNab, aren't all those earrings heavy on the lobe? You keep adding them on, you're going to start walking on a slant.'

'Fashion demands a heavy price. Here she comes. Zone five, yeah, yeah, sector A-B.' With a hand studded with rings, he shoved his plate off the chart he had spread over the desk. 'That puts us' – his limber fingers trailed over the chart, stopped – 'just about here. Here,' he said, raising his gaze to Eve. 'Right about where I'm sitting eating this really remarkable cow burger.'

'That's wrong.'

'I'll run it again, but it's telling me the transmission originated in this house, or on the grounds. This place takes up this entire sector.'

'Run it again,' she ordered and turned away.

'Yes, sir.'

'McNab, what's the error probability on that unit?'

He fiddled with the red ribbon he wore as a tie. 'Less than one percent.'

She pressed her lips together and turned back. 'I want to know if you can bury this for a while. I don't want a report going into Central on this data until I can . . . until I pursue another avenue of the investigation. Are you able to comply with that?'

Watching her, McNab sat back. 'You're the primary, Dallas. I figure it's your call. This kind of data's tricky, gets lost really easily. Takes some time to uncover it again.'

'I appreciate it.'

'I appreciate the burger. I'll go back over the steps, see what pops. Feeney says you're the best, and he ought to know. You figure there's something off, maybe there is. And if there is, I'm good enough to find it.'

'I'll count on that. Peabody?'

'Sir, just coming.' Loaded with a plate, Peabody started out.

'Bag that if you're hungry and saddle up. We're back on the clock.'

'Just give me a—' But since she was already talking to Eve's back, Peabody dropped the plate in front of McNab, 'Enjoy.'

'I will. See you, She-Body.' He wiggled his eyebrows when she turned and glared at him. And let out a little sigh when she stalked out. 'Sure is built,' he murmured, then pushed up his sleeves and got back to work.

Chapter Ten

'Recorder on, Peabody.'

Eve signaled the uniform to step away from the door, then used the master code to access the locks. She entered a parlor, lush and spacious, with a bank of fresh flowers in brilliant whites and blues sweeping beneath a waist-high wall of windows.

The spires and spears of New York rose beyond it, with the air traffic light and meandering. The blasting billboards that populated the West Side were banned here in the more exclusive Upper East.

Typical of most things Roarke owned, the hotel suite was beautifully appointed – thick cushions covered with jeweltoned silks and brocades, highly polished woods, carpet deep enough to wade in. An enormous basket of fruit and a bottle of sauvignon blanc, likely a welcome-to-the-Palace staple, sat on the pond sized coffee table.

The fruit had been riffled through, the wine opened. Jennie had had a few moments to enjoy the luxury, Eve thought, before she'd been lured away to death.

As far as Eve could see, nothing else had been disturbed. The entertainment and communication center was still discreetly tucked behind a silk screen of tropical birds, and the mood screen covering most of one wall was blank.

'Dallas, Lieutenant Eve and Peabody, Officer Delia commencing search of victim O'Leary's suite in Palace Hotel. We'll start in the bedroom, Peabody.'

Eve crossed over and entered a room where the sunlight filled a trio of windows and the peacock blue spread on a huge platform bed was neatly turned down for the night. Gold-foiled mints rested on plump pillows.

'Make a note to track down the maid who was on duty last night for this room. See what she touched, what she noticed.' As she spoke, Eve moved to the closet. Inside were three blouses, two pair of slacks, one day dress in plain blue cotton, and a cocktail suit in cream of an inexpensive fabric blend. Two pair of shoes were neatly lined beneath.

Routinely Eve checked the pockets, the inside of the shoes, ran a hand over the top shelf. 'Nothing here. Dresser drawers?'

'Underwear, hose, a cotton nightgown, and a small black evening bag, beaded.'

'She brought her best party dress.' Eve brushed her hand over the flounced hem of the cocktail suit. 'And never got the chance to wear it. She took the time to unpack – single suitcase in closet – brought enough clothes for three or four days. Jewelry?'

'I haven't found any so far.'

'She might have carried it with her. She'd have had something special for her evening wear. Run her 'link for incoming and outgoing. I'll check the bath.'

The bath offered a jet tub big enough to party in. A bottle of the hotel's complimentary bath foam sat on the lip. So she'd used the tub. Eve mused. It would have been hard to resist, she imagined, and Jennie had been waiting for contact.

Nervous? Eve wondered. Yes, she'd have been a little nervous. She hadn't seen Roarke for some time. She'd have worried about how she'd changed, aged, what he would see when they met again.

A woman would always worry about what a man like Roarke saw when he looked at her. They'd been lovers, she mused, studying the tidily arranged toiletries and cosmetics on the shell pink counter. Jennie would remember the way he'd touched her, the way he'd tasted. A woman wouldn't forget the power of a lover like Roarke.

And if she'd been human she would have wondered – hoped that he would touch her again. Had she submerged herself in that fragrant, frothy water imagining that?

Of course she had.

They'd been friends as well. Sharing laughs, perhaps secrets and dreams. They'd been young together, and foolish together. That was a link that was never completely broken.

And he'd summoned her, asked her to fly across an ocean. She hadn't hesitated.

She'd known there was trouble, but she'd dropped everything and come, and had waited. And had died.

'Dallas?'

Eve shook herself, turned to Peabody. 'What?'

'Nothing on the 'link, but I had the fax replay transmissions. You'll want to see this.'

The minifax was tucked inside a small, slanttop desk. It hummed patiently, waiting the next command. Peabody picked up the single sheet of paper it had spilled out and handed it to Eve.

Jennie, my dear,

Roarke wishes to convey his thanks for you agreeing to make this unexpected trip. We hope it hasn't caused you any great inconvenience. We trust your rooms are satisfactory. If you have any needs or desires that haven't been met, you have only to contact the concierge.

You're aware Roarke is concerned for your welfare. It's vital that he speak with you privately, and without the knowledge of the woman he chose to marry. He has information he wants to pass on to you as soon as possible. It's imperative that you meet him, and that you tell no one, not even those you trust, where you're going. Please go to the corner of Fifth and Sixty-second at five P.M. A black sedan with New York plates and a uniformed driver will meet you. The driver will escort you and has full instructions.

Forgive the intrigue, Jennie. A man in Roarke's position must be discreet. We ask that you destroy this communication.

Yours,

Summerset

'Clever boy,' Eve murmured. 'He gives her enough to be sure she goes along. He tells her to get rid of the copy of the fax, but he doesn't tell her to wipe the machine. He has to figure we'll check it, and he wants us to find this.'

'It's still circumstantial.' Peabody frowned at the communication. 'Anybody can send a fax, put any name on it. He's blocked the return code.'

'Yeah, on the hard copy, but I'll bet a year's pay that when we hand the unit over to McNab, he finesses the code, and that the code matches one of Roarke's fax lines. Bag it,' she ordered, passing the sheet to Peabody. 'Our boy drove the pickup car, waltzed her right into the room on the West Side. Then he took her down, physically or with drugs. The ME will tell us that part. Then he took his time setting it up. Everything he needs is in the car. Maybe he owns it, maybe he rented it. Slim chance he boosted it for the day, but we'll check on reports of stolen black sedans.'

She paused, took a slow survey of the room again. 'Calling the sweepers in here's a waste of the taxpayers' money, but we'll go by the book. I'll call it in, and run the sedan for what it's worth. You take the minifax to McNab at my home office. I'll meet you there when I can.'

'Where are you going?'

'To ask another favor,' Eve said as she walked out.

It was waiting to rain, and the air was moist and cool, the wind freshening. A few stubborn mums continued to bloom, adding unexpected splashes of color and scent. There was a fountain where water bubbled over the petals and stems of copper and brass water lilies. Well across the rolling lawn and sheltered by tall trees stood the big stone house, glowing in the dimming afternoon sun.

Dr Mira sighed. Such a place was built for peace and power, she thought. She wondered how often Eve settled for the first, how often she allowed herself to enjoy it.

'I've been expecting your call,' she began, watching as Eve stared at the house. 'I heard about the third murder.'

'Her name was Jennie O'Leary. It sounds like a song, doesn't it?' Surprised that she'd said such a thing, Eve shook her head. 'She and Roarke were friends. More than friends once.'

'I see. And the other two victims, they were both from Ireland?'

'He knew them, all of them.' She made herself turn.

Mira was tidy, as always, though the wind was fluttering her short, soft brown hair. Her suit was a deep green today, a change from the usual quiet colors she wore. Her eyes were patient and filled with compassion. And understanding.

Eve thought she looked every bit as efficient here, sitting on a stone bench under the denuded branches of an oak, as she did in her elegant office. She was the best criminal and behavioral psychologist New York, and possibly the country, had to offer.

'I appreciate you agreeing to meet me here.'

'I remember the grounds from your wedding.' Mira smiled.

It was difficult to nudge Eve over that first hurdle and into trust. 'It's a magnificent space. Carefully planned, lovingly tended.'

'I don't get out here much, I guess.' Feeling awkward, Eve jammed her hands in her pockets. 'I forget to look out the windows when I'm working here.'

'You're a focused individual, Eve. That's why you're an excellent cop. You don't come out here often, but I have no doubt you could describe the grounds exactly. You observe instinctively.'

'Cop's eyes.' Eve shrugged. 'Curse or blessing, who knows?'

'You're troubled.' Her feelings for Eve always went beyond the professional and tugged at Mira's heart. 'Are you going to let me help?'

'It's not me. It's not about me.'

But Mira thought it was, partly. The woman inside the cop was disturbed at facing the dead that Roarke had once been intimate with. 'Then you're sleeping well? Undisturbed.'

'Mostly.' Eve turned away again. She didn't want to delve into that area. Mira was one of the few people who knew the details of her past, the memories that came swimming back unexpectedly, the nightmares that plagued and terrified. 'Let's let that rest, okay?'

'All right.'

'I'm worried about Roarke.' She hadn't meant to say it, and regretted it instantly. 'That's personal,' she continued, turning around again. 'I didn't ask you to meet me to discuss that.'

Didn't you? Mira thought, but only nodded. 'Why did you ask me to meet you?'

'I need a consult on the case. I need a profile. I need help.' The discomfort of her position showed in anger in her eyes. 'I didn't want to do this in official surroundings because I'm going to ask you to skirt some of the rules. You're under no obligation to do so, and I'll understand perfectly if you not only refuse but decide to report this request.'

Mira's expression, mild and interested, didn't alter by a blink. 'Why don't you explain the situation to me, Eve, and let me make up my own mind?'

'The three murders are connected, and the probability that they're linked to a . . . series of events that took place several years ago is high. The motive is revenge. It's my opinion that Roarke is primary target and that Summerset is being used to get to him. There's circumstantial evidence attached to each murder that points to Summerset, and that evidence is piling up along with the bodies. If I believed he was responsible I'd close the cage door on him myself without a minute's regret, no matter what he means to Roarke. But it's a setup, cleverly planned and executed, and just obvious enough to be insulting to my intelligence.'

'You'd like me to do a profile on the killer; and examine Summerset for violent tendencies, unofficially.'

'No, I want those official. Black and white, by the book. I want to be able to turn them in to Whitney. I haven't given him a hell of a lot else.'

'I'll be happy to do both. You've only to clear it with your commander, get me the data. I can shift it to priority for you.'

'I'd appreciate it.'

'And the rest?'

Eve's palms went damp. Impatient, she swiped them on the thighs of her slacks. 'I have information that is vital to the investigation, and your profile, that I can't – no, that I won't – record in full. I'll only share this information with you under the scope of doctor-patient confidentiality. That protects you, doesn't it?'

Mira lifted her hands, folded her fingers. 'Anything you tell me as a patient is privileged. I can't report it.'

'And you're protected? Personally, professionally?' Eve insisted.

'I am, yes. How many people are you determined to protect here, Eve?'

'The ones who matter.'

Mira smiled now, a full bloom. 'Thank you.' She held out a hand. 'Sit, and tell me.'

Eve hesitated, then took the hand Mira offered. 'You . . . when I remembered what had happened to me in that room in Dallas. When I remembered my father coming in drunk, raping me again, hurting me again. When I remembered killing him that night, and I told you, you said it was pointless, even wrong, to punish the child. You said' – she had to clear her throat – 'you said I'd killed a monster, and that I'd made myself into something worthwhile, something I had no right to destroy because of what I'd done before.'

'You don't still doubt that?'

Eve shook her head, though there were times, there were still times she doubted it. 'Did you mean it? Do you really believe there are times, there are circumstances when taking the life of a monster is justified?'

'The state believed so until less than two decades ago when capital punishment was, yet again, abolished.'

'I'm asking you, as a person, a doctor, a woman.'

'Yes, I believe it. To survive, to protect your life or the life of another.'

'Only in self-defense?' Eve's eyes were intense on Mira's, reading every flicker. 'Is that the only justification?'

'I couldn't generalize in such a manner, Eve. Each circumstance, each person goes to defining the situation.'

'It used to be black and white for me,' Eve said quietly. 'The law.' She held up one fist. 'The breaking of it.' Then the other. On a long breath, she tapped the two fists together, held them close. 'Now . . . I need to tell you about Marlena.'

Mira didn't interrupt. She asked no questions, made no comments. It took Eve twenty minutes to tell it all. She was thorough, and made the effort to be dispassionate. Facts only, without opinion. And when she was finished, she was drained.

They sat in silence, while a few birds chattered, the fountain gurgled, and bruised clouds drifted over the sun.

'To lose a child that way,' Mira commented at length. 'There is nothing worse to be faced. I can't tell you the men who did that to her deserved to die, Eve. But I can tell you, as a woman, as a mother, that if she had been my child, I would have celebrated their deaths, and I would have sworn my gratitude to their executioner. That isn't scientific, it isn't the law. But it's human.'

'I don't know if I'm shielding Roarke because I believe what he did was justice or because I love him.'

'Why can't it be both? Oh, you complicate things, Eve.'

'I complicate things.' She nearly laughed, and pushed up from the bench. 'I have three murders that I can't investigate in an open, logical manner unless I want to see my husband locked away for the rest of this life. I've involved my aide, an e-detective I barely know, and you in the duplicity, and I'm busting my ass to keep that idiot Summerset out of lockup. And *I* complicate things.'

'I'm not saying circumstances aren't complicated, but there's no reason for you to internalize as much as you do. There's no need to try to segregate your heart from your intellect.'

Mira brushed a speck of dust from her skirt and spoke briskly. 'Now, from my end of it, I'd think it best if you make an official request for Summerset to be examined. In my office, tomorrow if possible. I'll do a complete testing scan and copy the results to you and Commander Whitney. If you can get me the data – official and otherwise – on your killer, I'll begin a profile right away.'

'The unofficial data can't be included in your workup.'

'Eve.' Now Mira laughed, a light, musical sound as charming as the fountain. 'If I'm not skilled enough to slide such things into a psychiatric profile without being specific, then I'd best turn in my license to practice. Believe me, you'll have

155

your profile, and, if you'll forgive me, it's highly unlikely my work will be questioned by anyone.'

'I need it fast. He doesn't wait long between rounds.'

'I'll have it to you as quickly as possible. Accuracy is every bit as important as speed. Now, on a personal level, would you like me to speak with Roarke?'

'Roarke?'

'I can read through even your closely guarded lines, Eve. You're worried about him. About his emotional state. You think he blames himself.'

'I don't know if he would talk to you. I don't know how he's going to feel about the fact that I've told you all this. Emotionally, he'll cope.' She began to worry her wedding ring around and around her finger with her thumb. 'My more immediate concern is his safety. I can't predict when the last round's coming. All I know is that Roarke's the finale.'

Eve shook that off, knowing that fear would cloud her thinking. 'If you'd come in now, I'll give you what I have, and we'll pin Summerset for testing tomorrow.'

'All right.' Mira rose and to Eve's surprise hooked arms with her. 'And I'd love a cup of tea.'

'I'm sorry, I should have thought. I'm lousy at the hostess thing.'

'I'd hoped we'd progressed beyond the point of hostess and guest and into friendship. Look, isn't that Mavis and her gentle giant getting out of a cab at your front door?'

Eve looked over. Who else but Mavis Freestone would be decked out in pink leather and green feathers on a week-day evening? Beside her, Leonardo looked huge and magnificent in an ankle skimming robe the color of good bordeaux. As fond as she was of both of them, Eve gusted out a sigh.

'What the hell am I supposed to do with them?'

'I'd say you're going to take a short break and be entertained.' With a laugh, Mira lifted an arm in a wave. 'I know I am.'

*

156

'So, you know, like this is all so bogus in the extreme.' Mavis helped herself to a glass of wine, gesturing with it as she clicked around the room on four-inch heels. Tiny golden fish swam within their clear spikes. 'Leonardo and me, we've caught most of the deets on the screen. I'd've been by before.' She gulped wine, gestured again. 'But I've got gigs scheduled back-to-back to prep for the recording session next month.'

'She's magnificent.' Leonardo beamed at her, his wide, golden face glowing with love.

'Oh, Leonardo.' She wrapped her arms around him, as far as they would go. 'You always say that.'

'It's always true. Turtle dove.'

She giggled, then spun around, the feathers decorating her breasts and shoulders fluttering. 'So, anyhow, we came to give Summerset our moral support.'

'I'm sure he appreciates it.' Since she could see no immediate escape, Eve reached for the wine herself. 'Dr Mira?'

'I'll wait for the tea, thank you. Mavis, is that one of Leonardo's designs you're wearing?'

'Absolutely. Frigid, isn't it?' She turned a circle in a flourish and had her currently lavender locks bouncing. 'You should see the mag rags he's got going for spring. He's got a show in Milan coming up.'

'I'd love to show you a preview of my corporate woman line, Dr Mira,' Leonardo offered.

'Well . . .' Mira ran her tongue around her teeth, eyeing Mavis's feathers, then, catching Eve's exaggerated eye roll, chuckled. 'I don't know if I'm as creative a model as Mavis.'

'Just a different style.' Leonardo's smile was sweet and guileless. 'You'd want classic lines, cool colors. I have some marvelous linen in a dusky pink that would be perfect for you.'

'Dusky pink,' Mira repeated, intrigued.

'Leonardo does the conservative jazz really well,' Mavis chimed in. 'Sexy lady of the manor, you know.'

'I might just have a look at that.' Sexy lady of the manor, Mira thought and smiled.

'There he is!' Mavis made a leap forward as Summerset rolled in a cart laden with a tea service, neat squares of apple pie, and rounds of frosted cakes. His color rose when Mavis locked herself and her feathers around him. 'We're behind you, Summerset. Don't you worry about a thing. Eve's the best there is. She took care of everything when I was in trouble. She'll look out for you.'

'I'm sure the lieutenant will settle the matter.' His gaze flicked to Eve. 'One way or the other.'

'Come on, lighten the load.' Mavis squeezed him. 'Have a drink. Want some wine?'

His eyes softened as his gaze returned to Mavis's eager face. 'Thank you, but I have duties.'

'He doesn't know if he wants to pat her head or jump her bones,' Eve muttered to Mira, causing the doctor to muffle a laugh into a cough.

'Roarke will be down momentarily,' Summerset continued. 'He's completing an interstellar transmission.'

Mavis caught up to him in the hall, tugged on his arm until he stopped and turned. 'Listen, I know what you're feeling. Been there, you know.' She offered a quick, crooked smile. 'When I was scared, when they put me in a cage and part of me thought they'd just leave me there, forever, you know, I got through it because I knew Dallas wouldn't let it happen. I knew she'd do it for me, no matter what it took.'

'Her affection for you is one of her finest qualities.'

'And you figure because the two of you don't rub smooth she'll let things slide?' Her eyes, colored to match her hair were round and sad. 'That's jerk thinking, Summerset. Dallas'll work till she drops to do right by you, and I figure you know it. If somebody came after you, she'd step between and take the hit, because that's who she is. I figure you know that, too.'

'I've done nothing.' He spoke stiffly now, refusing to acknowledge any shame. 'I would expect an efficient detective to deduce that, whatever her personal feelings.'

'You're down,' Mavis said gently. 'You want to ventilate sometime, just give me a call.' She teetered onto her toes to kiss his cheek. 'I'll bring the brew.'

'Your young man is very fortunate in you,' Summerset managed then hurried down the hallway and disappeared through an open door.

'That was well done, Mavis.' Roarke continued down the steps now and crossed to her to take her hands.

'He's bummed flat. Who can blame him?'

'And who could stay flat with you around?'

'It's like my mission to bubble things up. Let's see what we can do with the group in the parlor.' She slid a smile up at him. 'Am I staying for dinner?'

'I wouldn't have it any other way.'

Despite the company, Eve managed to slip away long enough to dismiss McNab and Peabody, gather their reports and file them for later view. She cornered Summerset and, after a nasty little conversation, convinced him it would be in his best interest to report to Dr Mira's office at eleven A.M. for testing.

At the end of it, her head throbbed badly enough for her to resort to a dose of painkiller. Roarke found her in the bathroom, scowling at the pills palmed in her hand.

'It must be unbearable, for you to even consider a pill.'

'It's been a long day,' she said with a shrug, and dumped the pills back into their tube. 'But I can handle it.'

'We'll run a bath. You need to relax.'

'I've got work.'

'Eve.' Firmly, he took her arms, turned her to face him. 'This is the part of your job I hate most. The shadows it puts under your eyes, and in them.'

'I don't have a lot of time on this one.'

'Time enough to take an hour for yourself.' Still watching her, he began to rub at the knots in her shoulders.

'I have to read the reports, extrapolate from them for the official record. I keep hitting walls.' There were nerves in her voice, and hearing them irritated her. 'I haven't been able to trace the tokens at all, and you hit it on the statue. Thousands of them available at God shops all over the known universe. Even at five hundred credits a pop, she's a popular lady.'

She started to pull back, but his hands held her still. 'I have to give Whitney something by tomorrow. I told Mira everything.'

His hands paused, a fraction of a moment, then continued kneading her muscles. 'I see.'

'Maybe I should have asked you first, but I did what I felt was necessary.'

'There's no need to apologize.'

'I'm not apologizing.' This time she shrugged him off. 'I'm saying.' She stalked into the bedroom. Even excellent coffee could start to burn a hole in the gut. Despite it, Eve jammed at the AutoChef to program a pot. 'I'm doing what needs to be done, and one of those duties is to advise you to increase your personal security until this case is closed.'

'I believe my security is more than adequate.'

'If that was the case, this bastard wouldn't have slipped through it to shoot transmissions from this house, to arrange for hotel rooms with one of your credit accounts, to draw a woman over from Ireland in your name.'

Roarke angled his head, nodded. 'Point taken. I'll have a look, personally, at my electronic security.'

'Fine, that's a start.' She slopped coffee into a cup. 'I'm putting a tag on Summerset.'

'I beg your pardon?'

'I'm tagging him.' The fury was bubbling, couldn't be stopped. 'For his own welfare. The next time I find a body, I want him well alibied. I put a tag on him, fit him with a security bracelet, or cage him. I figure the first is the easiest choice.'

'Perhaps it is.' Roarke decided brandy would go down easier than coffee. 'And do you intend to put a tag on me,' Lieutenant?'

'If I thought one could stick, damn right I would. Since you'd peel it off within an hour, it would be a waste of time.'

'Well.' He lifted his snifter in salute. 'We understand each other.'

'I think we do.' She drew a breath. 'I contacted the ME. There were traces of a tranq in Jennie O'Leary's system.'

Roarke stared into his brandy. 'Had she been raped?'

'No, there were no signs of sexual assault, no indication of struggle. She was still tranq'd when he strung her up. But the token – there was another token – the ME found it in her vagina. Again, there was no bruising or indication of force or struggle. It would appear that the token was inserted while she was unconscious. I'm sorry, but I thought you'd want the details.'

'I do, yes.'

'The ME reports that you've requested – as the victim has no next of kin – to be given possession of the body when it's released.'

'She'd want to go back to Ireland.'

'I assume you'll take the body back yourself.'

'Yes.'

The burn in her gut spread to her heart. 'I'd appreciate it if you'd let me know when you've finalized your plans.'

He looked up then, and the emotions swimming in those beautiful eyes stabbed her heart. 'Did you think I would send her back alone? That I would wash my hands of it and go about my business?'

'No. I've got work.'

'For Christ's sake.'

161

It was the tone, impatience, frustration, and just a whiff of amusement that had her whirling on him. 'Don't take that line with me, pal. Don't try to make me feel like an idiot. You loved her. Okay, fine. Do what you have to do, and so will I.'

He was swearing viciously by the time he caught her. Even the whiff of amusement was extinguished. 'Yes, I loved her, and what we once had was important to me. Even so it wasn't so much as a shadow against what I feel for you. Is that what you want to hear?'

Shame rushed over her, smothering temper. 'I don't know what's wrong with me. It's all pushing into my head.' Feeling helpless, she lifted her fingers to press at her temples. 'None of the others mattered because . . . I don't know, they just don't matter to me. She does, and I hate myself for being jealous, even for a minute, of a dead woman.'

'Eve.' He laid a hand on her cheek. 'From the first moment I met you, every other woman paled for me.'

She only felt more foolish. 'I wasn't groping, it's just—'

'You're all,' he murmured, touching his lips to each pounding temple in turn. 'You're only.'

The burning around her heart turned to an ache, sweet and strong. 'I need you.' Her arms came tight around him, her mouth fused to his. 'For so many things.'

'Thank God.' He deepened the kiss, gentled it until she sighed. 'We'll take that hour now. Together.'

Chapter Eleven

She could think again. Until she'd met Roarke, Eve hadn't realized how many benefits sex had to offer. Feeling limber, focused, and energized, she settled down in her office.

The new computer Roarke had arranged to have installed that morning was a beauty. Eve indulged herself, admiring it, tinkering with the tonal qualities. Her mood lifted even higher as it gobbled up the data she inputed like a hungry, yet well-mannered wolf.

'Oh, you honey,' she murmured and stroked its sleek, stylishly black armor. 'Okay, let's see what you can do. Run probability scan, file A data. What is the probability that victims Brennen, Conroy, and O'Leary were murdered by same perpetrator?'

Working, the computer announced in a creamy baritone enlivened with a hint of Parisian French. Before Eve could finish her grin, the scan was complete.

Probability ninety-nine point six three percent.

'Dandy, remain in file A. What is the probability that suspect Summerset committed murders?'

Working . . . Probability eighty-seven point eight percent. With current data arrest warrant for murder,

multiple, first degree, is recommended. Please advise
if list of available judges is desired.

'No thanks, Bruno, but I appreciate the advice.'

Please advise if you wish to contact the prosecuting
attorney's office.

'Eve.'

She looked over, saw Roarke in the doorway. 'Hold on,
Bruno.' Eve swiped her hair back, rolled her shoulders. 'I
told you I was going to work.'

'Yes, so you did.' He wore only jeans, unhooked at the
waist and obviously tugged on as an afterthought.

Despite the fact that her blood was still warm from him, it
heated now. She found herself fantasizing about tugging those
unfastened jeans off again, then maybe nipping her teeth into
his firm, naked butt for good measure.

'Huh?' she managed when his voice got through her fanta-
sy.

'I said . . .' He paused, then, recognizing the glint in her
eyes, arched a brow. 'Christ Jesus, Eve, what are you, a
rabbit?'

'I don't know what you mean.' She shifted back and stared
hard at her monitor.

'You certainly do, and I'm more than happy to accommodate
you . . . after you explain why you're running probabilities on
Summerset. I thought you agreed he was innocent.'

'I'm doing my job, and before you start,' she continued,
holding up a hand, 'I'll explain. I've run the probability from
my file A, which contains all the data, all the evidence that
I'm free to pass on through official channels at this time.
This analysis indicates that I'll be carting Summerset off to
maximum lockup in restraints. It's not a lock at under ninety
percent, but nobody would argue with the arrest.'

She rolled her shoulders again, blew her bangs out of her eyes. 'Now we'll run the scan using file B, which is everything I know, everything I have. Computer—'

'I thought its name was Bruno.'

'Just a joke,' Eve muttered. 'Computer, run probability scan, suspect Summerset, using file B.'

> Working . . . With additional data probability index drops to forty-seven point three eight percent. Warrant is not advised with available data.

'Cuts the probability by more than half. And I'd say with Mira's testing results logged in after tomorrow, it'll drop more. File A will drop some, too, maybe just enough to keep his ass from swinging.'

'I should have known.' Roarke moved behind her, leaned down to press his lips to the top of her head.

'He's not clear yet. The God guy's counting on me not being willing to trade you off for Summerset – and he's got that right.'

'But he's underestimated you.'

'Goddamn right. And he's overplayed, Roarke, I can use that with Whitney, too. A man smart enough to pull off these murders isn't stupid enough to leave such an obvious trail. It stinks from setup. And he's going to want to play again. Riddles. Games,' she mused, leaning back in her chair. 'He likes to fall back on God, but he likes his games. Games are for children.'

'Tell that to the linebacker for Big Apple Arena Ball and see where it gets you.'

She only shrugged. 'So, men are children.'

He barely sighed. 'Thank you so much.'

'Men are more into toys, games, gizmos as status symbols. You've got a house full of them.'

A bit nonplussed by her opinion, he slipped his hands into his pockets. 'I beg your pardon?'

'I don't just mean the toy toys like video and holo rooms.' Her forehead was furrowed now, the line between her brows deepening. 'Cars, planes, entertainment centers, spar droids, VR equipment, hell, your businesses are toys.'

Now Roarke rocked back on his heels. 'Darling Eve, if you want to tell me I'm shallow, don't be concerned with bruising my feelings.'

'You're not shallow,' she said with an absent, back of the hand gesture. 'You just overindulge.'

He opened his mouth, struggling to be insulted, and ended up laughing. 'Eve, I adore you.' He slid his hands down over her breasts, his mouth to her neck. 'Let's go overindulge each other.'

'Cut it out. I want to—' His fingers grazed over her nipples and caused her thigh muscles to thrum. 'I really have to – Jesus, you're good at that.' Her head fell back just enough to make her mouth vulnerable to his.

Before it had been soft and easy, a kind of healing both of them had needed. This was fire, hot and fast and all for greed. She reached up, circling her arms around his neck, and left herself open for him.

He made quick work of her robe, parting it so that his hands could roam flesh already damp, so he could race down and find her, already wet. She came with delightful ease, shuddering as she felt the climax roll through her and flood his hand.

Then she was struggling free, turning in the chair and rising on her knees to clutch at him. 'Now, now, now.' She gasped it out, punctuating each demand with nips and bites as she jerked at the jeans riding his hips.

He slid into the chair, gripping her hips as she straddled him. And he watched her throat, the lovely arch of it, the tiny pulse pushing in fast rhythm against the flesh as her head dipped back. She gripped the back of the chair, dizzy when he sucked her breast hard into his mouth, as the chair rocked, as she rocked, tormenting them both with the friction.

The pace was hers, and he let her ride, let himself be taken. His fingers dug into her hips while she drove him, while the breath strangled in his throat. And when it seemed his blood would burst from his veins like flames, he emptied himself into her.

Her hands slid limply down his damp shoulders. Her heart was still pumping viciously as she raced quick, delirious kisses over his neck and throat.

'Sometimes I just want to gobble you whole, eat you alive. You're so gorgeous. You're so beautiful.'

'What?' His senses were slowly swimming back, the roar in his ears subsiding like the tide.

She caught herself, appalled, mortified. Had she actually said that aloud? she wondered. Was she insane? 'Nothing. I was . . .' She took several deep breaths to level her system. 'I was just saying I only wanted to bite your ass.'

'You wanted to bite my ass.' He shook his head clear. 'Why?'

'Because it's there.' Relieved, spent, satisfied, she grinned at him. 'And it's a pretty great ass all in all.'

'I'm glad you—' He blinked, narrowed his eyes. 'Did you say I was beautiful?'

'Give me a break.' She snorted, then quickly wiggled off him. 'You must be hallucinating. Now, fun's fun.' She picked up her robe, pulled it on. 'But I have to get back to work.'

'Mmm-hmm. I'll get us some coffee.'

'There's no use both of us going without sleep.'

He smiled, ran a finger over her wedding band. 'Want some pie?'

'I guess I could choke some down.'

Within an hour Eve had moved the investigation into Roarke's private office. The lists she would run now couldn't be viewed by the all-seeing eye of CompuGuard.

'Six men,' she muttered. 'The six who killed Marlena

generate over fifty in family alone. What's with you Irish, haven't you ever heard of Zero Population?'

'We prefer the go forth and multiply rule.' Roarke pondered the list that took up two screens. 'I recognize a dozen or so. I might do better with faces.'

'Well, we'll eliminate the females, for now. The barmaid at the Shamrock said Shawn was talking to a man, the kid on the West Side—'

'His name's Kevin.'

'Yeah, the kid said a man. And the creep who's been calling me – even if he's using voice alteration to sound like a man – has a male rhythm to his speech. And typical male responses to insults and sarcasm.'

'It's illuminating for me,' Roarke said dryly, 'to discover your fascinating opinion on my gender.'

'When push comes, men are different, that's all. Computer, delete female names from screen.' Eve paced in front of it, nodding. 'That's a little more manageable. Best place to start is at the top. O'Malley's group, father, two brothers.'

'On screen three.' Commanding manually now, Roarke shifted the three names onto the next screen. 'Full data, with image. Ah, Shamus O'Malley, the patriarch, I do remember him. He and my father had some dealings together.'

'Looks like a violent tendency,' Eve commented. 'You can see it in the eyes. Major scar on the left cheek, a nose that's been broken more than once by the look of it. This makes him seventy-six, and he's currently a guest of the Irish government for first degree assault with a deadly.'

'A prince of a man.'

Eve hooked her thumbs in her robe pockets. 'I'm going to eliminate anyone doing time. It's impossible to say if our guy's acting alone, but we'll concentrate on him.'

'All right.' Roarke tapped a few keys and ten more names disappeared.

'That wipes the smiling O'Malleys.'

'They were always a bad lot, and not bright with it.'

'Go to the next.'

'Calhouns. Father, one brother, one son. Liam Calhoun,' Roarke mused. 'He ran a little food shop. He was a decent sort. The brother and the boy I don't remember at all.'

'The brother, James, no criminal record. Guy's a doctor, attached to the National Health Services. Forty-seven, one marriage, three children. Reads like pillar of the community.'

'I don't recall him. Obviously he didn't run in my circles.'

'Obviously,' Eve said so dryly Roarke laughed. 'The son, also Liam, is in college, following his uncle's footsteps it appears. Young Liam Calhoun. Good-looking . . . nineteen, single, top ten percent of his class.'

'I remember a boy, vaguely. Scruffy, quiet.' Roarke studied the image of a cheerful face and sober eyes. 'Looks like he's making something of himself from the academic data.'

'The sins of the father don't always transfer. Still, medical knowledge would have come in handy in these particular murders. We'll hold these two, but put them at the bottom of the list. Bring up the next group.'

'Rileys. Father, four brothers—'

'Four? God Almighty.'

'And all of them a terror to decent citizens everywhere. Take a good look at Brian Riley. He once kicked my head in. Of course two of his brothers and a close personal friend were holding me down at the time. Black Riley, he liked to be called.'

Roarke reached for a cigarette as the old, well-buried bitterness punched its way free. 'We're of an age, you see, and you could say Riley had a keen dislike for me.'

'And why was that?'

'Because I was faster, my fingers lighter.' He smiled a little. 'And the girls preferred me.'

'Well, your Black Riley's been in and out of cages most of his young life.' Eve angled her head. Another good-looking man, she mused, with fair hair and sulky green eyes. Ireland appeared to be filled with handsome men who looked for trouble. 'But he hasn't served any time in the last few years. Employment record's spotty, mostly as head knocker at bars and skin clubs. But this is interesting. He worked security for an electronics firm for nearly two years. He could have picked up quite a bit in that amount of time if he has a brain.'

'There was nothing wrong with his brain, it was his attitude.'

'Right. Can you get into his passport?'

'The official one, easily enough. Give me a minute.'

Eve studied the image while Roarke worked. Green eyes, she mused. The kid – Kevin – had said the man he'd seen had green eyes. Or he'd thought so. Of course eye color could be changed as easily as a spoiled child's mind.

'Immigration records, screen four,' Roarke told her.

'Yeah, he's visited our fair city a time or two,' Eve noted. 'Let's log these dates, and we'll see if we can find out what he was up to while he was here. Were the brothers close?'

'The Rileys were like wild dogs. They'd have torn out each other's throat for the same bone, but they'd form a pack against an outsider.'

'Well, let's take a good, close look at all four of them.'

By three A.M. she was losing her edge. The data and images on screen began to blur and run together. Names and faces, motives and murder. When she felt herself drifting to sleep where she stood, Eve pressed her fingers hard against her burning eyes.

'Coffee,' she muttered, but found herself staring at the AutoChef without a clue how to operate it.

'Sleep.' Roarke pressed a mechanism that had a bed sliding out of the wall.

'No, I just have to catch my second wind. We've got it down to ten possibles. And I want to look harder at that Francis Rowan who became a priest. We can—'

'Take a break.' He came up behind her, guided her toward the bed. 'We're tired.'

'Okay, we'll take a nap. An hour.' Head and body seemed to float apart as she slid onto the bed. 'You lie down too.'

'I will.' He lay beside her, gathered her close. He could feel her fall into sleep, a lazy tumble that had the arm she'd tossed around his waist going limp.

He stared at the screens a moment longer, into the void of his past. He'd separated himself from that, from them. The boy from Dublin's sad alleys had made himself rich, successful, respected, but he'd never forgotten what it was to be poor, a failure and disdained.

And he knew, as he lay in the soft bed on smooth linen sheets in a magnificent house in a city he'd made his home, that he would have to go back.

What he might find there, and in himself, troubled him.

'Lights out,' he ordered, and willed himself to follow Eve into sleep.

It was the beep of an incoming transmission that woke them both three hours later. Roarke swore when Eve jerked up and the top of her head caught him smartly on the jaw.

'Oh, sorry.' She rubbed her head. 'Is that yours or mine?'

'Mine.' Gingerly he rotated his jaw. 'It's a warning alarm. I have a conference call set up for six-thirty.'

'I've got McNab and Peabody here at seven. Christ.' She scrubbed her hands over her face and, when her fingers dipped below her eyes, studied him. 'How come you never look ragged in the morning?'

'Just one of those little gifts from God.' He scooped back his hair, which managed to look sexily tousled. 'I'll shower in here, save time. I should be finished up with this call by the time McNab gets here. I'd like to work with him this morning.'

'Roarke—'

'The transmission didn't come from this house. So I have an electronic leak somewhere. I know the setup here, in and out. He doesn't.' He added a bit of charm to his smile. 'I've worked with Feeney.'

'That's different.' But since she couldn't explain how it was different, she shrugged. 'McNab has to clear it. I won't order him to work with a civilian.'

'Fair enough.'

By eight, Eve had Peabody installed in a temporary office down the hall from her own. It was actually a small and elegant sitting room off a sweeping guest bedroom, but it was equipped with a tidy little communication and information center for the convenience of overnight associates who often visited.

Peabody gawked at the original pen-and-ink drawings covering the walls, the hand-knotted area rug, the deep silver cushions spread over an S-shaped settee.

'Pretty grand work space.'

'Don't get used to it,' Eve warned. 'I want to be back at Central by next week. I want this closed.'

'Sure, but I'll just enjoy this while it lasts.' She'd already eyed the mini AutoChef and speculated on what it might offer. 'How many rooms are in this place?'

'I don't know. Sometimes I think they mate at night and make more little rooms that grow into big rooms, and mate at night—' Eve stopped herself, shook her head. 'I didn't get much sleep. I'm punchy. I've got data here that needs a fresh eye and organizing.'

'I got eight straight. My eye's fresh.'

'Don't be smug.' Eve pinched the bridge of her nose. 'This data is unofficial, Peabody, but I think our man's in here, somewhere. There's a temporary block on this computer so that your work will bypass CompuGuard. I'm working on a way around that, but until I figure it out, there's no fancy way to put this. I'm asking you to break the law.'

Peabody considered for a moment. 'Is that AutoChef fully stocked?'

Eve had to smile. 'Around here? They always are. I have to get something to Whitney by this afternoon. I'm putting what I can together. Since this guy doesn't wait long between hits, we're in a squeeze.'

'Then I better get to work.'

Eve left her to it, but when she walked into her office, she found McNab and Roarke huddled together. The snazzy black armor of her computer was on the floor. Its guts were exposed, its dignity in ruins. Her desk 'link was in several unidentifiable pieces.

'What the hell are you two doing?'

'Men's work,' Roarke said and flashed her a grin. His hair was tied back, his sleeves rolled up, and he looked to be having the time of his life.

She would have mentioned men and their toys, but decided it would be a waste of breath.

'If you don't get this back together, I'm taking over your office.'

'Help yourself. You see here, Ian? If we interface this it should open the whole system long enough for us to see if there's a leak.'

'Don't you have a thing that does that?' she demanded. 'A scanner?'

'This is the best way to keep a scan from showing up.' McNab spared her a look that clearly told her she was in the way. 'We can search, and nobody – especially our mystery caller – will know we're looking.'

Intrigued now, Eve moved closer. 'So he stays confident. That's good. What does this do?'

'Don't touch anything.' McNab nearly smacked her hand before he remembered she outranked him. 'Sir.'

'I wasn't going to touch anything.' Annoyed, Eve jammed her hands into her pockets. 'Why'd you take my 'link apart?'

'Because,' McNab began with sighing patience, 'that's where the transmissions come through, isn't it?'

'Yeah, but—'

'Eve. Darling.' Roarke paused in his work long enough to pat her cheek. 'Go away.'

'Fine. I'll just go do some real cop work.' She maintained dignity until she slammed the office door.

'Whoa, she's going to make you pay for that one.'

'You don't know the half of it,' Roarke murmured. 'Let's run this, Ian, first level. See what we find.'

On her own, Eve struggled with the wording and tone of her official report. If she used the Marlena connection so that she could give Whitney the names of the men who'd killed her – justify the investigation of their families – she'd lock Roarke into it.

All the men had been murdered, all their cases remained open. So far even the International Center for Criminal Activity hadn't connected those murders. Could she use them now, and sell Whitney and the chief of police, the media, on one of those murders being the motive for her current investigation?

Maybe, if she was good enough, if she could lie with conviction and logic.

Step one: Build the facts and evidence that Summerset was being used. She needed Mira's findings to polish that up.

Step two: Build a logical theory that the setup was motivated by revenge – mistakenly targeted revenge. To do that she had to build a reasonable case that the six men who died had died by separate hands, for separate causes.

They had all been part of the crime community, had all associated with undesirables. Their deaths had been spread out over three years and had all been caused by different means.

Roarke was far from stupid, she mused. He'd taken his time, covered his tracks. All she had to do now was to see that they stayed covered.

If she had one break first, one solid, tangible piece of evidence to indicate a conspiracy. Anything she could put in Whitney's hand to help convince him to buy the rest.

She heard a shout from the next room and scowled, annoyed that she'd neglected to engage the sound control. But as she rose to do so, the excited voices on the other side of the door drew her through it.

'Okay, what's the big fucking deal? Did you find a new way to play Space Marauders?'

'I found an echo.' McNab was nearly dancing as he continually slapped Roarke on the back. 'I found a goddamn beautiful echo.'

'Take it to the Alps, pal, and you can have lots of echoes.'

'An electronic echo. The bastard's good, but I'm better. He bounced the transmission from the core system right here in the house, but he didn't send it from here. No indeed he didn't, because I have a fucking-A echo.'

'Good job, Ian. Here's another. See it?' Roarke pointed to a small needle gauge jury-rigged to the 'link. Eve saw nothing, but McNab hooted.

'Yeah, baby, that's the way. I can work with this, you bet your ass I can.'

'Wait a minute.' Eve muscled between them before they could slap backs again. 'Explain this in terms normal people can understand. No e-jabber.'

'Okay, try this.' McNab inched a hip onto her desk. He was wearing hearts in his ears today. A dozen tiny red hearts Eve tried not to focus on. 'The last incoming from mystery boy you received. I tracked it all over the damn place, and into here. Every indication showed the transmission originated from this building.'

'I got that.'

'But we don't want to believe that, so we open up the system for element scan. It's like – Do you cook?'

Roarke only chuckled. Eve sneered. 'Let's be serious.'

'Okay, I was going to say like a recipe where you separate the eggs from the sugar and like that.'

'I'm not a moron, McNab, I can follow that.'

'Good, great. When we're taking the elements for our cake and examining each one for, like, quality, maybe we see one's off, just a tad off. Like the milk's turned. So when we figure the milk's turned we want to know why. Now we find there's a leak in our refrigeration system. Just a tiny leak, microscopic, but enough to affect the quality, enough to let in germs. Your house system had a germ.'

'What does that have to do with echoes?'

'Ian.' Roarke held up a hand. 'Before you whip up a four-course meal, let me explain this. Electronic signals leave a pattern,' he told Eve patiently. 'And that pattern can be tracked and simulated. We've run the patterns for incomings on this unit for the last six weeks. We also ran patterns for outgoings from the main system for the same length of time. When doing so, and taking it through several levels, we discovered a shift in pattern on one incoming. The one that matters. An echo – or a shadow layered over the consistent pattern – which clearly indicates a different source.'

'You can prove the transmission didn't originate from here?'

'Exactly.'

'Is this the kind of proof you can put into black and white and I can take to Whitney?'

'You betcha.' McNab beamed at her. 'EDD's used this kind of evidence in hundreds of cases. It's standard. This one was buried deep and the pattern was nearly smooth. But we found her.'

'You found her,' Roarke corrected.

'I couldn't have done it without your equipment and your help. I missed it twice.'

'You came through.'

'Before I toddle off,' Eve interrupted, 'and leave you two

boys to bask in the glow of mutual admiration, would you mind taking just a moment to distill this evidence into hard copy and disc for my pesky report?'

'Lieutenant.' Roarke laid a hand on McNab's shoulder. 'You're embarrassing us with your praise and gratitude.'

'You want praise and gratitude?' On impulse, she grabbed Roarke's face in her hands and kissed him hard on the mouth. Then – what the hell – she did the same to McNab. 'I want the data within the hour,' she added as she strode out.

'Wow.' McNab pressed his lips together to hold on to the taste, then patted a hand on his heart. 'The lieutenant has some great mouth.'

'Don't make me hurt you, Ian, just when we're beginning such a beautiful friendship.'

'She got a sister? Cousin? Maiden aunt?'

'Lieutenant Dallas is one of a kind.' Roarke watched the needle give another, barely discernable jerk. 'Ian, let's distill this data for her, then wouldn't it be fun to see just how far we can follow this echo?'

McNab's brow furrowed. 'You want to try to track an echo this faint? Hell, Roarke, it takes days of man-hours and top equipment to track a solid one. I've never heard of anything below the scale of fifteen being tracked.'

'There's always a first time.'

McNab's eyes began to shine. 'Yeah, the boys in EDD would bow to me if I pulled it off.'

'More than enough reason to push forward, I'd say.'

Chapter Twelve

Eve paced the reception area outside Mira's office. What the hell was taking so long, she wondered, and checked her wrist unit once again. It was twelve-thirty. Summerset had been in testing for ninety minutes. Eve had until one to present her progress reports to her commander.

She needed Mira's findings.

To help herself wait, she practiced her oral backup to her written reports. The words she would use, the tone she would take. She felt like a second-rate actor running lines backstage. Sweat pooled at the base of her spine.

The minute the door opened, she leaped at Summerset. 'What's the deal?'

His eyes were dark and hard in a pale face, his jaw clenched, his mouth thin. Humiliation rolled greasily in his stomach. 'I've followed your orders, Lieutenant, and completed the required testing. I've sacrificed my privacy and my dignity. I hope that satisfies you.'

He stalked past her and through the outer doors.

'Screw it,' Eve muttered and walked straight into Mira's office.

Mira smiled, sipped her tea. She'd had no trouble hearing Summerset's bitter comments. 'He's a complicated man.'

'He's an ass, but that's irrelevant. Can you give me a bottom line?'

'It will take some time for me to review all the tests and complete my report.'

'I've got Whitney in twenty minutes. I'll take anything you can give me.'

'A preliminary opinion then.' Mira poured another cup of tea, gesturing for Eve to sit. 'He's a man with little respect for the law, and a great deal of respect for order.'

Eve took the tea but didn't drink. 'Which means?'

'He's most comfortable when things are in their place, and he's somewhat obsessive about keeping them there. The law itself, the laws society makes mean little to him as they are variable, often poorly designed, and quite often fail. Aesthetics are also important to him – his surroundings, appearances – as he appreciates the order in beauty. He's a creature of routine. This soothes him, this pattern, this stability. He arises at a certain hour and retires at a certain hour. His duties are clearly outlined and followed. Even his recreation, his free time is organized.'

'So, he's a tight-ass. I already knew that.'

'His way of dealing with the horrors he witnessed during the Urban Wars, the poverty and despair he escaped from, and the loss of his only child is to create a certain acceptable pattern, then follow it. But . . . in unclinical terms, yes, he's a tight-ass. However rigid he might be, however much he may sneer at the laws of society, he is one of the most nonviolent personalities I've encountered.'

'He's given me a few bruises,' Eve muttered under her breath.

'You disturb his need for order,' Mira said, not without sympathy. 'But the fact is, true violence is abhorrent to him. It offends his very rigid sense of order and place. And it's wasteful. He finds waste repellent. Again, I believe, because he saw far too much of it throughout his life. As I said, it will take a bit of time to review the tests, but I would say at this point it's my opinion that someone of his personality structure is unlikely to have committed the crimes you're investigating.'

For the first time in hours, Eve's stomach unknotted. 'This knocks him down the list. Way down. I appreciate you dealing with this so quickly.'

'I'm always happy to do a friend a favor, but after reading your data on this investigation, it's a bit more than that. Eve, you're dealing with a very dangerous, very canny, very determined and thorough killer. One who has had years to prepare, and be prepared. One who is both focused and unstable, and who has a massive and unstable ego. A sociopath with a holy mission, a sadist with skill. I'm afraid for you.'

'I'm closing in on him.'

'I hope you are, because I believe he's also closing in on you. Roarke may be his main target, but you stand between. He wants Roarke to bleed, and he wants him to suffer. Roarke's death puts an end to the mission, and the mission is his life. But you, you're his connection, his competitor, his audience. He has a black-and-white view of women. Chaste or whore.'

Eve let out a short laugh. 'Well, I can figure where I stand.'

'No.' Disturbed, Mira shook her head. 'It's more complicated with you. He admires you. You challenge him. And you anger him. I don't believe he's able to slip you into either mold and that only makes him more focused on you.'

Her eyes glinted. 'I want him focused on me.'

Mira held her hands up a moment to give herself time to gather her thoughts. 'I need further study, but in a nut-shell, his faith, his religion is catalyst – or excuse, if you prefer. He leaves the token – faith and luck – at every murder. He leaves the image of Mary as a symbol of her female power and her vulnerability. She's his real god.'

'I don't follow you.'

'The Mother. The Virgin. The pure and the loving. But an authority figure nonetheless. She is the witness to his acts, the audience to his mission. At this point, I'd have to say it's a woman who formed him. A strong and vital female figure of authority and love. He needs her approval, her guidance. He needs to please her. He needs her praise.'

'His mother,' Eve murmured. 'Do you think she's behind it all?'

'It's possible. Or just as possible that he sees his current behavior as a kind of homage to her. Mother, sister, aunt, wife. A wife is unlikely,' she added with a faint shake of her head. 'He's probably sexually repressed. Impotent. His god is a vengeful one, who permits no carnal pleasures. If he's using the statue to symbolize his own mother, he would view his conception as a miracle – immaculate – and see himself as invulnerable.'

'He said he was an angel. The angel of vengeance.'

'Yes, a soldier of his god, beyond the power of mortals. There is his ego again. What I am sure of is that there is a woman – or was a woman – whom he seeks to appease, and one he views as pure.'

For one sickening moment, Eve saw the image of Marlena in her mind. Golden hair, innocent eyes, and a snowy white dress. Pure, she thought. Virginal.

Wouldn't Summerset always see his martyred daughter exactly that way?

'It could be a child,' she said quietly. 'A lost child.'

'Marlena?' The compassion was ripe in the word. 'It's very unlikely, Eve. Does he mourn for her? Of course he does, and always will. But she isn't a symbol to him. For Summerset, Marlena is his child, and one he didn't protect. For your killer, this female figure is the protector – and the punisher. And you are another strong female figure of authority. He's drawn to you, wants your admiration. And he may, at some point, be compelled to destroy you.'

'I hope you're right.' Eve rose. 'Because this is a game I want to finish face-to-face.'

*

181

Eve convinced herself she was prepared for Whitney. But she hadn't been prepared to face both him and the chief of police and security. Tibble, his dark face unreadable, his hands clasped militarily behind his back, stood at the window in Whitney's office. Whitney remained behind his desk. Their positioning indicated to Eve that it was Whitney's show – until Tibble decided otherwise.

'Before you begin your report, Lieutenant, I'm informing you that a press conference is scheduled for four P.M. in the media information center at Police Tower.' Whitney inclined his head. 'Your presence and participation are required.'

'Yes, sir.'

'It has come to our attention that a member of the press has received certain communications which attack your credibility as primary in this investigation, and which indicate that you, and therefore the department, are suppressing certain data germane to said investigation, data that would implicate your husband in multiple murders.'

'That is both insulting to me, the department, and my husband, and absurd.' Her heart hitched, but her voice stayed low and steady. 'If these communications are deemed credible, why hasn't the member of the press reported same?'

'The accusations are so far anonymous and unsubstantiated, and this particular member of the press deemed it in his best interest to pass this information along to Chief Tibble. It's in your best interest, Lieutenant, to clear up this matter now, here.'

'Are you accusing me of suppressing evidence, Commander?'

'I'm requesting that you confirm or deny at this time.'

'I deny, at this time, and any time, that I have or would suppress evidence that would lead to the apprehension of a criminal or the closing of a case. And I take personal offense at the question.'

'Offense so noted,' Whitney said mildly. 'Sit down, Dallas.'

She didn't comply, but stepped forward. 'My record should stand for something. Over ten years of service should outweigh an anonymous accusation tossed to a hungry reporter.'

'So noted, Dallas,' Whitney repeated. 'Now—'

'I'm not finished, sir. I'd like to have my say here.'

He sat back, and though she kept her eyes on his she knew Tibble had yet to move. 'Very well, Lieutenant, have your say.'

'I'm very aware that my personal life, my marriage, is the source of speculation and interest in the department and with the public. I can live with that. I'm also aware that my husband's businesses, and his style of conducting his businesses, are also the source of speculation and interest. I have no particular problem with that. But I resent very much that my reputation and my husband's character should be questioned this way. From the media, Commander, it's to be expected, but not from my superior officer. Not from any member of the department I've served to the best of my ability. I want you to take note, Commander, that turning in my badge would be like cutting off my arm. But if it comes down to a choice between the job and my marriage, then I lose the arm.'

'No one is asking you to make a choice, Lieutenant, and I will offer my personal apologies for any offense given by this situation.'

'Personally, I hate chicken-shit anonymous sources.' Tibble spoke for the first time, his gaze steady on Eve's face. 'And I'd like to see you maintain that just-under-simmer righteous anger for the press conference when this matter comes up, Lieutenant. It will play very well on screen. Now I, for one, would like to hear the progress of your investigation.'

The anger helped her forget fear and nerves. She fell into rhythm, comfortable with the cop speak, the formality and the slang of it. She offered the names of the six men responsible for Marlena's murder, handed out hard copy of data on them, and proposed her theory.

'The caller stated that revenge was the name of his game. Therefore it's my belief that, acting alone or with a partner or partners, this individual is avenging the murder of one or more of these men. The connection's there. Marlena to Summerset, Summerset to Roarke. I've run the names and their cases through the ICCA.'

She said that briskly, as though it was no more than routine. And her stomach jumped like a pond of frogs on speeders. 'There is no evidence to link their murders to one individual. They were killed at different times over a three-year period, with different methods and in different geographical areas. The six men, however, were all linked to the same gambling organization based in Dublin, and that organization was investigated for illegal activities no less than twelve times by local authorities and the ICCA. Data supports that the men were killed individually and for separate motives, likely perpetrated by rivals or associates.'

'Then where's the connection to the deaths of Brennen, Conroy, and O'Leary?'

'In the killer's mind. Dr Mira is working on the profile, which I believe will support my suppositions. If you take it from his angle, Marlena was killed by these men as an example to Roarke, to discourage him from infringing on their territory.'

'That wasn't the conclusion of the investigating officer.'

'No, sir, but the investigating officer was a wrong cop, known to associate with this organization. He was in their pocket. Marlena was no more than a child.' Eve slid two photos out of her bag, one still taken from each of the hologram images. 'This is what was done to her. And the investigating officer spent precisely four and a half man-hours on closing her case and ruling it death by misadventure.'

Whitney stared down at the stills, and his eyes went grim. 'Misadventure, my ass. It's obviously a torture murder.'

'One defenseless girl brutalized by six men. And they got away with it clean. Men who can do that to a child are men who could brag about it. I believe those close to them knew, and when they were killed, one by one, at least one person decided Roarke and Summerset were responsible.'

Tibble turned the still of Marlena's body facedown. He'd been away from the streets long enough to know he'd be haunted by that image. 'And you don't believe that, Lieutenant? You want us to believe that those six deaths were unrelated, but that our current madman believes otherwise. And you want us to believe he's killing now, framing Summerset, and all to exact revenge on Roarke?'

'That's exactly right. I want you to believe that the man Mira described to me as a sadistic sociopath with a holy mission is using all the skill at his disposal to ruin Roarke. Framing Summerset was a miscalculation, and you'll see when Mira has completed her test evaluations on him. She's told me in a preliminary interview that Summerset is not only incapable of this range of violence, but is appalled by violence. The circumstantial evidence compiled against him is obvious enough for a cross-eyed five-year-old to see through.'

'I prefer to withhold judgment on that until I see Mira's completed evaluation,' Whitney told her.

'I can give you mine,' she said, and threw her weight on Summerset's end of the scale. 'The security discs at the Luxury Towers were doctored. We know this. However, the lobby sector – which clearly shows Summerset's entrance into the building – was untouched. Why? McNab has the disc of the twelfth floor being analyzed by the EDD compu-unit. I'm confident that we'll discover a blip for the period when Summerset exited the elevator and waited for Ms Morrell. And again, in the lobby sector where he's indicated he left the building at approximately twelve forty.'

'The extent of tampering you're indicating would require very specialized skill and equipment.'

'Yes, sir. So does jamming transmissions into Cop Central. Religion plays a vital part in the motive and method of these killings. The evidence points to a strong, if twisted, attachment to Catholicism. Summerset isn't Catholic nor is he particularly religious.'

'A man's faith,' Whitney put in, 'is often a private and intimate matter.'

'Not with this man it isn't. For him, it's a driving force. I have more. This morning Detective McNab, who was assigned to me from EDD, found what he referred to as an echo on my 'link transmission from the perpetrator. The transmission did not originate in my home, but someone went to a great deal of trouble to make it appear as if it did.'

Whitney said nothing until he'd scanned the report Eve offered. 'This is good work.'

'One of the Riley brothers did a stint on security for a large electronics firm – and he's also made several trips to New York in the last ten years. I'd like to pursue that angle.'

'Are you planning on going to Ireland, Lieutenant?'

Training prevented her from gaping. 'No, sir. I can access any necessary data from here.'

Whitney tapped a finger on the reports. 'I'd consider it, seriously consider it.'

Press conferences rarely put Eve in a cheery mood. The free-for-all at the media center was no exception. It was bad enough to be ordered to stand in front of a sea of reporters and tap dance around what was, what should be, and what wasn't, tricky enough when the questions batted to her dealt with her professional area. But many of the questions during the slated hour took a personal curve. She had to field them quickly, skillfully, and without breaking a sweat.

She knew damn well reporters could smell sweat.

'Lieutenant Dallas, as primary investigator, have you questioned Roarke in connection with these murders?'

'Roarke has cooperated with the department.'

'Was his cooperation elicited by the primary, or by his wife?'

Snake-eyed, flat-faced son of a bitch, Eve thought, staring the reporter down and ignoring the autotronic cameras that slid spiderlike in her direction. 'Roarke volunteered his statements and his assistance from the initiation of this investigation.'

'Isn't it true that your prime suspect is in Roarke's employ and resides in your home?'

'At this point in the investigation we have no prime suspect.' That brought on the growl from the wolf pack, the shouted questions, the demands. She waited them out. 'Lawrence Charles Summerset was interviewed formally and has voluntarily undergone testing. As a result of this, the department and the primary are now pursuing other investigative channels.'

'What is your response to the supposition that Summerset murdered three people on orders from his employer?'

The shouted question from the back had the effect of smothering the shouts. For the first time in nearly an hour, there was silence. Even as Chief Tibble stepped forward, Eve held up a hand. 'I'd like to answer that.' Fury might have clawed at her throat, but her voice was cold and level. 'My response is that suppositions of that nature have no place in this forum. They belong in tiny rooms where they can be discussed by tiny minds. Such a supposition when voiced publicly, particularly by a member of the media, falls into the category of criminal negligence. Such an innuendo, with no facts or evidence to support it, is an insult not only to the men involved, but to the dead. I have nothing more to say here.'

She stepped around Tibble and off the platform. She could hear the questions being shouted out at him, and his calm, reasonable voice answering. But she had blood in her eye and a bitter taste in her mouth.

'Dallas! Dallas, hold on.' Nadine Furst rushed after her, her camera operator in hot pursuit. 'Give me two minutes, come on. Two lousy minutes.'

Eve turned on her, knowing that it would be a miracle if she held on to her temper for two seconds. 'Don't get in my face here, Nadine.'

'Look, that last one was over the line, no question. But you've got to expect to take some heat here.'

'I can handle heat. I don't see why I have to handle morons, too.'

'I'm with you there.'

'Are you?' Out of the corner of her eye, Eve noted that the camera operator was recording.

'Let me help you out here.' Instinctively Nadine smoothed down her hair, hitched her jacket into a perfect line. 'Give me a statement, a quick one-on-one to balance things out.'

'Give you a ninety-second exclusive, you mean, and bump your rating points. Jesus.' Eve turned away before she could do or say something regrettable.

Then Mira's words came back to her. The massive and fragile ego of the murderer. His focus on her – the need for female approval. She wasn't certain if it was impulse or instinct, but she went with it.

She'd give Nadine her ratings boost, all right. And she'd take a nice hard slap at the killer. One she hoped he'd feel honor bound to try to return.

'Who the hell do you people think you are?' She whirled back, let her temper boil over. She had no doubt it would show, in her face, in her clenched fists. 'Using your First Amendment rights, your public's right to know, to interfere with a murder investigation.'

'Wait just a minute.'

'No, you wait.' Eve jabbed a finger into Nadine's shoulder, knocking her back a step. 'Three people are dead, children are orphaned, a woman is widowed, and all because some self-absorbed piece of shit with a God complex decided to play games. There's your story, pal. Some asshole who thinks Jesus speaks to him is playing the media like a damn banjo. The more air time you give him, the happier he is. He wants us to believe he has a higher purpose, but all he really wants is to win. And he won't. He won't because I'm better than he is. This jerk's an amateur who had a short run of luck. As long as he keeps screwing up I'll have him caged in a week.'

'And you'll stand by that, Lieutenant Dallas,' Nadine said coldly. 'You'll apprehend the killer within a week.'

'You can count on it. He's not the smartest I've gone after, he's not even the most pathetic. He's just one more tiny pimple on society's butt.'

She turned and stalked off.

'That's going to make great screen, Nadine.' The camera operator all but danced for joy. 'Ratings through the roof.'

'Yeah.' Nadine watched Eve slam into her car. 'And so much for friendship,' she muttered. 'Let's transmit it raw to the station. We'll have it on air in time for the five-thirty.'

Eve was counting on it. Her man would see it. Maybe he'd stew, maybe he'd explode, but she had no doubt he'd make a move. His ego would demand it.

And this time, he'd come after her.

She headed into Cop Central. She thought it would do her good to work a few hours in her usual environment. As an afterthought, she called home. When Roarke answered himself, Eve's eyebrows shot up.

'Where's Summerset?'

'In his quarters.'

'Sulking?'

'Painting, I believe. He thought it would relax him. And where are you, Lieutenant?'

'On my way in to Central for a while. Just wrapped up a press conference.'

'And we know how much you enjoy them. I'll be sure to tune in for the five-thirty.'

She didn't wince, at least not visibly. 'I wouldn't bother. It was pretty dull. Look, I figured you'd be at your head-quarters. There's no reason to put your world on hold because of this.'

'My world continues to revolve. I can handle details from here for a bit longer. Besides, Ian and I are having such a good time playing with our toys.'

'Getting anywhere?'

'I think so. It's slow.'

'I'll take a look when I get there. Couple of hours.'

'Fine. I believe we're having pizza.'

'Good, make mine loaded. See you.'

She cut transmission as she drove into the underground lot at Central. She took a minute to curse, as Lieutenant Medavoy from Anti-Crime had once again parked crookedly and infringed on her space. She squeezed in, indulged herself by rapping her door smartly against the side of his vehicle.

A new one, too, she thought, nothing the shiny surface now nicely dinged. *Where the hell does Anti-Crime get the budget?*

Fifteen minutes to air, she noted as she took the glide into the core of Central. She'd get herself some coffee, lock her office door, and watch the show.

She wasn't disappointed. Her impromptu statement to Nadine came across exactly as intended. She'd appeared furious, overconfident, and reckless. It was going to burn his ass, she decided, and wondered if she had time for another cup of coffee before Whitney summoned her.

She didn't have time for another sip.

She accepted the expected dressing down without argument or excuse, agreed that her comments had been unwise and overemotional.

'No pithy remarks, Lieutenant?'

'No, sir.'

'What are you up to here, Dallas?'

She shifted gears swiftly, smoothly, realizing she'd been just a bit too conciliatory. 'My armpit's in this investigation, one that is causing a great deal of stress on my personal life. I blew off steam, and I apologize. It won't happen again.'

'Be sure that it doesn't, and contact Ms Furst. I want you to offer her another one-on-one, this time with you in control of your emotions.'

Eve didn't have to feign the annoyance now. 'I'd like to avoid the media for the near future, Commander. I think—'

'That wasn't a request, Lieutenant. It was an order. You made the mess, now clean it up. And quickly.'

Eve closed her mouth, teeth first, and nodded.

She worked off her temper for the next hour by dealing with paperwork, and when that didn't do the trick, she contacted maintenance and scalded their ears over the as-yet unrepaired guidance system in her vehicle. Calmer, she drafted an e-message for Nadine offering another interview and shot it off before she could brood about it.

And throughout it all she waited for her 'link to beep. She wanted him to call, willed him to call. The sooner he made his move, the sloppier he would be.

Who is he? Sociopath, sadist, egotist. Yet, there was something weak and sad and even pathetic about him. Riddles and religion, she mused. Well, that wasn't so strange. Religion was a riddle to her. Believe this, and only this, because we say so. If you don't you're buying a one-way ticket to everlasting Hell.

Organized religion baffled her, made her vaguely uncomfortable. Each had followers who were so sure they were right, that their way was the only way. And throughout history they'd fought wars and shed oceans of blood to prove it.

Eve shrugged, idly picked up one of the three statues of the Madonna she'd lined on her desk. She'd been raised by the state, and a state education was forbidden, by law, to include even a whiff of religious training. Church groups were forever lobbying to change that, but Eve thought she'd done well enough. She'd formed her own opinions. There was right and wrong, the law and chaos, crime and punishment.

Still, religion, at its best, was supposed to guide and to comfort, wasn't it? She glanced at the pile of discs she'd amassed in her research of the Catholic faith. It remained a mystery to her, but she thought it was supposed to. That was its core, the mystery shrouded in pomp and pageantry. And its rituals were lovely and visually appealing.

Like the Virgin. Eve turned the statue in her hand, studying it. What had Roarke called her? The BVM. It made her sound friendly, accessible, like someone you could take your troubles to.

I can't quite work this one out, I'll ask the BVM.

Yet she was the holiest of women. The ultimate female figure. The Virgin Mother who'd been called on to bear the Son of God, then watch him die for the sins of man.

Now there was a madman using her image, twisting it, using it to stand witness to man's inhumanity to man.

But *mother* was the key, wasn't it? she mused. His mother, or someone he viewed as that figure of love and authority.

Eve couldn't remember her mother. Even in the dreams she was powerless to control there was nothing and no one in that role. No voice soft in lullaby or raised in anger, no hand stroking gently or slapping in annoyance.

Nothing.

Yet someone had carried her for nine months, had shot her from womb to world. Then had – what? Turned away, run away? Died? Left her alone to be beaten and broken and defiled. Left her shivering in cold, dirty rooms waiting for the next night of pain and abuse.

Doesn't matter, Eve reminded herself fiercely. That wasn't the point. It was this man's background that mattered now, what had formed him.

Eve Dallas had formed herself.

Gently she set the statue down again, staring into that serene and lovely face. 'Just another sin on his plate,' she murmured, 'using you as part of his obscenities. I have to stop him before he does it again. I could use a little help here.'

Eve caught herself, blinked in shock, then laughed a little as she ran a hand through her hair. The Catholics were pretty clever, she decided, with their statues. Before you knew it you were talking to them – and it was a hell of a lot like praying.

It isn't prayers that will bring him down, she reminded herself. It was police work, and she'd be more productive at home. A decent meal, a good night's sleep would keep her primed.

She discovered Medavoy's car was gone when she reached the garage, and since there was no memo stuck to her windshield she assumed he had yet to notice the new dent in his passenger-side door.

The garage echoed around her. She heard the whine of an engine starting up, the quick skid of tires on asphalt. Seconds later a unit bulleted by. The sirens hit the air as the car zipped out of the garage and into the night.

She uncoded her locks, reached for the handle. Footsteps sounded behind her. She whirled, her weapon in her hand, her body in a crouch.

The footsteps skidded to a halt, and the man threw up his hands. 'Whoa. At least read me my rights.'

She recognized the detective from her unit and reholstered her weapon. 'Sorry, Baxter.'

'Jumpy, aren't we, Dallas?'

'People shouldn't go skulking around garages.'

'Hey, I'm just heading to my vehicle.' He winked as he uncoded a car two down from hers. 'Got myself a hot date with a saucy señorita.'

'Olé, Baxter,' she muttered and, annoyed with herself, slid behind the wheel. It took three tries for the engine to catch. She decided she would go to maintenance personally in the morning and murder the first mechanic who crossed her path.

The temperature control hummed straight to warm, then shot into roast. Eve ordered it off with a snarl and settled for the late November chill.

She drove two blocks, hit a traffic snarl and sighed. For a time she simply tapped her fingers on the wheel and studied the new animated billboard over Gromley's Theater Complex. A dozen different videos were advertised. She watched an air chase between two sky-cycles over New Los Angeles that ended with a very impressive crash and display of flames. She pondered the beautiful couple who rolled across a spring meadow wearing little but glossy skin. The latest kid-flick was next in line and offered a trio of dancing spiders garbed in top hats and tails.

She inched forward, ignoring the bad-tempered honks and shouted curses of other drivers similarly situated.

A teenage couple riding tandem on an airboard surfed through the snarled traffic in a bright flash of color. The driver beside her resigned herself to a long wait by turning up her music system to an ear-splitting pitch and singing along in a loud, off-key voice.

Overhead an airbus blatted. There was something smug in the sound, Eve thought. *Yeah, yeah*, she mused, scowling up at it, *if more people took advantage of public transpo, we wouldn't be in this fix.*

Bored, Eve pulled out her communicator and tagged Peabody.

'You might as well call it a night,' Eve told her. 'I'm in a vehicle jam here and my ETA is anyone's guess.'

'There's this rumor about pizza.'

'Okay, enjoy then, but if you're still there when I get

in, you're going to have to give me a full report on the day's work.'

'For pizza, Lieutenant, I would face much worse.'

She watched it happen. It was perfectly choreographed for disaster. Three cars ahead of her, two Rapid Cabs shot into vertical lift at the same time. Their fenders brushed, bumped. The cabs shimmied. Even as Eve was shaking her head over idiocy, the cabs lost their lift and hit the street with resounding thuds.

'Well, damn.'

'Problem, Dallas? Thought I heard a crash.'

'Yeah, a couple of brain dead cabbies. Oh yeah, that's going to help. Now they're out of their rides and screaming at each other. This'll get traffic moving, all right.'

Her eyes narrowed as she saw one of the cabbies reach through his window and pull out a metal bat. 'That tears it. Peabody, call for a couple of black-and-white floaters, assault with deadly in progress, Tenth Avenue between Twenty-fifth and -sixth. Tell them to make it fast before we have a riot. Now I'm going to go give these assholes a lesson in driving courtesy.'

'Dallas, maybe you ought to wait for backup. I'll have—'

'Forget it. I'm sick of idiots.' She slammed her door, took three long-legged strides. And the world erupted.

She felt the hot fist of air punch her in the back, scoop her up like a doll, and fling her forward. Her eardrums sang with the force of the explosion as she flew. Something sharp, twisted, and flaming shot past her head. Someone screamed. She didn't think it was herself, as she couldn't seem to draw in air to breathe.

She bounced headfirst off the hood of a car, dimly saw the shocked, white face of its driver gaping at her, then hit the street hard enough to scrape flesh and rattle bones.

Something's burning, something's burning, she thought, but couldn't quite place it. Flesh, leather, fuel. Oh God. With wobbly effort, she pushed with her hands, managed to lift her head.

Behind her, people abandoned their cars like rats running from doomed ships. Someone stepped on her, but she barely felt it. Overhead, the traffic copters zoomed in to shine security beams and blast out cautions.

But eyes were dazzled by the fierce light, the shooting flames coming from her vehicle.

She wheezed in a breath, let it out. 'Son of a bitch.' And passed out cold.

Chapter Thirteen

Roarke muscled his way through crowds of people, lines of emergency vehicles. Airlifts hovered above, shooting out their streams of lights amid the shriek of sirens. There was a smell of sweat and blood and burning. A child was screaming in long, gulping wails. A woman sat on the ground, surrounded by sparkling, fist-sized diamonds of Duraglass, and wept silently into her hands.

He saw blackened faces, shocked eyes, but he didn't see Eve.

He refused to allow himself to think or to feel or to imagine.

He'd been in Eve's office, tinkering with McNab, when the hail for Peabody had come in. He'd continued to work, amusing himself by listening to Eve's voice, the irritation spiking it, then the disgust when she'd ordered Peabody to call for a floater.

Then the almost female shriek of the explosion had caused the communicator to jump in Peabody's hand. He hadn't waited, not even a heartbeat, but had been out of the room and gone even as Peabody had desperately tried to raise Eve again.

He'd abandoned his car a full block back, but was making good time on foot. Sheer force of will had people scrambling out of his way. Or perhaps it was the cold rage in his eyes as he scanned faces, forms.

Then he saw her vehicle – or what was left of it. The twisted hulk of steel and plastic was hulled out and coated with thick white foam. And his heart stopped.

He'd never know how long he stood there, unable to breathe, his body rocking with shock. Then he broke, started forward, with some wild notion of ripping the ruined car to pieces to find her.

'Goddamn it, I said I'm not going to any hospital. Just patch me up, for Christ's sake, and find me a fucking communicator before I kick your sorry ass over to the East Side.'

He whirled, his head whipping up like a wolf's scenting its mate. She was sitting on the running board of a medivan, snarling at a harassed medical technician who was struggling to coat her burns.

She was singed, bleeding, bruised, and furiously alive.

He didn't go to her at once. He needed a moment for his hands to stop shaking, for his heart to stop sputtering and beat normally again. Relief was like a drug, a spiked drink to make him giddy. He gulped it down, then found himself grinning like an idiot as she rammed her elbow into the MT's gut to prevent him from giving her a dose of medication.

'Keep that thing away from me. Did I tell you to get me a communicator?'

'I'm doing my job, Lieutenant. If you'd just cooperate—'

'Cooperate hell. Cooperate with you guys and I'll end up drooling and strapped to a gurney.'

'You need to go to a hospital or health center. You have a concussion, second-degree burns, contusions, lacerations. You're shocky.'

Eve reached up and grabbed him by the band collar of his uniform coat. 'One of us is going to be shocky, ace, if you don't get me a goddamn communicator.'

'Well, Lieutenant, I see you're in your usual form.'

She looked over, up, and, seeing Roarke, wiped the back of her hand over her bruised and sooty face. 'Hi. I was just trying to get this jerk to find me a communicator so I could call you. Let you know I'd be late for dinner.'

'I figured that out for myself when we heard your explosion.' He crouched down until they were eye to eye. There was a nasty scrape on her forehead, still seeping blood. Her jacket was gone, and the shirt she wore was ripped and singed. Blood stained the sleeve of her left arm from a six-inch gash. Her slacks were literally tatters.

'Darling,' he said mildly, 'you're not looking your best.'

'If this guy would just patch me up enough so I could – hey, hey, hey!' She jerked, slapped out, but wasn't quick enough to prevent the pressure syringe from shooting into her arm. 'What was that? What'd you give me?'

'Just a pain blocker. This is going to hurt some.'

'Ah shit, that's going to make me goofy. You know that stuff makes me goofy,' she said, appealing to Roarke. 'I hate when that happens.'

'I rather enjoy it myself.' He tipped her chin up as the MT went to work on her arm. 'How many devoted husbands do you see?'

'Just you. I don't have a concussion.'

'Yes, she does,' the MT said cheerfully. 'This gash is plenty dirty – got lots of street grit in it – but we'll clean her right up and close it.'

'Make it snappy then.' She was starting to shiver – part cold, part shock – but didn't notice. 'I've got to follow this up with the fire team and the explosive unit. And where the hell's Peabody, because I . . . . shit, shit, shit, it's happening. My tongue's getting thick.' Her head lolled, and she shook it back into place. She felt a snort of laughter building and fought to suppress it. 'Why don't they just give you a couple shots of Kentucky bourbon?'

'It isn't cost-effective. And you don't like bourbon.' Roarke sat on the running board beside her, took her free hand to examine the scrapes and burns himself.

'Yeah well, I don't like this either. Chemicals make you all otherwise.' She stared dully as the medic guided a suturing wand over her ripped flesh, neatly mending it. 'Don't you take me to the hospital. I'll be really pissed.'

He didn't see her beloved leather jacket anywhere and made a mental note to replace it. For now he stripped his own off and tucked it over her shoulders. 'Darling, in about ninety seconds you're not going to know what I do with you, or where I take you.'

Her body began a lovely slow float to nowhere. 'I will when I come out of it. Why, there she is. Hey, Peabody. And McNab, too. Don't they make a cute couple?'

'Adorable. Put your head back, Eve, and let the nice MT bandage it for you.'

'Okay, sure. Hiya, Peabody, you and McNab out on the town?'

'He drugged her,' Roarke explained. 'Tranqs always do this to her.'

'How bad are you hurt?' White-faced and shaken, Peabody knelt down. 'Dallas, how bad?'

'Oh.' She gestured widely, and managed to slap the long-suffering MT. 'Bumps and stuff. Boy, did I fly. Let me tell you, the up part can be pretty cool, but those landings suck space waste. Wham!' To demonstrate she attempted to slam her fist on her knee, missed and caught the medic in the crotch. 'Oops, sorry,' she said when he folded. 'Hey, Peabody, how's my vehicle?'

'It's a dead loss.'

'Damn. Well, good night.' She wrapped her arms around Roarke, nestled into him, and sighed.

The MT sucked his breath back then got shakily to his feet. 'That's the best I can do for her here. She's all yours.'

'Indeed she is. Come on, darling, let's go.'

'Did you save me some pizza? I don't want you carrying me, okay? It's embarrassing. I can walk fine.'

'Of course you can,' he assured her and hefted her into his arms.

'See, told you.' Her head dropped on his shoulder like lead. 'Mmm. You smell good.' She sniffed at his throat like a puppy. 'Isn't he pretty?' she said to no one in particular. 'He's all mine, too. All mine. Are we going home?'

'Mmm-hmm.' There was no need to mention the detour he intended to take to the nearest hospital.

'I need Peabody to stay for . . . I need her to stay for something. Yeah, for follow-up, get those bomb guys to spill it, Peabody.'

'Don't worry about it, Dallas. We'll have a full report for you in the morning.'

'Tonight. 'S only the shank of the evening.'

'Tomorrow,' Roarke murmured, shifting his gaze from Peabody to McNab. 'I want to know everything there is to know.'

'You'll have it,' McNab promised. He waited until Roarke carried Eve through the crowd, then turned to study the car. 'If she'd been inside when it went up . . .'

'She wasn't,' Peabody snapped. 'Let's get to work.'

Eve woke to silence. She had a vague recollection of being poked and prodded, and of swearing at someone – at several someones – during a physical examination. So her waking thought was panic, laced with fury.

No way were they keeping her in the damn hospital another five minutes.

She shot up in bed, and her head did one long, giddy reel. But it was relief that settled over her when she realized she was in her own bed.

'Going somewhere?' Roarke rose from the sitting area where he'd been keeping one eye on the scrolling stock reports on the monitor and one eye on his sleeping wife.

She didn't lay back. That was a matter of pride. 'Maybe. You took me to the hospital.'

'It's a little tradition of mine. Whenever my wife's been in an explosion, I like to make a quick trip to the hospital.' He sat on the edge of the bed, his eyes keen on her face, and held up three fingers. 'How many do you see?'

She remembered more now – being awakened half a dozen times through the night and seeing his face looming over her while he asked that same question. 'How many times are you going to ask me that?'

'It's become a habit now. It'll take me a while to break it. How many?'

'Thirty-six.' She smiled thinly when he simply continued to stare. 'Okay, three. Now get your fingers out of my face. I'm still mad at you.'

'Now I'm devastated.' When she started to shift he laid a hand on her shoulder. 'Stay.'

'What do I look like, a cocker spaniel?'

'Actually, there's a resemblance around the eyes.' He kept his hand firmly in place. 'Eve, you're staying in bed through the morning.'

'I am not—'

'Think of it this way. I can make you.' He reached out, caught her chin in his hand. 'Then you'd be humiliated. You really hate that. Think how much easier it would be on your pride and ego if you decided to stay in bed a couple more hours.'

They were fairly well matched physically, and Eve figured they were about even in takedowns. But there was a look in his eyes that warned he'd make good on his threat. And she wasn't feeling quite her best.

'Maybe I wouldn't mind staying in bed a couple hours, if I had some coffee.'

The hand on her shoulder slid up to her cheek. 'Maybe I'll get you some.' He leaned forward to kiss her lightly, then found himself holding her tight against him, burying his face

202

in her hair, rocking as every thought and fear he'd held back during the night flooded free. 'Oh God.'

The emotions that poured out of him in those two words swamped her. 'I'm all right. Don't worry. I'm all right.'

He thought he'd dealt with it, thought that through the long night he'd conquered this sick, shaky sensation in his gut. But it shot back now, overwhelmingly strong. His only defense was to hold her. Just hold.

'The explosion came through Peabody's communicator – loud and clear.' As his system began to settle again, he laid his cheek against hers. 'There was a long, timeless period of blind terror. Getting there, then getting through the chaos. Blood and glass and smoke.' He ran his hands briskly up and down her arms as he drew back. 'Then I heard you, sniping at the MT, and life snapped back into place for me.' He did kiss her now, lightly. 'I'll get your coffee.'

Eve studied her hands as Roarke walked across the room. The scrapes and abrasions had been treated, and treated well. There was barely a mark left to show for their violent meeting with asphalt. 'No one ever loved me before you.' She lifted her gaze to his as he sat on the bed again. 'I didn't think I'd ever get used to it, and maybe I won't. But I've gotten to depend on it.'

She took the coffee he offered, then his hand. 'I was giving the MT grief because he wouldn't get me a communicator. I had to get one to call you, to tell you I was okay. It was the first thing I thought of when I came to. Roarke. That was the first thing in my head.'

He brought their joined hands to his lips. 'We've gone and done it, haven't we?'

'Done what?'

'Become a unit.'

It made her smile. 'I guess we have. Are we okay now?'

'We're fine. Clear liquids were recommended as your upon

awakening meal, but I imagine we'd like something more substantial.'

'I could eat the best part of a cow still on the hoof.'

'I don't know that we have that particular delicacy in the pantry, but I'll see what I can come up with.'

It wasn't so bad, she decided, this being tended to. Not when it included breakfast in bed. She plowed her way through a mushroom and chive omelette made from eggs laid by pampered brown hens.

'I just needed fuel,' she managed over a bite of a cinnamon bagel. 'I feel fine now.'

Roarke chose one of the thumb-sized raspberries from her breakfast tray. 'You look amazingly well under the circumstances. Have you any idea how a bomb was planted in your official unit?'

'I've got a couple of theories. I need to—' She broke off, frowned a little when a knock sounded on the door.

'Peabody, I imagine. She'd be prompt.' He went to the door himself to let her in.

'How is she?' Peabody whispered. 'I thought they might have kept her overnight at the hospital.'

'They might have, but then she'd have hurt me.'

'No whispering,' Eve called out. 'Peabody, I want a report.'

'Yes, sir.' Peabody crossed over to the bed, then grinned from ear to ear. The woman in a red silk nightie, settled back on a mountain of pillows in a huge bed, a tray loaded with food on fine china settled over her lap, was not the usual image of Eve Dallas. 'You look like something out of an old movie,' she began. 'You know, like . . . Bette Crawford.'

'That would be Davis,' Roarke told her, after he'd disguised a chuckle with a cough. 'Or Joan Crawford.'

'Whatever. You look sort of glam, Dallas.'

Mortified, Eve straightened up. 'I don't believe I asked for a report on my appearance, Officer Peabody.'

'She's still a little testy,' Roarke commented. 'Would you like some coffee, Peabody, a bit of breakfast?'

'I had some . . .' Her eyes brightened. 'Are those raspberries? Wow.'

'They're fresh. I have an agri-dome nearby. Make yourself comfortable.'

'When you two finish socializing, maybe we could take a moment to discuss . . . oh, I don't know, how about car bombs?'

'I have the reports.' Drawn by the raspberries, Peabody sat on the side of the bed. She balanced her shiny black shoe on the knee of her starched uniform pants. 'The sweepers and bomb team put it together pretty fast. Thanks, this is great,' she added when Roarke supplied her with a tray of her own. 'We used to grow raspberries when I was a kid.' She sampled one and sighed. 'Takes me back.'

'Try to stay in this decade, Peabody.'

'Yes, sir. I—' She glanced over at the three quick raps on the door. 'Must be McNab.'

McNab poked his head around the door. 'All clear. Hey, some bedroom. Outstanding. Is that coffee I smell? Hey, Lieutenant, looking decent. What kind of berries are those?'

He crossed the room as he spoke, the cat jogging in behind him. When both of them made themselves cozy on the bed, Eve simply gaped.

'Make yourself right at home, McNab.'

'Thanks.' He helped himself to her bowl of berries. 'You look steady, Lieutenant. Glad to see it.'

'If someone doesn't give me a goddamn report, I'm going to look a lot more than steady. You,' she decided, pointing at Peabody. 'Because normally you're not an idiot.'

'Yes, sir. The explosive device was a homemade boomer, and whoever put it together knew their stuff. It had a short range, classic for car explosives, which is why it took out your vehicle, but had – relatively speaking – little effect on the surrounding area. If you hadn't been in a jam, cars locked in on all sides, there would have been basically no outside damage to speak of.'

'Were there any fatalities?'

'No, sir. The vehicles on your perimeters were affected, and there were about twenty injuries – only three were serious. The rest were treated and released. You sustained serious injuries as you were outside of the vehicle and unprotected at the time of the explosion.'

Eve remembered the two teenagers who'd boarded by only moments before. If they'd still been in range . . . She ordered herself to shake that image away. 'Was it on a timer? How was it cued?'

'I'll take that.' McNab gave Galahad an absent stroke on the back as the cat curled next to Eve's legs. 'He went for the standard car boom style – which was his mistake. If he'd used a timer, well, let's just say you wouldn't be eating berries this morning, Lieutenant. He linked it to the ignition, figuring it would trigger when you engaged the engine, Fortunately for our side, you drive – or drove – a departmental joke. The electrical system, the guidance system, the ignition system, well, just about every damn system in your vehicle was flawed. My guess is when you started it up yesterday, it hiccuped a few times.'

'It took me three tries to get it going.'

'There you are.' McNab gestured with a berry, then popped it in his mouth. 'It threw the link with the boomer off, skipped over the trigger. It was primed, could have gone off at any time from there. You hit a pothole, stop short, and boom.'

'I slammed the door,' Eve murmured. 'When those idiot cab drivers pissed me off, I got out and slammed the door.'

'That's likely what did it. Nothing wrong with the boomer. I took a look at the debris myself, and I can tell you he used top-grade components. It was just waiting for the signal to trigger.'

Eve drew a breath. 'So what you're telling me is I owe my life to budget cuts and a departmental maintenance crew who have their heads up their butts.'

'Couldn't have put it better.' McNab patted her knee. 'If you'd been driving one of those rockets like the boys in Anti-Crime, you'd have gone up in the garage at Central and become a legend.'

'The garage. How the hell did he get into the garage to plant it?'

'I'll take that.' Peabody did her best not to speak through clenched teeth. Not only did McNab report in an unsuitably casual style, but it should have been her damn report. 'I swung by Central and requested a copy of the security disc for yesterday. Whitney cleared it.'

'Have you got it?'

'Yes, sir.' Smug now, Peabody patted her bag. 'Right here.'

'Well, let's – Oh for Christ's sake.' Eve swore as someone banged on the door yet again. 'Just come the hell in. We should be selling tickets.'

'Dallas.' Nadine rushed in, all but leaped on the bed. Her usually shrewd eyes were clouded with tears. 'You're all right? You're really all right. I've been sick worrying. None of my sources could get the status. Summerset wouldn't say anything but that you were resting every time I called. I had to come see for myself.'

'As you can see, I'm dandy. Just hosting a little breakfast party.' She picked up the bowl of berries McNab was rapidly depleting. 'Hungry?'

Nadine pressed her fingers to her lips to control the trembling. 'I know this is my fault. I know you could have been killed because of what I did.'

'Look, Nadine—'

'It was easy enough to put together,' Nadine interrupted. 'I go on air with that statement I hammered out of you,

207

and a couple hours later, your car blows up. He came after you because he heard the report, because I put it on the air.'

'Which is exactly what I intended.' Eve set the bowl down again. The last thing she needed on her conscience was a hysterical, guilty reporter. 'You didn't hammer anything out of me. I said what I wanted to say, and what I wanted you to broadcast. I needed him to make a move, and I needed him to make it in my direction.'

'What do you mean you—' As it struck home, Nadine held up a hand. It took a moment before she was certain she could speak. 'You used me?'

'I'd say that was quid pro quo, Nadine. We used each other.'

Nadine took a step back. Her face was bone white now, her eyes blazing. 'Bitch. Goddamn cop bitch.'

'Yeah.' Weary again, Eve rubbed her eyes. 'Wait a minute. A minute,' she repeated before Nadine could stalk out. 'Would you all give Nadine and me some space here? Peabody, McNab, set up in my office. Roarke . . . please.'

Peabody and McNab were already out the door when he walked to the bed, leaned down close. 'I think we'll have to discuss this latest development, Lieutenant.'

She decided it was best to say nothing, and waited for him to go out and quietly close the door behind him. 'He's not going to understand,' she murmured, then looked over at Nadine. 'Maybe you will.'

'Oh, I get it, Dallas. I get it. You want to move your investigation along, why not fake a statement to a credible on-air reporter. Just use her – after all, what does she matter? She doesn't have any feelings. She's just another idiot reading the news.'

'The statement wasn't faked. It was what I wanted to say.' Eve set the breakfast tray aside. Doctor's recommendation or not, she wasn't going to have this confrontation while lounging in bed. 'It was what I felt, and what, under most circumstances, I'd have kept to myself.'

She tossed the covers aside, got to her feet. Then realizing her legs weren't quite ready to support her, she abandoned pride for dignity and sat on the edge of the bed.

'It was impulse. That's not an excuse. I knew exactly what I was doing, and where you would go with it. But one thing, Nadine. It wouldn't have happened if you hadn't come after me with a camera.'

'That's my fucking job.'

'Yeah, and it's my fucking job to catch this guy. I've got lives on the line here, Nadine, and one of them may be Roarke's. That means I'll do anything it takes. Even use a friend.'

'You could have told me.'

'I could have. I didn't.' Her head was starting to pound, so she rested it in her hands. Meds wearing off, she supposed. It was just as well. 'You want me to tell you something in confidence, Nadine, I will. And where you go with it is your choice. I'm scared.' She moved her hands to cover her face, just for a moment. 'I'm scared to the bone because I know the others are just layers. He's working his way through them to get to the core. And the core is Roarke.'

Nadine stared. She'd never seen Eve really vulnerable. Hadn't known she could be. But the woman sitting on the bed, her sleep shirt hiked on her thighs, her head in her hands, wasn't a cop. Not then. She was just a woman.

'So, you wanted to make sure they had to go through you first.'

'That was the idea.'

A softened heart couldn't hold anger. She sat on the bed beside Eve, draped an arm around her shoulders. 'I guess I do understand. And I wish I wasn't so damn jealous. I've scouted around a lot and never hunted up what you've got with Roarke.'

'I figure it doesn't work that way. It finds you, and it grabs you by the throat and you can't do a damn thing about it.' She pressed the heels of her hands against her eyes, then sighed. 'But I stepped over the line with you, and I'm sorry.'

'Jesus, you must have a big bruise on the brain if you're apologizing to me.'

'Since there's nobody else here, and I think you're feeling sorry for me, I'll tell you I feel like I've been run over by a fleet of airbuses.'

'Go back to bed, Dallas.'

'Can't.' She scrubbed her hands over her face, hard, rolled her aching shoulders. 'He's still a step or two ahead, and I'm going to fix that.' When the thought occurred, she turned her head and studied Nadine. 'But if some hotshot on-air reporter were to broadcast that Lieutenant Dallas's injuries are serious, that she is recuperating at home and is expected to be laid up for a couple days . . .'

'You want me to lie to the public?' Nadine arched a brow.

'My injuries are pretty serious. Everybody's been saying so until I want to deck them. And I am recuperating at home, aren't I? You can see that for yourself.'

'And you will be laid up, as you put it, for a couple of days.'

'It already feels like a couple of days. It might buy me time, Nadine. He'll want to wait until I'm on my feet again before he tries to take the next one out. He isn't playing solo. He wants an opponent.' She shook her head. 'No, he wants me. Particularly. I can't play if I'm flat on my back and tranq'd.'

'I'll do it.' She rose, looked down at Eve. 'And let me tell you, Dallas, I wouldn't be surprised if Roarke sees to it that you are flat on your back and tranq'd for the next few days.' Hitching her bag on her arm, Nadine smiled. 'Anyway, I am glad you're not dead.'

'Me, too.'

When Nadine left her, Eve managed to rise and make her

way slowly into the shower. Bracing both hands against the tile, she ordered water, full force at one hundred degrees. Ten minutes later, she felt steadier, and by the time she was dressed, nearly normal.

But when she walked into her office, it took only one long stare from Roarke to have her inching back.

'I figured I'd just stretch out in the sleep chair. I feel pretty straight,' she hurried on when he said nothing. 'I guess that stop at the hospital last night was a good move. I appreciate it.'

'Do you think you'll get around me that way?'

'It was worth a shot.' She tried a smile, then let it go. 'Look, I'm okay. And I need to do this.'

'Then you'll do it, won't you? I have some things to see to myself.' He moved to his office door, then flicked a glance over his shoulder. 'Let me know when you have a free moment, Lieutenant. For more personal matters.'

'Well, shit,' Eve sighed when his door shut.

'Never seen anybody steam that cold,' McNab commented. 'He even gave me the shakes.'

'Do you ever shut up, McNab? I want to see the disc, garage security.' Skirting the sleep chair, Eve sat behind her desk. 'Cue it up, Peabody, start at sixteen hundred. That's about the time I logged in to Central.'

Struggling not to sulk over more personal matters, Eve kept her eyes glued to the monitor as the image flicked on. 'Keep it on the access doors. He had to come from somewhere.'

They watched cars and vans pull in and out. Each time, the scanner eye above the access doors blinked green for cleared.

'That wouldn't be a problem for him, would it, McNab? Anybody who can pull the electronic magic he's been pulling could skim by the security eye for garage level.'

'Security's tight there. With the bombs in public buildings plague during the Urban Wars, all government and state facilities had new security installed at all access areas.' He nodded, kept watching. 'Even with budget cuts, they get maintained and upgraded twice a year. That's federal law. A specialized droid unit does spot inspections on a regular basis.'

'Could he do it?'

'He could, but it wouldn't be a round of Rocket Racers. And it's a hell of a lot riskier than a vid-game. If the alarm trips, all access and exit areas are automatically sealed. He'd be in a box.'

'He was pissed, and he's cocky.' Eve leaned back. 'He'd have risked it – and since he didn't trip any alarm, he pulled it off. He got into Cop Central garage, planted the boomer, and got out. That's the only place he could have gotten to my car during the time frame. Computer, split screen, second image section AB, level two. There's my vehicle, safe and sound.'

'You don't want to see it now,' Peabody commented and managed to suppress the shudder. 'They hauled it in to vehicle analysis. I shot through the automatic requisition for a new unit.'

'They'll probably stick a couple of bolts in it and expect me to make do.' However foolish and sentimental it was, she almost hoped they did. 'Idiot bureaucrats are always . . . wait, wait, what's this?'

Turbo-van, the computer told her helpfully. Model Jet-stream, manufactured 2056—

'Stop, freeze image. Look at this.' Eve gestured Peabody closer. 'The windows are privacy tinted. Surveillance vans aren't allowed to have that tint on the driver's area. And those plates, see the plates? That's not a van ID. It's a cab plate, for God's sake. Our boy's in there, Peabody.'

'Good catch, Dallas.' Impressed, McNab tapped some keys and had the frozen image printing out in hard copy. 'I'll run the plates for you.'

'Let's see what he does,' Eve murmured. 'Continue, computer.' They watched the van circle the first level, climb slowly to the next. And stop directly behind Eve's car. 'We've got him. I knew he'd get sloppy.'

The van door opened. The man who stepped out was concealed in a long coat, and his hat was pulled low. 'Police issue. That's a beat cop's overcoat. It's a uniform's hat . . . But he got the shoes wrong. He's wearing air treads. Damn it, you can't see his face. He's wearing sunshades.'

Then he turned, looked directly into the camera. Eve got a glimpse of white, white skin, just a hint of the curve of a cheek. Then he lifted a slim wand, pointed it, and the picture swam with color.

'Fucking hell, he jammed it. What the hell was that he had in his hand? Play back.'

'I've never seen a jammer like it.' McNab shook his head both in bafflement and admiration as the image replayed and froze. 'It's no more than six inches long, barely thicker than a ski pole. You ought to have Roarke look at it.'

'Later.' Eve waved that away. 'We've got coloring, we've got height and build. And we've got the make of a van. Let's see what we can do with it.'

She continued to stare at the screen as if she could somehow see through the concealing shades and hat to his face. To his eyes. 'Peabody, run the make and model of the van. I want a list of everyone who owns one. McNab, find out when that cabbie lost his tag. And figure this: He's driving into the garage at six twenty-three – that's less than one hour after Nadine's broadcast. Maybe he already had the boomer made up, but he had to have time to rig it for transport, to decide on a plan, to find my location. And you bet your ass he needed time to have a temper fit. How much time did he spend in transpo?'

She sat back again and smiled. 'I'm betting he's located downtown, within a ten-block radius of Cop Central. So we're going to start working our own backyard.'

Smiling, she ordered her computer to continue. She wanted to see just how long it took the son of a bitch to rig her car.

Chapter Fourteen

Eve wasn't in the mood for another marital bout, but she thought it best to get it over with. She needed Roarke's eye, his contacts – and, since she was going to follow her commander's request and travel to Ireland, his expertise in a foreign country.

Since Peabody and McNab had begun sniping at each other like longtime cohabitants, she'd separated them, shooing them off to different assignments in different locales. With their current competitive level, she hoped to have her answers from both of them by midday.

She paused outside Roarke's office door, sucked in a bracing breath, and gave what she hoped was a brisk and somewhat wifely knock.

When she entered, he held up a finger, signaling her to wait while he continued to address two hologram images. '. . . Until I'm free to travel to the resort personally, I'll trust you'll handle these relatively minor details. I expect Olympus to be fully operational by the target date. Understood?'

When there was no response other than respectful nods, he leaned back. 'End transmission.'

'Problem?' Eve asked when the holograms faded.

'A handful of minor ones.'

'Sorry to interrupt, but have you got a minute?'

Deliberately, he glanced at his wrist unit. 'Or two. What can I do for you, Lieutenant?'

'I really hate when you use that tone.'

'Do you? Pity.' He leaned back, steepled his fingers. 'Would you like to know what I hate?'

'Oh, I figure you'll tell me, but right now I'm pressed. I've got McNab and Peabody in the field chasing leads. I'm locked in here because I planted a story through Nadine that I'm busted up and recuperating at home.'

'You're getting good at that. Planting stories.'

She jammed her hands in her pockets. 'Okay, we'll run through it and clear the air. I made the statement, crossed the official line, to insult and challenge the killer to make a move on me. I'm supposed to serve and protect and I had to figure if he swung his aim in my direction, I'd buy time for whoever he'd targeted next. It worked, and as I'd calculated, he was pissed off enough to be sloppy, so we've got some leads we didn't have twenty-four hours ago.'

Roarke let her finish. To give himself time he rose, walked to the window. Absently he adjusted the tint of the glass to let in more light. 'When did you decide I was gullible, or simply stupid, or that I would be pleased to know that you had used yourself to shield me?'

So much for the cautious route, she decided. 'Gullible and stupid are the last things I believe you are. And I wasn't considering whether or not you'd be pleased that I deflected his attention from you to me. Having you alive's enough – even pissed off and alive is fine by me.'

'You had no right. No right to stand in front of me.' He turned back now, his eyes vividly blue with temper that had gone from frigid to blaze. 'No fucking right to risk yourself on my behalf.'

'Oh really. Is that so?' She stalked forward until they were toe to toe. 'Okay, you tell me. You keep looking me dead in the eye and you tell me you wouldn't have done the same if it was me in jeopardy.'

'That's entirely different.'

'Why?' Her chin came up and her finger jabbed hard into his chest. 'Because you have a penis?'

He opened his mouth, a dozen vile and furious words searing his tongue. It was the cool, utterly confident gleam in her eyes that stopped him. He turned away and braced both fists on the desk. 'I don't care for the fact that you have a point.'

'In that case I'll just finish it out so you can swallow it all in one lump. I love you, and I need you every bit as much as you love and need me. Maybe I don't say it as often or show it as smoothly, but that doesn't make it any less true. If it pricks your ego to know that I'd protect you, that's just too bad.'

He lifted his hands, dragged them up through his hair before he turned to her. 'That's a hell of a way to diffuse an argument.'

'Did I?'

'Since any argument I could attempt would make me sound like a fool, it would seem you have.'

'Good thinking.' She risked a grin at him. 'So, if you're finished being mad at me, can I run a few things by you?'

'I didn't say I was finished being mad, I said I was finished arguing with you.' He sat on the corner of his desk. 'But yes, feel free to run a few things by me.'

Satisfied with that, she handed him a disc. 'Put that in. I've got a still on it you can project on screen. Enhance it to full.'

He did as she requested, then studied the image. He could see the fingers of a gloved hand wrapped around a wand-shaped device. The hilt was blocked from view but the pattern of notches and buttons on the stem were clear. A light at the tip glowed green.

'It's a jammer,' he said. 'More sophisticated and certainly more compact than anything I've seen on the market.' He stepped closer to the screen. 'The manufacturer's ID – if there is one – is likely on the hilt and hidden by his hand, so that's no help. One of my R and D departments has been working on a smaller, more powerful jammer. I'll have to check the status.'

That caught her off guard. 'You're manufacturing this kind of thing?'

He caught the tone, smiled a little. 'Roarke Industries handles a number of contracts for the government – for a number of governments, as it happens. The Defense and Security Department is always looking for new toys such as this. And they pay well.'

'So a device like this might be in the works in one of your departments? Brennen was in communications. One of his research arms could have been working on one.'

'It's easy enough to find out. I'll check which one of my particular arms has something along these lines on the boards, and have one of my moles check Brennen's organization.'

'You have spies?'

'Data gatherers, darling. They object to being called spies. Have you got the rest of your man on here?'

'Click one back.'

'Computer, display previous image on screen.'

Roarke frowned at the picture and, using the vehicles for points of reference, speculated. 'About five-ten, probably about one-sixty by the way that coat hangs on him. He's very pale from the looks of that swatch of skin you can see. I wouldn't say he spends a lot of time outdoors, so his profession, if he has one, is likely white collar.'

Roarke tilted his head and continued. 'No way to tell age, except he . . . holds himself youthfully. You can see part of his mouth. He's smiling. Smug bastard. His taste in outerwear is miserably inferior.'

'It's a beat cop's topcoat,' Eve said dryly. 'But I'm inclined away from thinking he's got a connection with the department. Cops don't wear air treads, and no beat cop's going to have access to the kind of knowledge or equipment this guy has or EDD would have snatched him up. You can pick up one of those coats at a couple dozen outlets in New York alone.' She waited a beat. 'But we'll run it anyway.'

'The van?'

'We're checking. If he didn't boost it, and it's registered in the state of New York, we'll narrow the field considerably.'

'Considerably's optimistic, Eve. I probably have twenty of these vans registered in New York to various outlets. Delivery vans, maintenance units, interstaff transpos.'

'It's more than we started with.'

'Yes. Computer, disengage.' He turned to her. 'Peabody and McNab can handle a great deal of the legwork on this for the next day or two?'

'Sure. Then Feeney's back pretty soon and I'm grabbing him.'

'They're finished with Jennie's body. It's being released this afternoon.'

'Oh.'

'I need you to come with me, Eve, to Ireland. I realize the timing might not be convenient for you, but I'm asking you for two days.'

'Well, I—'

'I can't go without you.' The impatience surfaced, glowed in his eyes. 'I won't go without you. I can't take the chance of being three thousand miles away if this bastard tries to get to you again. I need you with me. I've already made the arrangements. We can leave in an hour.'

She thought it best to walk to the window so that he couldn't see she was fighting to hold back a grin. It was dishonest, she supposed, not to tell him she'd intended to ask him to go to Dublin with her that afternoon. But it was too sweet an opportunity to miss.

'It's important to you?'

'Yes, very.'

She turned back to smile at him with what she believed was admirable restraint. 'Then I'll go pack.'

'I want the data as it comes in.' Eve paced the cabin of Roarke's private plane and stared at Peabody's sober face in her palm 'link. 'Send everything to the hotel in Dublin, and send it coded.'

'I'm working on the van. There are over two hundred of that make and model with privacy tint registered in New York.'

'Run them down. Every one.' She skimmed a hand through her hair, determined not to let a single detail slip by. 'The shoes looked new. The computer should be able to estimate the size. Run the shoes, Peabody.'

'You want me to run the shoes?'

'That's what I said. Sales of that brand of air tread for the last two – no, make it three months. We could get lucky.'

'It's comforting to believe in miracles, Lieutenant.'

'Details, Peabody. You'd better believe in the details. Cross-check with sales of the beat cop's coat, cross-check that with sales of the statue. Is McNab working on the jammer?'

'He said so.' Peabody's voice chilled. 'I haven't heard from him in over two hours. He's supposed to be talking to the contact Roarke gave him in Electronic Future's research and development.'

'Same orders for him, all data, coded, as it's accessed.'

'Yes, sir. Mavis has called a couple times. Summerset told her that you were resting comfortably and under doctor's orders couldn't receive visitors. Dr Mira also called, and sent flowers.'

'Yeah?' Surprised and disconcerted by the idea, Eve paused. 'Maybe you should thank her or something. Damn, how sick am I supposed to be?'

'Pretty sick, Dallas.'

'I hate that. The bastard's probably celebrating. Let's make sure he doesn't party for long. Get me the data, Peabody. I'll be back inside of forty-eight hours, and I want to nail him.'

'Swinging the hammer as we speak, sir.'

219

'Don't bash your thumb,' Eve warned and ended transmission. She slipped the 'link back into her pocket and looked at Roarke. He'd been lost in his own thoughts throughout the flight, saying little. Eve wondered if it was time to tell him she'd already contacted the Dublin police and had an appointment with an Inspector Farrell.

She sat across from him, bounced her fingers on her knee. 'So . . . are you going to take me on a tour of the favored locales from your misspent youth?'

He didn't smile as she'd hoped, but he did shift his gaze from the window to her face. 'They wouldn't be particularly picturesque.'

'They may not be among the tourist hot spots, but it would be helpful to brush up with some of your former friends and companions.'

'Three of my former friends and companions are dead.'

'Roarke—'

'No.' Annoyed with himself, he held up a hand. 'Brooding doesn't help. I'll take you to the Penny Pig.'

'The Penny Pig?' She straightened quickly. 'Brennen's wife said he used to go there. A bar, right?'

'A pub.' Now he did smile. 'The social and cultural center of a race who goes from mother's milk straight to stout. And you should see Grafton Street. I used to pluck pockets there. Then there are the narrow alleyways of South Dublin where I ran games of chance until I moved my portable casino into the back room of Jimmy O'Neal's butcher shop.'

'Link sausage and loaded dice.'

'And more. Then there was the smuggling. An adventurous enterprise and the financial foundation for Roarke Industries.' He leaned forward, hooked her safety strap himself. 'And even with all that experience, I had my heart stolen by a cop and had to mend my ways.'

'Some of them.'

He laughed and glancing out the window watched Dublin

220

City rise toward them. 'Some of them. There's the River Liffey, and the bridges shine in the sun. A lovely place is Dublin Town of an evening.'

He was right, Eve decided when less than an hour later they were in the back of a limo and streaming along with traffic. She supposed she'd expected it to be more like New York, crowded and noisy and impatient. It certainly bustled, but there was a cheer beneath the pace.

Colorful doors brightened the buildings, arched bridges added charm. And though it was mid-November, flowers bloomed in abundance.

The hotel was a grand stone structure with arched windows and a castlelike air. She had only a glimpse of the lobby with its towering ceiling, regal furnishings, rich dark walls before they were whisked up to their suite.

Men like Roarke weren't expected to fuss with such pesky details as check-in. All was ready for their arrival. Huge urns of fresh flowers, massive bowls of fruit, and a generous decanter of fine Irish whiskey awaited them.

And the tall windows gleamed with the last red lights of the setting sun.

'I thought you'd prefer facing the street, so you could watch the city go by.'

'I do.' She was already at the windows, hands tucked in her back pockets. 'It's pretty, like . . . I don't know an animated painting. Did you see the glide-carts? Every one of them was shiny, the umbrellas stiff and bright. Even the gutters look like someone just swept them clean.'

'They still give tidy village awards in Ireland.'

She laughed at that, amused and touched. 'Tidy village?'

'It's a matter of pride, and a quality of life most are reluctant to give up. In the countryside you'll still see stone fences and fields green enough to startle the eye. Cottages and cabins with thatched roofs. Peat fires and flowers in the yard. The Irish grip their traditions in a firm hand.'

'Why did you leave here?'

'Because my traditions were less attractive and more easily let go.' He drew a bright yellow daisy from an arrangement and handed it to her. 'I want a shower, then I'll show you.'

She turned back to the window, twirling the daisy absently by its stem. And she wondered how much more she would see of the man she'd married before the night was over.

There were parts of Dublin that weren't so cheerful, where the alleys carried that universal smell of garbage gone over and thin cats slunk in shadows. Here she saw the underbelly of any city, men walking quickly, shoulders hunched, eyes shifting right and left. She heard harsh laughter with desperate undertones and the wail of a hungry baby.

She saw a group of boys, the oldest of them no more than ten. They walked casually, but Eve caught the cool, calculating gleam in their eyes. If she'd had her weapon, her hand would have been on it.

The street was their turf, and they knew it.

One bumped lightly into Roarke as they passed. 'Beg pardon,' he began, then cursed ripely when Roarke grabbed him by the scruff of the neck.

'Mind the hands, boyo. I don't care for any but my own in my pockets.'

'Turn me loose.' He swung, comically missed in a round-house as Roarke held him at arm's length. 'Bloody bastard, I never pinched nothing.'

'Only because you've thick hands. Christ, I was better than you when I was six.' He gave the boy a quick shake, more in exasperation of his clumsiness than in annoyance with the act itself. 'A drunk tourist from the west counties would have felt that grope. And you were obvious as well.' He looked down into the boy's furious face and shook his head. 'You'd do better as the pass-off man than the pincher.'

'That's great, Roarke, why don't you give him a few lessons on thievery while you're at it.'

At Eve's words the boy's eyes flickered and narrowed. He stopped struggling. 'They tell tales of a Roarke who used to work these streets. Lived in the shanties and made himself a right fortune off quick fingers and nerves.'

'You've got the nerves, but you don't have the fingers.'

'They work well enough on most.' Relaxed now, the boy flashed Roarke a quick and charming grin. 'And if they don't I can outrun any cop on two legs.'

Roarke leaned down, lowered his voice. 'This is my wife, you bonehead, and she's a cop.'

'Jay-sus.'

'Exactly.' He reached into his pocket, pulled out a handful of coins. 'I'd keep these for myself if I were you. Your associates scattered like rats. They didn't stand with you and don't deserve a share.'

'I won't be after dividing it.' The coins disappeared into his pocket. 'It's been a pleasure making your acquaintance.' He slid his gaze to Eve, nodded with surprising dignity. 'Missus,' he murmured, then ran like a rabbit into the dark.

'How much did you give him?' Eve asked.

'Enough to tickle his humor and not disturb his pride.' He slid his arm around her waist and began to walk again.

'Remind you of someone?'

'No indeed,' Roarke said with a cheer he hadn't expected to feel. 'I'd never have been caught so handily.'

'I don't see that it's anything to brag about. Besides, your fingers wouldn't be so light these days.'

'I'm sure you're right. A man loses his touch with age.' Smiling, he held out the badge he'd lifted out of her pocket. 'I think this is yours. Lieutenant.'

She snatched it back and struggled to be neither amused nor impressed. 'Show-off.'

'I could hardly let you disparage my reputation. And here

we are.' He stopped again, studying the pub. 'The Penny Pig. Hasn't changed much. A bit cleaner maybe.'

'It could be readying for competition for the tidy village award.'

It was unimposing from the outside. The grilled window boasted a painting of a sly-eyed white pig. No flowers bloomed here, but the glass was free of smears, the sidewalk free of litter.

The minute Roarke opened the door she felt the rush of heat, the jittery flow of voices and music, the cloud of beer fumes and smoke.

It was one long, narrow room. Men were lined at the old wooden bar. Others, including women and young children, were packed onto chairs around low tables where glasses crowded the space. At the far end at a tiny booth sat two men. One played a fiddle, the other a small box that squeezed out a jumpy tune.

High on the wall was a mini view screen with the sound turned off. On it a man struggled to ride a bicycle down a pitted lane and continued to take tumbles. No one appeared to be watching the show.

Behind the bar two men worked, pulling drafts, pouring liquor. Several people glanced over as they entered, but the conversations never lagged.

Roarke moved to the end of the bar. He recognized the older of the bartenders, a man of his own age who'd once been thin as a rail and filled with wicked humor.

While he waited for service, he lifted a hand to Eve's shoulder and rubbed absently. He was grateful to have her beside him when he took this short trip into the past.

'Guinness, a pint and a glass please.'

'On the way.'

'What am I going to be drinking?' Eve demanded.

'The heart of the realm,' Roarke murmured, and watched his old friend build the drinks with an admirable expertise.

'It's an acquired taste. If you don't care for it, we'll get you a Harp.'

Eve narrowed her eyes against the smoke. 'Don't they know tobacco's been banned in public places?'

'Not in Ireland it hasn't, not in the pubs.'

The bartender came back with the drinks. Eve lifted hers to sip while Roarke dug more coins from his pocket. Her brows drew together at the first sip, then she shook her head with the second. 'Tastes like something I should chew.'

Roarke chuckled and the bartender beamed. 'You're a Yank then. Your first Guinness?'

'Yeah.' Eve frowned at the glass, turning it slowly while examining the dark brown liquid with its foamy white head.

'And your last as well?'

She sipped again, holding the beer in her mouth for a moment, then swallowing. 'No. I think I like it.'

'That's fine then.' The bartender grinned widely, and neatly nudged Roarke's coins back. 'You'll have the first on me.'

'That's kind of you, Brian.' Roarke watched Brian turn from admiring Eve to study him.

'Do I know you? There's a familiar look about you that I'm not quite placing.'

'It's been fifteen years, more or less, so your memory might be dim even after all the times we had. I recognized you right enough, Brian Kelly, though you've added a stone or two. Perhaps three.' Roarke flashed a grin, and it was the grin that did it.

'Well, bloody hell, lock up your women. It's Roarke himself.' Brian's lips stretched in a mile-wide grin as he rammed a fist into Roarke's face.

'Christ Jesus' was the best Roarke could do as his head snapped back. He kept his balance, shook his head to clear it.

'Sucker punch,' Eve commented, and took another sip of stout. 'Nice pals you've got, Roarke.'

'I owed you that.' Brian shook a finger. 'You never did come back with the hundred pounds that was my fair share of the cargo money.'

Philosophically Roarke swiped the back of his hand over his cut lip to blot the blood. After the briefest of pauses, both the music and the hum of conversation continued. 'It would have cost me more than a hundred pounds to come back at that point with the guarda on the prowl.' Roarke picked up his pint, sipped to soothe his mouth. 'I thought I sent it to you.'

'Hell you did. But what's a hundred pounds between friends.' With a roaring laugh, Brian grabbed Roarke's shoulders, yanked him over the bar, and kissed him dead on his bleeding mouth. 'Welcome home, you bloody bastard. You there!' He shouted to the musicians. 'Play "The Wild Rover" for me old friend here, for that's what he ever was. And I've heard he's got gold in great store all right, enough to buy a round for the house.'

The patrons cheered and the music turned lively.

'I'll stand the house for a round, Bri, if you'll give me and my wife a few minutes of your time back in the snug.'

'Wife, is it?' He roared again and pulled Eve forward for a hearty kiss. 'Blessed Mary save us all. I'll give you a few minutes and more, for I own the place now. Michael O'Toole, you come on back and give Johnny a hand with the bar. I've got some catching up to do.'

He pressed a button beneath the bar and had a narrow door at the far end swinging open.

The snug, Eve discovered, was a tiny private room fitted out with a single table and a scattering of chairs. The light was dim, but the floor gleamed like a mirror. Through the closed door, the music piped.

'You married this reprobate,' Brian said, sighing as he lowered himself onto a chair that creaked beneath his weight.

'Yeah, well, he begged.'

'You've got yourself a pretty one here, boyo. A long one with eyes the color of the best Irish.'

'She'll do me.' Roarke took out his cigarettes, offered one to Brian.

'American.' He closed his eyes in pleasure as Roarke lighted it for him. 'We still have a hard time getting these here.'

'I'll send you a case to make up for the hundred.'

'I can sell off a case of Yanks for ten times that.' Brian grinned. 'So I'll take it. What brings you to the Penny Pig? I hear you come to Dublin now and again on your rich man's business, but you don't wander our way.'

'No, I haven't.' Roarke met his eyes. 'Ghosts.'

'Aye.' Brian nodded, understanding perfectly. 'They're thick in the streets and alleys. But you've come now, with your pretty wife.'

'I have. You'd have heard about Tommy Brennen and the others.'

'Murdered.' Brian poured from the bottle of whiskey he'd taken from beneath the bar. 'Tommy would come in now and again over the years. Not often, but now and again, and we'd have a song out of him. I saw him and his wife once, and his children, strolling on Grafton Street. He saw me as well, but it wasn't the time to speak to the likes of me. Tommy, well, he preferred keeping certain parts of what had been from his family.'

He lifted his glass more in resignation than toast. 'Shawn now, he was a rare one. He'd send word back from New York, always claiming he was making a fortune, and when he'd finished counting all his money, back he'd be. A fine liar was Shawn,' he said and drank to him.

'I've brought Jennie's body back with me.'

'Have you?' His wide and ruddy face sober, Brian nodded. 'That's the right thing. She'd have wanted that. She had a sweet heart, did Jennie. I hope they catch the bloody bastard who did her.'

'That's one of the reasons we're here, hoping you can help.'

'Now how could I do that, being an ocean away from where the deed was done?'

'Because it all started here, with Marlena.' Roarke took Eve's hand, 'I didn't properly introduce you to my wife, Brian. This is Eve. Lieutenant Eve Dallas, New York City Police and Security.'

Brian choked on his whiskey, thumped his chest to help the air into his lungs. His eyes watered. 'A cop? You married a bloody cop?'

'*I* married a bloody criminal,' Eve muttered, 'but nobody ever thinks of that.'

'I do, darling.' Amused, Roarke kissed her hand. 'Constantly.'

Brian let go another of his rollicking laughs and poured another shot. 'Here's to the pair of you. And to the icicles that are forming in Hell.'

He'd have to postpone the next.

He prayed for patience. After all, he'd waited so long already. But it was a sign from God, he understood that. He had veered from the path, acted on his own desires, when he had planted the bomb in her car.

He had sinned, and so prayed for forgiveness as well as patience. He had only to listen to the guiding force. He knew that, and was repentant. Tears blurred his vision as he knelt, accepting his penance, his punishment for his conceit and arrogance.

Like Moses, he had faltered in his mission and tested God.

The rosaries clinked musically in his hands as he moved from bead to bead, from decade to decade with a practiced ease and a deep devotion.

Hail Mary, full of grace.

He used no cushion for his knees, for he'd been taught that forgiveness demanded pain. Without it, he would have felt himself uncleansed. Votive candles, white for purity, flickered and carried the faint smell of wax pooling on wax.

Between them, the image of the Virgin watched him silently. Forgivingly.

His face was shadowed by the candlelight, and aglow with the visions of his own salvation.

Blessed art thou among women.

The anthem to the Virgin Mother was his favorite prayer, and no penance at all. It was comfort. As he completed the fifth of the nine rosaries he'd been given as penance, he pondered the Sorrowful Mysteries. He cleared his mind of worldly cares and carnal thoughts.

Like Mary, he was a virgin. He had been taught that his innocence and his purity were the paths to glory. Whenever lust crept its stealthy way into his heart, heating his blood, slickening his skin, he fought that whispering demon with all his might. Both his body, well trained, and his mind, well honed, were dedicated to his faith.

And the seeds of his faith were sown in blood, rooted in vengeance, and bloomed with death.

Chapter Fifteen

Eve could hear the low murmur of an international news report from the parlor screen when she awoke. Her body clock was a mass of confusion. She figured it was still the middle of the night according to her system, and a nice, rainy dawn where her body happened to be.

She didn't think Roarke had slept long, but accepted that he needed less sleep than anyone she'd ever known. He hadn't been talkative when they'd gotten back from the Penny Pig the night before, but he had been . . . hungry.

He'd made love like a man desperate to find something, or to lose it, and she had little choice but to grab hold and join the ride.

Now he'd already been up and working, she imagined. Scanning the news reports, the stock reports, making calls, pushing buttons. She decided it was best to leave him to it until her mind cleared.

She eyed the bathroom shower dubiously. It was a threesided affair of white tile that left the user's butt exposed to the room. Search as she might, she found no mechanism that would close her in and protect her privacy.

It was nearly six feet in length, with ceiling heads angled down to soak or spray. She went for spray, hot, and struggled to ignore the opening behind her as she soaped and rinsed.

Brian had been little help, she mused, though he had promised to put out the word, discreetly, and try to gather any information on the families of the men who'd killed Marlena. A few of them he knew personally and had laughed off the idea of any of them having the skill, the brains, or the nerve to choreograph a series of murders in New York.

Eve preferred to look at police records and solicit the opinion of a professional colleague. All she had to do was nudge Roarke in a different direction so that she would have the morning free to brainstorm with Inspector Farrell.

Confident that would only take a bit of maneuvering, she ordered the spray off, turned to step out of the shower, then yelped as if scalded.

Roarke was standing behind her, leaning back against the wall, hands dipped casually in his pockets.

'What the hell are you doing?'

'Getting you a towel.' Smiling, he reached for one on the warming rack. Then held it out of reach. 'Sleep well?'

'Yeah, well enough.'

'I ordered breakfast when I heard the shower running. Full Irish. You'll like it.'

She dragged her dripping hair out of her eyes. 'Okay. Are you going to give me that towel?'

'I'm thinking about it. What time is your appointment with the guarda?'

She'd started to make a grab for the towel, then pulled back, wary. 'Who?'

'The police, darling Eve. The Dublin cops. This morning, I imagine. Early. By, what, nine?'

She shifted, crossed her arms over her breasts, but it didn't help. 'I never said I was meeting anyone.' When he only lifted a brow, she swore. 'Know-it-alls are very irritating to mortals. Give me that damn towel.'

'I don't know it all, but I know you. Are you meeting someone in particular?'

'Listen, I can't have this conversation naked.'

'I like having conversations when you're naked.'

'That's because you're a sick man, Roarke. Give me that towel.'

He held it up by two fingers, and his eyes gleamed. 'Come and get it.'

'You're just going to try to get me back into bed.'

Now his smile spread and he moved toward her. 'I wasn't thinking of the bed.'

'Step back.' She held up a hand, feinted to the right. 'I'll hurt you.'

'God, I love when you threaten me. It excites me.'

'I'll give you excitement,' she promised. She'd just judged her chances of getting past him and out the door, found them passable, when he tossed the towel in her direction. When she grabbed for it, he caught her around the waist and had her pinned against the wall before she could decide whether to laugh or swear.

'I'm not fighting with you in here.' She blew at her wet hair. 'Everybody knows the majority of home accidents involving personal injuries happen in the bathroom. It's a death trap.'

'We'll have to risk it.' Slowly he lifted her hands over her head then scraped his teeth along her throat. 'You're wet, and you're warm, and you're tasty.'

Her blood fired, her muscles went lax. What the hell, she thought, she had at least two hours to spare. She turned her head and caught his mouth with hers. 'You're dressed,' she murmured. In a lightning move she tipped her weight, shifted, and reversed their positions. Hers eyes laughed into his. 'Just let me fix that for you.'

Wild vertical sex was a pretty good way to start the day, Eve decided, and when it was followed by what the Irish called breakfast, it was nirvana.

Eggs creamily scrambled, potatoes fried with onions, sausage and bacon and thick slabs of bread smothered with fresh butter, all topped off with coffee by the gallon.

'Um,' she managed, plowing her way through. 'Can't.'

'Can't what?'

'Can't eat like this every day. Whole country'd waddle to their death.'

It continually satisfied him to watch her eat, to see her stoke up that slim body that burned off fuel with nerves and energy. 'It's a now-and-again sort of thing. A weekend indulgence.'

'Good. Mmm. What's in this meat stuff here?'

Roarke eyed the blood pudding she shoveled in and shook his head. 'You'll thank me for not telling you. Just enjoy it.'

'Okay.' She paused for breath, flicked a glance at him. Sighed. 'I'm meeting Inspector Farrell at nine. I guess I should have told you.'

'You're telling me now,' he pointed out and glanced at his wrist unit for the time. 'That'll give me enough time to clean up a few details before we go.'

'*We?*' Eve set down her fork before she ate another bite and did permanent damage. 'Farrell is meeting with me – as in *me* – as a professional courtesy. And you know what? I bet she doesn't bring her husband along.'

He had his datebook out, checking appointments, and glanced up with an easy smile. 'Was that an attempt to put me in my place?'

'Figure it out.'

'All right, and you figure this.' Taking his time, he topped off both their coffee cups. 'You can pursue this investigation your way.' His gaze flicked up to hers, glimmered there. 'And I can pursue my interests in the matter in my way. Are you willing to risk my finding him first?'

He could be hard, she knew. And ruthless. He was undeniably clever. 'You've got twenty minutes to handle your details before we leave.'

'I'll be ready.'

Inspector Katherine Farrell was a striking woman. Perhaps forty-five, she had hair of blazing red neatly coiled at the nape of a long, slim neck. Her eyes were moss green, her skin the color of Irish cream. She wore a trim and tailored gray suit military in style that showcased lovely legs. She offered both Eve and Roarke her hand and a cup of tea.

'This would be your first trip to Ireland then, Lieutenant Dallas?'

'Yes.'

Though her tidy office was equipped with an AutoChef, Farrell poured the tea out of a white china pot. It was one of her small pleasures. And it gave her time to measure and judge the Yank cop and the man known only as Roarke. 'I hope you'll have time to see some of the country while you're here.'

'Not on this trip.'

'Pity.' She turned, teacups in hand, a smile on her lips. She found Eve both less and more than she'd expected. Less brittle than she chose to think of American police. And more tough than she expected to find a woman who had married a man with Roarke's reputation. 'And you're from Dublin originally,' she said to Roarke.

He recognized the speculation in her eyes, and the knowledge. He might not have a criminal record – officially – but he did have a reputation. And memories were long. 'I grew up in the shanties in South Dublin.'

'A difficult area, even now.' She sat, crossed her spectacular legs. 'And you have businesses – ah, enterprises so to speak, here still.'

'Several.'

'It's good for the economy. You've brought the body of Jennie O'Leary back to be waked and buried.'

'I have. We'll wake her tonight.'

Farrell nodded, sipped delicately at her tea. 'I've a cousin who once stayed at the B and B she ran in Wexford. I'm told it was a lovely place. Have you been there?'

'No.' He inclined his head, understanding the question

between the questions. 'I hadn't seen Jennie in over twelve years.'

'But you did contact her just before she went to New York and was killed.'

Eve set her cup aside with a click of china on wood. 'Inspector Farrell, this homicide and the others are under my jurisdiction. You don't have the authority to interview Roarke in this matter.'

Tough, Farrell thought again. *And territorial. Well, so am I.* 'All three of your dead were Irish citizens. We have an interest, a keen one, in your investigation.'

'It's simple enough to answer,' Roarke put in before Eve could fire up again. 'I contacted Jenny after Shawn Conroy was murdered. I was concerned for her safety.'

'Hers in particular?'

'Hers, and several others I'd been close to when I lived in Dublin.'

'Let's just put this on the table.' Eve drew Farrell's attention back to her, where she wanted to keep it. 'I received a transmission, expertly jammed and so far untraceable, from an individual who claimed his game was vengeance sanctioned by God, and he'd chosen me for his opponent. He gave me a Bible quote, and a riddle, and upon following them I discovered the mutilated body of Thomas Brennen in his New York residence. Subsequently I learned that Roarke had known Thomas Brennen when they had both lived in Dublin.'

'I've spoken with his widow myself,' Farrell put in. 'She said you were kind to her.'

Eve lifted her brows. 'We hardly ever kick widows around in the morgue anymore. It's bad for public relations.'

Farrell drew a breath and watched two tourist trams, bright in their green and white paint, pass her windows. 'Point taken, Lieutenant.'

'Good. The following day I received another transmission, another set of clues, and found the body of Shawn Conroy.

This pattern, and the fact that the second murder took place in one of Roarke's empty rental units, indicated that there was a connection to Roarke.'

'And following that you followed the path from yet another transmission and discovered the body of Jennie O'Leary in a hotel which Roarke also owns.'

'That's correct. A detective from our electronics division subsequently followed the transmission bounce, covering several points, one of which initially indicated that the transmission originated in our home. However, there was an echo which proved this to be false. At this time we are analyzing the echo and are confident that we will pinpoint the exact origin.'

'And at this time your prime suspect is a man in Roarke's employ, a man who also lived in Dublin at one time. Summerset,' she continued, smiling thinly at Roarke. 'We've been able to access very little background information on him.'

'You're a bit behind, Inspector,' Eve said dryly. 'Upon further investigation and personality testing, Summerset is no longer prime. Indications are that he was being used to mislead the investigation.'

'Yet the direction of all points back to Dublin, which is why you're here.'

'I received the cooperation of Roarke and Summerset. I believe that the motives for these crimes have their roots in the rape/murder of Summerset's minor daughter, Marlena, nearly twnety years ago. She was abducted and held by a group of men who threatened to harm her if Roarke didn't agree to their demands. However, his agreement was ignored and her body was dumped at the front door of the residence where Roarke, Summerset, and Marlena lived.'

'This happened here, in Dublin?'

'Blood was and is shed,' Roarke said coolly, 'even in your tidy streets, Inspector.'

Farrell's eyes hardened as she swiveled to her computer. 'When?'

It was Roarke who gave her the year, the month, the day, and then the hour.

'Marlena Summerset.'

'No. Kolchek. Her name was Marlena Kolchek.' *As Summerset's had been during that period*, Roarke thought, *but no records of Basil Kolchek exist. Not any longer. Summerset had come into existence only weeks after Marlena's death.* 'Not all children use their father's last name.'

Farrell sent him one quiet look, then called for the file.

'This matter was investigated and ruled death by misadventure. Investigating officer . . .' She trailed off, sighed. 'Inspector Maguire. You knew him?' she asked Roarke.

'Yes, I knew him.'

'I did not, not personally. But his reputation is not one this department has pride in. You knew the men who murdered this girl.'

'I knew them. They're dead.'

'I see.' Her gaze flickered. 'Their names, please.'

As Roarke listed each, Farrell pulled files, scanned them.

'They were not sterling citizens of our city,' she murmured. 'And they died badly. One could say . . . vengefully.'

'One could,' Roarke agreed.

'Men who choose that lifestyle often die badly,' Eve put in. 'It's my belief that due to the link to Marlena's murder, this killer has set out to avenge one or more of their deaths in the mistaken belief that Roarke was responsible. Those who died in New York also knew Marlena and the true circumstances of her death. Summerset was her father and maintains a close personal relationship with Roarke. I've distracted him for the moment, but we have another day or two at best before he kills the next.'

'Do you have any idea who will be next?'

'Nineteen years, Inspector,' Roarke said. 'I've contacted everyone I can think of who might be a target. But even that didn't help Jennie.'

237

'I can access official data on the families of these men,'
Eve began, 'but it's not enough. I need a personal take from a
professional eye. I need a cop's view, a cop who knows them,
their styles, their minds. I need a workable list of suspects.'

'Do you have a profile on your man?'

'I do.'

Farrell nodded. 'Then let's get to work.'

'Career criminals,' Farrell commented, tapping a slim black
pointer against her palm. They'd moved into a small, windowless
conference room with a trio of wall screens. She gestured
toward the first image. 'Ryan here, a bad one, I put him in
the nick myself five years back on armed robbery and assault.
He's vicious, but more a bully than a leader. He's been out for
six months – but it's doubtful he'll stay that way. He doesn't
fit your profile.'

Across the room Eve had tacked stills to a wide board,
victims on one side, possible suspects on the other. Taking
Farrell's word, she removed Ryan.

'O'Malley, Michael.'

'He was in the system the night Conroy was murdered.'
Eve frowned at the data beside the image. 'Drunk driving.'

'He has a problem with the bottle it seems.' Farrell scrolled
down, noted the dozens of violations for drunk and disorderly,
driving while intoxicated, disturbing the peace. 'And a wife
beater as well. A darling man.'

'He used to get pissed-faced then knock around the girl he
was courting. Annie, I think her name was.'

'Annie Murphy. And she married him and gets knocked
around even today.' Farrell sighed.

'A creep but not the killer.' Eve pulled down his still. 'How
about charmer number three.'

'Now here's a likely one. I've had dealings with Jamie
Rowan, and he's not a bonehead. Smart, smug. His mother's

family came from money that bought him a fine education. He has a taste for the high life.'

'Handsome son of a bitch,' Eve commented.

'That he is, and well aware of his charms. A gambling man is Jamie, and when those who lose don't pay quick enough, he has one of his spine crackers pay a visit. We questioned our boy here for accessory to murder just last year. It was one of his men right enough who did the deed on his orders. But we couldn't stick it.'

'Does he ever crack spines himself?'

'Not that we've ever proved.'

'We'll keep him up, but he looks too cool to me, more of a button pusher. Did you know him, Roarke?'

'Well enough to bloody his eye and loosen a few of his teeth.' Roarke smiled and lighted a cigarette. 'We would have been about twelve. He tried to shake me down. Didn't work.'

'Those are the last three of your main possibles. So now we're down to – what?' Farrell took a quick count of the stills. 'An even dozen. I'm inclined toward Rowan here, or Black Riley. The smartest of the lot.'

'Then we'll put them at the top. But it's not just brains,' Eve continued, walking around the conference table. 'It's temperament, and it's patience. And ego. And it's certainly his personal religion.'

'Odds are for Catholic if he's from one of these families. Most are churchgoers, attending Mass like the pious of a Sunday morning, after doing as they please on a Saturday night.'

'I don't know a lot about religion, Catholic or otherwise, but one of the transmissions he sent was identified as a Catholic Requiem Mass, and the statues he leaves at the scene are of Mary, so that's my take.' Absently Eve fingered the token in her pocket, pulled it out. 'This means something to him.'

'Luck,' Farrell said. 'Bad or good. We've a local artist who uses the shamrock as her signature on her paintings.' Farrell frowned when she turned it over. 'And a Christian symbol.

The fish. Well, there I'd say you have a man who thinks Irish. Pray to God and hope for luck.'

Eve slipped the token back in her pocket. 'How much luck will you have pulling these twelve in on something for questioning?'

Farrell laughed shortly. 'With this lot, if they're not brought in once a month or so they feel neglected. If you like, you can go have a bit of lunch, and we'll start a gathering.'

'I'd appreciate it. You'll let me observe the interviews?'

'Observe, Lieutenant, but not participate in.'

'Fair enough.'

'I can't stretch that to include civilians,' she said to Roarke. 'You might find the afternoon more profitable by looking up some of your old friends and standing them to a pint.'

'Understood. Thank you for your time.'

She took the hand Roarke offered, held it a moment while she looked into his eyes. 'I pinched your father once when I was a rookie. He took great exception to being arrested by a female – which was the mildest term he used for me. I was green, and he managed to split my lip before I restrained him.'

Roarke's eyes went cool and blank. He drew his hand free. 'I'm sorry for that.'

'You weren't there as I recall,' Farrell said mildly. 'Rookies rarely forget their first mistakes, so I remember him quite well. I expected to see some of him in you. But I don't. Not a bit. Good day to you, Roarke.'

'Good day to you, Inspector.'

By the time Eve got back to the hotel, lunch had worn off and jet lag was fuzzing her mind. She found the suite empty, but there were a half dozen coded faxes waiting on the machine. She added more coffee to her overburdened system while she scanned them.

She yawned until her jaw cracked, then put through a call to Peabody's palm 'link.

'Peabody.'

'Dallas. I just got in. Have the sweepers finished with the white van found abandoned downtown?'

'Yes, sir. Wrong trail. That van was used in a robbery in Jersey and dumped down on Canal. I'm still pursuing that lead, but it's going to take more time to eliminate vehicles. The cabdriver was a wash. He didn't even know his tags had been lifted.'

'McNab make any progress on the jammer?'

Peabody snorted, then sobered. 'He claims to be making some headway, though he phrases all of it in electro-ese and I can't make it out. He had a great time with some e-jockey of Roarke's. I think they're in love.'

'Your snotty side's showing, Peabody.'

'Not nearly as much as it could be. No transmissions have come through, so our boy's taking a break from mayhem. McNab is staying here at your home office tonight in case there's a send. I'm staying, too.'

'You and McNab are staying in my office tonight?'

Her mouth moved perilously close to a pout. 'If he's staying, I'm staying. Besides, the food's superior.'

'Try not to kill each other.'

'I'm showing admirable restraint in that particular area, sir.'

'Right. Is Summerset behaving himself?'

'He went to some art class, then out for coffee and brandy with his lady friend. I had him shadowed. It was all very dignified according to the report. He got back about twenty minutes ago.'

'See that he stays in.'

'I've got it covered. Any progress there?'

'That's debatable. We have a list of potentials, which was shorted by half during interviews. I'm going to take a closer look at six,' she said, rubbing her tired eyes. 'One's in New York, and one's supposed to be in Boston. I'll run them when I get in tomorrow. We should be back by noon.'

'We'll keep the home fires burning, Lieutenant.'

'Find that damn van, Peabody.' She disengaged the 'link and ordered herself not to wonder, or worry, about where Roarke could be.

He knew better than to go home. It was foolish and fruitless and irresistible. The shanties had changed little since he'd been a boy trying to crawl his way out of them. The buildings were cheaply constructed, with roofs sagging, windows broken. It was rare to see a flower bloom here, but a few hopeful souls had scratched out a stamp-sized garden at the doorstep of the six-flat building where he'd lived once.

But the flowers, however bright, couldn't overcome the odor of piss and vomit. And they couldn't lighten the air that lay thick with despair.

He didn't know why he went in, but he found himself standing inside the dim lobby with its sticky floors and peeling paint. And there were the stairs his father had once kicked him down because he hadn't made his quota lifting wallets.

Oh, but I had, Roarke thought now. What was a kick and tumble compared to the pounds he'd secreted away? The old man had been too drunk, and often too stupid, to have suspected his whipping boy of holding back any of the take.

Roarke had always held back. A pound here, a pound there could make a tidy sum for a determined boy willing to take his licks.

'He'd have given me his fist in my face in any case,' he murmured and gazed up those battered stairs.

He could hear someone cursing, someone else weeping. You would always hear cursing and weeping in such places. The odor of boiled cabbage was strong and turned his stomach so he sought the thick air outside again.

He saw a teenage boy in tight black pants and a mop of

242

fair hair watching him coolly from the curb. Across the street a couple of girls chalking the cracked sidewalk for hopscotch stopped to watch. He walked passed them, aware there were other eyes following him, peering out of windows and doorways.

A stranger in good shoes was both curiosity and insult.

The boy called out something vile in Gaelic. Roarke turned, met the boy's sneering eyes. 'I'm going back in the alley,' he said, using the same tongue, found it came more easily to his lips than he'd expected, 'if you've a mind to try your luck on me. I'm in the mood to hurt someone. Might as well be you as another.'

'Men have died in that alley. Might as well be you as another.'

'Come on then.' And Roarke smiled. 'Some say I killed my father there when I was half your age, sticking a knife in his throat the way you'd slaughter a pig.'

The boy shifted his weight, and his eyes changed. The sneering defiance turned to respect. 'You'd be Roarke then.'

'I would. Steer clear of me today and live to see your children.'

'I'll get out,' the boy shouted after him. 'I'll get out the way you did, and one day I'll walk in fine shoes. Damned if I'll come back.'

'That's what *I* thought,' Roarke sighed and stepped into the stinking alley between the narrow buildings.

The recycler was broken. Had been broken as long as he could remember. Trash and garbage were strewn, as always, over the pitted asphalt. The wind whipped his coat, his hair, as he stood, staring down at the ground, at the place where his father had been found, dead.

He hadn't put the knife in him. Oh, he'd dreamed of killing the man; every time he'd taken a beating by those vicious hands he'd thought of pounding back. But he'd only been twelve or so when his father had met the knife, and he'd yet to kill a man.

243

He'd crawled out of this place, out of this pit. He'd survived, even triumphed. And now, perhaps for the first time, he realized he'd changed.

He'd never again be like the mirror image of himself who had challenged him from the curb. He was a man grown into what he had chosen to be. He enjoyed the life he'd built for itself now, not simply for its opposition to what had been.

He had love in his heart, the hot-blooded love for a woman that could never have rooted if the ground had remained stony.

After all these years he discovered that coming back hadn't stirred the ghosts, but had put them to rest.

'Fuck you, bloody bastard,' he murmured, but with outrageous relief. 'You couldn't do me after all.'

He turned away from what had been, set his direction on what was, and what would come. He walked, content now, through the rain that began to fall as soft as tears.

Chapter Sixteen

Eve had never been to a wake before, and it surprised her that, given Roarke's usual style of doing things, he'd chosen to hold it in the Penny Pig.

The pub was closed to outside traffic, but crowded just the same. It seemed Jennie had left behind a lot of friends, if no family.

An Irish wake, Eve was to discover, meant pretty much what an Irish pub meant. Music, conversation, and drinking great quantities of liquor and beer.

It made her think of a viewing she'd attended only the month before, one that had led to more death and violence. There the dead had been laid out in a clear side-viewing casket, and the room had been heavy with red draperies and flowers. The mood had been sorrow, the voices hushed.

Here, the dead were remembered in a different manner.

'A fine girl was Jennie.' A man at the bar raised his glass, and his voice over the noise of the crowd. 'Never watered the whiskey or stinted when pouring it. And her smile was as warm as what she served you.'

'To Jennie then,' it was agreed, and the toast was drunk.

Stories were told, often winding their way from some virtue of the dearly departed and into a joke on one of those present. Roarke was a favored target.

'There's a night I remember,' Brian began, 'years back it was, when our Jennie was just a lass – and a fine figure of one was she – that she was serving the beer and the porter. That was when Maloney owned the place – God rest his thieving soul – and I was tending bar for a pittance.'

He paused, took a drink, then puffed into life one of the cigars Roarke had provided. 'I had an eye for Jennie – and what right-minded young lad wouldn't – but she had none for me. 'Twas Roarke she was after. On that evening, we had a fair crowd in, and all the young bucks were hoping to get a wink from young Jennie. I gave her all me best love-starved looks.'

He demonstrated with a hand over his heart and the heaviest of sighs so his audience hooted with laughter and cheered him on.

'But to me she paid no mind at all, for her attention was all for Roarke. And there himself sat, perhaps at the table where he's sitting where he is tonight. Though he wasn't dressed so fine as he is tonight, and I'd wager a punt to a penny that he didn't smell so fresh either. Though Jennie sashayed by him a dozen times or more, and leaned over, oh, leaned over close in a way that made my heart pound wishing I were exposed to such a fine and lovely view, and she would ask so sweetly could she fetch him another pint.'

He sighed again, wet his throat, and went on with it. 'But Roarke, he was blind to the signals she was sending, deaf to the invitation in that warm voice. There he sat with the girl of my dreams offering him glory, and he kept noting figures in a tattered little book, adding them up, calculating his profits. For a businessman he ever was. Then Jennie, for a determined girl was she when her mind was set, and it was set on Roarke, asked him please would he give her a hand for just a moment in the back room, for she couldn't reach what she needed on the high shelf. And him being so tall, and strong with it, could he fetch it down for her.'

Brian rolled his eyes at that while one of the women leaned over the booth where Roarke sat with Eve and good-naturedly pinched his biceps. 'Well, the boy wasn't a cad for all his wicked ways,' Brian continued, 'and he put his book away in his pocket and went off with her into the back. A frightful long time they were gone I'm after telling you, with my heart broken to bits behind Maloney's bar. When come out they did, with hair all mused and clothes askew, and a bright-eyed look about them, I knew Jenny was lost to me. For not a bloody thing did he carry back for her from the high shelf in the back room. All he did was sit again, give her a wicked, quick grin and take out his book and count his profits.

'Sixteen years old we were, the three of us, and still dreaming about what our lives might be. Now Maloney's pub is mine, Roarke's profits too many to count, and Jennie, sweet Jennie, is with the angels.'

There were a few tears at the end of it, and conversation began again in murmurs. Bringing his glass, Brian walked over, sat across from Roarke. 'Do you remember that night?'

'I do. It's a good memory you brought back.'

'Perhaps it was ill-mannered of me. I hope you didn't take offense to it, Eve.'

'I'd need a heart of stone to do that.' Maybe it was the air, or the music, or the voices, but they made her sentimental. 'Did she know how you felt about her?'

'Then, no.' Brian shook his head, and there was a warm gleam in his eye. 'And later, we were too much friends for else. My heart always leaned toward her, but it was in a different way as time passed. It was the thought of her I loved.'

He seemed to shake himself, then tapped a finger on Roarke's glass. 'Well now, you're barely drinking. Have you lost your head for good Irish whiskey living among the Yanks?'

'My head was always better than yours, wherever I was living.'

'You had a good one,' Brian admitted. 'But I remember a night. Oh, it was after you'd sold off a shipment of a fine

French bordeaux you'd smuggled in from Calais – begging your pardon, Lieutenant darling. Are you remembering that, Roarke?'

Roarke's lips moved into a smirk, and his hand brushed its way down Eve's hair. 'I smuggled more than one shipment of French wine in my career.'

'Oh, no doubt, no doubt, but this night in particular, you kept a half dozen bottles out, and were in a light and sharing frame of mind. You pulled together a game – a friendly one for a change – and we sat and drank every drop. You and me and Jack Bodine and that bloody fool Mick Connelly who got himself killed in a knife fight in Liverpool a few years back. Let me tell you, Lieutenant darling, this man of yours got drunk as six sailors in port and still won all our money.'

Roarke picked up his glass now and savored a sip. 'I recall being a bit light in the pocket the next morning when I woke up.'

'Well.' Brian grinned hugely. 'Get drunk with thieves and what does it get you? But it was good wine, Roarke. It was damn good wine. I'll have them play one of the old tunes. "Black Velvet Band." You'll sing?'

'No.'

'Sing?' Eve sat up. 'He sings?'

'No,' Roarke said again, definitely, while Brian laughed.

'Prod him enough, and keep his glass full, and you'd get a tune out of him.'

'He hardly even sings in the shower.' She stared thoughtfully at Roarke. 'You sing?'

Struggling between amusement and embarrassment, he shook his head and lifted his glass. 'No,' he said again. 'And I don't plan to get drunk enough to prove myself a liar.'

'Well, we'll work on that some.' Brian winked and rose. 'For now then I'm going to have them play a reel. Will you dance with me, Eve?'

'I might.' She watched him walk off to liven up the music.

'Getting drunk, singing in pubs, and tickling barmaids in the back room. Hmmm.' She shot a long, speculative look at the man she married. 'This is very interesting.'

'You do the first, the others come easy.'

'I might like to see you drunk.' She put a hand on his cheek, glad to see the sadness had faded from his eyes. Wherever he had gone that afternoon was his secret, and she was satisfied that it had done him good.

He leaned forward to touch his lips to hers. 'So I could tickle you in the back room? There's your reel,' he added when the music brightened.

Eve glanced over, saw Brian coming back her way with neat, bouncing little steps. 'I like him.'

'So do I. I'd forgotten how much.'

Sunshine and rain fell together and turned the light into a pearl. In the churchyard stood ancient stone crosses, pitted from age and wind. The dead rested close to each other, intimates of fate. The sound of the sea rose up from beyond rocky cliffs in a constant muted roar that proved time continued, even here.

There wasn't a single airbike or tram to spoil the sky where clouds layered over the blue like folded gray blankets. And the grass that covered the hills that rose up toward that sky was the deep emerald of hopes and dreams.

It made Eve think of an old video, or a hologram program.

The priest wore long traditional robes and spoke in Gaelic. The burying of the dead was a ritual only the rich could afford. It was a rare sight, and a crowd gathered outside the gates, respectively silent as the casket was lowered into its fresh pit.

Roarke rested his cheek on the top of Eve's head, gathering comfort as the mourners made the sign of the cross. He was putting more than a friend into the ground, and knew it. He was putting part of himself, a part he'd already thought long buried.

'I need to speak with the priest a moment.'

She lifted a hand to the one he'd laid on her shoulder. 'I'll wait here.'

As he moved off, Brian stepped up to her. 'He's done well by Jennie. She'll rest here – have the shade of the ash in the summer.' With his hands comfortably at his sides, he looked out over the churchyard. 'And they still ring the bells in the belfry of a Sunday morning. Not a recording, but the bells themselves. It's a fine sound.'

'He loved her.'

'There's nothing quite so sweet as the first love of the young and the lonely. You remember your childhood sweetheart?'

'I didn't have one. But I understand it.'

Brian laid a hand on her shoulder, gave it a quick squeeze. 'He couldn't have done better than you, even if you did make the unfortunate mistake of becoming a cop. Are you a good one, Lieutenant darling?'

'Yeah.' Something in the way he'd asked had her looking over, into his face. 'It's what I'm best at.'

He nodded, and his thoughts seemed to drift as he shifted his gaze. 'Christ knows how much money Roarke's passing the priest in that envelope.'

'Do you resent that? His money?'

'No indeed.' And he laughed a little. 'Not that I don't wish I had it as well. He earned it. Always was the next game, the next deal with our lad Roarke. All I wanted was the pub, and since I have my heart's desire, I suppose I'm rich as well.'

Brian looked down at the simple black skirt of her suit, the unadorned black pumps Eve wore. 'You're not dressed for cliff walking, but would you take my arm and stroll along that way with me?'

'All right.' There was something on his mind, she thought, and decided he wanted privacy to share it.

'Do you know, I've never been across that sea to England,' Brian began as he walked slowly over the uneven ground.

'Never had the wanting to. A man can go anywhere, on-or off-planet, and in less time than it takes to think of it, but I've never been off this island. Do you see those boats down there?'

Eve looked over the cliffs, down into the restless sea. Hydro-jetties streamed back and forth, skimming the waves like pretty stones. 'Commuters and tourists?'

'Aye, rushing over to England, rushing over here. Day after day, year after year. Ireland's still poor compared to its neighbors, so an ambitious laborer might take a job over there, ride the jetties, or the airbus if he's plumper in pocket. It'll cost him ten percent of his wages for the privilege of living in one country and working in another, as governments always find an angle, don't they, for nipping into a man's pocket. At night, back he comes. And where does it get him, this rushing over and back, over and back for the most of his life?' He shrugged. 'Me, I'd as soon stay in one spot and watch the parade.'

'What's on your mind, Brian?'

'Many things, Lieutenant darling. A host of things.'

As Roarke walked toward them he remembered that the first time he'd seen Eve they'd been at a funeral. Another woman whose life had been stolen. It had been cold, and Eve had forgotten her gloves. She'd worn a hideous gray suit with a loose button on the jacket. He slipped a hand into his pocket now, idly fingering the button that had fallen off that baggy gray jacket.

'Are you flirting with my wife, Brian?'

'I would if I thought I stood a chance with her. The fact is I've something that will interest you both. I had a call early this morning, from Summerset.'

'Why would he call you?' Roarke demanded.

'To tell me you wanted me in New York, urgently, and at your expense.'

'When did it come in?' Eve was already pulling out her palm 'link to contact Peabody.

'Eight o'clock. It's a matter of dire importance that can't be divulged except face-to-face. I'm to fly over this very day, and check in to the Central Park Arms, where I'll have a suite, and wait to be contacted.'

'How do you know it was Summerset?' Roarke asked.

'By God, Roarke, it looked like him, sounded like him. Stiffer, older, but I wouldn't have questioned it. Though he wouldn't make conversation, and ended the call abruptly when I pressed him.'

'Peabody. Slap yourself awake there.'

'What?' Peabody, puffy-eyed and disheveled, yawned. 'Sorry, sir. Yes, sir. Awake.'

'Kick McNab out of whatever bed he's in and have him check the mainframe on the 'links. I need to know if there's been a transmission to Ireland – it would have been at, shit, what's the time difference here? – like three A.M.'

'Kicking him out of bed immediately, Lieutenant.'

'And contact me the minute you have the answer. I need to take your 'link log into evidence,' she told Brian as she stuffed the palm 'link back in her pocket. 'We'll dupe it for Inspector Farrell, but I need the original.'

'Well, I thought you might.' Brian took out a disc. 'Anticipating that, I brought it with me.'

'Good thinking. What did you tell the man who called you?'

'Oh, that I had a business to run, that I couldn't just be traipsing off across the Atlantic on a whim. I tried to draw him out, asked after Roarke here. He only insisted that I come, straight off, and Roarke would make it worth my while.' He smiled thinly. 'A tempting offer. First-class transpo and accomodations, and twenty thousand pounds a day while I'm away from home. A man would have to be mad to say no to that.'

'You'll stay in Dublin.' Roarke's voice was sharp, edged with fury, and put Brian's back up.

'Maybe I've a mind to go to New York City and give this murdering bastard a taste of Brian Kelly.'

'You'll stay in Dublin,' Roarke repeated, eyes narrowed and cold, fists clenched and ready. 'If I have to beat you unconscious first, then that's fine.'

'You think you can take me down, do you?' Primed for a fight, Brian started to strip off his topcoat. 'Let's have a go.'

'Stop it, you idiots.' Eve stepped between them, prepared to deck both if necessary. 'You're staying in Dublin, Brian, because the only thing this bastard's getting a taste of is me. I'll have your travel visa blocked, and if you try to leave the country you'll spend some quality time in lockup.'

'Travel visa be damned—'

'Shut up. And you,' she continued, swinging to Roarke. 'Step back. Nobody's beating anyone unconscious unless it's me. A couple days in Ireland and all you can think of is punching somebody. Must be the air.'

Her 'link beeped. 'That's Peabody. Now, the two of you remember: People who act like assholes get treated like assholes.'

She stalked away to take the call. Brian's face broke out in a wide grin as he slapped Roarke on the back. 'That's a woman, isn't it?'

'Delicate as a rose, my Eve. Fragile and quiet natured.' He grinned himself when he heard her curse, loud and vicious. 'A voice like a flute.'

'And you're sloppy in love with her.'

'Pitifully.' He remained silent a moment, then spoke quietly. 'Stay in Dublin, Brian. I know you can get around a blocked visa as easily as crossing High Street, but I'm asking you to do this. It's too soon after burying Jennie for me to risk losing another friend.'

Brian heaved out a breath. 'I wasn't thinking of going until you ordered me not to.'

'The son of a bitch sent me flowers,' Eve fumed as she

stalked back. 'Hey.' When Roarke grabbed her lapels, she slapped at his hands and scowled.

'Explain.'

'A couple dozen roses just arrived – with a note that hopes I'll be back on my feet and ready for the next match soon. Something about a novena – whatever that is – being said in my name for my full and speedy recovery, too. Peabody's called a bomb unit, just in case, and she's holding the delivery boy, but he looks genuine. No direct transmission from our 'links this morning. McNab needs Brian's disc to run it for bounces.' When his hands relaxed slightly, she put hers over them. 'I've got to go back . . . Now.'

'Yes, we'll go straight back. Do you need a lift back to Dublin, Brian?'

'No, go on. I've my own ride. Take a care, Roarke,' he said and wrapped his arms around him. 'And come back.'

'I will.'

'And bring your lovely wife.' While Eve blinked in surprise, Brian gathered her up in a bear hug, then kissed her long and lavishly. 'Godspeed, Lieutenant darling, and you keep our lad here on the narrow if not the straight.'

'Watch your back, Brian,' Roarke called out as they walked away.

'And the rest of me as well,' Brian promised, then turned to watch the fast boats streak across the water.

It was barely eight A.M. on the East Coast when Eve settled in to her office. She eyed the young, gawky delivery boy coolly while he sat fidgeting in the chair across from her desk.

'You get a call to deliver roses before six A.M. and that doesn't seem weird to you, Bobby?'

'Well, ma'am – sir – Lieutenant, we get that sometimes. We got this twenty-four-hour delivery service because people want the convenience. This one time I delivered a fern to the

East Side at three A.M. This guy, see, he'd forgotten his lady's birthday, and she'd given him grief, and so he—'

'Yeah, yeah.' Eve brushed it off. 'Tell me again about the order.'

'Okay, sure. No problem.' His voice bobbed up and down like a cork on a restless sea. 'I'm on call, see, for the midnight-to-eight shift. What happens is anybody who calls in to the shop, the transmission gets bounced to my beeper. I read the order on the screen, then I gotta go in, put the order together, and get it where it's going. I got a master for the flower shop so I can get in when it's closed. My aunt owns the joint, so she, like, trusts me, and I'm going to school on the three-day-week thing, so it gives me some pocket credit.'

'Officer Peabody has your beeper.'

'Yeah, I handed it over. No perspiration, no debate. You want it, you got it.'

'And you, personally, put the flowers in the box.'

'Oh yeah. It's no whoop. You just dump in some greenery, coupla sprigs of those little white flowers, then lay on the roses. My aunt keeps the boxes and tissues and ribbons all together so we can slap the orders together fast. The officer, she, like, called my aunt and verified. Do I need a lawyer?'

'No, Bobby, you don't need a lawyer. I appreciate you waiting until I could talk to you.'

'So, like, I could go.'

'Yeah, you can go.'

He got up, grinning shakily. 'I never really, like, talked to a cop before. It's not so bad.'

'We hardly ever torture our witnesses these days.'

He paled, then laughed. 'That's, like, a joke, right?'

'You bet. Beat it, Bobby.'

Eve shook her head, then signaled for Peabody to come in. 'McNab get anything off the beeper?'

'The order was shot in on a public 'link, from Grand Central. It was keyed in, no voiceprint – and the order was paid for via electronic transfer of cash, point of order scrambled. We couldn't trace it with a fleet of bloodhound droids.'

'I didn't figure he'd slip up again, not so soon. The van?'

'Nothing solid yet. I'm working on the shoes, too. Computer estimates a size eight. That's small for a man's shoe. That style hit the market only six months ago – high-end price range. It's the epitome of air tread for the stylish jock. So far, I'm down to six hundred pair of size eights sold in the city.'

'Keep running it. And the coat?'

'I've only got about thirty purchases for the same three-month period. No matches yet. And none on the statue.'

'McNab?'

Seconds later, he stuck his head in the doorway. 'Yo.'

'Full progress and status report.'

'Let's start with the wand.' He made himself at home by sitting on Eve's desk. 'I like our chances there. That e-jock of Roarke's knows his shit. Down at Trident Security and Communications – that's Roarke's gig – they've been working on a jammer of this style and power for over a year. A. A. says they've nearly worked out the bugs.'

'A. A.?'

'That's the jock. Plenty of brain cells there. Anyway, he projects they'll have a model under wraps within six months – four if they get lucky. Rumor is that several other e-firms are working on the same deal. One of those firms is Brennen's. The take from the industrial espionage people is that Brennen's is the closest competition.'

'Does anyone have a prototype?'

'A. A. showed me one. It's fairly icy, but only hits the mark as of now at extreme close range. The remote capability's giving them some grief. It's still got some major power fluctuation.'

'So how did our man get his hands on one that doesn't give him grief?'

'Good question. I'm thinking he's put some time in at R and D himself.'

'Yeah, I'd agree with that. We'll run the six most likely from Inspector Farrell's shakedown and see if any of them pop.'

'And I wonder if the unit he used is a one-shot.'

Eve narrowed her eyes. 'Only good for one jam at a time? What would you do, recharge it? Toss it? Reconfigure?'

'Recharge or recon, I'd say. I'm working with A. A. on it.'

'Good, keep at it. Any luck with the echo?'

'I can't lock it. Driving me bat-shit. But I did scrape the layers off the disc you brought back from the Emerald Isle. Projected image. Hologram.'

'A holo? You're sure?'

'Don't I look sure?' He let his cocky smile go when Eve only stared coolly at him. 'Yeah, it was a holo. Damn good one, but I enhanced, did heat and light testing. The image was projected.'

'Good.' It was one more stone to weigh on Summerset's side. 'Any hits yet on the analysis of the security discs on the Luxury Towers?'

'They're whining in EDD. Backlog. I used your name and got them to promise we'd have results within the next forty-eight.'

Feeney, Eve thought, *where the hell are you?* 'What else have you got?'

'The transmission had the same echo as the others. Exact match.'

'Even better. Now find the source.' She rose. 'It's time for me to put in a public appearance. Let's get this jerk now that I'm up for another round. Peabody, you're with me.'

'My favorite place, Lieutenant.'

'Sucking up noted.' She pulled her palm 'link as she started out, coded in for Nadine Furst at Channel 75.

'Hey, Dallas, you look pretty good for an invalid.'

'Get this. Lieutenant Eve Dallas has recovered from her injuries and is reporting back to duty. She remains in charge of the investigation involving the murders of Brennen, Conroy, and O'Leary. She is confident a suspect will be in custody shortly.'

'Hold it, let me get my recorder.'

'That's all you get, pal. Put it on.' She clicked off as she jogged down the stairs. There, draped across the newel post, was a new and butter-smooth leather jacket of golden brown. 'He doesn't miss a trick,' Eve murmured as she picked it up.

'Man oh man.' Unable to resist, Peabody stroked a hand down the sleeve as Eve shrugged into it. 'Like a baby's bottom.'

'It had to cost ten times what my old one did, and I'll have it banged up in a week. I don't know why he – Shit, where's Roarke?' She turned to the house computer. 'Locate Roarke.'

Roarke is not on the premises at this time.

'Well, hell,' Eve muttered. 'Where the hell did he go so fast? He damn well better be out buying some country and not poking into this.'

'Does he really buy countries?' Peabody wanted to know as she hurried outside after Eve.

'How the hell do I know? I stay out of his business, which is more than he does for me. Central Park Arms.' She swore, suddenly sure that's where he'd gone. Then she stopped, stared at the empty space in front of the steps. 'I don't have a vehicle,' she remembered. 'Goddamn it, I don't have a ride.'

'Auto requisition hasn't come through. You can make a personal order.'

'Oh yeah, that'll only take a week or two. Shit.' Jamming her hands in new, silky pockets, she jogged to the end of the house.

The garage attachment melded with the main structure.

The massive doors were wood with thick brass fittings. The windows, arched and majestic, were sunscreened to keep the finish on the vehicles housed there from fading. Inside the temperature would be kept, year-round, at a comfortable seventy-two degrees.

Eve uncoded the locks, identified herself through voice and palm print. The doors swung gracefully open.

So did Peabody's mouth. 'Holy cow.'

'It's excessive,' Eve said, sniffing. 'It's ridiculous and such a clichéd man-thing.'

'It's frigid,' Peabody said reverently.

Vehicles were housed in individual bays, on two levels. Sports cars, limos, air cycles, all-terrains, sedate sedans, and sleek solo-riders. Colors ranged from flashy neon shades to classic blacks. Peabody stared dreamily at a tandem-style air cycle and imagined herself riding the skies, wind in her hair, with some muscled hunk behind her.

She snapped out of it when she saw Eve heading toward a discreet compact model in industrial gray.

'Dallas, how about this one?' Hopefully, Peabody gestured up to a snazzy electric blue sportster, its silver wheels gleaming, its narrow grille a piece of automotive art.

'That's a fuck-me car, and you know it.'

'Well, yeah, maybe, but it's got to be fast, and really efficient. It'd be loaded, too.' She smiled winningly.

'Everything in here's loaded.'

Peabody danced forward when Eve reached for the button to release the sedan. 'Come on, Dallas, live a little. Don't you want to see how she moves? And it's only temporary. You'll be back in some departmental clunker before you know it. It's a 6000XX.' Her voice came perilously close to a whine. 'Most people live their whole lives without even touching one. Just one ride. What could it hurt?'

'Don't beg,' Eve muttered. 'Jesus.' But she gave in and lowered the sportster to the scrubbed tile floor.

'Oh, look at the interior. It's real leather, isn't it? White leather.' Unable to control herself, Peabody opened the door of the car and breathed deep. 'Just smell it. Oh, oh, check the controls. It's even got an airjet gauge. We could be on the beach in New L.A. in under three hours in this baby.'

'Get a hold of yourself, Peabody, or it's back to the sedan.'

'No way.' Peabody all but dived inside. 'You're not getting me out with a hydro-lift until I get a ride.'

'I wouldn't think a woman raised by Free-Agers would be so shallow and materialistic.'

'I had to work on it, but I've almost got it down.' She smiled happily when Eve slipped in beside her. 'Dallas, this rocks. Can I try the music system?'

'No. Strap in. We'll look for your dignity later.' But because the car called for it, Eve engaged ignition and took off like a rocket.

It took less than ten minutes to reach the Central Park Arms.

'Did you see the way this honey handled the turns? You took that last one at sixty and there wasn't even a shimmy. Imagine what she'd do in the air. Why don't we try it when we leave. Man, I think I had an orgasm rounding Sixty-second.'

'I don't need to know about that.' Eve climbed out, tossed her key code to the doorman. When she flashed her badge, the hand he'd held out for a tip retreated. 'I want that vehicle kept close. I don't want to wait more than thirty seconds for it when I come out.'

Without waiting for an answer, she swung through the auto-doors and crossed the mosaic tiles of the lobby toward the massive front desk.

'You have a suite registered to a Brian Kelly,' she said, holding up her badge.

'Yes, Lieutenant, scheduled for arrival and occupancy this afternoon. Penthouse B, Tower Level.'

'Clear me through.'

'I believe that suite is occupied at the moment. However, if you'd like to wait until—'

'Clear me through,' she repeated. 'Now.'

'Right away. The private elevator is down this corridor and to the left. It's clearly marked. Your key code will access both the elevator and the doors, parlor and bedroom.'

'Any transmissions, messages, deliveries come in for that suite, send them directly up.'

'Of course.'

The clerk winced as she strode off, then quickly rang Penthouse B. 'I beg your pardon, sir, but a Lieutenant Dallas and a uniformed officer are on their way up. Excuse me? Ah, yes, sir, of course. I'll see to it right away.'

Baffled, the clerk hung up, then contacted room service and ordered coffee, tea cakes, and fresh fruit for three.

Outside Penthouse B, Eve drew her weapon. At her signal, Peabody flanked the opposite side of the door. Eve slid her key code toward the lock, gave her aide a quick nod.

They went in low and fast.

She hissed at Roarke, who continued to smile and lounge on the silk-covered sofa pit. 'I don't think the weapon's necessary, darling. I've ordered coffee, and the service here is very swift and efficient.'

'I ought to give you a jolt, just for the hell of it.'

'You'd be sorry later. Hello, Peabody, you look a bit windblown. Very attractive.'

Flushing, she brushed at her straight black hair. 'Well, I put the sky roof down for a minute on the XX.'

'Sexy little ride, isn't it? Well, shall we discuss how to lay the trap now, or wait for the coffee?'

Resigned, Eve shoved her weapon back in its harness. 'We'll wait for the coffee.'

Chapter Seventeen

'We're nearly set up here, Commander. If he calls, we'll be ready.'

'*If* he calls, Lieutenant, and if he follows the same pattern he used to abduct O'Leary.'

'He used the same pattern when he contacted Brian Kelly this morning.' Beneath the range of the 'link monitor, she jerked a hand so that McNab would stop the chatter. Christ, the man ran his mouth at light speed. 'We can take him down here, Commander. All he has to do is move in this direction.'

'You better hope he does, and quickly, Dallas, or both of us are going to get our butts singed.'

'I planted the bait. He'll take it.'

'Contact me the minute you hear from him.'

'You'll be the first,' she murmured as the screen went blank. 'You guys want to keep it down? This isn't the damn party suite.'

McNab and two EDD drones were chirping away as they set up equipment in the bedroom that was the temporary command center. Eve worried that she'd thrown this task force together too quickly, but time was the enemy. There were tracers and bypass units, three sets of porta-links, all with headsets and voice mufflers. Recorders were set to clock on with the first beep of the first 'link. McNab had already interfaced it with her office unit.

She'd had all the equipment brought from Central in a

delivery van. If her man had the hotel under surveillance, all he would have seen was yet another commerical vehicle pulling into the hotel's rear dock.

No uniforms, no black and whites.

Six cops were on surveillance in the lobby posing as bellstaff, clerks, maintenance. A detective from her squad had taken over for the doorman. She had two more in the kitchen as line chefs, another two covering the penthouse floor as housekeeping staff.

The man power and equipment were eating a moon-sized hole in the departmental budget. If it went wrong, there would be hell to pay, and she'd be the one to pay it.

She wasn't going to let it go wrong.

Restless, she moved out into the spacious parlor. The bank of windows was privacy screened there, as were the bedroom windows. Only Roarke, as owner of the hotel, and his manager were aware of the infiltration of police. At two P.M., one hour after the flight from Dublin landed at Kennedy, another cop would check in to the hotel as Brian Kelly.

It was going to work. All he had to do was call Eve's 'link.

Why the hell didn't he call?

Roarke came in from the second bedroom and saw her frowning at the screened windows. 'You've covered all the details, Eve.'

'I've gone over it and over it. He can't wait long to move on Brian. He won't risk Brian contacting you on his own and finding out it's all a scam. On his call to Jennie he got her to promise she wouldn't try to contact anyone, that she wouldn't speak to anyone unless it came through you. But Brian wouldn't commit, wouldn't promise anything.'

'And if our man knows him at all, he'd know Brian tends to do as he chooses.'

'That's right, so he'll arrange for the meet quickly. He's already got the place where he'll kill him set up. And he's not going to want to take chances. Brian's a tough, muscular man in his prime. And he's street smart. He'd put up a hell of a fight.'

'He'd have to be taken by surprise,' Roarke agreed, 'caught off guard.'

'Exactly. My guess is he plans to do it all right here. Brian'll be expecting a driver, a messenger, a liaison for you, so he'll open the door. He would have to get a tranq in him then and there, quick, quiet.'

'Lieutenant,' Roarke said and held out a hand, and when Eve automatically put hers in it, he smiled and squeezed. 'If I'd had a minipopper in my hand, you'd be tranqued just that fast and easy. They were popular in certain unsettled areas during the twenties, only they were most often laced with strychnine rather than a dozer. Shaking hands became quite unfashionable for several years.'

'You're a fount of the most disturbing trivia.'

'Wonderful icebreaker at parties.'

'He should have called by now.' She spun away to pace. 'With each one he's narrowed the time between the murder and the earliest possibility of discovery. He wants me to get close, really close. It makes him feel more superior. It's more of a rush when he knows I'm right behind him, while the blood's still fresh.'

'He may be planning to call from here, once he's locked in his prey for this round.'

'I've thought of that. It won't matter. We'll still get him. He'll have to call this room. The cop who's posing as Brian for check-in is a good match in coloring and build. McNab's already added the jazz to trip the voice into Brian's tone over the 'link. And he's got the video fuzzy. But he's not going to move until he calls me. He wants to make sure I'm ready.'

She looked at her wrist unit, swore. 'Jackison's going to check in as Brian in fifteen minutes. Where is that son of a—'

The second the bedroom 'link beeped, she was streaking inside. 'Back off,' she ordered. 'All porta-links into the next room. No chatter. Hologram backdrop, McNab.'

'Engaged.' He nodded as an imaged reproduction of her office flickered on around her. 'Sitting pretty, Dallas.'

'Trace this bastard,' she ordered and answered. 'Dallas, Homicide.'

'So glad you're feeling better, Lieutenant.'

It was the same voice, the same swimming colors on screen. 'Did you miss me? Sending me flowers was such a nice touch, especially since blowing me up didn't quite work out for you.'

'You were so . . . discourteous in your statement to the press. I found your lack of manners very rude.'

'You know what I find rude, pal? Taking someone's life before they've finished using it. That kind of thing really ticks me off.'

'I'm sure we could debate the value of our personal annoyances for quite a while, but I know how desperately you're trying to tape this transmission, with your inferior equipment and your undereducated technicians.'

'I know a couple e-detectives who would find that statement very rude.'

His laughter came through the speaker, genuine and amused. And, she thought as her ear cocked, *young*.

'Oh, under different circumstances I'm sure I could be very fond of you, Lieutenant. If not for your deplorable lack of taste. What do you see in that Irish street rat you married?'

'He's great in bed.' Hoping he had clear video, she leaned back and smiled. 'I've got an expert's profile here that says you're likely lacking in that arena. Maybe you should try some Stay-Up. It's available at your local pharmacy everywhere.'

His breathing hitched once clearly through the speakers. 'I am pure of heart and body, sanctified.'

'Is that another word for impotent?'

'You bitch. You don't know anything about me. Do you think I want to lie with you, is that it? Maybe I will, when this is over, maybe God will demand it. "Better to spill seed in the belly of a whore than on the ground."'

'Have trouble jacking off, too? That's rough. Maybe if you tried to keep your mother out of your head when you're working on yourself you'd finish off and have a cheerier personality.'

'Don't you speak of my mother.' His voice went ragged and thin, wavering on a high note.

Bingo, Eve thought. Mommy equals female authority figure.

'What's she like? Is she still yanking your chain, pal, or is she at home, keeping the lights burning without a clue how you spend your free time?' She thought of the ritual she'd witnessed just that morning in a little church near the cliffs. 'Do you still go to Mass with her every Sunday? Is that where you go to find your vengeful god?'

'The blood of my enemies flows like tainted wine into Hell. You'll know such pain before I kill you.'

'You already tried once. You missed. Why don't you come closer. Take me on, one on one. Do you have the balls for it?'

'When the time comes. I won't be seduced by the words of a harlot to stray from the path.'

His voice broke, shuddered, making Eve tilt her head as if to catch the nuance. Was he crying?

'No time like the present.'

'My mission isn't completed. It isn't over. I say when, I tell you when. The fourth damned soul meets God's judgment today. Two hours.' He let out a long, shuddering breath. 'Two hours is all you've got to find the pig and save him from slaughter. "By his own iniquities the wicked man will be caught, in the meshes of his own sin he will be held fast; He will die from lack of discipline, through the greatness of his folly he will be lost."'

'Proverbs again? There's never any variety with you.'

'All that is necessary for life is found in the Bible. He's walking into my arms, a squealing pig into the land of sleek and pampered dogs and underpaid nannies.'

'That's not much of a clue. Am I getting too close for you to play a fair game?'

'The game's fair enough, but here's another. The sun sets behind, and before it drops to night, the next Judas will pay dearly for his betrayal. Two hours. Starting now.'

'Give me good news, McNab.' Eve demanded when the transmission ended.

McNab looked up, his green eyes shining. 'I got him.'

Eve rose slowly, disengaging the hologram herself. 'Don't toy with me, McNab.'

'Transmission source is sector D, grid fifty-four.'

Eve strode over to the chart, scanned quickly. 'Son of a bitch, the Luxury Towers is in that grid. The fucker's in there. He's working out of the building were he did the first murder.'

'Do we move on him there?' Peabody demanded.

Eve held up a hand to halt the questions until she could think it through. 'He said I had less than two hours. He doesn't rush through his work, so he'll want at least one of those hours in here. He'll be contacting this room any minute. Did Jackison get in?'

'He's in the next room.'

'All right, let's give our boy a little time. He's already got his tools packed. He doesn't leave anything to the last minute. He'll get his transpo, and he won't break any traffic laws getting here. He's on a timetable. We need a second team over at the Luxury Towers, but I don't want them moving in. If he's working with anyone and they stay behind, they could tip him off.'

She pulled out her communicator, contacting Whitney to report and outline strategy for the next stage. Her blood was cool, her mind clear as she began snapping out orders.

She broke off when the room fax beeped. 'He's made contact, Commander. I'm reading it now. He's giving instructions for the mark to expect a uniformed driver within fifteen minutes. He wants the mark to wait in the room. This indicates the hit is meant to go down here, as anticipated. Mark is requested to release the elevator when signaled by 'link from the lobby. Three beeps. Transmission's ended. He'll be moving now.'

'A second team will stake out the Luxury Towers. I can give you two detectives from the Homicide Division and three officers.'

'In civilian attire, Commander. And I need at least one man from EDD to run a trace sweep.'

'You already have three there, Dallas. You're straining the resources.'

She set her teeth, wishing desperately to be in two places at once. 'I'll send McNab to coordinate with the second team.'

'I'll squeeze out a van with the necessary equipment. Keep this frequency open.'

'Yes, sir. McNab.'

Insult radiated from him. 'You're kicking me now, when it's going down?'

'I need you to find his hole.'

'He's coming here. We can scoop him up.'

'I need you to find his hole,' she repeated, 'because God help us if he gets past us and crawls back in it. You find it, McNab, and you block it off. That's an order, Detective.'

Steaming, he grabbed his coat. 'Homicide figures all EDD's good for is ghost work. Fine when you don't have the answers, but when you do it's back to the recorders.'

'I haven't got time for temper tantrums. See that the other e-men here are fully briefed, then turn it over.' She brushed by him and into the parlor. 'Everybody out of this room but Jackison. Take your positions. Weapons on low stun. We want him coherent.'

She lifted her eyebrows at Roarke. 'Civilians, in the spare

268

room.' She picked up one of the remote monitors. 'You can watch.'

'I'm sure it would be entertaining. Lieutenant, you've just shorted yourself one e-man. I'll take his position. Bend the rules a little,' he said before she could object. 'It'll do you more good than having me twiddle my thumbs.'

She had reason to know he was better with the equipment than the two men she had left. 'First bedroom,' she decided. 'You're better off where I can keep an eye on you anyway. Jackison, stay clear of the door. When he rings in, wait for my signal to answer. Peabody, I want you at the door of the second bedroom. Use the security peep. Keep alert.'

She spoke into her communicator as she walked back into the control room. 'Team A, in position. Team B. Team C. It's going down here. Observe but do not approach or delay any uniformed drivers. Suspect will employ house or palm 'link on arrival and use penthouse elevator. Repeat, observe only. No one moves on him. We want him up here. When he's boxed, you'll get my signal and close in on this sector.'

'I love it when you talk cop,' Roarke murmured in her ear.

'No civilian chatter.' Eve planted herself in front of the monitors, scanning each to satisfy herself that all her troops were in position. 'He's coming,' she murmured. 'Any minute now. Come on, you little prick, walk into *my* arms.'

She saw McNab exit the elevator into the lobby. Still steamed, she thought, noting his grim face and stiff posture. He was going to have to learn the value of teamwork. She watched him scan the lobby, and did so herself.

A droid walked a pair of silky, long-haired dogs across the colorful tiles. A woman in a severe black business suit sat on the circular bench surrounding the central fountain and snarled into a palm 'link. A bellman guided an electric cart loaded with luggage toward the main doors. A woman came through them, leading a toy poodle on a silver leash. Both woman and dog were sleekly groomed, with matching silver bows decking their hair. Behind her came a domestic droid loaded down with shopping bags and boxes.

Rich tourist, Eve thought. Early Christmas shopping.

Then she saw him. He came in directly behind the droid, wearing the long dark coat, a chauffeur's cap pulled low, sunshades concealing his eyes. 'He's in.' She barely breathed it. 'Possible target entering through main doors. Male, five-ten, black coat, gray hat, sunshades. He's carrying a black valise. Team leaders copy?'

'Copy that, Lieutenant. In sights. Suspect is taking palm 'link from left coat pocket, moving left of fountain now.'

Then it all went wrong. The poodle started it. Eve saw that for herself. The little dog began to bark manically, broke from her mistress and streaked, yapping and snarling, toward the pair of Afghans.

A vicious little battle ensued, full of noise and fury. In her rush to save her poodle, the woman with the silver ribbons raced over the tiles and shoved past the businesswoman who'd risen to watch the commotion, nearly sending her into the fountain.

The businesswoman's palm 'link went flying and cracked directly between the surprised eyes of a cop in bellman's gear. He went down like a felled tree.

There were screams and curses, a major crash when one of the participants rammed a table holding a duet of crystal vases. Three bellmen dashed to assist, the first to arrive receiving a slash of canine teeth for his trouble. One of the Afghans bounded clear and raced toward the main doors and escape.

The dog caught McNab at the back of the knees and sent him headlong into the door he'd just been approaching. Outside it, Eve saw one of her men reach under his doorman's coat for his weapon.

'Keep your weapons out of view. Goddamn it, don't draw your weapons. It's a fucking dogfight.'

But she saw, because her attention was focused on the target throughout the thirty-second battle, the exact moment they were made. The palm 'link was shoved back in his pocket, his stance went stiff with shock, and he bolted.

'He's made us. Suspect is proceeding on foot to the south entrance. Block south entrance,' she ordered as she ran from the suite and toward the elevator. 'Repeat. Block the south entrance. Suspect's rabbiting, consider him armed and dangerous.' She didn't bother to glance over when Roarke pushed into the elevator with her.

'He's nearly to the doors,' Roarke told her, and she saw now that he'd had the foresight to grab up one of the minimonitors.

'Ellsworth, your location's hot.'

'I see him, Dallas. I've got him.'

The instant the elevator doors opened, she was streaking across the lobby. Ellsworth was inside the south doors, and out cold. 'Tranq'd him. Jesus.' She pulled her weapon and went through the doors.

'Suspect is out of controlled area. I've got an officer down at the south entrance. Suspect is on foot—'

She heard the scream as she raced for the corner. He was dragging a woman out of a car. Even as Eve reached the curb and brought up her weapon, he'd tossed her onto the street and had dived behind the wheel.

Pivoting, she pounded to the sportster she'd parked at the entrance.

'I'll drive.' Roarke beat her to the car by a stride. 'I know the car better.'

With no time to argue, she jumped into the passenger seat. 'Suspect's jacked a vehicle, is heading east on Seventy-fourth in a white minijet, N-Y-C license C-H-A-R-L-I-E. That's Charles Abel Roger Loser Ice Even. This is Dallas in pursuit. I need ground and air support. He's got a four-block lead, now approaching Lex.'

Roarke shoved the sportster into turbo, rocketed.

'Make that three blocks,' she murmured, eyes straight ahead when they swung around a commuter tram with a layer of paint to spare.

'He didn't boost a snail,' Roarke commented, zigzagging through traffic without a single tap for the brakes. 'Those minijets have muscle if he knows how to use it. But he shouldn't be able to outrun us in the long haul.'

As he approached a red light, Roarke gauged the timing, punched for power, and streaked his way through the crossing traffic, leaving tire squeals and blasting horns in his wake.

'Not if we live through it. Suspect is turning south on Lexington, heading downtown. Where is my goddamn air support?' she barked into the communicator.

'Air support is being deployed.' Whitney's words sliced through like shards of glass. 'Ground units heading in from east and west, should join your pursuit at Forty-fifty and Lex.'

'I'm in a civilian vehicle, Commander,' she told him, then finished with a description. 'We're less than two blocks behind him now and closing. Suspect crossing Fiftieth.'

She barely hissed when a maxi-bus lumbered across their path. Roarke punched for vertical, sending the car in a long sweeping rise that had Eve's stomach pitching. They leapfrogged over the bus and dived for the street.

But the bus had blocked their view just long enough. 'He's turned off. Damn it. Which way?'

'Right,' Roarke decided. 'He was shifting to the right lane before the fucking bus.'

'Suspect believed to now be traveling west on Forty-ninth. Ground and air support adjust direction to pursue.'

The light changed as they reached the corner. Roarke readied to whip for the turn. New Yorkers being what they were, pedestrians surged forward into the street as the light beamed yellow and, in defiance of the electric blue bullet bearing down on them, didn't give an inch.

'Idiots, assholes.' Eve barely had time to finish the thought before Roarke was airborne again and skimming down the sidewalk. 'Don't kill anyone, for Christ's sake.'

He nearly nipped the outer edge of a glide-cart umbrella, terrorized a trio of Hasidic Jews carrying their briefcases of gems to market. A Bosc pear heaved by the cart operator sailed past Eve's window.

She caught sight of the fishtailing rear of the minijet as it rounded the corner on Fifth Avenue. The glide-cart on that corner wasn't as lucky. She saw the unit upend and the operator go sprawling.

'We're losing ground here. He's on Fifth now.' She checked the skies and ground her teeth when she spotted media copters rather than cops. 'Commander, I need my air support.'

'A hitch at Control. Support delayed. Deployment in five minutes.'

'That's too late, too goddamn late,' she murmured, and felt little satisfaction when she heard the scream of sirens approaching from the rear.

'We'll take the long shot,' Roarke decided. His smile was as sharp and deadly as a laser when he punched the sportster into sharp vertical, into full-speed nose lift that had the blood draining out of Eve's face and her fingers digging hard into the buttery leather of her seat.

'Oh Christ, I hate this.'

'Just hang on. We go up and diagonal, we'll cut his lead.'

And over twenty-story buildings at approximately a hundred miles an hour.

The street dropped away as they rose up into the arena of tourist blimps and air tram commuters. Eve got a much closer look at the New York City Tourist Board's pride and joy than she cared to. The monotonous recording touting the joys of the Diamond District blared in her ears.

'There!' She had to shout over the noise, pointed due west. 'White minijet. He's caught in a jam on Fifth, between Forty-sixth and Forty-fifth.' Then she spotted another, half a block ahead of the first. 'Shit, there are two of them. Take us down, park it on the sidewalk if you have to. All units, two white minijets on Fifth, both stopped. One between Forty-sixth and Forty-fifth, the second between Forty-fifth and Forty-fourth. Block southbound traffic on Fifth at Forty-third.'

Her stomach tripped over her throat as Roarke took them into a dive. He leveled off ten feet above street level, set down with barely a shimmy in a maxi-bus lane directly across from the northernmost minijet.

Eve leaped out, aimed her weapon at the driver. 'NYPSD. Out of the car, keep your hands where I can see them.'

The driver was male, midtwenties. He was wearing a lime green Day-Glo jacket and matching pegged pants. Sweat poured down his face as he got out of the car. 'Don't stun me, for God's sake, I'm just a runner, that's all. Just making a living.'

'In the position.' She reached out, spun him around. 'Hands on the roof of the car.'

'I don't want my wife to know about this. I want a lawyer,' he demanded as she patted him down. 'I've only been doing runs for six months. Give me a fucking break.'

She dragged her restraints from her pocket, dragged his arms behind his back. Even as she snapped them on, she knew he wasn't her man.

'Move one inch from this spot and I'll zap you unconscious.'

She started off at a jog, then slowed as she watched Roarke walk back toward her from the other car. 'All I got is an illegals runner with the brains of a toadstool.'

'The other car's empty,' he told her. 'He's ditched it.' Jaw set, he scanned the street crowded with vehicular and pedestrian traffic. Three criss-crossing sky-glides were jammed with people. Grand Central was a crosstown block away. 'We lost him.'

Chapter Eighteen

Two hours later, Eve was in the Tower, explaining the failure of the operation to Chief Tibble.

'I take full responsibility for the unsatisfactory outcome of the operation, sir. The performance of the officers involved in the task force is not to blame.'

'Fucking circus.' Tibble tapped a huge fist lightly on the surface of his desk. 'Dogfights, injured civilians, the primary officer hot-rodding around and over the city in a souped-up, two-hundred-thousand-dollar sports jet. The damn media fly-bys caught you shooting across town in it. That's going to look just dandy for the departmental image on screen.'

'Excuse me, sir,' Eve said stiffly. 'My department-issue unit was recently destroyed and has yet to be replaced. I opted to utilize a personal vehicle until my new unit is issued. Departmental procedure allows for this contingency.'

His fist stopped pounding as he narrowed his eyes at her. 'Why the hell hasn't your unit been replaced?'

'The automatic requisition was not processed, for reasons I can't explain, Chief Tibble. My aide applied again today for a replacement, and was told that it would take approximately a week to never.'

He let out a long breath. 'Idiot paper pushers. You'll have your replacement by oh eight hundred, Lieutenant.'

'Thank you, sir. There's no question that the operation today was unsatisfactory. However, Detective McNab has pinpointed the Luxury Towers as the source of today's transmission. I'd like to join the sweep and search team deployed there.'

'How many angles of this investigation do you intend to handle personally, Lieutenant?'

'All of them, sir.'

'And have you considered that your objectivity might be in question in this matter? That you've begun to pit your ego against the killer's. Are you investigating a series of homicides, Lieutenant, or are you playing his games?'

She accepted the slap, agreed that she deserved it, but she wouldn't back off. 'At this point in time, sir, I don't believe I can do one without doing the other. I realize that my performance in this matter has been substandard. It won't continue to be.'

'I'd like to know how the hell I'm supposed to give you a dressing-down when you keep beating me to it.' He pushed away from the desk and rose. 'Consider your wrist officially slapped. Privately, I'll tell you that I don't find your performance in this matter substandard. I've watched the recordings of the operation. You command well, Lieutenant, with authority and without hesitation. Your strategy to entrap this perpetrator can't be faulted. Damn poodle,' he said under his breath. 'And you were denied air support due to some foul-up at control – a foul-up that will be fully investigated. Consider yourself officially supported.

'Now . . .' He lifted a small clear globe filled with glinting blue fluid, turned it so that the tiny enclosed sea ebbed and flowed. 'The media will no doubt enjoy our embarrassment today. We'll just take that on the chin. Will he contact you again?'

'He won't be able to stop himself. He's likely to have a period of silence. He'll sulk, have a temper fit, and he'll attempt to find some way to harm me physically. I'd say he'd consider that I cheated, and it's his game. Cheating would be a sin, and he'll want God to punish me. He'll be scared, but he'll be pissed, too.'

She hesitated, then decided to lay out her thoughts. 'I don't believe he'll return to the Luxury Towers. Whatever he is, Chief, he's smart. He'll know that if we could get as close as we did today, it's likely we've begun to track his transmissions. He made us in the lobby today, so he's got sharp instincts when it comes to cops. He walked into us at the hotel and we blew it. But if we can find his equipment, if we can find his hole, we'll find him.'

'Then find his hole, Dallas, and bury it.'

She swung by her office to make copies of all audio and video discs from the failed operation. She intended to study every second of every disc.

'I told you to go on home,' she said when she saw Roarke waiting for her.

He rose, walked over, and rubbed his knuckles over her cheek. 'How much skin did Tibble leave on your hide?'

'He barely stripped any, considering.'

'This wasn't your fault.'

'Fault doesn't matter, responsibility does. And this was mine.'

Understanding, he rubbed her shoulders. 'Want to go out and kick some poodles?'

She let out a short laugh. 'Maybe later. I've got to get my record copies then I'm heading over to join the search and sweep team.'

'You haven't eaten in hours,' he pointed out.

'I'll grab something at a QuickMart.' Disgusted, she scrubbed her hands over her face. 'Goddamn it, Roarke, we were inches away. Inches. Did he see Baxter go for his weapon through the door? Did one of the team look too hard in his direction? Did he just smell us?'

'Why don't you let me look at the records, with the eye of a veteran cop-spotter?'

'It couldn't hurt.' She turned to her computer, ordered dupes of all operational files. 'We should have plenty of full views of him on the lobby file. There's not much of his face, but maybe you'll spot something that clicks. You've got to know him, Roarke.'

'I'll do what I can.'

'I don't know when I'll be home.' She handed him the copies. 'But don't wait up.'

She grabbed a cheese phyllo and an energy bar at a QuickMart and settled for a tube of Pepsi rather than their notoriously poisonous coffee. She carried the miserable meal with her into the second-floor conference room where McNab was heading the electronic sweep.

'Anything?'

'Plenty of hits on mega-links, laser faxes. The building's lousy with high-end electronics. We're checking floor to floor, but there's nothing on the scale of what our guy plays with.'

Eve set the bag down, then reached out and turned McNab's face toward her with a firm thumb to his chin. There was a bruising knot on his forehead and a long thin scrap just above his right eye. 'Get the MTs to look at that ugly face of yours?'

'Just a bump. Damn dog came at me like an Arena Ball tackle.' He shifted in his chair so that the gold rings in his ears jangled. 'I'd like to apologize for my insubordination during the operation, Lieutenant.'

'No, you wouldn't. You were pissed and you still are.' She pulled out her tube of Pepsi, broke the safety seal. 'You were wrong, and you still are. So stuff the apology. Don't ever question an order from a superior officer during an operation, McNab, or you'll end up skulking in some little dark room listening to sex noises for a private security hack instead of rising through the ranks of the illustrious EDD.'

While his temper bobbed up and down, he meticulously manipulated his scanner, noting the location of a dual communication unit on floor eighteen.

'Okay, maybe I'm still a little steamed, and maybe I know I was over the line. I'm lucky if I get out of my cube at Central once a month. This was the closest I've come to action, then you yanked me.'

Looking at him, at that young, smooth, eager face, she felt incredibly old and jaded. 'McNab, have you ever participated in hand-to-hand other than in training?'

'No, but—'

'Have you ever discharged your weapon at anything other than a heat target?'

His mouth went sulky. 'No. So I'm not a warrior.'

'Your strengths are right here.' She tapped a finger on his scanner, then pulled out her energy bar. 'You know as well as I do how many applicants wash out of the EDD program every year. They only take the top. And you're good. I've worked with the best,' she said, thinking of Feeney, 'so I know. This is where I need you to take this fucker down.'

Then none too gently, she tapped her finger on the swollen bruise on his forehead. 'And action mostly just hurts like a bitch.'

'Guys are going to rag me for weeks. Getting taken down by a dog.'

'It was a pretty big dog.' Sympathetic now, Eve took out the phyllo and gave it to him. 'Really big teeth. Lorimar took a bite in the ankle.'

'Yeah?' Somewhat cheered, McNab bit into the bread and cheese. 'I hadn't heard.' A series of beeps had him frowning at the scanner. 'Lots of goodies on nineteen, east wing apartment.' He shifted to his communicator. 'Blue team, check on nineteen twenty-three. It looks like some rich kid's entertainment center, but it's loaded.'

'I'll go check on the door-to-doors,' Eve said. 'You get any interesting hits, pass them on to me.'

'You first, Dallas. Thanks for the food. Say, ah, where's Peabody?'

Eve lifted a brow as she glanced back over her shoulder. 'Overseeing the breakdown of equipment in the penthouse at the Arms. She doesn't like you, McNab.'

'I know.' He flashed a grin. 'I find that really attractive in a woman.' He turned back to his scanner, humming as he went through the complicated task of separating the beeps into known components.

At midnight, she ordered in a new crew, sent McNab home for eight hours off, and packed it in. It didn't surprise her to find Roarke up, in his office, enjoying a glass of wine while he studied the recordings.

'I had the first team wrap for the night. They were getting punchy.'

'You look a bit punchy yourself, Lieutenant. Shall I pour you a glass of wine?'

'No, I don't want anything.' She walked over, noted that he paused the recording at the point where McNab made abrupt contact with the stationary panel of the main doors. 'I don't think he'd consider that suitable for framing.'

'No luck locking in on his communication center?'

'McNab's worried he's shut it down.' She rubbed at the stiffness at the base of her neck. 'So am I. He could have done it by remote while he was on the run, or contacted someone he's working with. Mira's profile indicates he'd want constant praise and attention during the game, so it's possible he's got a partner – likely a female, strong personality. Authority figure.'

'Mother?'

'That would be my first guess. But a remote's just as likely as him having Mommy by his side. He wants to believe he's running the show, so he probably has his own place.'

She stepped forward, closer to the screen, staring hard at the image of the man in the long coat and chauffeur's cap. 'It's like a costume,' she murmured. 'Another part of the game. He's dressing up. It's concealing, but it's also, I don't know, dramatic. Like in a play, and he's the star. But right here, you can see that we've thrown him a cue he wasn't expecting. See the shock, the panic in the body language. His weight's off balance because he took a step back. Instinctive retreat. His free hand's coming up, a defensive gesture. I bet his eyes are moon wide with shock behind the sunshades.'

Something caught her, made her frown and step even closer. 'Can't see what the hell he's looking at. You can't see where his eyes are focused. Just the angle of his head. Is he looking at Baxter going for his weapon on the other side of the glass? Or is he looking at McNab crash headfirst into the panel?'

'From his angle, you'd see both.'

'Yeah. Baxter look like a cop going for his stunner to you? Couldn't he be a doorman, alerted by the commotion, reaching for his security beeper?'

'I'd go for cop,' Roarke told her. 'Look at the way he moves.' He ordered the recorder to rewind thirty seconds, then play. The room erupted with noise so he muted audio. 'Watch – it's a textbook cop move. The spin, knees bent, body braced, the right hand sweeping inside the coat at the armpit. Doormen wear beepers on their belts, so his grab's too high for that.'

'But it happened fast, look how fast.'

'If he knows cops, has had many dealings with them, it could have been enough. McNab doesn't look anything like a cop, doesn't move like one. The only way that would have tipped him is if he recognized Ian, knew him to be a cop.'

'McNab doesn't do much field work, as he complained to me tonight. But they're both electronics jocks, so it's not impossible they've brushed up against each other. Damn it, I should have thought of that before I sent him out.'

'You're Monday morning quarterbacking, darling Eve.'

'What?'

'We really have to do something about your lack of interest in sports other than baseball. It's useless to second-guess yourself here. I watched you run that operation, and you did it with a cool and steady hand.'

'I still fumbled.' She smiled thinly. 'How's that for sports?'

'The fat lady has yet to sing,' he said and laughed at her confused stare. 'Meaning the game isn't over. But tonight is. You're going to bed.'

She'd been about to say the same, but it was always hard to resist arguing. 'Says who?'

'The man you married for sex.'

She ran her tongue around her teeth, hooked her thumbs in her front pockets. 'I just said that to needle a sexually repressed, homicidal maniac.'

'I see. So you didn't marry me for sex.'

'The sex is an entertaining element.'

'An element you're too tired to explore tonight.'

Because her eyes were drooping, she narrowed them. 'Says who?'

He had to laugh, slipping an arm around her waist to walk with her to the elevator so she wouldn't have to climb stairs. 'Darling Eve, you would argue with the devil himself.'

'I thought I was.' She yawned, let herself lean on him a little. In the bedroom, she stripped, let her clothes lay where they fell. 'They're doing a full scan on the car he left in front of the hotel,' she murmured as she crawled into bed. 'It's a rental – charged to Summerset's secondary credit account.'

'I've shifted all my accounts and numbers.' He lay beside her. 'I'll see that the same is done with Summerset's in the morning. He won't find it as easy to access now.'

'No latents on the scan so far. Gloves. Swept some strands

of hair. Might be his. Couple foreign carpet fibers. Coulda come off his shoes. Running them.'

'That's fine.' He stroked her hair. 'Turn it off now.'

'He'll shift targets. Didn't get his points today.' When her voice thickened, he turned so she could curl against him. 'It's gonna be soon.'

Roarke thought she was right. But the target wouldn't be her, not for now. For now she was curled up warm against him, and asleep.

Patrick Murray was drunker than usual. In the normal scheme of things, he avoided sobriety but didn't care to stumble or piss on his hands. But tonight, when the Mermaid Club closed its doors at three in the morning, he had done both, more than once.

His wife had left him. Again.

He loved his Loretta with a rare passion, but could admit he too often loved a cozy bottle of Jamison's more. He'd met his darling at that very club five years before. She'd been naked as the wind and swimming like a fish in the aquatic floor show the club was renowned for, but it had been – for Pat – love at first sight.

He thought of it now as he tripped over the chair he'd been about to upend on the table directly in front of him. Too many pulls of whiskey blurred his vision and hampered him in his maintenance duties. It was his lot in life to mop up the spilled liquor and bodily fluids, to scour the toilets and sinks, to be sure the privacy rooms were aired so they didn't smell like someone else's come the following day.

He'd hired on at the club to do just that five years and two months before, and had been struck by Cupid's arrow when he'd seen Loretta execute a watery pirouette in the show tank.

Her skin, the color of barrel-aged scotch, had gleamed so wet. Her twisty curls of ebony hair had flowed through the virulently dyed blue water. Her eyes behind their protective lenses had gleamed a brilliant lavender.

Pat righted himself, and the chair, before reaching in his pocket for the mini bottle of whiskey. He drained it in a swallow, and though he wobbled, he tucked it neatly in the nearest recycle slot.

He'd been twenty-seven when he'd first set eyes on the magnificent Loretta, and it had been only his second day in America. He'd been forced to leave Ireland in a hurry, due to a bit of a brushup with the law and a certain disagreement over some gambling debts. But he'd found his destiny in the city of New York.

Five years later, he was scraping the same floor clean of unmentionable substances, pocketing the loose credits dropped by patrons who were often more drunk than Pat himself, and mourning, once again, the loss of his Loretta.

He had to admit she didn't have much tolerance for a man who liked his liquor by the quart.

She was what some would call the giant economy size. At five-ten and two hundred fiery pounds, she made nearly two of Patrick Murray. He was a compact man who'd once had dreams of jockeying thoroughbreds on the flat, but he'd tended to miss too many morning exercise rounds due to the inconvenience of a splitting head. He was barely five-five, no more than a hundred and twenty pounds even after a dip in the aquatic show floor tank.

His hair was orange as a fresh carrot, his face splattered with a sandblast of freckles of the same hue. And Loretta had often told him it was his sad and boyish blue eyes that had won over her heart.

He'd paid her for sex the first time, naturally. After all, it was her living. The second time he'd paid her fee he'd asked if perhaps she might enjoy a piece of pie and a bit of conversation.

She'd charged him for that as well, for the two hours spent, but he hadn't minded. And the third time he'd brought her a two-pound box of near-chocolates and she'd given him the sex for nothing.

A few weeks later they'd been married. He'd stayed almost sober for three months. Then the wagon had tipped, he'd fallen off, and Loretta had lowered the boom.

So it had been, on and off that wagon, for five years. He'd promised her he'd take the cure – the sweat box and shots down at the East Side Substance Abuse Clinic. And he'd meant to. But he'd gotten a little drunk and gone off to the track instead.

He still loved the horses.

Now she was talking divorce, and his heart was broken. Pat leaned on his string mop and sighed at the glinting waters of the empty tank.

Loretta had done two shows tonight. She was a career woman, and he respected that. He'd gotten over his initial discomfort when she'd insisted on keeping her sex license up to date. Sex paid better than sweeping, even better than entertainment, and they sometimes talked of buying a place in the suburbs.

She hadn't spoken to him that evening, no matter how he'd tried to draw her out. When the show ended, she'd climbed down the ladder, wrapped herself in the striped robe he'd given her for her last birthday, and swished off with the other water beauties.

She'd locked him out of their apartment, out of her life, and, he was afraid, out of her heart.

When the buzzer sounded from the delivery entrance, he shook his head sadly. 'Where'd the time go?' he wondered. 'Morning already.'

He made his bleary way into the back, fumbled twice with the code before getting it right, and hauled open the steel-enforced door. He puzzled a moment, standing framed there, with the security light beeping and the black-coated figure smiling in at him.

'It's still dark, isn't it?' Pat said.

'It's always darkest before the dawn, so they say.' He stepped forward, offering a gloved hand. 'Do you remember me, Paddy?'

'Do I know you? Are you from home?' Pat took the offered hand and never even felt the slight pinch as he pitched forward.

'Oh, I'm from home, Paddy, and I'll be sending you there.' He let the unconscious man slide to the floor before turning and carefully recoding the locks.

It was easy enough to drag a man of Pat's size from the back room into the main lounge. Once there, he set his valise on a table, carefully unpacked what he would need.

He tested the laser – one quick shot to the ceiling – and smiled in approval. The shackles were lightweight and fashioned from a material approved by NASA II. The 'link was heavier, loaded as it was with its maxi-battery and interfaced jammer. He found a handy outlet behind the bar and quickly set up his communications.

Humming a little, he turned the tank system to drain. It sounded like one huge and slightly clogged toilet flushing, he thought, amused, then walked back to kick Pat sharply in the ribs.

Not a stir, not a whimper.

With a sigh he bent down, efficiently checking vital signs. The man was stinking drunk, he realized. And he'd used too much of the tranq. Vaguely irritated by the miscalculation, he took a pressure syringe filled with amphetamine and jabbed it against Pat's limp arm.

There was barely a stir, hardly a whimper.

The anger built quickly, until he shook with it. 'Wake up, you bastard.' Rearing back, he slapped Pat's face, front handed, then back, over and over. He wanted him awake and aware for all of it. When the slaps didn't work, he used his fists, pummeling until blood spurted and soaked his gloves.

Pat only moaned.

His breathing was ragged now, his eyes beginning to sting with tears. He only had two hours, for God's sake. Was he supposed to work miracles? Was he supposed to think of everything?

Had God abandoned him after all, for his failures?

If it hadn't been for Dallas, he'd have finished with the pig Brian by now, and Pat would have waited another day or two. Another day or two to observe more closely his habits and patterns and he wouldn't have been in such a hurry to put him under.

He heard a crash, blinked dully. He realized he'd thrown a chair and broken the mirror behind the bar.

Well, so what? It was just a filthy sex club in a filthy city. He'd like to destroy it, to smash every glass, set fire to it, watch it burn.

Christ Himself had destroyed the marketplace, hadn't he? In righteous anger at the moneylenders, the harlots and sinners.

But there wasn't time. That wasn't his mission.

Pat Murray was his mission tonight.

Resigned, he picked up the laser. He'd just have to remove the eye while Pat was unconscious. It didn't matter, he decided, and bent to his work. There would be plenty of fun after that. More than enough entertainment.

It pleased him that he removed the eye so neatly, so efficiently. Like a surgeon. The first time he'd been sloppy. He could admit that now. His hand had shaken, and nerves had screamed. Still he'd done it, hadn't he, as he'd been bidden. He'd finished what he started. And he would finish it all. Finish them all.

He took a moment to slip the organ into a small bottle of clear fluid. He would have to leave this one behind, of course. He'd accepted that too. If the plan was to move forward, he wouldn't be able to add Pat Murray's eye to his collection.

It was enough to have taken it. An eye for an eye.

Pat began to moan again as he dragged him to the tank. 'Ah, now you wake up, you drunken sinner.' Sucking in his breath, he heaved Pat over his shoulder and, with the shackles dangling over his arm, climbed the ladder.

He was proud that he was strong enough to do this, carry a grown man on his back. He hadn't always been so fit. He'd been sickly as a child, puny and weak. But he'd been motivated to change that. He'd listened to what he was told, did what was necessary. He'd exercised both body and mind until he was ready. Until he was perfect. Until the time was right.

Inside the empty tank he laid Pat down, took a small diamond bit drill from his pocket. He hummed a favorite hymn as he punched the small holes into the tank floor. He fit the shackles onto clamps, tested them by standing and pulling with all his strength. Satisfied they wouldn't give, he turned to remove Pat's clothing.

'Naked we're born and naked we die,' he said cheerfully, then locked the shackles over Pat's thin ankles. He studied the battered face, noted the slight flicker of the eyelid. 'How loud will you scream for mercy, I wonder?'

He slipped a token from his pocket, then dropped it with a clink on the floor of the tank. The statue of the Virgin Mother was kissed reverently then affixed to the floor facing the sinner.

'Do you remember me, Paddy?'

There was red-hot pain and stomach cramping nausea as Pat swam toward consciousness. He groaned with it, whimpered, then screamed.

'Oh Jesus, sweet Jesus, what is it?'

'Retribution.'

Sobbing, Pat pushed a hand to his face, trying to cover the worse part of the agony. And he found what had been done to him and wailed. 'My God, my eye, my God, I've lost my eye.'

'It's not lost.' Now he laughed, laughed so hard he had to hold his sides. 'It's on the table out there.'

'What's happening? What's done?' Desperate and cold sober, Pat dragged at the shackles. Pain boiled through him like acid. 'You want money, they don't leave anything after closing. I don't have the code for the lock box. I'm just the janitor.'

'I don't want money.'

'What do you want? What have you done to me? Oh, sweet Mary. What do you want?'

'Don't use her name.' Fired again, he struck Pat hard in the face with a balled fist. 'I don't want her name in your filthy tongue. Use it again, and I'll cut it out of your sinful mouth.'

'I don't understand.' Pat wept it. The blow had knocked him to his knees. 'What do you want from me?'

'Your life. I want to take your life. I've waited fifteen years and it's tonight.'

Tears swam out of the eye he had left and the pain was a hideous thing. But still he swung out, tried to grab a leg. When his fingers swept air, he tried again, cursing now, threatening, weeping.

'This would be fun, but I have a schedule.' He moved to the ladder, climbed nimbly while Pat's pleas and threats echoed up to him. 'It'll take nearly an hour for the water to cover your head at the speed I'll use. An hour,' he repeated, grinning at Pat through the glass wall as he climbed down. 'You'll be nearly insane by then. The water will rise, inch by inch. Ankles, knees, waist. You'll be straining against the shackles until your ankles are raw and bleeding and burning but it won't help. Waist, chest, neck.'

Still smiling he turned to the controls, adjusting until the water poured through the side channels.

'Why are you doing this, you bloody bastard?'

'You have nearly an hour to think about that.'

He knelt, crossed himself, folded his hands, and offered a prayer of celebration and gratitude.

'You're praying? You're praying?' Struggling to focus, Pat stared at the statue of the Virgin as the water rose over her robes. 'Mother of God,' he whispered. 'Dear Mother of God.' And he prayed himself, as fiercely, as fervently as he ever had in his life. If she would intercede on his behalf, he would swear by her mercy never to lift a bottle to his lips again.

For a silent five minutes, the supplicates, one in the tank, one outside it, mirrored each other.

Then one rose lightly and smiled. 'It's too late for prayers. You've been damned since you sold a life to a devil for profit.'

'I never did. I don't know you.' The water licked slyly at his knees, urging Pat to struggle up. 'You've got the wrong man.'

'No, you're just one ahead of schedule.' Because he had time before he needed to make the necessary calls, he went behind the bar and helped himself to a soft drink as Pat shouted and begged for mercy. No spirits had ever passed his lips.

'I hope you remember me before you're dead, Pat. I hope you remember who I am and who I come from.'

He broke the seal on the tube, carried it around the bar. Humming again, he set a chair directly in front of the tank and took his seat. And, sipping, watched the show.

It was exactly five A.M. when the 'link woke her. She shot up, fully alert, heart roaring in her chest. It took only an instant to realize it wasn't the 'link signal that had her pulse racing, but the dream it had interrupted.

And she knew it was him.

'Block video, set trace.' She held a hand behind her to nudge Roarke back. 'Dallas.'

'You thought you could win by cheating, but you were wrong. All you did was postpone fate. I'll still kill Brian Kelly. A different time, a different place.'

'You screwed up, pal. I could see you sweating when you

realized we were waiting for you. We knew exactly what you were going to do, and how you planned to do it.'

'You didn't stop me. You couldn't get near me.'

'We're so close you feel our breath on the back of your neck.'

'Not so close. "Who scream? Who shriek? Who have strife? Who have anxiety? Who have wounds for nothing? Who have black eyes? Those who linger long over wine, those who engage in trails of blended wine." I'm watching a man die. He's dying now. Do you want to hear who screams and shrieks?'

Quickly he switched off the filter and opened the 'link to the room.

Screams and sobs exploded through Eve's speaker and iced her blood. 'Now who's cheating?' she demanded. 'You're going to kill him, then give me a clue. That's what you did with Brennen. What kind of game is it if you don't take any risks?'

'He's not dead yet. I think you have almost, almost enough time.'

She was already out of bed and dragging on clothes. 'Where's the clue?'

'I'm even going to make this one easy for you. Dine and dance and watch the naked mermaids. It's after hours, but come on in. The water's fine. He's starting to gurgle, Lieutenant. Don't take too long.'

Sick of him, she cut the transmission herself. 'It's a club,' she said to Roarke as she strapped on her weapon harness.

'The Mermaid Club. Naked water dancers.'

'Then that's our best shot.' She stepped into the elevator with him. 'He's going to drown this one.' She looked at Roarke as she pulled out her communicator to call in. 'You don't own the Mermaid Club, do you?'

'No.' His eyes were hard. 'But I used to.'

Chapter Nineteen

The sun was breaking over the East River as they shot southward through the still-slumbering uptown. Clouds scooted over the light, moving lazily, making it the thick color of powder.

Roarke chose to keep the car on manual, and avoided Broadway with its never-ending party and unfriendly traffic. He could feel Eve's frustration riding with them like a third passenger crowding the car.

'It isn't possible to outguess a madman.'

'He's got a pattern, but it's coming apart. I can't get the threads of it.' *Think, think, think*, she ordered herself as they bulleted through the change-of-shift traffic in midtown. 'Do you know who owns the Mermaid Club?'

'Not personally. It was something I picked up years ago. One of my first downtown properties. Actually I won it in a dice game, kept it a couple of years, then sold it off at a tidy profit.' Spotting a loaded commuter tram stalled across Seventh, he whipped west and headed crosstown.

'Has to be the owner or someone who works there.' Eve pulled out her personal palm computer. Her teeth snapped together when Roarke hit one of the potholes neglected by the city's road and infrastructure teams. 'Silas Tikinika? Ring a bell?'

'No.'

'Then he's probably sleeping peacefully tonight. I'll run employees.'

'We're nearly there,' Roarke told her. 'We'll know soon enough.'

The animated mermaid, naked but for her glossy green tail, was dark and still over the safety grilled window. He pulled up at the all but empty curb. It was rare for people in this ugly little section of town to have personal transportation. Without the auto-shield and security feature on Roarke's car, it wouldn't be waiting when he came out.

He caught a glimpse of a couple of street ghosts hovering in a doorway two buildings down. They drifted out in the murky dawn, then faded back at the scream of approaching sirens.

'I'm not waiting for the backup,' she told Roarke, pulling both her weapon and her master code. Then she reached down, tugged a stunner from her boot. 'Take my clinch piece – and make sure it disappears when the uniforms get here.' Her eyes held his for one quick moment. 'You take the left.'

Wild light and wilder music met them when they went through the door. Eve swung right, sweeping. Then sprinted forward with a shout of warning for the man clinging to the ladder on the side of the show tank.

'Stop! Keep your hands where I can see them.'

'I've got to get him out.' Summerset's knuckles scraped metal as he slid down a rung. 'He's drowning.'

'Get the hell out of my way.' She all but dragged him off the ladder and threw him at Roarke. 'Find the drain switch, for God's sake, Hurry.' Then she was scrambling up, and diving in.

Strings of blood swam in the water like exotic fish. The man who was bolted to the floor of the tank was blue around the lips, his single eye open and staring. She could see both his fingers and ankles were raw from fighting the shackles. She grabbed his battered face, fit her mouth over his, and gave him her breath.

Lungs burning, she pushed off, fought her way to the surface, and sucked in more air. Without wasting the breath on words, she dived again. Her gaze flicked briefly to the face of the Madonna, its carved eyes watching tortured death with absolute serenity.

Eve shuddered once, then fought for life.

On her third trip up, she thought the surface was closer, and swimming down, she turned her head and got a watery view of Roarke coming up the ladder.

He'd taken time to pull off his shoes and jacket. When he reached the floor of the tank, he yanked her arm, jerked a thumb for her to go up. So they worked in tandem, one drawing in air, the other giving it while the water swirled down.

When she could stand, her head above water, she coughed violently. 'Summerset,' she managed.

'He won't go anywhere. For God's sake, Eve.'

'I haven't got time to argue about it. Can you pick the locks on the restraints?'

Dripping, still gasping for air, he stared at her. Then he dug in his pocket for his penknife. 'Here come your men.'

'I'll deal with them. See what you can do down there.'

She flipped her wet hair out of her eyes as four uniforms charged inside the club. 'Dallas,' she shouted. 'Lieutenant Eve. Get some med-techs here, fast. Resuscitation equipment. Drowning victim. I don't know how long he was under, but there's no pulse. And someone turn that goddamn music off. Glove up. I want this scene preserved as much as possible.'

The water was down to her knees now, and the air was making her shiver in her wet clothes. Her muscles ached from supporting the dead weight of the victim. She saw Roarke finesse the lock on the first shackle and shifted to adjust.

The minute the second ankle was free, she laid the body down in the few remaining inches of water and, straddling it, began pumping his chest.

'I want a CPR kit in here, some blankets.' The last word echoed as the music shut abruptly off. Now she could hear her ears ringing. 'Come on, come on, come back,' she panted, then leaned forward and forced air into his mouth.

'Let me do it.' Roarke knelt beside her. 'You've got a crime scene to secure.'

'The MTs.' She continued to count the chest pumps in her head. 'They'll be here any minute. You can't stop until they get here.'

'I won't stop.'

At her nod, he placed his hands over hers, picked up her rhythm. 'Who is he, Roarke?'

'I don't know.' He glanced up briefly as Eve got to her feet. 'I just don't know.'

It was a great deal harder climbing out of the tank than it had been getting in, Eve realized. She was winded by the time she reached the lip. She took a moment to catch her breath, to draw it into lungs that felt seared and scraped. Then she swung her leg over and started down.

Peabody was waiting at the bottom. 'The MTs were right behind me, Dallas.'

'He's pretty far gone. Don't know if they can bring him back.' She looked through the glass, watched Roarke working steadily. 'Take the uniforms. Form two teams and do a search. You won't find him, but look anyway. Secure all doors. Engage recorders.'

Peabody looked over Eve's shoulder to where Summerset stood, hands at his sides, watching Roarke from the far end of the tank. 'What are you going to do?'

'My job. You do yours. I want this scene secured and a sweep team ordered. Do you have a field kit with you?'

'I don't have a detective kit, just my street and scene bag.'

'I'll use that.' She took the bag Peabody offered. 'Get started,' she ordered, then signaled the emergency medical team that rushed in. 'Inside the tank. Drowning victim, no pulse. CPR in progress for approximately ten minutes.'

She turned away, knowing there was nothing more she

could do there. Water squelched in her boots, dripped from her hair and face as she walked over to Summerset. Because her leather jacket weighed on her like a stone, she stripped it off and slammed it on the table.

'Goddamn it, Summerset, you're under arrest. Suspicion of attempted murder. You have the right to—'

'He was alive when I got here. I'm almost sure he was alive.' His voice sounded thin and thoughtful. Eve recognized the symptoms of shock in it, and in his glassy eyes. 'I thought I saw him move.'

'You'd be smart to wait until I've told you your rights and obligations before you make any statement.' She lowered her voice. 'You'd be real smart to say nothing, not a fucking thing, until Roarke rounds you up his fancy lawyers. Now be smart and shut up.'

But he refused the lawyers. When Eve walked into the interview room where he was being guarded by a uniform, Summerset sat stiffly and continued to stare straight ahead.

'I won't need you,' she told the guard. She came around the table and sat when the guard left the room. She'd taken time to change into dry clothes, warm up her system with coffee; and she had checked with the medical team that had brought the man identified as Patrick Murray back to life, and the doctors who were fighting to keep him that way.

'It's still attempted murder,' she said conversationally. 'They brought Murray back from the dead, but he's in a coma, and if he makes it he may be brain damaged.'

'Murray?'

'Patrick Murray, another Dublin boy.'

'I don't remember a Patrick Murray.' His bony fingers moved through his disordered hair. His eyes looked blindly around the room. 'I would – I would like some water.'

'Sure, fine.' She rose to fill a pitcher. 'Why aren't you letting Roarke set up the lawyers?'

'This isn't his doing. And I have nothing to hide.'

'You're an idiot.' She slammed the pitcher in front of him. 'You don't know how bad it can be once I turn the recorder on and start on you. You were at the scene of an attempted murder, caught by the primary investigator climbing out—'

'In,' he snapped. Her tone had torn away the mists that kept closing in on his mind. 'I was going into the tank.'

'You're going to have to prove that. I'm the first one you're going to have to convince.' She raked both hands through her hair in a gesture of fatigue and frustration that made Summerset frown. Her eyes, he noted, were reddened from the water, and deeply shadowed.

'I can't hold back with you this time,' she warned him.

'I expect nothing from you.'

'Good. Then we start even. Engage recorder. Interview with subject Summerset, Lawrence Charles, in the matter of the attempted murder of Patrick Murray on this date. Interview conducted by primary, Dallas, Lieutenant Eve. Commence oh eight fifteen. Subject has been Mirandized and has waived counsel and representation at this time. Is that correct?'

'That is correct.'

'What were you doing in the Mermaid Club at six-thirty in the morning?'

'I received a transmission at about six-fifteen. The caller didn't identify himself. He told me to go there, immediately and alone.'

'And you always go to sex clubs when some anonymous guy calls you up at dawn and tells you to?'

Summerset sent her a withering look, which cheered her a bit. He wasn't down yet, she decided.

'I was told that a friend of mine was being held there, and that she would be harmed if I didn't obey instructions.'

'What friend?'

He poured the water now, drank one small sip. 'Audrey Morrell.'

'Yeah, she was your alibi for Brennen's killing. That didn't pan out too well for you. Sure you want to use her again?'

'There's no need for sarcasm, Lieutenant. The transmission came in. It will be on the log.'

'And we'll check that. So this anonymous caller tells you to get over to the Mermaid Club – you knew where it was?'

'No, I didn't. I am not in the habit of patronizing such establishments,' he said so primly she had to stifle a snort. 'He provided the address.'

'Damn considerate of him. He tells you to get there or your girlfriend'll be in dire straights.'

'He said – he indicated that he would do to her what had been done to Marlena.'

A jolt of pity, of understanding, of great regret thudded through her. But she couldn't offer it. 'Okay, you've got a cop in the house, but you don't bother to tell this cop of a possible abduction and/or assault.'

His eyes were dark and cold on hers, but she saw the fear riding just behind the pride. 'I am not in the habit of depending on the police department.'

'If your story's clean, you wouldn't be sitting here if you had.' Their eyes held as she leaned forward. 'You're aware that there have been three murders and that you were under suspicion for those three murders. Though the evidence is circumstantial, and your testing results were negative, you weren't sitting on a garden bench there.'

She wanted to shake him for being stupid, for disliking her so intensely he hadn't asked for help even when she would have had no choice but to give it. 'Now, you claim to have gotten an anonymous call and end up on the scene of an attempted murder.'

'It isn't a claim, it's a fact. I couldn't risk someone else I cared for being hurt.' It was as much as he could bear to give, that one reminder of his daughter. 'I wouldn't risk it. When the transmission came through, I acted as I thought I had to act.'

It would have been easier if she hadn't understood. She eased back again. 'The scene and method of this attempted murder follows the same pattern as the three more successful murders.'

She reached down into the bag she'd brought in and took out a small glass jar. It wasn't Patrick Murray's eye that floated in it. The surgeons had hope they could reattach it. But the simulation carried the same impact.

She watched as Summerset stared at the small, floating organ, then turned her head away.

'Do you believe in an eye for an eye?'

'I thought I did.' His voice trembled, then he steadied it. 'I don't know what I believe.'

Saying nothing, she reached down again and picked out the statue of the Madonna. 'The Virgin. Marlena was innocent. She was pure.'

'She was fourteen. Only fourteen.' Tears swam in his eyes, paining them both. 'I have to believe she's at peace. To survive I have to believe. Do you think I could do what's been done here, in her name?' He closed his eyes, desperate for control. 'She was gentle, and unspoiled. I won't answer any more questions about her. Not to you.'

She nodded and rose. But before she turned he caught the pity dark and deep in her eyes. He'd opened his mouth without any idea what he would say, when she spoke again.

'Are you aware that electronics play a primary part in said crimes, and that your incoming log is worth squat?'

Again he opened his mouth, closed it again. What kind of woman was it, he wondered, who could go from melting compassion to whiplash in less than a blink. This time he took a deeper drink. 'The transmission came in, just as I've said.'

Steady again, Eve came back, sat. The image of Marlena was ruthlessly blocked from her mind. 'Did you attempt to contact Audrey Morrell and access her status?'

'No, I—'

'How did you travel to the Mermaid Club?'

'I took my personal vehicle and, following the instructions I was given, parked near the side entrance of the club on Fifteenth Street.'

'How did you get in?'

'The side door was unlocked.'

'What happened then?'

'I called out. No one answered, but the music was very loud. All the lights were on. I went into the lounge area. I saw him right away, in the tank. He – I think he was moving. I thought I saw his lips move. His eye – his eye was gone and his face was battered.'

He began to lose color as he spoke, as the image played back in his head. 'Water was still going into the tank. I didn't know how to shut it off. I started up the ladder, thinking I could pull him out. Then you came in.'

'How were you going to pull him out when he was cuffed to the tank floor?'

'I didn't see that. I didn't see. I only saw his face.'

'You knew Patrick Murray in Dublin?'

'I knew a number of people. I don't remember a Patrick Murray.'

'Okay, let's try this again.'

She worked him for two hours, and worked him hard. His story never shifted by an inch. When she stepped out of Interview, she signaled to Peabody. 'Check and see if my new vehicle's come through and what slot I'll find it in. Let me know, then meet me there in five minutes.'

'Yes, sir. He held up,' she commented. 'If I got hammered that hard in Interview, I'd probably confess just to get some peace.'

He'd held up, she thought, but he'd looked ten years older when she'd finished with him. Old and ill and fragile. Her stomach rolled with guilt. 'The only thing he did this morning

300

was win a stupidity prize,' Eve muttered as she marched down the corridor.

She found Roarke, as she'd expected, waiting in her office. 'I'm getting you ten minutes with him. Talk him into letting you lawyer him. I don't care how you do it.'

'What happened? What was he doing there?'

'I don't have time. He'll tell you. I've got some legwork, shouldn't take more than an hour. Then I'm going home, with Peabody. We have to do a search. Technically, I don't need a warrant to sweep his quarters as it's on your property. But you could make it sticky.'

'I've no intention of making this sticky. I want this put away as much as you do.'

'Then do us all a favor – stay away from the house, and see that he stays away once your lawyers spring bail, until after three this afternoon.'

'All right. Do you have an ID on the victim?'

'He's alive, barely, and his name is Patrick Murray. He was the floor scraper at the club. I've got to contact his wife.'

'Pat Murray. Jesus, I didn't recognize him.'

'But you knew him.'

'More professionally than personally. He liked to gamble, I provided games.' His recollection was vague and misty. 'He sold me a tip on where I could find Rory McNee. He must have told someone about it. I certainly didn't, and we weren't friends. The fact is he often ran numbers and minor errands for O'Malley and the others. I never thought of him.' He lifted his hand, let it fall. 'The tip was a dead end, so I never thought of him.'

'Someone did. Doesn't matter if the tip was bogus or not. He sold it to you and that makes him a traitor. Which makes him a target.' Her communicator beeped. 'Dallas.'

'Got your vehicle, Lieutenant, garage section D, level three, slot 101.'

'On my way. I've got to go,' she said to Roarke. 'Call the lawyers.'

He managed to smile a little. 'I did that an hour ago. They should be convincing a judge to grant bail about now.'

Because she was in a hurry, Eve took the motor glide to section D – or as far as section C, where it broke down. She jumped off without bothering to swear and covered the next level at a fast clip. She located slot 101 and found Peabody gawking at a slick new Sunspot with an angled-down hood, converto-roof, and deflector fins, front and rear.

'I thought you said 101.'

'I did.'

'Where's my replacement vehicle?'

'This is it.' Peabody turned with wide eyes. 'Right here. This one.'

Eve only snorted. 'Nobody in Homicide gets one of these muscle jobs – not even the captains.'

'Serial plates match. I checked the key code.' She held out a thin metal plate that could be used by the operator if the code was forgotten. 'It works. I started to call in to Vehicular Requisitions, then figured why be stupid.'

'Well.' Eve pursed her lips, whistled lightly. The color might have been an unfortunate pea green, but everything else about it was prime. 'Wow. Somebody screwed up, but we might as well enjoy it while we can. Get in.'

'You don't have to twist my arm.' Peabody scooted under the upward-opening door and wiggled down until her butt settled comfortably. 'Nice seats. You can program initial for your voiceprint.'

'We'll play with it later.' Eve engaged the ignition manually and lifted a brow in approval at the big cat purr of the engine. 'Not one hiss or hiccup. This could be the beginning of a fine new partnership. I hope the security shield and jacking deflectors are operational.'

'Any particular reason?'

302

'Yeah.' Eve backed up, swung around, and headed down the levels. 'We're going back to the Mermaid Club to search out a couple of street ghosts I spotted this morning. Car like this – cop plates or not – someone's going to try to boost it.'

'It comes with full shields, deflectors, and a thievery deterrent – graduating electrical shocks.'

'That ought to work,' Eve mused. When she reached for her car 'link, Peabody shook her head.

'That's a hands-free. You just tap the second button down on your wheel stem to engage.

'I love technology.' Eve did so and watched the 'link screen go to holding blue. 'Audrey Morrell, Luxury Towers, New York City. Search number and contact.'

Searching . . . Number is on public list. Contacting . . .

An efficient two beeps later, Audrey's face came on screen. There was a smear of bright yellow paint on her right cheek and a distracted look in her eyes. 'Lieutenant Dallas, Ms Morrell.'

'Oh, yes, Lieutenant.' Audrey lifted a hand dotted with cerulean blue to her hair. 'What can I do for you?'

'Could you tell me where you were between five and seven A.M. this morning?'

'Here, here in my apartment. I didn't get up until just after seven o'clock. I've been in all morning working. Why?'

'Just routine. I'd like to set up a follow-up interview with you. Tomorrow morning, at your residence if that's convenient.'

'Well, I, yes, I suppose so. At nine if it won't take more than an hour. I have a private lesson here at ten-thirty.'

'Nine's fine. Thank you. Transmission concluded.' Eve pulled up at the rear of a line of traffic waiting for the light. 'Whoever called Summerset this morning had to know that he's got a thing for Artsy Audrey – as tough as it is to imagine that dried-up stick having a thing for anyone.'

'I've been giving it some thought.'

'And?'

'It can't be one person acting alone – not if we proceed with the belief that Summerset is innocent. It's not just the murders, but the setup. The killer has to know Summerset's routine, and he has to be certain he doesn't deviate from it. Someone's got to be staking him out, following him, while the killer acts. And the killer, according to profile, requires praise, attention, and rewards. Someone has to be giving them to him.'

'That's good, Peabody.'

Peabody said nothing for a moment, then sighed. 'But you already knew all that.'

'It doesn't matter. It's good. Half of detective work is following logic, and you followed it.'

'What's the other half?'

'Following illogic.' She pulled up in front of the Mermaid Club, noted the police seal on the door was blinking red and the security grilles on the windows were still down and locked.

'Street ghosts don't walk much in daylight,' Peabody commented.

'The car will lure them out.' Eve stepped onto the street, waited until Peabody stood on the sidewalk. 'Engage all tampering deflectors and security measures.'

The locks had barely slammed home when she caught the slight movement in the doorway just across from her. 'I've got fifty credits for information,' she said without bothering to raise her voice. Street ghosts heard everything they wanted to hear. 'If I get it, my aide and I won't have to follow through on a tip we got that there are illegal substances in the building.'

'It's twenty credits just to ask. Thirty more for an answer.'

'Fair enough.' She dug in her pocket, pulled a single twenty chip out.

The figure that came toward her was gray. Skin, hair, eyes all the same dust tone as the street sweeping coat he wore. His voice was whisper soft, and the fingers that plucked the credit from Eve's palm did so without touching flesh.

'Do you know Patrick Murray, the floor scraper?'

'Seen him, heard him, don't know him. Dead now though.'

'No, he's not quite dead.' Like you, she thought, he's in some half world. But Patrick still had a chance to come all the way back. 'Did you see anybody go in the club after hours this morning?'

'Seen him.' The ghost's gray lips split open over gray teeth in a horrid smile. 'Heard him. Don't know him.'

'What time?'

'There is no time. Just day, just night. One came when it was more night than day. One came when it was more day than night.'

'Two?' Her eyes sharpened. 'You saw two different people go in, at two different times.'

'First one rang in, second didn't.'

'What did the first one look like?'

'One head, two arms, two legs. Everyone looks the same to me. Nice coat. Thick and black.'

'Was he still here when the second man came?'

'They passed like ghosts.' He smiled again. 'One goes out, the other goes in. Then you came.'

'You got your coffin up there?' She jerked a thumb at the building.

'I should be in it now. It's too day out here.'

'You keep it there.' She passed him another thirty credits. 'If I need you and come back, there'll be another fifty for you.'

'Easy money,' he said and faded back.

'Get me a name on him, Peabody. Run the building for tenants.'

'Yes, sir.' She climbed back in the car. 'Two men. That backs Summerset's story.'

'Our killer doesn't know enough about ghosts to have covered himself there. All he had to do was pass over money and promise more.'

'Those types give me the creeps.' Peabody punched in the request, waited for her ppc to search and find. 'You'd think they could walk through walls, the way they look.'

'You fix on Tranquility for a few years, you'd look the same. File all the names in case our ghost decided to load up his coffin and find another graveyard. Then contact McNab, have him meet us at the house.'

'McNab?'

'Don't be pissy,' Eve ordered, engaging wipers as a thin, wet snow began to fall. 'I need Summerset's 'link logs checked.' She engaged the car 'link again and contacted the hospital for an update on Murray.

'He could come out of it,' she said as she drove through the gates of her home. 'There's more brain wave activity, and he responded to VR stimulus. His wife's with him.'

She barely stopped the car when she noted another vehicle scooting down the drive behind her. Her initial annoyance at the interruption faded when she recognized the car.

'Feeney.'

He got out of his car, his skin pink from the Mexican sun, his clothes rumpled, his wiry red hair topped by an incredibly silly straw hat.

'Hey, kid.' He dragged a box out of the car and, nearly staggering under its weight, carried it toward her. 'Just got back, and the wife wanted me to bring you over a little thank-you for lending us the place. Some place.'

He rolled his eyes. 'Peabody, you gotta tag Dallas for a

couple weeks there. It's a frigging Mex palace right on a damn cliff. You can be lying in bed, reach out the window and pluck a mango right off the tree. Got a pool the size of a lake and a droid to do everything but zip your fly in the morning. You going to let me in? This thing weighs fifty pounds if it weighs an ounce.'

'Sure. I didn't think you were coming back till . . .' She trailed off when she reached the door and realized today was the day he was due back. 'I lost track.'

He dumped the box on a table in the foyer, rolled his shoulders. 'So, what's new?'

'Nothing much. I got three homicides and an attempted, connected. Mutilations. Guy contacted me personally, set it up as a game with religious overtones. Last victim's in a coma, but will probably pull through. Roarke knew all the victims back in Dublin and Summerset just bounced to the top of the suspect list.'

Feeney shook his head. 'Never changes. I tell you I never turned on the screen for two weeks for anything but sports and—' He stopped and his droopy eyes went wide. 'Summerset?'

'I'll fill you in while we do the search. McNab's on his way over.'

'McNab.' Feeney danced after her, ditching his straw hat and his vacation mood as he went. 'EDD's working with you on this?'

'Our guy's an electronics and communications whiz. He's got a high-end jammer among his toys. McNab's been cutting through the layers, and he managed to nail the source. But we haven't found his hole.'

'McNab. The boy's good. I've been bringing him along.'

'You can talk techno-jazz when he gets here. Right now I've got a straight search – and a 'link log to verify.' She paused at the entrance to Summerset's quarters: 'You want in, or do you want to go back and find your party hat?'

'I'll just call the wife and tell her I won't be home for supper.'

Eve grinned. 'I missed you, Feeney. Damned if I didn't.'

He grinned wickedly. 'The wife took six hours of video. She wants you and Roarke to come over for dinner next week, and the show.' Wiggling his brows, he turned to Peabody. 'You come too.'

'Oh, well, Captain, I wouldn't want to horn in on—'

'Stow it, Peabody. If I have to suffer, you have to suffer too. That's chain of command.'

'Another incentive,' Peabody decided, 'for increasing my rank. Thank you, Lieutenant.'

'No problem. Recorder on. Dallas, Lieutenant Eve; Feeney, Captain Ryan; Peabody, Officer Delia entering quarters of Summerset, Lawrence Charles, standard search for evidence.'

She'd never been inside Summerset's private domain. It was just one more surprise. Where she'd expected the stark and utilitarian, straight edges and minimal style, was a lovely living area with soft, blending tones of blue and green, pretty trinkets on tables of honey-hued wood, generous, giving cushions, and an air of welcome.

'Who'd have figured it?' Eve shook her head. 'You look at this and picture a guy who enjoys life, even has friends. Feeney, take the communications center, will you. Peabody – That'll be McNab,' she said when the buzz sounded from the recessed house monitor on the south wall. 'Clear him through, Peabody, then I want you to start in here. I'll take the bedroom.'

Four rooms spread out from the living area like ribs of a fan. The first was an efficient office and control center where Feeney rubbed his hands together and dived into the equipment. Opposite that was an equally efficient kitchen that Eve ignored for now.

Two bedrooms faced each other, but one was doubling now as an artist's studio. Eve pursed her lips, studied the watercolor still life in progress on the easel. She knew it was fruit because she saw the huge bowl with overflowing grapes and glossy apples on the table under the window. On the canvas, however, the fruit was having a very bad season.

'Don't quit your day job,' she murmured and turned in to his bedroom.

The bed was big, with an elaborate pewter headboard that twisted into vines and silvery leaves. The duvet was thick and spread neatly over the mattress without a wrinkle. The closet held two dozen suits, all black, all so similar in style they might have been cloned. Shoes, again black, were housed in clear protective boxes and ruthlessly polished.

That's where she started, checking pockets, searching for anything that would signal a false wall.

When she came out fifteen minutes later, she could hear Feeney and McNab happily chirping about mainframes and signal capacitors. She went through the bureau drawer by drawer and shut down any threatening shudder that she was pawing through Summerset's underwear.

She'd been at it an hour, and was just about to call Peabody in to help her flip the mattress when she looked at the single watercolor over a table decked with hothouse roses.

Odd, she thought, all the other paintings – and the man had an art house supply of them – were in groupings on the walls. This one stood alone. It was a good piece of work, she supposed, moving closer to study the soft strokes, the dreamy colors. A young boy was the centerpiece, his face angelic and wreathed with smiles, his arms loaded with flowers. Wild flowers that spilled over and onto the ground.

Why should the kid in the painting look familiar? she wondered. Something about the eyes. She moved closer yet, peering into that softly painted face. *Who the hell are you?* she asked silently. *And what are you doing on Summerset's wall?*

It couldn't be Summerset's work, not after the canvas she'd

seen in his studio. This artist had talent and style. And knew the child. Eve was almost certain of that.

For a better look, she lifted it from the wall and carried it to the window. Down in the corner she could see a sweep of writing. *Audrey.*

The girlfriend, she mused. She supposed that's why he'd hung it separately, underplanting it with fresh roses. Christ, the man was actually love struck.

She nearly rehung the painting, then laid it on the bed instead. *Something about the boy*, she thought again, and her heart picked up in pace. *Where have I seen him? Why would I have seen him? The eyes. Damn it.*

Frustrated, she turned the painting over and began to pry it from its gilded frame.

'Find something, Dallas?' Peabody asked from the doorway.

'No – I don't know. Something about this painting. This kid. Audrey. I want to see if there's a title – a name on the back of the canvas. Hell with it.' Annoyed, she reached up to tear off the backing.

'Wait. I've got a penknife.' Peabody hurried over. 'If you just slit the backing up here, you can reseal it. This is a nice, professional job.' She slipped the tip of her knife under the thin white paper, lifted it gently. 'I used to do the backings for my cousin. She could paint, but she couldn't turn a screw with a laser drill. I can fix this when—'

'Stop.' Eve clamped a hand on Peabody's wrist when she spotted the tiny silver disc under the backing. 'Get Feeney and McNab. The fucking painting's bugged.'

Alone, Eve lifted the painting out of its frame and, turning it, looked down in the signature corner. Below Audrey's name, deep in the corner that had been covered by the frame, was a green shamrock.

Chapter Twenty

'They could keep an eye on him during his personal time,' Eve said as she drove hard to the Luxury Towers. 'Odds are Feeney and McNab will find another couple paintings of hers through his quarters, wired.'

'Shouldn't Roarke's bug eaters have tapped them?'

'Feeney'll find out why they went undetected. You got anything on her yet?'

'No, sir. All I get from the run is that she's forty-seven, born in Connecticut. She studied at Julliard, did three years at the Sorbonne in Paris, another two at the art colony on Rembrandt Station. She teaches privately and donates instruction time at Culture Exchange. She's lived in New York for four years.'

'She's connected. He's diddled with her records. I'll eat Feeney's ugly new hat if she's from Connecticut. Run the females on the Irish link. All female relatives on the six men who did Marlena. Put it on the monitor so I can see.'

'Take a minute.' Peabody opened Eve's file, found the labeled disc, and inserted it. 'Display females only, with full data.'

Eve pulled over a block from the Luxury Towers as the faces began to run. 'No.' She shook her head, signaling Peabody to go on to the next, and the next. She cursed under her breath, snarled at a glide-cart operator who slid up to try to hawk his wares. 'No, damn it. She's in here, I know it. Wait, hold on, go back one.'

'Mary Patricia Calhoun,' Peabody read off. 'Née McNally, widow of Liam Calhoun. Resides Doolin, Ireland. Artist. Her tax-exempt number's up to date. Age forty-six, one son, also Liam, student.'

'It's the eyes, just like the kid in the painting. She's changed her hair, brown from blond, had some face work done. Longer, thinner nose now, more cheekbone, less chin, but that's her. Split screen, display image of Liam Calhoun, son.'

The picture popped, joining mother and son. 'That's him, from the painting.' She stared hard into the older and no less angelic face, the bright and brilliant green eyes. 'Got you, bastard,' she murmured, then shot back into traffic.

The doorman from their first visit paled when he saw them. It only took a jerk of Eve's thumb to have him moving aside.

'They must have planned this for years, starting with her.' Eve stepped to the center of the glass elevator. 'He'd have been about five when his father died.'

'Before the age of reason,' Peabody commented.

'Right. And she'd have given him the reason. She gave him the mission, the motive. She turned him into a killer. Her only son. Maybe the tendencies were there, heredity and genetics, but she exploited them, used them. Dominated him. That's what Mira said. A dominating female authority figure. Toss in religion and lean it toward vengeance, add in a good brain for electronics, and the training, you can make yourself a monster.'

Eve rang the bell, then laid a hand on the butt of her weapon. Audrey opened the door, offered a hesitant smile. 'Lieutenant. I thought we'd agreed on tomorrow morning. Have I mixed up times again?'

'No, change of plan.' She stepped in, careful to block the door as she scanned the living area. 'We have some questions for you, Widow Calhoun.'

Audrey's eyes flickered, then went dead cold, but her voice remained smooth. 'I beg your pardon?'

'This round's mine. We made you, and your only begotten son.'

'What have you done to Liam?' Audrey curled her hands into claws and leaped forward, aiming for the eyes. Eve dipped under the swipe, pivoted, and wrapped an arm tight around Audrey's neck. She was half Eve's size and no match for a choke hold.

'Her Irish is up, Peabody? Did you hear it? Connecticut, my butt.' With her free hand, Eve reached into her back pocket for her restraints. 'It's a musical accent, isn't it?'

'My personal favorite.' She took Audrey's arm once Eve had clapped on the cuffs.

'We're going to have a nice long chat, Mary Pat, about murder, about mutilation, about motherhood. The three M's, you know?'

'If you've harmed a hair on my boy's head, I'll pull out your heart and eat it.'

'If *I've* harmed him.' Eve lifted her brows, and beneath them her eyes were iced. 'You doomed him the first time you tucked him in with a bedtime story of revenge.'

Disgusted, she turned away, pulled out her communicator. 'Commander, there's been a break in the case. I require a search and seizure warrant for the premises and personal effects of Audrey Morrell.' She paused. 'Also known as Mary Patricia Calhoun.'

They found Liam's hole behind a false wall in a converted pantry. Along with the equipment was a small table covered with a cloth of white Irish lace. Candles sat on it, surrounding a beautifully sculpted marble statue of the Mother of God. Above her, her Son hung from the golden cross.

Is that how she'd wanted Liam to see themselves? Eve wondered. As saints and sufferers? As divine mother and sanctified child? And Audrey herself as the untouched, the wise, the chosen.

'I bet she'd bring him a nice cup of tea and a sandwich with the crusts cut off while he was baiting traps in here. Then pray with him before she sent him off to kill.'

Feeney barely heard Eve's comment as he ran reverent hands over the equipment. 'Have you ever seen the like of this, Ian McNab? This oscillator? What a beauty. And the cross-transmitter with multitask options. Nothing like this on the market.'

'There will be, by next spring,' McNab told him. 'I saw this unit down at Roarke's R and D division. More than half of these components are his, and nearly half of them aren't on the market yet.'

Eve grabbed his arm. 'Who'd you talk to down at Roarke's? Who'd you work with. Every name, McNab.'

'Only three techs. Roarke kept it low-key, didn't want the whole department to know there was a cop sniffing around. Suwan-Lee, Billings Nibb, and A. A. Dillard.'

'Suwan, female?'

'Yeah, tidy little Oriental dish. She was—'

'Nibb?'

'E-lifer. Knows everything. The teams joke that he was around when Bell called Watson.'

'Dillard?'

'Smart. I told you about him. Got great hands.'

'Fair, green eyes, about twenty, five-ten, a hundred sixty?'

'Yeah, how did you—'

'Christ, Roarke's been paying the son of a bitch. Feeney can you get this equipment up and running, fully analyzed?'

'You bet.'

'Let's go, Peabody.'

'Are we going to interview Mary Calhoun?'

'Soon enough. Right now we're going to give A. A. Dillard his fucking pink slip.'

A. A. had missed his shift. It was the first such incident, she

314

was told by Nibb, the department manager. A. A. was a model employee, prompt, efficient, cooperative, and creative.

'I need to see all his files, personnel, works completed, works in progress, status, reports, the whole shot.'

Nibb – who wasn't quite old enough to have known A. G. Bell, but who had celebrated his centennial the past summer, crossed his arms. Behind a thick white moustache, his mouth went hard.

'A great deal of those records include confidential material. Research and development in the electronics field is highly competitive. Cutthroat. One leak and—'

'This is a murder investigation, Nibb. And I'm hardly going to sell data to my husband's competitors.'

'Nonetheless, Lieutenant, I can't give you files on works in progress without the boss's personal consent.'

'You have it,' Roarke said as he walked up.

'What are you doing here?' Eve demanded.

'Following my nose – correctly, I see. Nibb, get the lieutenant everything she requested,' he added, then drew Eve aside. 'I reviewed the recording of the dustup in the lobby of the Arms again, then ran it through an analysis procedure we're working on here. Not to be technical, it assessed angles, distances, and so forth. The probability quotient that the killer was focused on McNab rather than the cop outside was very high.'

'So you asked yourself who might be connected to you, on some level, who would make McNab as a cop.'

'And the answer was someone in this department. I've just run a personnel scan. A. A. most closely fits the physical description.'

'You'd make a halfway decent cop.'

'I see no reason to insult me. I'd just accessed A. A.'s home address when the word came through we had cops sniffing. I assume our noses had caught the same scent.'

'What's the address? I want some uniforms to pick him up.'

'Saint Patrick's Cathedral. I doubt you'll find him nibbling his lunch there.'

'That's sloppy of your personnel department, Roarke.'

His smile was not amused. 'Believe me, they'll be so informed. What have you got?'

'He's Liam Calhoun, the son. And I've got his queen, Roarke. I've got his mama.' She filled him in, watching as his eyes grew darker, colder. 'Feeney and McNab are working on the equipment we found in Audrey's apartment. And they'll analyze the bugs we took from Summerset's quarters. Where is he now? Summerset.'

'Home. Bail was set and paid.' His jaw set. 'They put a bracelet on him.'

'The charges will be dropped – and it'll come off. I'll take care of it as soon as I get to Central. Whitney's meeting me to observe the interview with the mother.'

'I believe you'll find we manufacture the bugs here, and we're testing a new shield coat that protects them from detection from currently marketed scanners. I've been bankrolling his game all along. Wonderfully ironic.'

'We've got him pinned, Roarke. Even if he's been tipped somehow and he's running, we'll have him. We've got his mother. Every indication is he can't and won't function without her. He'll stay close. I'll take the data from here back to Central and key it in under my name and Feeney's only. You have a right to that protection under the law.' She blew out a breath. 'I'm going straight into Interview, and odds are it's going to be a long haul. I'll be home late.'

'Obviously I have quite a bit of work to do here. I'll probably be later. I spoke to the head of Pat Murray's medical team. He's regained consciousness. At this point he isn't able to speak or move his legs, but they believe with proper treatment, he'll make a full recovery.'

She knew Roarke would be paying for that proper treatment,

and touched his arm briefly. 'I've got two uniforms on his room. I'll get over there myself tomorrow.'

'We'll go.' He spotted Nibb bringing a box of disc files. 'Good hunting, Lieutenant.'

In hour five of the interview with Audrey, Eve switched from coffee to water. The simulated caffeine the station house offered its weary cops tended to eat stomach lining on continued use.

Audrey insisted on tea by the gallon, and though she sipped it hour after hour with delicacy, her polish was wearing thin. Her hair was losing its shape and starting to straggle. It was damp and sticky at the temples from sweat. Cosmetics were fading, leaving her skin overly pale, her mouth thin and hard without the softening color. The whites of her eyes were beginning to streak with red.

'Why don't I encapsulate for this session? When your husband was killed—'

'Was murdered,' Audrey interrupted. 'Murdered in cold blood by that street-rat bastard Roarke, murdered over a little harlot so that I lived a widow and my son lived without a father all his life.'

'So you wanted your son to believe. You fed him that, day after day, year after year, twisting his mind, darkening his heart. He was to be your tool for vengeance.'

'I told him nothing but God's truth from the day he was born. I was to be a nun, to go through my life without knowing a man. But Liam Calhoun was sent to me. An angel called me to him, and so I laid with him and conceived a son.'

'An angel,' Eve repeated and leaned back.

'A bright light,' she said her eyes gleaming. 'A golden light. So I married the man who was only an instrument to create the boy. Then he was murdered, his life taken, and I understood the purpose of his son. He wasn't born to die for sins, but to avenge them.'

'You taught him that. That his purpose in life was to kill.'

'To take what had been taken. To balance the scales. He was a sickly boy. He suffered to purify himself for his mission. I dedicated my life to him, to teaching him.' Her lips curved. 'And I taught him well. You'll never find him. He's too smart. A fine mind has my boy. A genius, he is. And a soul as white as new snow. We are,' she said with a chilling smile, 'beyond you.'

'Your son's a killer, a sociopath with a god-complex. And you made sure he got a good education, in the area you'd decided would be most useful.'

'His mind was his sword.'

And what of his soul? Eve wondered. If there were such things, what had she done to his soul? 'You took nearly fifteen years to train him, to mold him, before you set him loose. You're a clever woman yourself, Mary Pat.'

'Audrey, my name is Audrey now. It says so on all my records.'

'He fixed that for you, too. Created Audrey for you. You had money, plenty of it to pour into your project. And you had patience, patience enough to wait, to plan, to fine down the details. He doesn't have as much patience as you, Audrey. What do you suppose he'll do now, without you to guide him?'

'He'll be fine. He'll finish what he's begun. He was born for it.'

'You think you programmed him that well? I hope you're right because when he comes in for the next round, I'll break him. He's got more equipment stashed, hasn't he? Not far from here.'

Audrey smiled, sipped her tea. 'You'll never find him in your big filthy city. Your Sodom and Gomorrah. But he'll know where you are, you and your lover with the bloody hands. I did my part, God is my witness to that. I sacrificed, I offered it all up when I let that fool Summerset touch me.

318

Not too much touching, for Audrey's a dignified woman, and I wanted the man to keep coming back. He wanted me, oh yes, he did. Quiet evenings in his quarters, listening to music and painting.'

'And you planting bugs.'

'Easy enough, he was blind where I was concerned. I told him the painting I gave him belonged on that wall in the bedroom, and so he put it there. And we could watch him, know what he did and when he did it. He made a fine pawn for my Liam.'

'Did you tell Liam to rig my car?' Eve smiled when she saw Audrey's lips thin. 'I didn't think so. You're too subtle for such things, and you didn't want me taken out so early. He did that on his own. He's got a trigger that slips if you're not right there to control it. You're not there now.'

'He did penance for that. He won't stray from the path again.'

'Won't he? Or will he screw up now, walk right into my hands? It could get ugly, Audrey. He could be killed. You could lose him. If you tell me where he is, I can take him alive. I can promise you that he won't be hurt.'

'Do you think I want him living out his life in a cage, in an institution?' She rose out of her seat, leaning forward. 'I'd rather he die, like a man, a martyr, with righteous vengeance in his heart, with the blood of his father at last at peace. Honor thy father and mother. The wisest of the commandments, for they bring you life. He won't forget it. He won't forget it, I promise you. He'll be thinking of it when he finishes what he started.'

'There's no moving her,' Eve said to Whitney when Audrey was removed to a cell. 'She won't give him up even to save him, and she'll cheer if he dies finishing what she started.'

'She'll be tested, most likely live out her life in a facility for people with violent tendencies and mental defectives.'

'She's not as crazy as she pretends, and it's not enough. The kid might have had a chance. You never know, he might have become something else without her ugly mothering.'

'There's no changing the past. Go home, Dallas. You've done all you can do tonight.'

'I'll just check in with Feeney first.'

'No need. He and McNab have that situation under control. If they break through and locate his other cache of equipment, they'll contact you. Go home, Lieutenant,' he repeated before she could make an excuse. 'You've got to be running on empty by now. Refuel, start again in the morning.'

'Yes, sir.' It was after nine P.M. in any case, she thought as she headed down to the garage. She'd go home, eat, find out what Roarke had uncovered on his end. Maybe if they ran names again with Roarke's equipment they'd find a few probable locations.

It was a big city for someone who wanted to hide. And if he didn't yet know about his mother . . . Eve engaged the 'link. 'Nadine Furst, Channel 75.'

'This is Nadine Furst, I'm not in this location, please leave a message or contact me via e-mail or fax.'

'Transfer call to home residence. Damn it, Nadine, what are you doing taking a night off?'

'Hello. This is Nadine. I'm unavailable right now. If you'd—'

'Shit. Nadine, if you're screening, pick up. I've got a ratings buster for you.'

'Why didn't you say so?' Nadine's face popped on screen. 'Working late, Dallas?'

'Later than you.'

'Hey, humans occasionally take an evening off.'

'We're talking about reporters, not humans. You'll want to get this on air tonight. Police have made an arrest in the matter of the recent series of homicides. Mary Patricia Calhoun, also known as Audrey Morrell, is in custody tonight as an accessory to the murders of Thomas X. Brennen, Shawn Conroy, and

Jennie O'Leary. She is also charged with accessory before and after the fact in the attempted murder of Patrick Murray.'

'Hold it, hold on, I've barely got my recorder going.'

'First and last chance,' Eve said without sympathy. 'Authorities are looking for her son, Liam Calhoun, in connection with these crimes. Call Public Relations at Cop Central if you want pictures of the alleged murderers.'

'I will. I want a one-on-one with the mother tonight.'

'Keep believing in miracles, Nadine. It's real sweet.'

'Dallas—'

Eve ended transmission and smiled into the dark. If Nadine was up to par, the broadcast would play within thirty minutes.

By the time she pulled through the gates and headed toward home her eyes were burning with fatigue, but her system was wired. She could put in another couple of hours on hard data, she decided. Just needed some food, maybe a quick shower, at most a power nap.

She left her car in front and, rolling the kinks out of her neck and shoulders, walked up the steps. In the foyer, she shrugged out of her jacket, tossed it over the newel post. And sighed. She'd have preferred avoiding Summerset, but he deserved to know that he was completely off the hook. Normally he would have simply materialized, scowl first.

'Sulking somewhere,' Eve muttered and turned to the house screener. 'Locate Summerset.'

Summerset is in the main parlor.

'Sulking all right.' She blew out a breath. 'You heard me come in, bone ass. Much as I prefer the cold shoulder to your usual raft of complaints . . .' she began as she strode toward the parlor.

Then she stopped. The hand that itched for her weapon rose slowly up, until she held both in plain sight, palms out.

321

'A self-starter. I appreciate that.' Liam smiled from behind the chair where Summerset was secured with cord. 'Do you know what this is?' he asked, moving the thin silver tool he held a hairbreadth from Summerset's right eye.

'No, but it looks efficient.'

'Laser scalpel. One of the finest medical tools currently in use. I've only to engage it to destroy his eye. And with him, a whoremonger, I'd keep going until I'd sliced right through the brain.'

'I don't know, Liam, his brain's pretty small. You might miss it.'

'You don't even like him.' His grin widened as Summerset simply closed his eyes. For an instant, he was a young, attractive man with sparkling eyes and a smile full of charm and promise. 'That was part of the fun I enjoyed the most. You worked so hard on his behalf, and you must hate him as much as I do.'

'Nah. I'm more ambivalent, really. Why don't you ease back on the laser? Unless you're into droids, good help's really hard to find these days.'

'I need you to take out your weapon, Lieutenant, using your thumb and index finger. Put it on the floor, moving very carefully, then kick it over here. I can see you hesitate,' he added. 'I should tell you I've adjusted this particular instrument. Its range is extended.' Amused, he turned it, aimed it at her head. 'It'll reach you, I promise, and go through your brain instead.'

'I hate doctors.' She took out her weapon. But as she crouched down as if to lay it on the floor, she flipped it into her hand. A beam shot out from the scalpel, sending a line of fire burning across her biceps. Her fingers went numb, and the stunner clattered to the floor.

'I'm afraid I anticipated that. I do know you well.' He crossed the room as he spoke, picking up her weapon as Eve fought to rise over the pain and focus. 'I'm told the pain from

322

a laser incision is excruciating. We recommend anesthesia.' He laughed and stepped back. 'But you'll live. You may want to bind up that arm. You're getting blood all over the floor.' Willing to oblige, he leaned over and ripped the sleeve of her shirt, dropped it into her lap. 'Try that.'

He watched her fumble to wrap it around the wound. Listened to her labored breathing as she fought to tie it with one hand and her teeth. 'You're a tenacious opponent, Lieutenant, and fairly clever. But you've failed. You were doomed to fail from the beginning. Only the righteous triumph.'

'Spare me the religious crap, Liam. Under all that holy talk, it's all just a game to you.'

'Make a joyful noise, Lieutenant. Enjoying God's work is a tribute to His powers, not a sin.'

'And you've enjoyed this.'

'Very much. Every step you took, every move you made brought us here, tonight, where it was always meant for me to be. God's will.'

'Your god's an asshole.'

He struck her across the face, backhanded. 'Don't dare blaspheme. Don't ever deride God in my presence, you whore.' He left her curled on the floor and picked up the glass of wine he'd poured while waiting for her. 'Jesus drank the fruit of the grape while sitting among his enemies.' He sipped, calmed. 'When Roarke arrives, the circle will be complete. I have the power of the Lord in my hands.' He grinned down at the two weapons. 'And the technology of the ages.'

'He isn't coming.' Summerset's voice was slurred from the drugs Liam had pumped into him. 'I told you he isn't coming.'

'He'll be here. He can't keep away from his harlot.'

Eve clamped down on the pain and managed to get to her knees. When she looked into Liam's face, she knew it was far too late for him. The madness his mother had planted in the child had rooted deep in the man.

'How the hell did you let this Bible-thumping fuckhead into our house?'

'Do you want me to hurt you again?' Liam demanded. 'Do you want more pain?'

'I wasn't talking to you.'

'I thought he was the police,' Summerset said wearily. 'He was driving a cruiser, wearing a uniform. He said you'd sent him.'

'Couldn't break the security field here, could you, Liam. Just a little over your head.'

'With time I would have.' His face went sulky, like a child's denied a favored treat. 'There's nothing I can't do. But I'm tired of waiting.'

'You missed the last two times, didn't you?' Eve forced herself to her feet, clamped her teeth together as the pain sang through her. 'You didn't get Brian, and you didn't finish Pat Murray. He's going to make a full recovery, and he'll point across the courtroom at you at your trial.'

'They were simply tests of my commitment. God always tests His disciples.' But he pressed his fingers to his lips, rubbed them there. 'It's almost over now. It's the last round, and you lose.' Eyes bright as a bird's, he cocked his head. 'You might want to sit down, Lieutenant. You lost some blood, and you're looking very pale.'

'I'll stand. Aren't you going to tell me your game plan? That's how it works. What's the point in ending it if you don't brag first?'

'I don't consider it bragging. I'm honoring my father, avenging his death. Point by bloody point. When I'm done here, I'll go back for Kelly and Murray and one more. Suffocation, drowning, then poison. Six sinners for the six martyred, and three to make nine for the novena. After that, he'll rest in peace.'

He set the laser down to run a finger down the folds of the veil of the Virgin Mother he'd placed on a table. 'The

324

order's changed, but God understands. Tonight, Roarke will walk into his own private hell. His longtime companion, his trusted friend, dead. His whore, his slut cop, dead. It will look as if they did away with each other. A terrible fight right here in his own home, a fight for life, for death. For a moment, just for a moment, he'll believe that.'

He smiled at Eve. 'Then I'll step out and he'll know the truth. The pain will be worse then, unbearable, excruciating. He'll know what it is to lose, to have all that matters stolen from him. He'll know that by his own evil he brought the angel of death into this house. The avenging sword.'

'Angel. Avenging Angel.' She had to risk it, play on his madness. 'A. A.? Is that where you got your cover? We know all about you. Everything. How you infiltrated Roarke's company, worked on his equipment. Stole from him.' She stepped closer, keeping her eyes steady on his. 'We know where you came from, where you've been. We found your hole. Your picture's on the news right now. Right next to your mother's.'

'You're lying. Lying whore.'

'How do I know who you are? How do I know about A. A.? And the dinky little room in your mother's apartment where you kept your equipment. And the other place, downtown.' *It has to be downtown*, she told herself. 'The bugs your mother planted in Summerset's quarters. We played the game, Liam, and we beat you. What we didn't find out, Audrey filled in. Right before I locked her in a cage.'

'You're lying!' He screamed it, and rushed her.

Braced and ready, Eve met the attack, using her uninjured arm to block the blow, her elbow jabbing into his stomach. She got her foot under him, threw her weight into the move, and sent them both tumbling to the floor. She ignored the eye-searing pain when he fell on her injured arm; slamming her fist up, she connected with bone. But she'd miscalculated the strength rage would bring him.

It was she who screamed when he dug his fingers into her wound, and the room swam blackly. When her vision cleared he had her weapon on her throat, where firing it even at midsetting could be fatal.

'You lying cunt bitch. I'll cut out your tongue for your lies.'

'Turn on the screen.' She wanted to curl up, hide from the agony screaming in her arm. 'See for yourself. Go ahead, Liam, turn it on. Channel 75.'

When he released his grip on her arm she had to swallow a sob. He bounded off her, raced to the recessed unit. 'She's lying, she's lying. She doesn't know anything.' He talked to himself in a sing-song tone as he switched on the viewing screen. 'Hail Mary, full of grace. She's going to die. They're all going to die. The valley of the shadow of death, but they'll fear. God will destroy them, all of them, through me. It's for me.'

'You have to stop this.' Summerset strained against his bonds as Eve crawled to him. 'Get out. He's mad. You can get out while he's involved with the screen. He doesn't even know where he is now. You can get out. He'll kill you if you don't.'

'I'd never make it to the door.' Her wound was bleeding again, dripping through the makeshift bandage. 'I have to keep him focused on me. As long as he is, he's not interested in you. I have to keep him busy, distracted, and he might not hear Roarke come in.' She dragged herself up to her knees. 'If he doesn't hear Roarke, he'll have a chance.'

'Audrey's his mother?'

'Yeah.' She gained her feet. 'She's responsible for all of it.' She looked over as Liam screamed at the images on the screen. 'For everything. For him.' She steadied herself, bearing down when her knees threatened to fold under her. 'Liam, I'll take you to her. You want to see your mother, don't you? She asked to see you. You want to see her, don't you? I'll take you.'

326

'Did you hurt her?' Tears began to leak from his eyes.

'No, of course not.' She took a shaky step forward. 'She's fine. She's waiting for you. She'll tell you what to do next. She always tells you what to do, doesn't she?'

'She always knows. God speaks through her.' He started to lower the weapon, as if it were forgotten. 'She's blessed,' he whispered. 'And I'm her only son. I'm the light.'

'She wants you now.' *One more step*, Eve thought. *Just one more*. She only had to get the stunner away from him.

'She told me God's plan.' The weapon came up again, and Eve froze. 'To kill you. God demands the sacrifice. Him first,' he said with a sly smile as he shifted the weapon toward Summerset.

'Wait—' Instinctively Eve stepped between, and took the hit.

The jolt sizzling through her nervous system dropped her. Her body forgot how to breathe, her eyes forgot how to see. Even pain was gone. She never felt him kick her, bruising ribs as he screamed and cursed and stormed through the room.

'You try to spoil everything. Everything!' He ranted as he shoved over a table and its beautiful old Ming vase. 'Cheater. Whore. Sinner. Even your weapon's inferior. Look at this – pitiful. You have to manually increase power. Just as well, just as well, why kill you all at once?'

'She needs a doctor,' Summerset said. His breath was ragged, his arms and wrists raw and trembling from struggling with his bonds. 'She needs medical attention.'

'I could have been a doctor, the way my uncle wanted, but it wasn't God's plan. My mother knew that. She knew that. My father loved me, he provided for me. Then he was taken from us. Vengeance is mine, sayeth the Lord. I am his vengeance.'

Shuddering with pain, Eve rolled onto her side. If she was going to die, by Christ she would have the last word. 'You're nothing but a pathetic and defective tool used by a woman who cared more about herself than her own son. Now both of you are going to spend the rest of your lives in a cage.'

'God will show me a sign. He'll direct my path.' Liam walked over and stood above her, weapon aimed down and on full power. 'As soon as I send you to Hell.'

Eve kept her eyes open and kicked upward with what strength she had left. The blow caught him at the knees, sent him staggering back. She pushed herself up, hoping for one last grab at the weapon. But the whine of a stunner came from the doorway, shooting Liam back against the wall.

His body jittered in a death dance she'd seen before. The nervous system went into overdrive, sent the dying body shaking like a puppet, then shut down.

He was sliding to the floor when Roarke rushed across the room.

'Game over,' Eve said dully. 'Amen.'

'Oh God, Eve, look at you. You're a mess.'

Little white dots circled in front of her eyes so that she barely saw Roarke face as he dropped beside her. 'I almost had him.'

'Of course.' Even as he gathered her up, rocked her, she fainted. 'Of course you did.'

When she came to she was on the sofa, with Summerset efficiently treating her arm. 'Get the hell away from me.'

'This needs tending. You're badly injured, but Roarke seems to believe you'll be more cooperative here than at a health center.'

'I have to call this in.'

'Another few moments won't matter. The boy won't be less dead.'

She closed her eyes, too tired and battered to argue. Her side was screaming, and whatever Summerset was doing to her arm was just one more small torture.

His hands were as gentle as a mother's with an infant, but he knew he hurt her. 'You saved my life. You stepped in front of me. Why?'

'It's my job, don't take it personally. It wasn't set on full power anyway. Oh shit.' The moan escaped her clenched teeth. 'Ten years I've been a cop. First time I took a stunner hit full body. Christ, it really hurts, everywhere, all at once. Where's Roarke?'

'He'll be right here.' Instinctively he stroked her hair back from her damp face. 'Don't squirm. It'll only cause you more discomfort.'

'Nothing could.' She opened her eyes again, looked into his. 'I fired the weapon that killed Liam Calhoun. I fired it before Roarke came in. Do you understand?'

Summerset studied her for a long moment. Pain swam in her eyes, must have been screaming through her system. But she thought of Roarke. 'Yes, Lieutenant. I understand.'

'No, you didn't kill him,' Roarke corrected. 'Summerset, I expect you to give a clear and truthful statement. You're not going through Testing for this, Eve. Not for this. Here, you need to sit up a bit to drink this.'

'You shouldn't have had the weapon. It'll complicate – Where did you get the weapon?'

'You gave it to me.' He smiled as he eased her up, his arm supporting her neck. 'Your clinch piece. I never gave it back.'

'I forgot.'

'I hardly think the authorities are going to give me any trouble about it. Drink this.'

'What is it? I don't want it.'

'Don't be such a baby. It's just a soother – mild, I promise. It'll help the pain.'

'No, I—' She choked a bit when Roarke simply poured some of the tranq down her throat. 'I have to call this in.'

Roarke sighed. 'Summerset, would you contact Commander Whitney and tell him what's happened here tonight?'

'Yes.' He hesitated, then gathered up the bloody cloth. 'I'm

329

very obliged to you, Lieutenant, and I regret that you were injured performing you duties.'

When he walked out she pursed her lips. 'I'll have to get blasted more often. He didn't even sneer at me.'

'He told me what happened. And that you're the most courageous and foolish woman he's ever known. At the moment, I have to agree.'

'Yeah, well, we lived. I'll take the rest of that soother now that he's gone. The arm's some better, but my side's killing me.'

'You took a kick.' Gently, Roarke lifted her higher so that he could sit down with her resting against him. 'My brave and foolish cop. I love you.'

'I know. He was only nineteen.'

'Evil isn't the exclusive territory of adults.'

'No.' She closed her eyes as the pain eased away toward numbness. 'I wanted to take him alive. You wanted him dead. He swung the tide in your favor.' She turned her head. 'You'd have killed him anyway.'

'Do you want me to deny it?' He lowered his lips to her brow. 'Justice, Eve, is weak and thin without the underpinning of retribution.'

She sighed, rested her head, closed her eyes again. 'What the hell are we doing together anyway?'

'Leading lives that are often too interesting. Darling Eve, I wouldn't change a moment.'

She looked around the wreckage of the lovely room, at the wasted boy on the floor. And felt Roarke's lips brush over her hair. 'Me either.'

If you enjoyed *Vengeance in Death*,
you won't want to miss
J. D. Robb's next novel . . .

HOLIDAY

IN

DEATH

She didn't exactly sneak out of the house, but she was quiet about it. Maybe it was barely five in the morning, but she didn't doubt Summerset was around somewhere. She preferred, whenever possible, to avoid Roarke's sergeant-major – or whatever term you'd use for a man who knew everything, did everything, and poked his bony nose into what Eve considered her private business entirely too often.

Since her last case had shoved the two of them closer together than either was comfortable with, she suspected he'd been avoiding her as carefully as she had him for the past couple of weeks.

Reminded of it, she rubbed a hand absently just under her shoulder. It still troubled her a bit in the morning, or after a long day. Taking a full blast from her own weapon was an experience she didn't want to repeat in this or any other lifetime. Somehow worse was the way Summerset had poured meds down her throat afterward, when she'd been too weak to knock him on his ass.

She closed the door behind her, took one deep breath of the frigid December air, then cursed viciously.

She'd left her vehicle at the base of the steps – mostly because it drove Summerset crazy. And he'd moved it – because it pissed her off. Grumbling because she hadn't bothered to bring along the remote for the garage door or her vehicle, she trooped around the house, boots crunching on frosted grass. The tips of her ears began to sting with cold, her nose to run with it.

She bared her teeth and she punched in the code with gloveless fingers, then stepped into the pristine and blissfully warm garage.

There were two gleaming levels of cars, bikes, sky-scooters, even a single passenger mini-copter. Her city issue vehicle in industrial beige looked like a mutt among sleek, glossy hounds. But it was new, she reminded herself as she slid behind the wheel. And everything worked.

It started like a dream. The engine purred. At her command, the heat began to whir softly through the vents. The cockpit glowed with lights, indicating the initial check run, then the bland voice of the recording assured her all systems were in operational order.

She'd have suffered the tortures of the damned before she would admit she missed the capriciousness and outright crankiness of her old unit.

At a smooth pace, she glided out of the garage and down the curved drive toward the iron gates. They parted smoothly, soundlessly for her.

The streets in this exclusive neighborhood were quiet, clean. Trees on the verge of the great park were coated in a thin sheen of glittery frost like a skinsuit of diamond dust. Deep inside its shadows, chemi-heads and spine crackers might be finishing up the night's work, but here, there were only polished stone buildings, wide avenues and the quiet dark before dawn.

She was blocks away before the first billboard loomed up, spitting garish light and motion into the night. Santa, red-cheeked and with a manic grin that made her think of an oversized elf on Zeus, rode through the sky behind his fleet of reindeer and blasted out ho-ho-hos, while warning the populace of just how many shopping days they had left before Christmas.

'Yeah, yeah, I hear you. You fat son of a bitch.' She scowled as she braked for a light. She'd never had to worry about the holiday before. It had just been a matter of finding something ridiculous for Mavis, maybe something edible for Feeney.

There'd been no one else in her life to wrap gifts for.

And what the hell did she buy for a man who not only had

everything, but owned most of the plants and factories that made it? For a woman who'd prefer a blow with a blunt instrument to shopping for an afternoon, it was a serious dilemma.

Christmas, she decided, as Santa began to tout the variety of stores and selections in the Big Apple Sky Mall, was a pain in the ass.

Still, her mood lifted as she hit the predictably snared traffic on Broadway. Twenty-four hours a day, seven days a week, there was a party going on. The people glides were jammed with pedestrians, most of whom were drunk, stoned or both. Glide-cart operators shivered in the cold while their grills smoked. If a vendor had a spot on this street, he held it in a tight, ready fist.

She cracked her window a sliver, caught the scent of roasting chestnuts, soy dogs, smoke and humanity. Someone was singing out in a strident monotone about the end of the world. A cabbie blasted his horn well over noise pollution laws as pedestrians flowed into the street on his light. Overhead the early airbuses farted cheerfully, and the first advertising blimps began to hawk the city's wares.

She watched a fistfight break out between two women. Street lcs, Eve mused. Licensed companions had to guard their turf here as fiercely as the vendors of food and drink. She considered getting out and breaking it up, but the little blonde decked the big redhead, then darted off into the crowd like a rabbit.

Good thinking, Eve approved, as the redhead was already on her feet, shaking her head clear and shouting inventive obscenities.

This, Eve thought with affection, was her New York.

With some regret, she bumped over to the relative quiet of Seventh, then headed downtown. She needed to get back into action, she thought. The weeks of disability had made her feel edgy and useless. Weak. She'd ditched the recommended last week off, had insisted on taking the required physical.

And, she knew, had passed it by the skin of her teeth.

But she'd passed, and was back on the job. Now if she could just convince her commander to get her off desk duty, she'd be a happy woman.

When her radio sounded, she tuned in with half an ear. She wasn't even on call for another three hours.

Any units in the vicinity, a 1222 reported at 6843 Seventh Avenue, apartment 18B. No confirmation available. See the man in apartment 2A. Any units in the vicinity . . .

Eve clicked on before Dispatch could repeat the signal. 'Dispatch, this is Dallas, Lieutenant Eve. I'm two minutes from the Seventh Avenue location. Am responding.'

Received Dallas, Lieutenant Eve, Please report status upon arrival.

'Affirmative. Dallas out.'

She glided to the curb, flicked a glance up at the steel gray building. A few lights glimmered through windows, but she saw only darkness on the eighteenth floor. A 1222 meant there'd been an anonymous call reporting a domestic dispute.

Eve stepped out of her vehicle, slid an absent hand over her side where her weapon sat snug. She didn't mind starting out the day with trouble, but there wasn't a cop alive or dead who didn't dread a domestic.

There seemed to be nothing a husband, wife or same-sex spouse enjoyed more than turning on the poor bastard who tried to keep them from killing each other over the rent money.

The fact that she'd volunteered to take it was a reflection of her dissatisfaction with her current assignments.

Eve jogged up the short flight of stairs and looked up the man in 2A.

She flashed her badge when he spoke through the security peep, shoved it into his beady little eyes when he opened the door a stingy crack. 'You got trouble here?'

'I dunno. Cops called me. I'm the manager. I don't know anything.'

'I can see that.' He smelled of stale sheets, and inexplicably, of cheese. 'You want to let me into 18B?'

'You got a master, don't you?'

'Yeah, fine.' She sized him up quickly. Short, skinny, smelly, and scared. 'How about filling me in on the occupants before I go in?'

'Only one. Woman, single woman. Divorced or something. Keeps to herself.'

'Don't they all,' Eve muttered. 'You got a name on her?'

'Hawley. Marianna. About thirty, thirty-five. Nice looker. Been here about six years. No trouble. Look, I didn't hear anything, I didn't see anything. I don't know anything. It's five-fucking-thirty in the morning. She's done any damage to the unit, I want to know about it. Otherwise, it's none of my nevermind.'

'Fine,' Eve said as the door clicked shut in her face. 'Go back to your hole, you little weasel.' She rolled her shoulders once, then walked across the corridor to the elevator. As she stepped inside, she pulled out her communicator. 'Dallas, Lieutenant Eve. I'm at the Seventh Avenue location. Building manager is a wash. I'll report back after interviewing Hawley, Marianna, resident of 18B.'

Do you require backup?

'Not at this time. Dallas out.'

She slipped the communicator back into her pocket as she stepped out into the hallway on eighteen. A quick glimpse up showed her security cameras in place. The hall was church quiet. From its location and style, she pegged most of the residents as white collar, middle income. Most wouldn't stir from their beds until after seven. They'd grab their morning coffee, dash out to the airbus or subway stop. More fortunate ones would just plug into the office from their home station.

337

Some would have children to see off to school. Others would kiss their spouses good-bye and wait for their lovers.

Ordinary lives in an ordinary place.

It flipped through her mind to wonder if Roarke owned the damn building, but she pushed the idea aside and stepped up to 18B.

The security light was blinking green. Deactivated. Instinctively she stepped to the side of the door as she pushed the buzzer. She couldn't hear its muffled echo and decided the unit was soundproofed. Whatever went on inside, stayed inside. Vaguely annoyed, she took out her master code and bypassed the locks.

Before entering, she called out. Nothing worse, she mused, then scaring some sleeping civilian into coming at you with a homemade stunner or a kitchen knife.

'Ms Hawley? Police. We have a report of trouble in your unit. Lights,' she ordered, and the overheads in the living area flashed on.

It was pretty enough in a quiet way. Soft colors, simple lines. The view screen was programmed to an old video. Two impossibly attractive people were rolling around naked on a bed scattered with rose petals. They moaned theatrically.

There was a candy dish on the table in front of the long, misty-green sofa. It was filled to the brim with sugar-dashed gumdrops. Silver and red candle pillars were grouped beside it, burned artistically down to varying heights.

The entire room smelled of cranberry and pine.

She saw where the pine scent originated. A small, perfectly formed tree lay on its side in front of a window. Its festive lights and sweet-faced angel ornaments were smashed, its boughs snapped.

At least a dozen festively wrapped boxes were crushed under it.

She reached for her weapon, drew it, and circled the room. There was no other obvious sign of violence. The couple on the view screen reached simultaneous climax with throaty, animal moans. Eve sidestepped past it. Listened, listened.

Heard music. Quiet, cheerful, monotonous. She didn't know the tune, but recognized it as one of the insidious Christmas ditties that played everywhere for weeks during the season.

She swept her weapon over a short corridor. Two doors, both open. In one she could see a sink, a toilet, the edge of a tub, all in gleaming white. Keeping her back to the wall, she slid toward the second door where the music played on and on.

She smelled it, fresh death. Both metallic and fruity. Easing the door all the way open, she found it.

She moved into the room, swinging right, then left, eyes sharp, ears alert. But she knew she was alone with what had been Marianna Hawley. Still she checked the closet, behind the drapes, then left the room to search the rest of the apartment before she relaxed her guard.

Only then did she approach the bed.

2A had been right, she thought. The woman had been a looker. Not stunning, not an eye-popper, but a pretty woman with soft brown hair and deep green eyes. Death hadn't robbed her of that, not yet.

Her eyes were wide and startled as the dead's often were. Against the dull pallor of her cheeks careful and subtle color had been applied. Her lashes were darkened, her lips painted a festive cherry red. An ornament had been pinned to her hair just above the right ear – a small glittery tree with a plump gilded bird on one of its silver branches.

She was naked but for that and the sparkling silver garland that had been artistically wrapped around her body. Eve wondered as she studied the raw bruising around the neck, if that was what had been used to strangle her.

There was more bruising on the wrists, on the ankles, indicating the victim had been bound, and had likely had time to struggle.

On the entertainment unit beside the bed, the singer suggested she have herself a merry little Christmas.

Sighing, Eve pulled out her communicator. 'Dispatch, this is Dallas, Lieutenant Eve. I have a homicide.'

'Heck of a way to start the day.' Officer Peabody stifled a yawn and studied the victim with dark, cop's eyes. Despite the atrociously early hour, Peabody's uniform was crisp and pressed, her dark-brown bowl-cut hair ruthlessly tamed.

The only thing that indicated she'd been rudely roused out of bed was the sleep crease lining her left cheek.

'Heck of a way to end one,' Eve muttered. 'Prelim on scene indicates death occurred at twenty-four hundred hours, almost to the minute.' She shifted aside to let the team from the Medical Examiner's office verify her findings. 'Indications are cause of death was strangulation. The lack of defensive wounds further indicate the victim didn't struggle until after she was bound.'

Gently, Eve lifted the dead woman's left ankle and examined the raw skin. 'Vaginal and anal bruising indicate she was sexually molested before she was killed. The unit's soundproofed. She could have screamed her lungs out.'

'I didn't see any signs of forced entry, no signs of struggle in the living area except for the Christmas tree. That looked deliberate to me.'

Eve nodded, slanted Peabody a look. 'Good eye. See the man in 2A, Peabody, and get the security discs for this floor. Let's see who came calling.'

'Right away.'

'Set a couple of uniforms on the door-to-door,' Eve added as she walked over to the tele-link by the side of the bed. 'Somebody turn that damn music off.'

'You don't sound like you're in the holiday spirit.' Peabody hit the off button on the sound system with a clear-sealed finger. 'Sir.'

'Christmas is a pain in the ass. You finished here?' she demanded of the ME's team. 'Let's turn her over before she's bagged.'

The blood had found its lowest level, settling in the buttocks and turning them a sickly red. Bowel and bladder had emptied, the waste of death. Through the seal coat on her hands, Eve felt the waxy-doll texture of the skin.

'This looks fresh,' she murmured. 'Peabody, get this on video before you go down.' Eve studied the bright tattoo on the right shoulder blade as Peabody moved in to document it.

'My True Love.' Peabody pursed her lips over the bright red letters that flowed in old-fashioned script over the white flesh.

'Looks like a temporary to me.' Eve bent lower until her nose all but brushed the curve of shoulder, sniffed. 'Recently applied. We'll check where she gets bodywork done.'

'Partridge in a pear tree.'

Eve straightened, lifted a brow at her aide. 'What?'

'In her hair, the pin in her hair. On the first day of Christmas.' Because Eve continued to look blank, Peabody shook her head. 'It's an old Christmas song, Lieutenant. "The Twelve Days of Christmas." The guys gives his true love something on every day, starting with a partridge in a pear tree on the first day.'

'What the hell is anybody supposed to do with a bird in a tree? Stupid gift.' But a sick suspicion churned in her gut. 'Let's hope this was his only true love. Get me those tapes. Bag her,' she ordered, then turned once more to the bedside 'link.

While the body was being removed, she ordered all incoming and outgoing transmissions for the previous twenty-four hours.

The first came in at just past eighteen hundred hours – a cheerful conversation between the victim and her mother. As Eve listened, studied the mother's laughing face, she thought

341

of how that same face would look when she called and told the woman her daughter was dead.

The only other transmission was an outgoing. Good-looking guy, Eve mused as she studied the image on screen. Mid-thirties, quick smile, soulful brown eyes. Jerry, the victim called him. Or Jer. Lots of sexual byplay, teasing. A lover then. Maybe her true love.

Eve removed the disc, sealed it, and slipped it into her bag. She located Marianna's daybook, porta-link, her address book in the desk under the window. A quick scroll through the entries netted her one Jeremy Vandoren.

Alone now, Eve turned back to the bed. Stained sheets were tangled at the foot. The clothes that had been carefully cut off the victim and tossed to the floor were bagged for evidence. The apartment was silent.

She'd let him in, Eve mused. Opened the door to him. Did she come in here with him voluntarily, or did he subdue her first? The tox report would tell her if there were any illegals in the bloodstream.

Once he had her in the bedroom, he tied her. Hands and feet, likely hooking the restraints around the short posts at all four corners, spreading her out like a banquet.

Then he'd cut off her clothes. Carefully, no hurry. It hadn't been rage or fury or even a desperate kind of need. Calculated, planned, ordered. Then he'd raped her, sodomized her because he could. He had the power.

She'd struggled, cried out, probably begged. He'd enjoyed that, fed on that. Rapists did, she thought and took several, deep, steadying breaths because her mind wanted to veer toward her father.

When he was done, he'd strangled her, watching, watching, while her eyes bulged. Then he'd brushed her hair, painted her face, draped her in festive silver garland. Had he brought the hair pin with him, or had it belonged to her? Had she amused herself with the tattoo, or had he decorated her body himself?

342

She moved into the neighboring bathroom. White tile sparkled like ice, and there was an underlying scent of disinfectant.

He'd cleaned up here when he was finished, Eve decided. Washing himself, even grooming, then wiping down and spraying the room to remove any evidence.

Well, she'd put the sweepers on it in any case. One lousy pubic hair could hang him.

She'd had a mother who loved her, Eve thought. One who'd laughed with her, making holiday plans, talking about sugar cookies.

'Sir? Lieutenant?'

Eve glanced over her shoulder, saw Peabody in the center of the hallway. 'What?'

'I have the security discs. Two uniforms are initiating door-to-doors.'

'Okay.' Eve rubbed her hands over her face. 'Let's seal the place up, take everything to Central. I have to inform the next of kin.' She shouldered her bag picked up her field kit. 'You're right, Peabody. It's a heck of a way to start the day.'

VISIONS IN DEATH

Nora Roberts writing as J.D. Robb

'The summer had been long hot and bloody. Fall, with its cooler temperatures, was coming. Maybe people wouldn't be as inclined to kill each other. But she doubted it.'

Eve Dallas' latest case involves the murder of a young mother, found raped and strangled in the park. As Eve starts investigating the victim's friends and family, an offer of help comes from an unlikely source. Psychic Celina Sanchez claims to be having visions of the killer and can recite precise details of the case – details not released to the press. She is also no glory-hunter – haunted by the visions of death that she sees, all she wants to do is help Eve catch the murderer so that she is left in peace.

Though Eve remains sceptical of Celina's abilities, she serves the greater good, and she will use all the resources she can to track down the killer before he strikes again . . .

978-0-7499-3499-6

SURVIVOR IN DEATH

Nora Roberts writing as J.D. Robb

'Murder was always an insult, and had been since the first human hand had smashed a stone into the first human skull. But the murder, bloody and brutal, of an entire family in their own home, in their own beds, was a different form of evil.'

When Eve Dallas is called to a multiple homicide at the Swisher family home, she discovers a blood-bath. The killers breached an elaborate security system, slashed the throat of each victim while they slept and were in and out of the house in less than ten minutes. But they did make one mistake. They left a survivor . . .

While her parents, brother and best friend lay in their beds, oblivious to the danger, nine-year-old Nixie Swisher was in the kitchen and saw far too much.

Offering Nixie temporary refuge is easy, but dealing with the emotional needs of a girl who has lost everything isn't. Eve can at least promise Nixie justice, but she's chasing professionals who don't like leaving loose ends. And leaving Nixie Swisher alive is one loose end too many . . .

978-0-7499-3584-9